Nourishment

Gerard Woodward

W F HOWES LTD

This large print edition published in 2010 by
W F Howes Ltd
Unit 4, Rearsby Business Park, Gaddesby Lane,
Rearsby, Leicester LE7 4YH

1 3 5 7 9 10 8 6 4 2

First published in the United Kingdom in 2010
by Picador

A CIP catalogue record for this book is available
from the British Library

ISBN 978 1 40746 545 6

Typeset by Palimpsest Book Production Limited,
Falkirk, Stirlingshire
Printed and bound in Great Britain
by MPG Books Ltd, Bodmin, Cornwall

'Uncover, dogs, and lap.'

Timon of Athens

PART I

CHAPTER 1

Shortly after the outbreak of war, Emily Head, known by everyone, including her late husband Arthur and her daughter Tory, simply as Mrs Head, returned to London after a brief sojourn in the marshland village of Waseminster (Anglo-Saxon for *the church in the mud*, according to Tory's husband Donald), possessed of an unshakeable belief that her daughter, and London generally, needed her.

Tory did her best to conceal her dismay at her mother's return, and to hide the shock she felt to see Mrs Head looking so windswept and craggy as she stepped shakily down from a horse-drawn hackney (the last such vehicle to survive in London, so the cab driver claimed), clinging to her hat of bedraggled turkey plumage, parrying forth a tatty parasol, and bringing Tory's short reign as matriarch of the little house in Peter Street to an end.

In truth, Mrs Head was hardly needed. Donald had already been called up, and was receiving his basic training somewhere near Durdle Door; the children had been evacuated to a very pretty part

1

of the Cotswolds, Lower Slaughter (or was it Upper? Mrs Head could never remember), and Tory might have joined them, had not her mother made her intentions known of returning to help with the battle on the home front. She'd said she would do all the cooking and shopping, all the cleaning and other domestic chores, while Tory got on with her war work in a gelatine factory (no one denied the importance of gelatine production in the war effort, though no one quite understood it either). Tory had written tactfully dissuasive letters, pointing out that with the prospect of air raids and gas attacks, she would be much safer staying put. Her mother had replied that she had no intention of biding her time on the Thames Marshes while London burned and, using a logic that would soon seem absurd, regarded the city as a sanctuary, imagining that the bombers, when they came, would pick off all the little villages one by one as they approached the capital. She would be much safer as one among the many millions. Furthermore, she seemed to regard the muddy shores of Waseminster Parish as an ideal landing spot for an invasion. *'Every time there's a knock at the door I wonder if it's Adolf,'* she wrote.

Mrs Head had been a resident of Waseminster for little more than a year and was, she confessed, beginning to think that the move had been a great mistake. Despite the fervour with which she had described country pursuits in her letters – *'to see the pheasants falling as heavily as Christmas puddings is such a glorious affirmation of the superiority of man over nature'* – she was not a proper countrywoman, and although she had connections to the area (it had been the birthplace of her late husband, Tory's father) she was not made to feel welcome. Few of Arthur's bloodline remained in the village, and her attempts at ingratiation were met with little warmth. No one really understood why a woman who'd lived in the city all her life should suddenly want to live in the countryside; her friends thought it faintly treacherous, while her new neighbours regarded her with suspicion.

'It *is* a lovely little house,' Mrs Head remarked gratefully as she walked up the path with her hand on Tory's arm (who was carrying her bag), as though she'd been debating this aspect of 17 Peter Street all the way up on the train from Kent.

And so mother and daughter now lived alone in the house that had once been so busy and crowded, and each seemed more shocked by this fact than by the bombs that, some time after Mrs Head's return, began to rain down upon the city.

Mrs Head stuck to her word, shopping and cooking with heroic, redoubtable zeal. With the children gone, she had no other role, despite the fact that neither she nor her daughter had a great appetite, and Tory could obtain free meals in the factory canteen. This was just as well, because there wasn't much in the shops for Mrs Head to

3

buy. Good meat was soon scarce. But Mrs Head was a tenacious and dogged shopper, queuing for however long it took, remonstrating with shop-keepers (most of whom she believed were corrupt) and waving her ration book as a token of right-eousness and entitlement.

She had a particularly troubled relationship with Icarus Dando, the butcher who had supplied her with meat for more years than she cared to remember. He was an outwardly jolly sort, with yellow mutton chops and watery, laughter-filled eyes, but she had never liked him. His talk could get too risqué, even for a butcher, so much so that she had been reluctant to take her children into the shop when they were little, in case they caught one of Dando's gristly innuendoes. He tried to soften these with displays of salty charm. He would claim to be in love with Mrs Head, would even serenade her, cleaver in one hand and steel in the other, handprints of blood all over his apron, as though he had been tickled by Lady Macbeth. But now that there was a war on, she realized she was many rungs down on his ladder of preference. There were younger mothers now, women of Tory's generation, whom he could woo and serenade anew, and who responded with far more favour than she would have thought seemly.

She had several times been told that he had no steak, and then later that evening had caught the pungent tang of a piece of rump frying in

Mrs Richards' kitchen. Mrs Richards was a favourite of Mr Dando.

In fact, things had become so fraught between Mrs Head and Mr Dando that she couldn't help feeling rather pleased when his shop was bombed out of existence one Tuesday night.

It had been a particularly heavy raid, coming at a time when the residents of that corner of south-east London were beginning to wonder if the Germans were showing mercy for their humble, Thames-side district. It was hardly likely since their suburb included a barracks and a munitions factory, both wonderfully disguised as leafy forests, so it seemed to be only by chance that so few bombs had troubled their sturdy terraced streets and parades in the months since the raids had begun. Mrs Head and her daughter had even taken to sleeping in their own beds, and not bothering with the public shelter (their house was too small and crooked to have shelters of its own), since most of the raids went north of the river, towards the Royal Docks and the factory land surrounding them. It hardly seemed to make sense to Mrs Head. 'How can you bomb a dock? If you're on target, you'll merely be making a big splash. If you're off target, you'll only be making the dock bigger.' She was herself defiantly indifferent to aerial attack. She had once, from the top of Shooters Hill, watched an air raid over London. The bombs seemed to her no more than little scratches of flame. The might of the German Air Force appeared like someone throwing lighted cigarette ends at a huge black bull. The immense body of the city hardly seemed to notice them.

Well, it didn't seem like that now, with the bombing of Old Parade, where Mr Dando's shop had been. She'd heard it fall at four o'clock in the morning. It had woken her out of the deep sleep she enjoyed every night, and she had opened her eyes, thinking she was back in her cottage in Waseminster, and that Major Brandish, her closest Waseminster neighbour, had fallen down the stairs. She was delirious enough to run to the stairs with the intention of picking him up, when she realized what the sound had actually been. A bomb. Close enough to rattle the windows and doors, and make every floorboard in the house wheeze. Then the horrible moment when she waited to see if it had any companions, as bombs so often did, falling in twos, threes and fours, sometimes fives, a street or two apart. But this bomb seemed to be alone. A stray, loosed by chance, or merely jettisoned by a plane that had only one bomb left and had let it go without a thought so that the crew could get home to the peat bogs of Saxony in time for breakfast. Mother and daughter had stood on the landing in the dark, having emerged from their neighbouring bedrooms, neither quite sure whether they should make for somewhere safer (wherever that might be), and looking in a slightly abashed way at the ceiling, as though they might see if there were any more bombs to come, before feeling, once more, safe. Their local bomb seemed to be the last of the night.

'I hope no one I know has copped it,' Mrs Head muttered, before they went back to bed.

It was a neighbour, Mrs Long, who had called to tell her, breathlessly but with a peculiar hint of relish, that the shops at Old Parade, suppliers of food and other wares for all the households in the area, had been destroyed. Tory had already left for work so Mrs Head went alone to see the devastation, wearing her thick woollen coat and taking, out of habit, her shopping basket, an act which seemed unwittingly to mock the sight that greeted her. It was heartbreaking to see all those lovely little shops in ruins. And Dando's seemed to have taken the full impact, as though he had been specifically targeted (perhaps by a vegetarian Luftwaffe pilot, Mrs Head chuckled sadly to herself), and his shop could hardly have been more neatly dispatched. It had simply disappeared, as though removed, like a book from a shelf.

The shops either side of the butcher's were so badly damaged they would surely have to be pulled down. The baker's was only half there, the rest of it a scree of bricks and joists. The little tobacconist's on the other side was in a similar condition. It had burnt the longer, someone joked, because of all the uncut shag. Other shops were hardly recognizable:

signs had been blown off completely or were hanging at an angle, windows were open, as though flung to greet the day, their shredded curtains and blinds overspilling.

By this vision of things hanging and crooked or otherwise out of place, it seemed to Mrs Head that the main purpose of bombs was not destruction, so much as the creation of disorder and untidiness. It was only the little area beneath the bomb itself that was ever destroyed, but it spread about it a great ring of cluttered mess that would take a huge effort of will to put right. To her surprise the process had already begun. Bricks filled the road in tidy heaps, as though they were bargain items. Mrs Head learnt later that this was because they had already been sorted by the rescue teams who had spent all morning lifting them, one by one, searching for survivors. She approached as closely as she could, right up to the rope that had been set up, and where a small gaggle of her shopping acquaintances had gathered.

There was Mrs Richards, in the same turban and pearls that had, only yesterday, charmed Mr Dando into passing her some fillet steak. When Mrs Head, who had glimpsed the exchange when passing the window, challenged him about this he had claimed it was liver. 'You are a tricky little spiv, Mr Dando,' she had called through the shop doorway, then done her best to slam the door, not waiting for Mr Dando's retort, 'It was liver, love! LIVER, my lovely!' Well, she had a right to be angry. He had sold her nothing but ox tails, trotters, cow heels and tripe for weeks.

The mothers, roped off, exclaimed in surprise when one spotted what looked like victims of the explosion. At the distant end of the parade, only partly visible, bodies were arranged on the ground, on their backs, in fashionable but tattered clothes, stiffly raising arms to the heavens that had rained death upon them. It was a moment before anyone realized the dead were in fact shop mannequins, rescued from Mr Carter's dress emporium. He emerged with some more while they were watching, a woman under each arm. Mrs Head and the other gathered housewives couldn't help smiling at the spectacle: the little bald-headed chap looked like the Sheikh of Araby carting off his harem.

'Do you think anyone really was – hurt?' said Mrs Lippiatt, a sad and rather turtle-like woman, who always had trouble with her neck.

'I wouldn't have thought so,' said Mrs Sparrow, wiping her nose aggressively. 'I don't think anyone lived over those shops . . .'

'What about Mr Dando?' said Mrs Richards, in her sandpapery voice.

No one seemed quite to know where the butcher lived, or what his habits were. It was odd that he wasn't on the scene to inspect the damage. Perhaps he'd been already and was busy making his arrangements, whatever they might be. There was clearly nothing that could be salvaged from his shop, so there was probably little point in staying around.

There were lots of suitcases in the road, scattered, splayed, empty. Handbags as well, little brown leather ones, also empty. It was as if the residents of Old Parade had seen what was coming and had boldly made to escape, but just a minute too late. In fact the bags came from the luggage shop, Bon Voyage, whose merchandise had all been blown out through its windows. A sign was propped on the rubble, in dripping red: 'Looters Will Be V Severly Delt With.'

'I think Mr Larkin must have written that,' said Mrs Taylor. Mr Larkin was, at that moment, gathering up the apples and oranges that had fallen from his greengrocer's.

'I don't know where we're going to do our shopping now,' said Mrs Pinner, who also had her shopping bag, making Mrs Head feel less foolish. 'There isn't a decent butcher's within a mile of here.'

'And if we do find one, will we be able to register?'

'We'll have to. They can't let us starve.'

'Why not? In Silvertown they were fighting each other over bags of flour . . .'

'The high street must be the nearest. There's several there. Shouldn't be any trouble, as long as the trams are running. Otherwise it's a two-mile walk.'

'Perhaps they can deliver . . .'

10

Mrs Head began making plans in her mind almost immediately. All the housewives of Peter Street, and Mark Street, and John Street, and all the tough little terraces around here, they would all be making for the high street, elbowing each other out of the way to get to the best butcher. The jostling for position would begin all over again. She would need to plan her campaign, practise her charm (her one serious failing) and, above all, strengthen her legs. A two-mile walk every day was more than she'd bargained for on returning from Waseminster.

The conversation petered out and the housewives began to drift away, empty-handed, to their homes. Mrs Head would have been among the first to make her way back and prepare for the expedition to the high street, but she was transfixed by the details of the devastation. She had already noted the mannequins, the suitcases and handbags, the apples and oranges, now she began to notice the upper storeys of the bombed shops. The tall interior walls disclosed apparently lived-in spaces, marked by the stained zigzags of fallen staircases, and the macaroni ends of wrenched piping (some trickling pathetically) standing feebly out from tiled corners. Faded wallpaper, exposed to the glare of daylight for the first time, had pictures hanging on it. A wardrobe was lying half shattered and aslant on a heap of rubble. Thirty feet in the air, a little black fireplace was stranded in a wall,

11

its mantelpiece (surely not) had what looked like an ornament still in position.

At ground level groups of men in dusty clothes were hastily trying to assemble scaffolding poles and salvaged timber to shore up the teetering walls. Mrs Head moved away, across the wide, strewn expanse of Old Parade itself to the opposite pavement, noting the damage on this side, the gaping windows, and the deeply pocked brickwork, which had taken the full impact of shrapnel. Further along, firemen were still hosing water into a smouldering shopfront.

Directly opposite where Dando's had been was Timothy's, a large bakery, confectioner and chocolatier, which had done rather well since opening a few years back but had suffered since the shortages had taken hold and had seemed, recently, to be on the point of going out of business – as much for the scarcity of its wares, Mrs Head sometimes suspected, as for its suspiciously continental leanings. It liked to sell what it called Austrian Apple Cake and Bavarian Gateau, as well as Swiss Pralines (slightly more acceptable).

As she looked closely at the shopfront of Timothy's now she could see, among the many scars and mini-craters of a building that had been exposed to a bomb blast, other matter. Yes, she was sure of it. There was actually a rasher of bacon stuck to the wall over the main window, perfectly flat against the brickwork, as though it had been cemented there. And then she saw another, and then another, fanned out across the façade, an array of streaky bacon. Then other materials that must have been flung with terrific force from the exploding butcher's across the street – that thing up there, over the door, that was surely a sausage. It was flattened and burst, but it was definitely one of Mr Dando's notoriously gristly bangers. (It was said that sawdust was a prime ingredient.)

There was much else. Dollops of mince, pieces of liver, kidneys, other offal, all stuck fast. And, Mrs Head felt like raising a fist in self-vindicating triumph, there was steak. The tricky little victualler who had denied his shop contained an ounce of beef now had his lies stuck fast over Timothy's for the world to see. His shop had been veritably overflowing with beefsteak. There must have been so much steak in Dando's shop he probably couldn't close his refrigerator doors for it. She turned to the busy crowds of rescuers and onlookers, ready to cry out, 'I told you so! You want proof, here it is, the sins of the butcher written on the walls of the confectioner's . . .' She didn't shout it. There wasn't anyone nearby anyway. No one was even looking in her direction. And Mrs Head turned back to her tableau of exposed meat, and briefly wished that the bomb hadn't thrown it so high.

She turned her attention to ground level and saw, for the first time, what seemed to her an almost perfect leg of pork, just sitting there on the pavement. Or, rather, it was resting, tucked slightly behind a piece of timber (probably part of a window frame), and was off the ground and quite hidden. Furthermore, it was covered with the same layer of dust as everything else in the area and so was well camouflaged.

After a moment's thought, Mrs Head bent down, picked up the joint and put it in her shopping bag, feeling grateful that she had decided to bring that piece of equipment after all.

Had anyone called Mrs Head a looter she would have expressed great indignation, even outrage, though the thought did cross her mind, as she hurried home, as to whether, if spotted, she would have been 'v. severly delt with' in the manner of that crudely written sign. Apart from the fact that Mr Dando was always lying about how much meat he had in stock, which in itself was justification for taking it when it had become available, such goods were perishable and would only spoil if they weren't used. It could hardly be compared to stealing tins of food or dresses or wireless sets.

When home she gave the meat a long, investigative sniff. She looked closely for any signs that it might have been nibbled by rats. She ran her fingers over its surface, feeling for any splinters of broken glass. There were none. She brushed off the little pieces of grit and ash, ran it under the kitchen tap for a full five minutes, dabbed it with a kitchen towel, then wondered what she should do with it.

Cleaned up, the meat looked excellent. A lovely

deep, almost purply pink, with a nice hairless skin covering a layer of snowy-white fat. It seemed to cry out, 'Roast me, roast me.' Mrs Head thought of the wonderful crackling such a joint would give, and she wouldn't have hesitated, except that it was a Wednesday. A stew would have been more appropriate for a Wednesday. On the other hand, the meat might not keep until Sunday. She didn't like the thought of it lying around in her house uncooked for four days. And the look of excitement she would see on Tory's face when she got home from work, to smell a joint of pork roasting in the oven, would be worth it in itself. They hadn't had a joint for many months. Apart from that, she had some apples and could make a good sauce to go with it. And the cold pork would keep them in sandwiches for days.

So, that afternoon, instead of going to stake her claim on the butchers of the distant high street, Mrs Head prepared the roast dinner of her life, using the joint of pork she had found near the site of a bombed butcher's shop.

And still no one seemed to know what had become of Mr Dando.

CHAPTER 2

Mrs Head was a little disappointed with her daughter, in almost every way. She had not attained the beauty that had seemed possible when, as a ten-year-old, she had possessed the most lovely eyes. In adulthood they seemed, instead, to bulge slightly. In the same way her face, going through the mill of puberty, had been pulled out of shape. All the bones were wrong. Her forehead was too high, her chin too small. Such things might not have mattered, but Mrs Head was beginning to believe that all her other little failings seemed to stem from this one – the failure to be beautiful.

If beautiful, she could have attracted a more worthwhile husband than the little Scottish painter and decorator she had married, without much obvious enthusiasm, in 1930, and who now had been missing in action for more than six months. With more beauty she could have found more appropriate, more glamorous war work than toiling in the packing department of a gelatine factory. Above all, she would have attracted and benefited from the attentions of the world: her

16

teachers would have taught her more, her friends would have shared their best things with her. She would, like all beautiful people, have had a trust fund set up on her behalf for the world to fill with its riches. She would have had vitality.

Instead, it seemed to Mrs Head, Tory not only lacked vitality, she seemed, at just thirty-four years old, to be spent, exhausted, defeated. Each day she looked greyer. She came home from work each evening red-eyed and chap-lipped and, after a silent, small dinner, would shut herself in the sitting room for most of the evening. Hardly a word passed between them on most nights.

Well, perhaps things would be different this evening, Mrs Head thought, when Tory caught the whiff of a real roast dinner. It was a troublesome thing for Mrs Head, thinking of her own child in such poor terms, and she wondered if she was making sufficient allowances for her. She must, of course, be missing her children terribly, and was probably rather upset about Donald (whom she seemed to think for certain was dead), and if she wasn't the radiant beauty Mrs Head had been expecting, it was going too far to say she was ugly. Just a quarter of an inch off the forehead, a bit more on the chin, a rounding-off of the face to lose that horrible squareness it had developed, and she would be quite good-looking. If only she would make the best of what she had. She didn't even bother with makeup these days. And this evening, the evening of the roast-pork

17

dinner, she arrived home, not for the first time, with her hair still in the factory-issue nets under her own slightly crumpled hat.

She entered the dining room utterly indifferent to the smell that filled it, or the sound of a spitting joint that could be heard from the kitchen and, still in her chunky, too-masculine raincoat, flopped into an armchair by the mantelpiece, took out the newspaper that was folded under her arm and dropped it onto the dining-table beside her.

Mrs Head told her about the bombing of Old Parade and the destruction of the shops, how terrible it had been to see all those lovely little shops blown inside out, and how difficult it was going to be now to do the shopping, but she, Mrs Head, was not going to be put off and she was going down to the high street first thing tomorrow and would get herself registered with the best butcher she could find . . .

Tory took all this in, or at least seemed to, in a passive, disinterested way, leaning back in her chair with her eyes closed, working her head gently from side to side, as though to ease some tension in her neck. Having told Tory everything she could think of about the bomb, Mrs Head came to a stop, trying her best not to show frustration at her daughter's indifference, both to the news and to the cooking smells she should have noticed by now. She felt, as she stood there in the middle of the room facing her seated daughter, rather like

18

an actor who had forgotten their lines. Then she said, 'Hungry?'

'No, not really.' It was the expected answer.

'Oh, but you must be. I've got something special tonight, really special.'

'Oh, yes?' She seemed to be waiting to be told what it was.

'Can't you smell it?'

'I can smell something.'

'We're having roast pork. A real treat. And I've made apple sauce, and roast potatoes, and we're going to have the most marvellous gravy, well . . .'

Tory managed a nod and a smile, as if she was, in some remote corner of her mind, surprised and pleased.

'Aren't you going to change for dinner?' said Mrs Head, setting the table, using her cork place mats for once, and the Noah's Ark condiment set – indicators that this was indeed to be a very special meal.

'Into what?' said Tory, lifting her head.

'You could at least take your coat off, and take your hair out.'

Mrs Head had worried a little about her daughter's hygiene since she had started working at Farraway's. Her clothes always smelt of animals, her fingernails were usually black, and there was often a grimy tincture to her skin, as though someone had scribbled all over her with a pencil. In the early days Mrs Head had set up the bath in the sitting room ready for her when she got home,

19

but now Tory only bathed once or twice during the week, although she usually washed her hands and face at the basin. Farraway's had a reputation locally. If you found yourself downwind of it, you'd better shut all your windows and doors. It seemed such a pity that her daughter should soil herself with such tawdry manufacturing. Gelatine of all things. Who needed gelatine now?

'Can't I change afterwards, Mama? My body feels like it's bound with red-hot iron hoops.'

'All the more reason to change, I would have thought, and to have a wash as well. At least give your hands a clean.'

'I washed them at the factory,' said Tory, as her mother entered from the kitchen, with her oven gloves on, which made her hands look as soft and bulky as a bear's paws. The gloves were joined together, which made her seem like a bear in chains.

'I'm just about to get it out of the oven,' Mrs Head said, flourishing the gloves.

Tory stood up and took off her coat, and went out into the hall to hang it up. In the hall mirror she released her hair from its netting, shook it out, was briefly appalled by the rat-tails that appeared at her shoulders but which she managed to knead back into the main body of her hair. She was aware that she was a little grimy, that her eyes looked tired, that her lips were pale and cracked, but it wasn't as though she was going anywhere tonight. It was only her mother who had to look at her, and she felt a certain pleasure in presenting such a tired, dirty face to her, just to remind her of how much she was suffering in this war. She didn't realize her mother had had exactly the same thoughts, and deliberately stooped and left her hair partially unpinned for the same reason.

By the time she re-entered the dining room, the joint of roast pork was on the table, and Mrs Head was standing before it with a carving knife.

'It's at times like this you realize how much you miss men,' said Mrs Head, immediately biting her lip, for she hadn't really wanted to invoke the absent fathers of the family, deceased Arthur and missing Donald.

'Why should we assume that carving is a man's job?' said Tory, taking her seat at the table – somewhat reluctantly, it seemed to Mrs Head. She had still shown no sign of appreciation for the spread that had been put out: thick gravy in a china boat that hadn't been used for years, roast potatoes and buttered sprouts in servers under floral lids, even ringed napkins beside the coasters.

'Well, the one who provides, I suppose, also does the carving, but then, by that logic, it's right that I should carve, since I'm the provider this time.'

This brought a little smile to Tory's tired face. Mrs Head inserted the tines of a carving fork into the meat. The crackling cracked, juice bubbled up and flowed down. The knife was put against the roasted skin, a few cautious strokes were made, the sharpened edge moving against the hard skin,

21

which yielded nothing. Then suddenly, with a little pressure, she was through; the skin had broken and the meat was coming away under the knife. With a few strokes a slice had been produced, which flopped to the side, like the page of a book turning. Mrs Head worked quickly.

'Even if I say so myself,' she remarked, delivering the first pink slice to Tory's plate, 'this meat is done to perfection.'

Tory had to agree, as the excellent crackling clinked onto the plate. She was even beginning to feel quite hungry. She bent down to sniff it, in a way that her mother thought was rather rude. 'So where did you get it?' she said.

'Where did I get it?' Mrs Head hesitated, suddenly struck by the trickiness of this question, shocked that she hadn't anticipated it. 'Where did I get it? Well, where do you think I got it?'

'You've just been telling me about how Dando's has been completely destroyed, and how you haven't been able to buy any meat there for days, and how there aren't any other butchers for miles around, and that you'll set off early to visit them tomorrow . . .'

'Yes,' said Mrs Head in a lingering sort of voice, 'yes, I did say that, didn't I?' She was going through all the possible fabrications she could tell, and wondering how they compared with the truth. In the end there just wasn't time for her to work out a story.

'Well, you could say I did get it from Dando's after all . . .'

Tory, about to put some of the meat into her mouth, instead returned it carefully to her plate. 'What do you mean, Mother?'

'I suppose you could say I was lucky, Tory. Very lucky. Blessed, you could say.'

Now Tory put down her knife and fork. 'Are you trying to tell me you found this meat in the ruins of the shop?'

'No, no, no,' said Mrs Head, as though affronted. 'No, not in his shop at all, no. It had been thrown right across to the other side of the street.'

Tory closed her eyes and hung her head, as though having trouble comprehending the simple words her mother was speaking. She lifted her head and spoke. 'Where exactly did you find it?' She still had her eyes closed, as though dreading the answer.

'Now, Tory, there is absolutely nothing wrong with this meat. I've thoroughly cleaned it, I inspected it very closely . . .'

'You're telling me that this meat has been lying on the pavement since the small hours of this morning?'

'Tory please, be practical . . .'

Tory stood up and moved away from the table, as though merely being near the meat could be dangerous. She stood in the middle of the room with her arms folded. 'This is wrong in so many ways,' she said, 'I hardly know where to begin. Leave aside the question of looting for the moment. This meat has been lying in the open air since around three o'clock in the morning before you found it. Goodness knows what creatures could have run their rheumy snouts over it and dragged their dirty little feet across it, or sat on it with their dirty little bottoms. Then there is the question of what exactly this meat is. You say it is leg of pork. I wonder how you know it is even animal meat at all.'

'What are you saying, Tory? Don't be ridiculous. Of course it's pork.'

'Were there any casualties in this air raid? I heard people on the tram saying there had been some . . .'

'It's leg of pork, Tory, trust me. I have been visiting butchers' shops for more than forty years and I know my cuts of meat. No bomb could joint a piece of meat so neatly. And I know how Dando cuts his pork . . .'

Mrs Head knew that she had not succeeded in convincing her daughter of the meat's cleanliness, its wholesomeness. And now she, too, was starting to have her doubts. It had never once occurred to her that the meat might not be animal at all, but the remains of some poor devil caught in the bomb blast. Trust Tory to think of this possibility. She remembered how her daughter had put her off black pudding. A few months ago Tory had refused to eat any when Mrs Head had brought some home. She claimed to have heard it on good authority that the Government was using human blood for its manufacture. It was a way of making

24

use of the surplus that had built up at the blood banks since the outbreak of war, when everyone was queuing up to 'give'. Her mother wondered how she could know these things, and presumed that the gelatine factory was privy to such information.

'It's tantamount to cannibalism,' Tory had said.

That was one way of looking at it. But it hadn't stopped Mrs Head frying some up with the previous day's mashed potato for a solitary lunch. She didn't tell Tory she'd eaten it, nor that it had tasted, to her, better than normal. So good, so filling, that she'd had to lie down for an hour afterwards. It had confirmed her own feelings about herself, that she was a strong woman who could withstand anything.

A black cat entered the room, its tail perpendicular, and sniffed the air eagerly. Mrs Head, still seated at the table, lifted a small slice of pork off her plate and held it out for the cat who, as though having a fantasy realized, darted across and grabbed the meat in its teeth, making Mrs Head laugh. 'Sambo doesn't care,' she said, as the cat hurried to a corner of the room and ate with his back to the humans.

Though she recognized that cats did this thing with their food, of eating defensively in corners, Tory wondered if he didn't look a little bit ashamed. 'The day we look to cats for moral guidance will be the day that civilization ends,' she said.

'They're very practical creatures, aren't you, Sambo?'

He had finished his morsel and come back for more.

'All animals are practical, Mother. They're also thoughtless.'

'I don't know about that, Tory. Sometimes I look at Sambo and he seems to see right through me. And you know what they say about following a cat in an air raid.' Both women contemplated him for a few moments. 'You know how difficult it is to come by good meat, Tory, and now that Dando's has gone, we need to make the best of what we can get. This may be the last piece of decent meat we see for a very long time. And you can rest assured that I would never knowingly eat someone . . .'

Tory laughed at the statement, made so sincerely by her mother, who failed to see what was funny. The ensuing discussion grew quite heated but only served, in the end, to strengthen Tory's conviction that there was something wrong about the meat. The more they spoke of cannibalism (in all but name), the more likely it seemed that the meat on the plate was human. Perhaps it was even Mr Dando himself. With such a possibility foremost in her mind, Tory now even found the sight of the meat repulsive, and believed that she was, indeed, very close to vomiting. At the same time she was so damn hungry.

The argument had the opposite effect on her

mother. The more they discussed cannibalism, the more rigid her resolve to eat the meat, even if it was only to prove how firmly she believed it was safe. So it was Mrs Head who took the first bite at the pork of doubtful origin. Stabbing a piece with her fork, popping it into her mouth and chewing, she was careful not to meet her daughter's eye, but to glance elsewhere with as much casual indifference as to what was in her mouth as she could muster. She took another forkful, carefully selecting the biggest, juiciest piece of pork she could find on her plate. She chewed slowly and thoughtfully. Chewing had replaced speech in their discussion. She could say all she needed to say on the subject simply by chewing.

Tory watched the spectacle, her lips set a tiny bit lopsidedly, not quite grimacing, but close to it. She sat down again and took a drink from the glass of water next to her.

'It's getting cold,' her mother said, as she poked around on her plate for the next morsel. 'It would be the most awful crime, in these times of scarcity, to waste good food like this. Absolutely criminal. And so tasty . . .' She sprinkled some salt and pepper onto her meal. 'If you don't eat it, Tory, I – well, I don't know what the world would think of you, if it knew . . .'

The likelihood of the roast dinner containing human meat was very, very slight. No one lived over those shops, she was sure, and certainly not

Mr Dando (she hadn't seen the fallen wardrobe, of course, or the pictures on the wall, or the ornament on the stranded mantelpiece). And there wouldn't have been anyone out in the street at that time of night during a raid. Which could only mean that the meat was stock from the butcher's shop, thrust forth by the bomb blast. But then – it was very unlikely that Dando's was so richly stocked with meat that there was much to keep overnight. Surely any meat that came in was gone within minutes.

'I'm sorry,' said Tory, picking up her fork, 'I'm sure you know best.' She was giving the meat the benefit of the doubt. Besides, it was producing the most appealing, tempting smell. Human meat, surely, would not give off such savouriness. She picked up a piece on her fork, opened her mouth and filled it.

Mrs Head was very pleased. If she herself had any doubts about the food that had entered her digestive tract, if she discerned the faintest unwholesome taint to what was now slowly progressing through her gut, it seemed instantly dispelled the moment Tory joined her in her meal. This was because she sincerely believed that Tory would not, for a moment, have considered eating the pork if there had been any doubt in her mind that it might be human flesh. She was good in that way. Had Mrs Head been told that she had eaten human meat, she would merely have felt that an unfortunate misunderstanding had occurred. She

28

might have felt uncomfortable, even a little nauseous, but that would have passed once the digestive process had reached its discreet conclusion. Tory, on the other hand, would have believed that her soul had been indelibly stained. She was not, as far as her mother knew, a particularly religious person (if she was, it certainly wasn't her parents' doing) and yet she seemed to have an almost spiritual understanding of right and wrong. She had what her father had called a sound moral foundation. He should have known, of course, because, at six years old, Tory had reported him to the police for breaking a promise to take her kite-flying. This was something for her mother to be proud of, but it irked her sometimes because she was often made to feel bad in the radiant light of her daughter's goodness.

But Tory didn't eat much. If she was to be a cannibal (so she seemed to imply with her leftovers), she wasn't going to be a greedy cannibal. By contrast Mrs Head was again made to feel a little bit bad by finishing her portion entirely and wiping up the juices with some bread.

CHAPTER 3

The rest of the evening followed a well-established pattern, though Tory couldn't rid herself of the lingering suspicion that she had been transformed in some irrevocable way. It was a similar feeling to the aftershock of being kissed for the first time (Clarence Dundry, chief teller at her father's bank, on the common after a tea of kidneys and lemonade at the English Rose Tea Rooms). She would look at her face in the mirror and say, 'Tory Head has been kissed by a man,' and wonder why the face looking back at her was the same face that had always looked back at her, and not a different one, a woman's one. Now she might look in the mirror and say, 'Tory Pace has eaten human flesh and no longer deserves to live amongst civilized people,' but again it would have been the same tired face that had looked back at her for the last ten years. The tired, drawn face of the mother-of-three and wife-to-one.

She changed her clothes and brushed her hair, then went into the living room to write some letters at the escritoire. She wrote letters nearly every day, usually to the children, a separate letter each. This torrent of postage was met with a trickle in reply, but she didn't expect much more. At first they had written brave, unhappy letters from the Cotswolds. Paulette, her older daughter, had written, *'Do not worry about us, Mother. I have devised a machine for disarming ogres. It uses trick chocolate . . .'*

Tom, her studious eldest, had written, *'We are very sorry that Father is dead, but we doubt he would have wanted to be part of a world like the one that is taking shape around us . . .'*

This letter had alarmed Tory. While she herself had decided that Donald was no longer alive, she couldn't remember passing this belief on to the children. And they seemed to have accepted it so matter-of-factly, or at least Tom had. But then none of them had been particularly close to their father, or had appeared especially fond of him.

She tried hard to imagine her son. It had become difficult. She didn't have any recent photographs. She remembered him more by his actions than his appearance: she could picture him changing the wheel of his bike, or mixing things in a test tube from his chemistry set, or plotting the passage of sunlight across the living room, or sitting in a corner of the kitchen with his face hidden behind a big, serious book. The only feature she could recall with certainty was his spectacles, because they were so black and heavy-framed. She tried to imagine him explaining the death of their father

31

to the two girls, in his matter-of-fact way. She imagined that they had sat under a haystack, the girls sobbing while Tom spoke: 'There's no point in crying, you know. There's a war on and people have to die. That's the whole point of a war . . .'

She sometimes wondered why she bothered writing to her clever son at all. He clearly found her letters unsatisfying. She was reading his most recent one to her, which began

Dear Mama,

I refer you to your letter dated 16–1–41, in which you tell us about your work at Farraway's Gelatine Factory. Your most recent letter (dated 21–3–41) repeats a lot of this information. There is really little point in writing to us unless you have something new to tell.

I have bought a magnifying glass.

Yours sincerely

Tom

He seemed to think he was writing on behalf of the girls as well. They rarely wrote, and when they did, the results were even briefer. Albertina, her youngest, had once written her the following:

Dra Mama,

I cant think of anything to rite

Your truly

Albertina

'At least she's honest,' Mrs Head had said, and it had amused Tory, seeing the sweated labour evident in every crooked downstroke. In fact it had moved her to tears, the simple, contradictory honesty of her little girl's letter, so painstakingly rendered in clumsy pencil. But this evening she felt Albertina's sentiments acutely as her own. She couldn't think of anything to write. The bombing of the butcher's shop was not something that she thought they would like to hear about, although perhaps it would do them good, occasionally, to be reminded of why they'd been evacuated in the first place. She played over to herself the words that were actually struggling for expression: '*Mrs Head and I had the most gorgeous roast dinner this evening. The only problem was that we couldn't be sure the meat was not human, perhaps even a portion of Mr Dando's leg, which made it rather difficult to enjoy . . .*'

She emerged from the sitting room an hour later, defeated and nauseous, and sat in the armchair opposite her mother at the fireplace. Her mother was, unusually, reading the paper that Tory had brought home that evening. Mrs Head did very

33

little reading, even of newspapers. She was a woman who liked to be always doing things, and she didn't regard reading as an activity. Somewhat reluctantly, Tory picked up her knitting. She was in the middle of making a stripy bobble hat for Albertina, but it wasn't going well. Tory was not a natural knitter, unlike her mother, and she'd several times already had to unravel the thing and start again. Knitting within visual range of her mother was always a risk since it invited commentary.

But this evening Mrs Head seemed unusually quiet. The pair of them sat there in a silence interrupted only by the curious noises their respective digestive systems gave, alimentary howls and cat-calls, as that evening's meal was, apparently with some difficulty, processed. It was as though two forest animals were calling to each other in the dark, little yelps and shrieks from Mrs Head's intestines answered by gorilla-yodels and perversely masculine grumbles from Tory's petite insides. Suddenly a new voice was added, as Mrs Head spoke.

'There we are,' she said, turning the pages of the newspaper to face her daughter. 'What did I tell you?' She pointed to a news item that described the safe return home of several prisoners of war after a daring escape from a German camp. 'I expect Donald is at this very moment digging some sort of tunnel, like those fellows did.'

'Donald is dead, Mother. I would be wearing mourning if it was available on rationing.'

'Quite right that it isn't,' said Mrs Head, who

hadn't worn black when her Arthur had died, even though it had happened long before clothing coupons came in. 'It's extravagant, illogical and unchristian. Why should you want to draw attention to yourself and demand sympathy? But that ignores the main fact that your husband, as we're all sure, apart from you for some unknown reason, is not dead.'

Tory didn't speak, but struggled with a stitch instead.

'Why do you insist on believing this nonsense, Tory? I think it's criminal. You've even convinced the children when there isn't a shred of evidence—'

'It's been six months, Mother,' her daughter snapped, 'six months since he was declared missing in action . . .'

'But it can take a long time before news comes through. That's what the letter said. It can take months . . .' But even she had to concede, privately, that the chances of Donald being alive were small. The losses in North Africa had been heavy, and the Germans had shown little mercy. She wished it was otherwise, since she dreaded the thought of her daughter becoming a widow – it was a role she cherished for herself alone. At the same time she couldn't help secretly (or so she hoped) nursing feelings of blazing self-righteousness and supreme vindication when her son-in-law was declared missing in action after only three months in the Army. She wondered why on earth anyone, let alone those who should have known better, would think he might serve any useful purpose as a fighting soldier. She was up visiting from Waseminster the very day his call-up papers came, and she couldn't quite believe it.

'What would the Army want with you?' she'd said.

Donald had given her one of his disgruntled tomcat looks, thinking she was being sarcastic before realizing she was genuinely puzzled. 'It's conscription,' he explained. 'Everybody has to go.'

'But surely they mean every able-bodied man . . .'

Jokingly, Donald had rolled up his right sleeve and flexed his biceps, displaying the little white muscle that suddenly appeared there, like a boiled egg. 'You're forgetting I'm from Glasgae,' he said, exaggerating his nearly lost Gorbals accent. 'We were slaughtering Visigoths while you lot were still treading grapes with the Gauls.'

Mrs Head suspected different periods of history were mixed up in that little put-down, but didn't feel able to question Donald's scholarship. He was a very bookish chap. 'Well, it's a long road,' she said, 'that leads from wallpapering the pantries of Plumstead Common to the battlefields of the Eastern Front, whenever there may be one . . .' She'd been rather pleased with that retort, and afterwards she couldn't stop giggling at the picture in her mind, of Donald running on his silly little legs to paste rolls of wallpaper over the approaching German tanks. 'God help us,' she half whispered to herself.

He had sent regular letters but wasn't allowed to say where he was, though they guessed, from his continual references to sand, heat, scorpions, camels and pyramids, that he was somewhere in North Africa.

Then the letter from the Army Records Office arrived.

Dear Sir or Madam,

I regret to have to inform you that a report has been received from the War Office to the effect that

No. (54769)

Rank (Pte)

Name *Pace, Donald Midlothian*

Was posted *'missing'* **on the** *(date unknown)*

The report that he is missing does not necessarily mean that he has been killed, as he may be a prisoner of war or temporarily separated from his regiment. Official reports that men are prisoners of war take some time to reach this country, and if he has been captured by the enemy it is probable that unofficial news will reach you first. In that case I am to ask you to forward any postcard or letter received at once to

37

this office, and it will be returned to you as soon as possible.

Should any further information be received it will be at once communicated to you.

I am,
Sir or Madam,
Your obedient servant,

H. J. Hiscock

Officer in charge of Records

'They do not take prisoners in the desert,' had been Tory's first remark, after she and her mother, shoulder to shoulder, had read the letter together. She had made up her mind that quickly, and hadn't altered her position since.

'It's unpatriotic of you,' Mrs Head now said to her daughter, 'to suppose that your husband is dead.'

'Patriotism has got nothing to do with it,' said Tory, quietly, without looking up from her knitting.

'Well, I don't like to say this, Tory, but in my opinion you seem too ready to believe the worst where Donald is concerned. Any other wife would be clinging to the hope that he had survived as a prisoner of war, but you almost seem to want him to have been killed.'

This made Tory look up in alarm. About to remonstrate angrily, she checked herself, then looked down again at her needles. There were tears forming, her mother was pleased to note. One or two had dropped into her wool.

'It's not that I don't want to believe that he's alive,' she said. 'It's just that I don't really think Donald is much of a survivor.'

Donald was physically tough, in his small, wiry way, but he tended to keel over when confronted with an obstacle. She remembered a bossy, needle-nosed spinster who'd refused to pay him when he'd spent a fortnight brightening up her gloomy little parlour. After a few doorstep arguments he had just thrown in the towel, said, 'Have it your own way', and gone on to the next job. It had shocked her that he should give up so quickly. She even went round to the spinster's house herself to try to reason with her. It was a particularly lean time and they needed every penny. How Donald had laughed when she, too, came home empty-handed. 'I told you. No point in wasting energy with someone like that.' She supposed he thought the same when confronted with enemy divisions.

Sometimes there came to her mind a picture of Donald as a skeleton, picked clean and bleached white, drowning in sand.

'Well, I think that's a rather pitiful thing to think about your own husband . . .'

'I don't want to talk about it, Mama.'

And so they didn't. They said very little for the rest of the evening.

They went to bed without wishing each other goodnight, feeling hungry and unloved.

CHAPTER 4

Mrs Head set off early next morning for her journey to the high street, which she decided to walk, despite there being trams available, just to see if she could do it. She chose a special hat for the occasion, determined to make an early impression on the distant butchers, in the manner of Mrs Richards, and so bedecked herself in a turquoise toque garnished with osprey feathers, forgetting how down at heel the high street had become in recent years, and not realizing how jarringly she would stand out among the grey crowds there. She was pleased to see that there were many butchers in the high street. In fact, there seemed to be more than she would have thought necessary. She found it easy to register with the one she considered the most promising (from the relative abundance of red meat in his window), and was able to buy some fatty little chump chops and streaky bacon that very morning. Perhaps the bombing of Dando's, she thought to herself as she made the long walk back, was to be a blessing in disguise.

She was quite unprepared for the shock that was to greet her on her return. Opening the front door she found a letter on the mat, realizing even before she picked it up that it was a powerfully official communication. The blue envelope bore German writing in one corner that, just by virtue of its dark, prickly typeface, looked threatening. It made her hesitate as she stooped to pick it up, and in the end she lifted the envelope carefully, as though it was a piece of broken glass.

Kriegsgefangenenpost was written across the top. She knew that this meant it was a letter from a prisoner of war. And there was Donald's hand-writing, overshadowed and cowering, it seemed, beneath the rubber stamps of officials and censors. STALAG-VII-C. A red crown with the word 'passed' underneath. A German eagle. Hands from both sides of the war had touched this envelope, had read its contents. Enemies had co-operated in its journey across Europe. It thrilled Mrs Head a little, and she became breathless.

'So the little Scotchman painter and decorator is alive after all,' she gasped to herself, as she hurried with the letter into the kitchen, 'wiling away his days in a prisoner-of-war camp.' She giggled nerv-ously. 'Well, he could have written sooner.'

She fought the temptation to open the letter, unable to understand whether the soaring feelings of excitement she was experiencing were for the knowledge that Donald was alive and that her daughter was no longer a widow, or that she could tell her daughter how wrong and mean-spirited she had been all this time in assuming Donald to be

41

dead. She became so excited about the letter that she was wondering whether she should go down to the factory and give it to her there, but she was tired enough after her shopping expedition to feel that the longer trip would be too much for her.

She told Mrs Wilson next door, when she went out into the yard to hang up some washing, and then she told Mrs Allen on the other side.

'Tory's Donald is alive,' she told them, with an air of pride, forgetting those scornful remarks she had made to her neighbour shortly after he was declared missing in action, that she'd never supposed he would last long in the Army anyway, that he would be among the first to be killed or captured, the puny little Scotchman. Now she proclaimed him as a hero to her neighbours. The truth was that the news Donald was still alive lifted her heart far more than she would have expected. Dead he was rather a disgrace, but captured – that meant there might still be a chance for her family to distinguish itself in the war effort.

'Have you opened it?' said Mrs Wilson.

'No, of course not. It's addressed to Tory.'

'He'll be asking for food. That's what they all ask for. Mrs Adams's son's a PoW, and the first thing they write about is to ask for a food parcel. Bovril, Oxo cubes, ointment, chocolate, cocoa, tea, all that sort of stuff. You can claim extra rations if you've got a PoW in the family.'

But Donald didn't ask for any of these things. When Tory finally came home, a little later than usual, she took the envelope down from the mantelpiece where it had been propped all day, watched by Mrs Head with the same inert concentration as the china spaniels that sat obediently at either end of the mantelpiece. She didn't register as quickly as her mother that she was holding a letter from her husband, and pored for some time over the peculiar markings on the envelope, looking across for explanation.

'There! Aren't you ashamed of yourself? You said he was dead all this time – well, dead men don't write letters.'

The letter suddenly felt heavy in Tory's hands, as though it had been written on sheets of lead. That was when she began shaking – it seemed to take all her effort to keep the envelope from dropping out of her grasp.

She couldn't say anything.

'Aren't you going to open it, child?' Her mother liked nothing better than sending Tory back to her infancy.

'I can't.' She meant this literally: her fingers couldn't find an edge to pull. After a few moments she held the letter out, still shakily, towards her mother. 'Can't you do it for me?'

'Child, surely you can open a letter from your husband.'

Tory took a moment to re-examine the front of the envelope.

'This is dated December . . .'

'Well, just be thankful it got here at all – who

knows what obstacles that little piece of paper has had to overcome to get here? Now open it . . .'

'I can't,' Tory repeated. 'I'm shaking too much.' She didn't want to say what she was really thinking: that a letter so old was no proof that her husband was alive, that he could have died since. Eventually Mrs Head took the letter and tore it open. Glancing to check that it was indeed from Donald, she held forth the extracted sheet of blue paper, covered with awkward, square-looking handwriting, for her daughter to read.

'Please,' said Tory, 'you read it.'

Mrs Head feigned reluctance to do this, but secretly she was delighted to be the first reader of Donald's letter. She had long since recovered from the shock of knowing that Donald was alive and, as the afternoon had drawn on, had even become a little bored by the fact, but now the opportunity of a little performance, to be the herald of important news – she relished the prospect.

'Very well, Tory. Why don't you sit down and prepare yourself? Would you like a cup of tea first?'

'No,' said Tory, as she sat on one of the stiff, wheelbacked dining-chairs. 'Just read it.'

There was a little moment of fuss as Mrs Head hunted down her spectacles. Then, with Tory nervously seated, she held the letter before her, cleared her throat, and began. *My Dearest Darling Sweetheart Tory . . .*

Tory couldn't help but let out a yelp of passion at hearing herself so addressed by the man she had convinced herself was long dead, and Mrs Head paused to let her recover. Her daughter was sobbing, and the tears were falling fast. She went on:

'At last the Germans have given us pens and paper and allowed us to write letters home. They have only given us one sheet each and told us to write in block capitals, so that they can read them, I suppose. Well, now I've said all that I've got hardly any room left to say anything else.'

Mrs Head and her daughter both laughed, Tory in the most relieved sort of way, as her mother held the letter so that she could see the big block capitals it was written in.

'Wonderful that he's kept his sense of humour,' said Mrs Head.

'I'm doing pretty well considering. Was captured near Libyan border, defending an airfield, and was shipped over the Med and transported north through Italy. Don't know where the hell I am now, though. Good crowd here, some Australians and Canadians. We play cards quite a lot. Food not so bad.

'We were right, Tory, weren't we, when we said he was in North Africa? I told you. I'm so glad he wasn't badly hurt.

45

'Nothing else troubles me, apart from not being able to . . .'

Here Mrs Head stopped abruptly, and was silent for a few moments as she read on to herself. Tory, who had been hanging her head for most of the time, suddenly looked up. 'Apart from not being able to what?'

'Oh dear,' said Mrs Head.

'What is it? What has he written?'

'I'm afraid I can't say, Tory. Your husband seems to have quite lost his mind.'

'Show me.'

Tory reached for the letter but Mrs Head drew back, cautiously.

'What are you doing? It's my letter, you shouldn't even be reading it.'

'But you asked me to.'

Tory seemed to have regained her composure after the shock of receiving the letter and was now standing up. For a moment it seemed that there might be an absurd chase through the house, the daughter after her mother in pursuit of a letter from her own husband. Before this could happen Mrs Head seemed to concede defeat and allowed the letter to pass into her daughter's hands. She quickly scanned through it to the final paragraph.

Nothing else troubles me apart from not being able to pull your knickers down and give you

46

*a good fuck. Instead, could you write me a
dirty letter, by return of post? I mean really
filthy, full of all the dirtiest words and deeds
you can think of.*

I require this most urgently.

Love to your ma

Donald

XXX

Mother and daughter were silent for a few
moments after Tory, having taken far longer than
seemed necessary, had finished reading. Neither
knew quite what to say. Tory read through it again,
squinting closely, as though having trouble de-
ciphering the very clear handwriting.

'Oh, for heaven's sake, how many times do you
have to read it?' Mrs Head finally blurted.

'He's not himself,' said Tory, with a sense of
hard-won resolve. 'I can tell by the handwriting.
He's not himself. After all he's been through, he's
confused. His head's been turned.'

Mrs Head coughed theatrically. 'I don't care what
he's been through, there is absolutely no excuse
for that – sort of thing. We can only hope that he's
not in his right state of mind, as you say. He seems
to have forgotten completely that he even has any
children.'

Tory felt as though she had frozen into a solid

47

lump. For a few moments she couldn't move or speak. She stood by the mantelpiece, the letter hanging in her hand like the shred of a burst balloon. The porcelain spaniels each patiently examined one of her ears. She was experiencing no emotion, apart from a distant sense of panic, such as she sometimes felt on a railway platform when gripped by the absurd thought that the innocent old lady behind her might push her into the path of the express. Her mother had identified the truly horrifying thing about the letter, that it contained no reference whatsoever to Tom, Paulette and Albertina.

'You'd better give me the letter, Tory.' Mrs Head was holding out her hand.

'What? Why?'

'So that I may dispose of it properly, of course.'

Tory had by now put the letter carefully back in its envelope, and she held it close to her. 'I don't know what I'm going to do with it, Mama, but I'm going to keep it for the moment.'

'But you can't possibly be thinking of replying in the manner he demands. Make a note of the address so that you can write him a sensible reply, but let me destroy that letter. It pains me too much to think what might happen if someone should find it.'

'No one will find it. Why should they?'

'Well, where are you going to put it? In some box of keepsakes so that when the war is over and Donald is safely home you can go through your casket of treasured memories? What'll happen then? You'll read this letter and all the filth it contains . . .

48

Or you'll leave it for your children to discover when you're long gone, and what'll they think of their war-hero father then? These things have a habit of turning up . . .' Her argument trailed off.

Tory had folded the letter and was holding it against her breast in a rather defiant way. She had no intention of giving it up. 'You're judging Donald too harshly, just as you have always done. We can't begin to understand what he might have been through. Of course he puts a brave face on things in this letter, but that's his way, never complaining. It could only be a kind of madness that made him write that last paragraph, especially as he must have realized it was likely to be read by people other than me.'

'You're beginning to sound a little as though you're making excuses for him. He's a British soldier, for heaven's sake. This letter has been read by officials of the Nazi war machine – look at their stamp on the top of the letter. What sort of impression is that going to give of our moral health?'

This thought did give Tory some pause. The idea that some jackbooted Nazi had read this letter from her husband, imagining the sort of wife who would comply with such a demand without a second thought, imagining some lipsticked, viridian eye-shadowed she-devil with a Passing Cloud hanging from her lips . . . Her mother was right, such correspondence could easily be used to give an impression of the British housewife as morally depraved.

'Don't worry, Mama,' said Tory irritably, 'it will not be seen by anyone. But I must keep it for the moment.'

Mrs Head shook her head pityingly and went back into the kitchen. Tory went in the opposite direction, to the sitting room, where she shut the door behind her and then leant with her back against it. She began crying.

Over the months this room had become her own private space. In the past it had only ever been used for entertaining visitors and her mother rarely went in there. Tory derived great comfort from its plusher, classier furnishings. The little velvet chaise longue, the mahogany escritoire, the china pots and vases with their healthy-looking plants. There was a smell in there she had come to recognize as one that offered great comfort, the smell of polished wood and venerable old cushions and upholstery. It was a churchy smell. Old without being merely dilapidated and worn (which could not be said for the dining room and kitchen), it was a smell that seemed to speak of long lives lived in one place, generation after generation.

When the tears had subsided, which they did rather quickly, Tory read Donald's letter again. 'Oh, Donald, how could you?' she said croakily to herself. The letter should have been the moment of Donald's heroic return to the world of the living. Instead he had made a fool of himself and had soiled the occasion with a most uncharacteristic lurch into sexual vulgarity.

Tory calmed herself by writing letters to the children, one for all three of them this time

Dear Tom, Paulette, and Albertina

Prepare yourselves for some truly wonderful news. Your father is alive and well! Yes, that's right, your sincerest wish has come true. I received a letter from your father this very morning, and in it he said he wanted me to tell you how proud he is of you all, and that he is thinking of you every day and night.

She did her best to write a letter that conveyed a sense of rejoicing and celebration, such as the children (she hoped) would be feeling when they read this letter, but it was a hard struggle and she soon found that she had said all she could on that subject, and filled the rest of the page with inconsequential news.

She would have written immediately to Donald, had he not included that final request. It threw her into an emotional turmoil. She dismissed from her mind immediately any idea that she would try to meet his demand, but at the same time she had to deal with it somehow. She had to answer it. What should she say in her letter? How should she make reference to his request? How should she refuse him?

Having sealed the children's letter safely into an envelope, she took another sheet of writing paper out of the escritoire's tray, and tried drafting a reply.

Dearest Donald,

I thank heaven that you are alive and apparently well. You didn't ask how I, my mother or the children are, but I am sure you would like to know that we and they are also well. I am afraid, however, that I cannot meet your request for what you call a 'dirty letter'. In fact, I feel quite insulted that you think I am capable of producing such a document. I will put your request down to a moment of brain fever, brought on by the stresses of your situation.

Please let me know if there is anything else I can do for you. Would you like me to send you some chocolate?

Your loving wife

Tory

It took Tory nearly an hour to write this letter, and less than a minute to realize that she could never post it. *I sound so cold,* she thought. It had the blunt officiousness of the letters her father must have written to overdrawn customers. Tory had spent her first few years of employment as a clerk in her father's bank, and the scrupulous procedural efficiency of the work had left its mark on her. She hated waste, ambiguity and inaccuracy. She also hated dishonesty. Even if she was capable of writing a dirty letter, it would have had to be a work of fiction, and therefore dishonest.

Now, by drafting a reply, all she had done was bring another document into being whose existence would need to be covered up. There was a small fire burning in the grate, and Tory gave her letter to its little yellow flames. She wondered for a moment if she should do the same with Donald's. It would have been the most obvious solution, making a note of the address, as her mother had said, and then simply destroying the horrible thing. But it was the only piece of evidence that her husband was still in the world, and no matter how soiled it seemed, it was precious for that reason alone.

She decided she should not be hasty in replying. Supposing, after all, that Donald had actually written the letter in a state of delirium, and had no memory of adding that final paragraph. What would he then make of her reply, if she was to meet his demand? Apart from that, the letter had been four months in transit. Surely Donald, in all those months of waiting, had written again. Perhaps that letter was following quickly behind the first one. Perhaps she should wait a week or two to see if another letter arrived. If that letter made no lewd demands, she could put the whole incident down to madness, pretend that the first had never existed, and let the matter pass into oblivion.

★   ★   ★

53

At work Tory was rather alarmed to find that news of Donald's survival had arrived ahead of her. Doreen, one of the matronly elders, had got everyone to make Union Jacks out of red, white and blue packing paper and sack thread, draping them all around the bare brick walls. An impromptu party was held, and she was toasted with mugs of strong sweet tea and congratulated all round by the packing women. She had made no real friends among these people so was a little surprised by the warmth of her reception. Several other women had husbands or other close relatives in prisoner-of-war camps, and they were eager to share information. After her initial fear, Tory felt assured that whatever gossipy network had brought the news from Peter Street to here (emanating, no doubt, from one of Mrs Head's over-the-garden-wall chinwags) it hadn't included the news about the sordid coda to Donald's letter. There was no sniggering or blushing among the grey-skinned packing women.

'I've brought a tin of cocoa in for you, darling, so that you can send it to him,' said Verity, pushing it into her hands.

'How's he doing, love? Are they feeding him? I've brought in some shortbread I been saving since Christmas – for you to send to your Don.'

Tory didn't even know the name of this woman. And Don? She had never called him Don.

'For your Donny,' said Win, one of the oldest of the group, landing a heavy cylindrical object into her lap at tea break. 'Made it specially.'

The object was a pound cake.

'Thank you so much,' said Tory, genuinely moved.

'Well, we've got to think of the men, haven't we? Sooner they win this war and come home, the sooner we can pack in these awful jobs.'

'Oh, I like the way you said "pack in", Winnie,' said Verity. 'That's so droll.'

By lunchtime Tory had accumulated a stack of gifts and goods for Donald that she would never be able to take home in one go. But she did manage to talk for a little while to Dorothy, one of the women with a husband in a camp.

'Does he write many letters?' Tory asked.

'Quite a regular flow, yes.'

'What does he write about?'

Dorothy looked at Tory as though she'd said something strange. 'Just stuff, like what people always put in letters, asking how you're keeping, what's the weather like, the weather here's drizzly, et cetera, et cetera'

'Does he ever write about anything else?'

'Sometimes he gets a bit maudlin and says how he misses home, then I write to him to tell him to pull himself together, and then he writes to say he'll soldier on regardless. Just needs a kick in the pants now and then, that's all.'

Tory so longed to ask Dorothy if she'd ever been required to write a dirty letter or, if not, what she would do if she was. But it simply wasn't possible even to broach the subject. There was no one else Tory could turn to. Her best friend had emigrated to Canada just before the war, and of her other friends, there were none with whom she felt it appropriate to share such information.

She returned home that evening, heavily laden with chocolate, biscuits and cakes to send to Donald. Perhaps under the welter of so much sugar his lustiness might dissolve. She would bombard him with sweet and sticky things so that he could forget about his other desires.

She entered the kitchen exhausted, and loaded her goods on to the table. Mrs Head was in her chair, staring at the mantelpiece. There was another blue envelope up there, covered with stamps and seals, waiting for her inspection.

'It's postmarked two weeks after the first one,' said Mrs Head, 'but has still taken nearly four months to get here.'

Mrs Head looked at Tory with one eyebrow raised, the look she might give to a naughty child who was thinking about being naughty a second time. She was dying to know, just as Tory was, whether the two-week interval between the letters had been enough time for Donald's sanity to return. The letter began:

Dearest Darling Sweetheart Tory,

I don't know if you ever received my last letter, but I wrote to you about two weeks ago to tell you that I'm fine and that I'm out here in the middle of nowhere in some Godforsaken part of the German empire, being held as a prisoner of war. I was captured in the desert, shipped across the Med then conveyed north through Italy in a cattle truck. Food not too bad, the other chaps are a good crowd – some Canadians and Australians. The English and the Aussies are teaching the Canadians how to play cricket.

My one problem is that I am starved of sex and I can't seem to take my mind off the thought of giving you good ol' fucking. You are always on my mind, Tory, but it is a lonely business when you are not here to do your duty. I therefore beg you to write me a dirty letter by return, as dirty as you can possibly make it, full of filthy thoughts and deeds. Even better would be if you could send me a photo of your-self with no clothes on – I know, it would be a difficult thing to fix. Perhaps you could get a camera from somewhere, and use a mirror. I'm running out of room, damn block caps.

Love to your ma

Donald

XXX(merry Xmas!)

'Well?' said Mrs Head, after Tory had read Donald's letter to herself, remaining silent and motionless long after she had finished reading. 'Am I to take it from your contemplative immobility that your husband has repeated his earlier request?'

'Not just repeated it,' said Tory, offering her mother the letter, 'he has asked more.'

Mrs Head read it quickly. 'The nerve,' was all she could say for a few moments. 'The nerve.'

More letters arrived in the following days. Sometimes two or three were delivered in the same post. They had all been written at fortnightly intervals, yet were delivered in the space of a few days. Donald's despair and frustration had spanned several months, yet for Tory they were compressed to about a week and a half. Perhaps if she had received them fortnightly she would have felt differently, would have had more time to be persuaded by their insistence and urgency, but to receive them *en masse,* to have the months of Donald's frustration crushed into the space of a few days, gave them such density and weight – it was as though she had been struck by a bomb made of words.

Each letter repeated the request made in the first, though phrased differently, with variations each time, and with relentlessly increasing coarseness.

Dearest Tory,

I have been writing letters to you for some time now and I do not know if they have reached you. Letters here arrive sometimes months after they were written, so I am hoping that there has simply been a delay with the post. My news is that I was captured in the desert and transported

58

across the Med, then up the leg of Italy to here. I think we're in the east of Germany somewhere.

I am a bit worried that you may have been offended by something I said in my earlier letters. I know it was a bit of a sauce of me, but I have this most burning desire for carnal gratification that only a wife can satisfy. In my earlier letters I asked that you write me a dirty letter. Please forgive me if you find that rude or bad of me. I do not know what else to do. I also wrote that I would like a nude photo of yourself. I know that was a crazy thing to ask because how would you get it developed, even if you could take it? Well a chap here knows of a photographer's studio in Stepney where they will develop such pictures with no questions asked. If you change your mind, here is the address: 17 Barrow Street, Stepney E1. The fellow there is called Watts.

Yours lovingly

Donald

Dear Tory,

The mail is coming and going quite smoothly out here so I am beginning to think that you are ignoring me. Perhaps you are offended by my requests or are too shy to reply. Come on, old girl! Don't be a prissy little missy (that's what the Canadians call 'em). You will do me great wrong by not complying – you might even be breaking the law (denying a husband his conjugal rights is grounds for divorce, you know), so take your knickers down, dip your nib in your fanny and write me a letter full of juice!!!!!!

Love to your ma (ask her for some writing tips!!),

Donald

From this letter onwards Donald's correspondence became so filthy that Tory could not bear to read it. Furthermore, he had begun illustrating his missives with drawings, of herself and Donald (she supposed), naked and with monstrously large private parts. This was quite enough for Tory, and she finally decided that Donald's letters had to be destroyed immediately. She burnt them in the sitting-room fireplace, with Mrs Head's overseeing approval. The last two letters she gave to the flames without even opening the envelopes.

The depravity of his later letters made it easier for Tory to reply. She was not only upset by the experience, she was disgusted and angry, and she wrote to Donald immediately.

Dear Donald,

Your letters were delayed in the post and have arrived all at once this past week. I have destroyed them. Please do not write me any more letters like those. If you do so I will destroy

all further communication from you without opening it, and will not write to you again.
You have offended me grievously.

Yours sincerely

Tory Pace

After Tory had posted this letter, she considered the fact that if Donald had not gone so far she might, eventually, have thought about how she might comply. But she was truly shocked by the depths to which her husband seemed to have sunk, and she was thus saved the trouble of tackling the problem of writing a dirty letter. Instead she had written what she supposed was the exact opposite – a cold, clinical, remonstrative epistle that could have come from the pen of a bewigged denizen of the Temple Inn. In fact, Tory was rather proud of the letter: she felt she had written something as pointed and as efficient as an arrow. She imagined it nailing any future indecent letters from Donald, pinning them to the floor so that they would never reach her. It would have an effect on Donald, she was sure. He was someone who appreciated words very much, someone who always corrected her when she misused them. He was a self-educated man, and very proud of the fact. It was this, among other considerations of Donald's character, that made the letters so very puzzling and shocking.

★   ★   ★

More letters came, which had left Germany several weeks before and so would not be an answer to her own. Tentatively Tory opened them and glanced at their contents, in the hope of detecting signs that Donald had mended his attitude. Instead she would see the now familiar graffiti and would not even attempt to read any of the words. The letters went into the fire, like the others. Then, after a gap of about two weeks:

My Dearest Tory,

Once again I have only a little page in which to say so much. Let me tell you how sorry I am for causing you offence. That was never my intention (quite the opposite, actually). But there is something about warfare that affects a man's spirits in the strangest ways. I did not ask those things of you from mere desire for recreation but out of a strong sense that my survival as a man depends upon it. I cannot describe for you the horrors I have seen, and continue to see. I think my desires for you act in part as an antidote to those horrors. A letter of the kind I describe will lighten so much of my suffering. I am asking you to think again, dearest Tory.
  No space left.

Donald

'Just because he can put it into those long sentences doesn't make it any less smutty,' was Mrs Head's verdict on the letter.

Tory was less sure. She immediately wondered if she was being too harsh on Donald. There was something beautiful about his last letter – for a painter and decorator he really did have an exceptionally sharp and sensitive mind. Well, painting and decorating was a type of art, after all. As Donald himself sometimes said, he shared a profession with Michelangelo, the greatest painter and decorator of them all. Not to mention Giotto. There was something in this letter that worked deeply at Tory's sense of marital duty – the faintest suspicion that, in ignoring Donald's request, she was failing in her wifely obligations.

She no longer even heard the bombs falling. At night her thoughts were with Donald and his terrible letters, trying to imagine the circumstances that could have wrought such changes in the man. What must he have seen and suffered to open up such stark and base longings? And who was she, from the relative comfort and security of blitzed London where, although the raids continued nightly, she had yet to see a dead body (unless, of course, the pork Mrs Head had found turned out to be what they most feared), who was she to deny a battle-worn prisoner of the Nazi regime the right to a moment of written lovemaking? It would only be doing what she would normally do as a wife but by post instead.

It was just that, before, Donald had never made much of a fuss about the thing. He performed the deed (always his word for it) perhaps once a month, using a prophylactic that Tory had never seen but which she could smell (it smelt of erasers and olive oil) and occasionally hear as a snapping sound before and after use. The whole business seemed to go on above Tory's head, with Donald up there, silent and sweating, grinding back and forth, trying to make the bed shake as little as possible, and always in the dark. It was not a wholly unpleasant experience and, in a curious way, Tory had come to miss it in the months since Donald had left. Behind the abrasive, sharp-boned, rough texture of the event, there was something warm and comforting.

As for writing a letter that would substitute for the act itself (if that was what was expected), she was at a complete loss. As a mother of three children she did not lack experience, but when it came to finding the words, her pen seemed to freeze in her hand and all the warmth drained out of those remembered moments. She began to think of their lovemaking as something taking place in a landscape of snow, two motionless bodies locked beneath a frosty counterpane, icicles hanging from the headboard . . .

A letter had come from the children, or from Tom at least, a couple of weeks after she had written to them with news of their father. It was a letter she liked to read and reread.

Dearest Mama,

In reference to your letter of 21 March 1941, we have some important information we would like you to give to Daddy. These are escape plans. The best one is No. 1, a tunnel, but since we do not know the layout or soil type of Daddy's prison, we have got some other escape plans. No. 2 is the human catapult. This is Paulette's plan. A catapult, like the ones the Romans used in sieges, could be constructed, and the escaper (with parachute) could be fired over the fence or wall. The parachute could be made from hankies. This would be best done at night. No. 3 is Albertina's plan, which is a bit silly but I have put it in anyway because she cried. She said Daddy should start a trampolining class, and have all the prisoners practising on trampolines next to the fence or wall. Then, when the signal is given, they could jump over. The trampolines could be made from hankies.

Please pass these plans on to Daddy as soon as you can, but don't say we thought of them in case they go wrong.

Yours sincerely,

Tom

The enclosed plans were very detailed, with diagrams, measurements, weight ratios and trajectories. The siege catapult had been carefully drawn, with a dotted, arcing line showing the path through the air to be taken by Donald (represented by a matchstick figure in mid-flight). Tom seemed to have inherited Donald's practical sense and artistic skills – the diagrams had the same sureness of line as Donald's pornographic cartoons, she was slightly perturbed to realize. She thought she would forward this letter to her husband to remind him of how much he still figured in the minds of his children. If only he would mention them once in his letters.

There was something about Tom's letter that inspired her. It was her children who had seen immediately what Donald needed – escape – but why hadn't she? She read through Tom's letter on the evening she had set aside for writing, finally, to Donald. She thought she would enclose it with her own letter, once she had written it. Sitting at the escritoire, she began,

Dearest Donald,

Forgive me if I seemed harsh in my earlier letter. We have been apart for a long time and it has taken me a while to try to see things from your position. I understand, now, how difficult things must have been for you, and how the struggles and sufferings you have endured must have

66

affected your thinking, and your memory. I'm sure this is why you have not asked about your children and their circumstances, or mine and Mrs Head's. First, let me tell you about the children. They have been very lucky in finding good foster families, and they are living in such a beautiful part of the world I feel quite jealous. They were, of course, overjoyed to learn that you are alive and well. I have only been able to visit them once since they were evacuated, but we write regularly. They have devised some plans for your escape which I think you will find amusing.

Mrs Head and I live in quiet and peaceful coexistence. Mrs H keep herself busy with shopping and cooking and visiting her friends, while I have taken work in a factory. I did spend some time as a searchlight operator, but I'm afraid I wasn't very good at it, and would have let hundreds of German planes sneak past unilluminated had I stayed in the job, so was glad to be relieved. I can do much less damage to the world in a gelatine factory, though I do sometimes wish I was doing something a little more important than packing gelatine.

The raids continue nearly every night. I do not know how much longer the city can take this sort of attack, although our part has escaped the worst so far (apart from a single bomb that fell on Old Parade, destroying Dando's and several other shops), but I do

67

know that the spirit of the people of London has not been broken and never will be, no matter what happens.

She added that last sentence after realizing her letter would be read by Germans. This thought also made it hard to decide how she would write what she thought she should write next.

Donald, I am thinking of what you asked for in your earlier letters . . .

She sat back, nibbled the end of her pencil nervously, glanced up at the wall, on which hung a framed photograph of Mr and Mr and Mrs Head, Mama and Papa, taken to commemorate their engagement, though you would not think this from the expressions on their faces – passive, stern, bored, two sepia-toned Victorians, her hand on his arm, gazing into space. For some reason the studio setting of this photograph was of the seashore. There were pebbles strewn on the floor, a starfish, and white cliffs were painted rather badly onto the draped background. At least they were not looking at her directly as she wrote. On the wall to the left there was a little engraving of Leonardo's *Last Supper*. Donald had said this picture was all wrong, that Jesus and his disciples had eaten like the Romans, reclining on couches.

She half closed her eyes and wrote:

I imagine you taking me in your manly arms,
my love, and then putting one of your hands
on my behind.

She wrote this sentence as if hurrying out of a smoke-filled building – blindly, stumblingly and fast. She signed her name, then sealed the letter in the envelope quickly, deciding at the last moment that she couldn't possibly include Tom's with her own. She gave another abashed glance at the photograph on the wall – could it be possible that they now looked a little bit shocked?

After posting the letter into the leering red mouth of the box on the corner of Peter Street and Mark Street, she imagined, at the other end, prison-camp guards in jackboots and those horrible streamlined helmets, ripping open her letter and laughing loudly at its last sentence. She imagined it being passed around the guardhouse for the amusement of the whole patrol. She couldn't help cherishing the hope that whatever van, boat or other vehicle helped carry communication across the battlefields would come under fire and her little letter be destroyed.

But afterwards, walking back to the house, she felt the lifting of a great weight. It was as though she'd finally found the money to pay a debt that had been owing for many years.

CHAPTER 5

Tory tried to think back to times that Donald had talked about sex. She could not recall a single remark. She wasn't even sure that she had ever heard him make mention of any of the nether parts of the human anatomy. And she had never heard him use a swear word stronger than 'blast'.

There was one occasion that stood out in her memory, but she wasn't sure that it counted. They hadn't been married for long, and they were walking on the common where they had taken many romantic walks in the days of their courtship, and they came upon a row of very old beech trees. Wonderful, misshapen things, swollen and bloated with age, with many stumps and scars from decades of pruning and lopping. They were little more than torsos, with stumps and sockets instead of limbs. And it was in observation of one of these trees that Donald said his rude word. He said, 'That tree, it looks like it's got an arsehole.'

Tory was so shocked that all she could say was 'Donald!'

But Donald wasn't at all ashamed, and in fact seemed keen, having taken the word out of whatever place he'd been keeping it, to give it a good airing.

'In fact, it looks like it's got two arseholes.' Then he went a little bit further, noting the same anatomical feature in other trees, and Tory gave up even trying to respond to these statements. The fact that Donald saw so many of them in the trees (and she could see them as well – those puckered rings of bark, thickening round the hollowness left by a fallen or chopped-off branch) meant that she saw them, and the woods generally, in a slightly different way from then on, and she mourned less their loss when they were felled some years later, as though they had been rather indecent, the poor, venerable things. He never used that word again.

It was one of the many occasions that Donald had said something odd, peculiar, even unsettling. It was very difficult to know when he was being serious. She remembered what he had said the day his call-up papers arrived.

'When I was a boy I used to think, How the hell am I going to get through the next sixty years or so without killing someone? Well, now it looks like I won't have to.'

Then there was that thing he had said just after she'd accepted his proposal of marriage: 'I'm so glad, Tory. I've always thought you were too good for me, you see.'

Oddly, she'd always thought exactly the opposite, that she couldn't possibly be good enough for the strictly moral painter and decorator.

'What do you mean, too good for you?'

'Let me put it this way, Tory. I've always felt that you are made of gold while I am a man of lead.'

It was only years later that she understood he was paraphrasing something from Plato's *Republic*, a book he often carried around with him and would brandish at certain moments of intellectual anxiety, at which times he would also revert to his broadest Gorbals accent: 'Ye need to take a look a' this wee book. Nivver min' *Mein Kampf*, ye want tae read *Thae Republic*.'

Such remarks cut little ice with Tory's mother, who didn't care for books, but to Tory they gave her husband an authority and stature she had not seen in her family before.

'You are an ideal of goodness,' he said, 'the lost half of my spirit double . . .'

She didn't know, quite, what he meant by this, but she loved the words.

They had met when she was working as a waitress in the English Rose Tea Rooms. She had taken up a position there shortly after leaving her job at her father's bank (a necessity when things had turned sour with her fellow teller, Clarence Dundry). Donald had been a regular customer at the bank and was now a regular customer at the

Tea Rooms. 'I'm not following you, you understand.' Despite its name, the English Rose was not a genteel establishment frequented by Victorian ladies sipping Darjeeling. It was, rather, a rough and ready eating house, serving hot-pots and pies to hungry working men and women, clerks from the nearby council offices, shopworkers from the high street, artisans who ate chops with their fingers and then loudly licked the tips of them. Butchers used to come in, Tory now recalled, bloodstained and sweaty, for their steaks. There was one who had taken the cheese and onion flan for lunch every day, as though he could not stand the sight of any more blood.

Donald always had devils on horseback with a glass of milk.

She felt she'd got to know Donald from the top down, because in the early days of their relationship she would stand over him while he sat at a table, choosing from the menu. She became familiar with the crown of his head, with its brushed-back wiry hair that sometimes stood up in spikes that trembled or vibrated, like tuning forks, when Donald spoke. She got to know the over-furrowed brow, which was very high, giving him the tousled widow's peak of the soon-to-be-bald. (In fact, to her surprise, Donald had done a good job of keeping his hair, just the littlest bald spot opening at the top after a few years.) Then she came to know the eyes, which would turn up to look at her with a mysterious twinkle when he ordered his devils on horseback, making a little joke each time about how he was struggling with the choice, then ordered the same thing yet again. 'Let me see, what'll I have? My, my so much choice, so little time. Well, just for a change I think I'll be daring and have . . . devils on horseback.' He could be funny when he wanted to.

But mostly he was serious. He had a way of speaking that made everything he said sound profoundly important. Perhaps it was the accent, which Tory always associated with bank managers, solicitors and other purveyors of probity and prudence. He would underscore statements with a piercing stare from rather feline eyes, which made it impossible to doubt anything he said. Once under his spell, there was no escape for Tory. Not that she ever desired escape, not seriously anyway. Occasionally she experienced an engulfing sense of dread that she had made some awful mistake in marrying Donald and should instead have thrown in her lot with Clarence Dundry and a life similar to her mother's, that of a bank clerk's wife. But such fears were usually shortlived. Donald's maturity, learning and practical sense made him seem a sensible yet adventurous option. He was a craftsman, a businessman, a self-made intellectual. As their marriage progressed Tory slowly began to feel it wasn't love she was experiencing, rather a sense of awe and admiration. They had lived their first few years together in a spirit of mutual respect. Tory felt that she was not so much loved as curated. Donald treated her as a precious and rare specimen, always concerned for her safety and comfort, and proud to show her off to his friends. She, in turn, enjoyed the way his talk soared far above the heads of all around them.

Things began to change when the children arrived. They seemed to unsettle and disconcert him. He didn't know quite what to do with them. His aura of authority and wisdom began to wane. He became distant and distracted. He was embarrassed when, for financial reasons, they had to move back into Peter Street, and he did little to disguise his glee when Mrs Head emigrated to the estuary. The children seemed to embarrass him as well – when they were babies at least. As they grew up, and he started to take more notice of them, he became a strict father, though he was never particularly severe. She only had one clear memory of him playing with the children when, one Christmas, he picked up a rug and pretended to be wrestling with a lion. On the whole, though, it seemed clear that his children, in his eyes, were not quite good enough.

She thought of Donald's oft-repeated remark that she was too good for him as she waited for his response to her letter. It came quickly, the usual blue envelope covered with stamps and the imprints of military officials. This was what appalled her most about the correspondence that had begun between them – that it was conducted through so many different levels of officialdom, from the bullet-dodging couriers (so she imagined) to the border guards, the censors. Great pains and, risks had been taken to negotiate the exchange of mail between prisoners of war and the outside world, and all Private Donald Pace and his wife could think to do was exchange indecent thoughts.

When she opened this latest communication she was puzzled. Even without reading it she could see that the envelope contained her own letter, the one she had sent to her husband two weeks earlier. She thought for a moment that perhaps the censor had not allowed it through. Surely her postscript was not strong enough to earn that degree of censure. Perhaps there had been some mistake. When she looked through the letter her eyes were immediately drawn to the bold red letters that had been scrawled in the margin. Not the censor's hand, but her husband's. In harsh, angry block capitals he had written *'NOT GOOD ENOUGH!!!'* And several arrows pointing to the offendingly inadequate sentence.

How the officials on both sides of the border must have laughed. The jackbooted guards who had previously leered and chuckled over the letter on its way in must have laughed even louder on its way out. Her humiliation was official and international. The frigid, inadequate wife unable to satisfy her husband's simple demands for sexual satisfaction – all he'd wanted was a few dirty words and the best she could come up with was 'behind'.

If it wasn't bad enough to have her erotic writing so closely examined, it seemed even worse to have it deemed inadequate. What he meant, of course, was that she was not bad enough.

In her next letter she tried pleading with her husband:

> *Dearest, I must ask you to stop making these requests. I know you do not mean anything serious by them, but you must know that anything – how shall I say? – 'earthy' will be blacked out by the English censor . . .*

He replied:

> *Do you not think the English censor might be a wee bit more sympathetic to my needs than you yourself seem to be? Do you think he will really run his pencil through lines of passionate love between an estranged wife and her husband? Other men here have wives who oblige – I haven't seen their letters, of course, they are always private, but I know they are full of lovely things. I shall not cease from asking you for this, Tory, no matter how many months or years this war lasts or how many years I am a prisoner of it. I need it as much as I need food and drink, and I am a starving man, Tory. I have precious memories of our many nights of passion, when*

you were as energetic and as lustful as I. They are my only sustenance at this time, but they are fading fast.

Love to the weans, and your ma,

Donald

PS if you are stuck for what to write, why don't you ask some of the girls at your factory? You know what they say about factory girls.

CHAPTER 6

Tory didn't know what they said about factory girls, and she didn't like the implications. Whatever they said, she was a factory girl now. Did that mean they said it about her?

She also wondered what sort of nights Donald remembered, and why they seemed so different from the ones that had stuck in her own mind. Energy was not something she associated with them, at least from her viewpoint: it was Donald who had done all the work, striving away above her in the darkness, as busy as a picador. She lay in bed one night trying her best to recall the occasions when Donald had done the deed, and the kinds of words that came to her – sweaty, rough, friction, grease – were not the sort she imagined Donald wanted. She did remember thinking, on one of the first occasions they'd done it, how he had treated her rather like an awkward corner of a room that needed sanding and papering. Examining her closely, brushing her skin with his lips, then blowing, as if to remove shavings or dust. Then re-examining her, his brows knotted, frowning, as though she was such an awkward, difficult thing. A problem. Then he was sanding her down again, brushing her off. He was abrasive, rough, though not wilfully. It was just that he had an angular, hard, stubbly body. And he smelt of turpentine, and in his wiry hair there were always little flecks of white paint. Were those the sort of details he required? *How I miss the reek of turpentine in my nostrils as you dig your sharp little Scottish elbows into my ribs . . . I want nothing more than to feel your unshaven chin sandpapering my breast . . .*

Reluctantly Tory began to think that perhaps the answer did lie in the factory somewhere. Surely there was someone, among all those careworn, lovesick and battle-scarred women, who knew how to write the sort of letter Donald wanted.

Farraway's was not a good place to think about matters of a carnal nature since it dealt with such matters itself in the most pitiless and brutal way. She had not given gelatine a moment's thought before arriving at the factory for work. She was aware of the existence of Farraway's, and that it had a reputation as an originator of bad smells. One of the reasons she had been conscripted there for her war work was that very few women could be found to go there out of choice. If the wind was blowing a certain way, people within range of the factory took their washing in, so it was said, to avoid it becoming saturated with that odour – what was it? Tory had never found it particularly offensive: a rich, spicy, faintly animal smell, similar to that which you find in a zoo, but Tory loved zoos. Then she saw

80

what caused the smells: animal parts, stewed and simmered for days on end, vats bubbling with calves' feet and hides, barrows heaped with bones.

One of the managers had given the new recruits a tour before allocating them to their departments, or 'rooms', as they were called. She'd seen the Skin Cutting Room, where the sad, flattened pelts of once beautiful creatures were shredded in vicious guillotines, and the Melting Room, where the stewing took place and the gelatine formed as a scum to be lifted off and spread over sheets of glass to cool in the Slabbing Room. There were many other such departments, equally grim, where she could have found herself allocated, so she was greatly relieved when she found she had been assigned to the Packing Room, where she spent her days among rows of girls sewing the granulated gelatine into canvas sacks, or folding sheet gelatine into crates with greaseproof paper.

Since Donald's resurrection she had begun to find the sights and sounds of Farraway's rather disturbing. At the beginning and end of each shift she had to walk the cobbled yards between the tall brick sheds, the Packing Room being (against what seemed practical common sense) at the far end of the maze-like complex, and each time it became more and more like a journey through Hell. Well, 'a hell for animals', anyway – all the odds and ends of magnificent beasts being processed. She once came across a trolley of calves' heads, with eyes and tongues protruding, as though outraged at their

81

treatment. The trolley was harnessed to a patient but tired-looking dray. It was as though the entire animal kingdom had been betrayed. That was the first time the horrors of Farraway's had struck her, and she was in tears as she passed the gate porter so couldn't return his customary pleasantries.

When she told her mother about it Mrs Head scorned her for her softness.

'They are only doing what we've always done. I've been boiling up bones and trotters to make jelly since I was girl. We were all thankful when powdered gelatine arrived, and we could save ourselves the trouble . . .'

But Tory was also bothered by the apparent uselessness of her labours. She had imagined, when she offered herself for employment, that she would be going to work in the munitions factory, manufacturing the weapons that would eventually win the war. What a waste to put so many able-bodied women to such trivial use, enabling the continued production of jellies and blancmanges. But she didn't say anything. It was assumed by everyone that they were doing important work, and that gelatine must be put to uses they had no inkling of. Perhaps it was a vital ingredient in certain explosives. Wasn't there an explosive called gelignite? Perhaps a little bit of their gelatine found its way into the bombs that were being dropped on Hanover and Frankfurt. Remembering the gurning calves' heads, it seemed a far more fitting destination than a children's birthday party.

She was a little disappointed not to have made any close friends among the women in the Packing Room. They were not hostile towards her – in fact, quite the opposite. Some of the older ladies especially went out of their way to make her feel at home, and they had been so generous with their parcels for Donald. But, despite all this, she had developed no confiding intimacy with any of the other women.

Tory soon became aware that there was a well-established pecking order, intricately formed according to various degrees of status, and roughly corresponding to seating arrangements on the long bench. At the far end was a group of women who had worked in the Packing Room since before the war, and who were simply carrying on their regular jobs. They clearly thought themselves above the common herd of conscripted packers and made sure everyone was aware of their exalted rank. Next came the older women, ladies who had worked in other factories and knew the rules and traditions of factory life. Then there were the slightly younger women, who had never worked in a factory before but who came from working-class or lower-middle-class households, who might have fathers, husbands or brothers in factory work. Then came the women of modest education, who had never expected to find themselves anywhere near a factory, and were rather uncomfortable, even embarrassed, at being so positioned. Tory belonged somewhere in this group, though she felt no distaste for her working environment. She was married to a manual worker, after all, and her bank-clerk father, if truth be told, was only one rung above this sort of life.

Lowest of the pecking order were the younger women and girls, childless and unmarried, who might well have worked in such a factory as this anyway. They formed a noisy posse at the near end, cackling and giggling all through the long mornings and afternoons. It was among this group that Tory thought she might be able to find someone who could help her. Seated near their end, she could overhear their conversations sometimes, and was shocked at how crude they could become. There was one girl, called Amy, a little blonde with a face like a knife, who was particularly loud in her conversations and would use words that Tory could only guess were grossly indecent. Sometimes they sat together at tea break, Amy slurping loudly, often spilling her drink in fits of giggling. She would tell everyone stories about her family, about how her sister was having her fourth baby and she was only twenty-one, about her own boyfriend, who was only sixteen and worked in the sugar factory over the river. These stories were always on the edge of respectability. Amy once came back from the lavatory doubled up with laughter, saying she'd heard a funny noise in the next cubicle, only able to say, after a long effort of self-control, 'She went *hisss* plop-plop-plop . . .' then doubled up in tearful laughter again.

'Who did, dear?' said someone.

'The lady in the next cubicle, and guess who it was.' She claimed it was Clara, their uppity shift manager, who took her tea breaks alone.

'Well, that's nothing to get worked up about, dear,' said one of the older women. 'We all go hiss plop-plop-plop sometimes.'

'Well, I just thought it was funny, that's all.'

Thinking it probably unwise, but doing it anyway, Tory confided in Amy, when she could get her alone. She showed her one of Donald's letters and confessed that she had no idea what she should write.

But Amy was a terrible disappointment, and Tory soon realized she had far overestimated her maturity. The letter from Donald seemed to shock her even more than it had Tory. She read it slowly and carefully, went bright red in the face and seemed unable to speak, looking up at Tory with slit eyes.

'I'm sorry,' said Tory, taking the letter out of Amy's hands, which was as easy as taking a petal from a wilting rose. 'I shouldn't have troubled you with it.'

After some opening and shutting, Amy's mouth produced some muffled words: 'I – I won't tell,' she stammered.

'No, please don't.' The horrible thought occurred to her that Amy had somehow misunderstood her reason for showing her the letter, that it was not simply a request for help in constructing a reply, but a sharing of intimate marital details to one who had so often talked about her boyfriend's prowess and lustiness. Did Amy think she was perhaps displaying her own husband's masculine virtues in reply? The thought was reinforced by the faint smirk that was beginning to appear on Amy's face.

Then the worst possible thing happened. Amy was overtaken with spasms of uncontrollable laughter. Luckily this occurrence was so frequent that no one else in the department took any notice. It was just Amy laughing again.

'This has been very distressing for me, Amy,' Tory said, over the laughter, feeling urgently the need to reinforce the seriousness of her situation, to make it clear that she was not just sharing a piece of marital smut with a work colleague. 'Having a husband who is a prisoner of war puts one in a very difficult position . . .'

Amy regained some self-control, and gave Tory a twinkling, dangerous smile. 'No – it's when he gets out you want to be worried about,' she said. 'What's he going to be like by then? Like a tomcat that's been locked in a shed for the summer. You'll need to put chains on him – you'll need to padlock him to the bedpost . . .'

'Yes, well, thanks so much for your help.' Tory left, having issued more reminders about confidentiality, to the hoarse chuckles of the gelatine guttersnipe, wondering how she could have been so stupid as to turn to someone like that for help.

She realized that it was a measure of her desperation that she had done so. There was no one else. How she longed for a sister who might have married an artist or worked as a nude model in Paris. Oh, for a Bohemian in the family, a believer in free love, a frequenter of back-street abortionists, a denizen of the opium dens of Limehouse Reach, someone who knew the lingo, the vocabulary, someone who knew what the sex-starved male would like to read about. Her own sisters were far from that type: stern, aloof, they had both married prosperous men in distant counties. Adelle had married a hotelier in Clevedon, who was now an officer in the air force. Mabel had wedded an antiques dealer in Epsom, and ran a tea shop.

She negotiated the bloody cobbles on her way out of Farraway's, and took a wrong turning between the Skin Cutting Room and the Melting Room, finding herself in a part of the complex she'd never visited before. The sense of being lost provided, to her surprise, some relief from the thoughts that had been troubling her, and she decided to explore this undiscovered corner of the factory. She was intrigued by a sound that she hadn't heard before, and wondered if some part of the gelatine-production process had been missed out on her original tour. The sound was rhythmic, but soft, the sound that a machine designed for testing the durability of pillows might make, but not quite regular enough in its rhythm to suggest automated power. She noticed that the noise was coming from a small, low building tucked away around the corner behind the Skin Cutting Room. This was not a much-used part of the complex. The yard was filled with what looked like useless or redundant machinery. There was a guillotine, with its rows of savage steel blades, like a masculine version of a loom: instead of shuttles and frames there were jaws and teeth. But this contraption was entering decrepitude, covered with blobs of jackdaw and raven droppings (many such birds nested on the high, cliff-like walls of the factory), and rusting. She walked past a barrel of shin bones. Sawn in half lengthways, they looked like a heap of giant broken pencils. As she approached the bones she saw that they were crawling with bluebottles, which suddenly erupted in hysterical clouds. The cobblestones of the yard were slippery with grease. She batted a brave hand at the dizzy flies which, as though having collectively lifted a single baffled head, lowered it again to minute inspection of the bones.

By now it was apparent that the noise that had first attracted her was human in origin. She imagined something being chopped up by a team of people with cleavers, and there was a new smell now, as she approached the open door, a sharp, powerful stink, not unpleasant but not entirely wholesome either. Cautiously she put a toe over the threshold, seeing a surprisingly big space within and sensing that the source of the noise was to the right. For a moment she thought she had entered some illicit, corrupt or otherwise depraved world. Up on a sort of stage two mad men were attacking each other. Then she saw the ropes that ringed the 'stage', the weights and dumbbells, the punchbags and exercise benches, the bulbous gloves hanging on hooks, the sweaty young men engaged in various training routines in different corners of the room, and realized that the men on stage, in the boxing ring, were not mad – at least, not in the ordinary sense. They were wearing soft helmets tied under the chin, odd apparel that made them look as though their heads were badly swollen.

Ordinarily she wouldn't have lingered in such a place, no more so than if she had blundered into a gentlemen's lavatory, and she would certainly not have admitted to herself that she was in any way aroused by the spectacle of young men thus engaged. It was more an innate sense of concern that caused her to hesitate. The original sense that the two men in the ring were set upon harming each other, which remained true even after she thought about it, confused her somewhat, and she couldn't quite leave the scene until she felt satisfied that they were not. They had no audience, apart from two or three men standing beside the ropes: monitors, supervisors, closely observing every detail of the fight and occasionally shouting instruction. One man among them stood out, partly because he was of a higher, thicker bearing than the rest, but also because he was smoking a cigar. He was the only one in the room to notice her presence, turning slightly to regard her, then smiling at the sight. Tory stepped back, suddenly realizing what she must look like, a lone woman spying on young male bodies in the middle of athletic exertions. She fled before any ribald commentary could be made, feeling as though she had just escaped from a cage of wild animals.

She'd recognized the man who'd turned to look at her. It was George Farraway himself, the owner of the factory, the man whose name, written vertically, adorned the vast chimney that sent bluish grey smoke across the river to soil the washing lines of Silvertown. She had seen him on several occasions. His presence in the Packing Room always silenced the girls, who would glance over their shoulders to get a glimpse, then turn back red-faced if they thought he'd caught their eye. Others would carry on their work with exaggerated nonchalance, doing their utmost to express their indifference, which only served to sharpen the atmosphere even more. The first time it happened – Mr Farraway standing at the far end in close conference with the dispatch manager and some others – Tory hadn't known who he was. When he left, she was made to feel curiously ashamed of the fact, almost as if she'd been caught out in church as an unbeliever. It wasn't that George Farraway was worshipped exactly, it was more a sense that you didn't really belong until you knew who he was.

But perhaps there was an element of worship as well. He was a very striking figure, after all. Handsome in a heavy, slightly clumsy way, he had the sort of slapdash face that looked as though it had been put together in a few seconds, and was only handsome by lucky accident. Dark-haired, but starting to grey, he had a finely shaped beard that jutted forward emphatically. And now she remembered the stories about his early career – that he had been a boxer. A good one, she supposed. Famous enough to make some money and start up a successful business when he retired. But she'd no idea he still kept a hand in, running a boxing gym for factory workers. When she asked the girls, they all seemed to know.

The sight of the young men boxing stayed in her mind. It seemed odd to see them there, fighting, in a time of war. All that energy and aggression going to such waste, to be soaked up by punch-bags and skipping ropes. They were too young, she supposed, for call-up, but old enough to be as powerful as little bulls. One didn't see men like that around any more. They had become rare and exotic. She pictured Donald in a boxing ring and thought how miserably lightweight he seemed in comparison, even though he was strong in a wiry way, able to lift surprisingly heavy things (a whole motorbike once). He *looked* puny, however.

She continued to think about the young boxers after she'd got home. In a land where healthy young men had all but disappeared, it was as though she had come across a secret stock of them. An ark for the male of the species, where their precious bullishness was encouraged and preserved so that there would be new generations of fighters and fathers. She had been reassured, she supposed, that there was a future.

CHAPTER 7

She began to think again about Donald and all he'd been through. Since he had told her nothing of his capture and his experiences since then, she could only use her imagination (which she found to be as inadequate to this task as to the unsavoury one), and so she tried her hardest to think of what a terrible time he must have had. He must have seen battle, dead bodies, victorious enemies barking instructions. He must have been marched, starved, tied, blindfolded. He had spent many months in prison, maybe mana- cled (she had little idea of what a prisoner-of-war camp must be like and could only imagine some- thing like the Bastille, with thick walls and tiny windows, where the little Scotsman would be chained to a mossy pillar). He was probably bearded too, by now. A long, scruffy growth hanging from his chin.

Was it really such a bad thing he was asking, given his circumstances? Perhaps there was some peculiar aspect of the male body's design that meant it actually needed sexual congress as much as it needed food. Was she, in withholding her co-operation in this respect, actually starving him? She pondered this for a little while – it really did seem a possibility, and would certainly account for the curious hunger men displayed in their courtship practices, and which she remembered with horror from her own courtship days. Even Clarence Dundry had exhibited the tendency, showing her his collection of foreign banknotes with trembling, sweaty hands one moment, pawing hungrily at her chest and reaching for her lips with his own the next. And Donald did make strange gobbling noises during his lovemaking (as she remembered now), and would even, occasionally, bite her. But then, she wondered, what about all the healthy, glowing bachelors she knew? What about monks and Catholic priests? They seemed perfectly nourished despite their sexless lifestyles – or did they all secretly visit brothels? Perhaps that was the very reason for the existence of brothels – to prevent the unmarried men of the world suffering a slow and agonizing death . . .

She dismissed the thought, and told herself off for being silly.

The house itself seemed to have been tainted by the ingress of Donald's correspondence. Whatever Tory or Mrs Head did or said, it was against a background of sinister, grubby machinations. Even the kettle coming to the boil on the stove, rocking back and forth with barely contained eagerness, ejecting that long plume of steam as though in resplendent satisfaction, seemed in on the secret. The bombing seemed to have stopped, at least for a while. There hadn't been a raid for two weeks, and this made the unsavoury vista of Donald's imagination all the more prominent. Sometimes Mrs Head would doze off in her chair and start muttering in her sleep. Tory was sure that one evening she was saying, 'The Filth! The Filth!' over and over again.

She consulted a medical encyclopedia among the house's small library of books and was unsurprised to find that the subject of sexual intercourse had been omitted altogether. There was only the briefest chapter on human reproduction, which concentrated on the gestative phase and ignored conception altogether. Did 'womb' count as an erotic word? She doubted it. She perused one of the diagrams in the book, an exploded view of a child *In utero*, the womb itself looking rather like a rugby ball, cut open and peeled back to reveal the crouching, inverted, huge-headed figure within. The cold objectivity of the grey diagram appalled her, and she closed the book quickly.

One evening at the escritoire, she took a sheet of paper and wrote a list of all the words she could think of that related to the subject of sex. She wrote them down the left-hand margin of the page, afterwards realizing she had placed them, more or less, in alphabetical order (she wondered why there were so many Bs). It didn't take Tory long to exhaust her sexual vocabulary, although she was surprised by the number of words she produced. She was

94

also surprised by the fact that the process left her feeling hot and breathless. She could see in the bureau mirror that her cheeks were blushing. She fanned her face with her jotter, and opened the top button of her blouse to let some air in. There was something rather thrilling, she half admitted to herself, in doing something so silly as writing a list of dirty words. When she read them back to herself she couldn't quite suppress a giggle. The words were, after all, so very silly. They couldn't possibly be used to construct a piece of erotic writing. At the same time, there was something oddly powerful about them. She had never seen them on paper, as far as she could recall (apart from the one or two that had polite as well as impolite uses), and as such she felt as though she had done something rather special. She felt like a witch who had just cast a spell, or that she had somehow rent the fabric of the familiar world to glimpse a different one beyond, a libidinous landscape with unfrocked peasantry continually fornicating in the hedgerows. It was, evidently, where Donald now lived, among the overly endowed and the wretchedly hedonistic.

Perhaps she should just send him the list. Perhaps that would be enough, would do the trick. Then, thinking that she needed to write to the children now (at that same desk! With that same pen and notepad!), she hurriedly crumpled her list of dirty words and threw it on to the still-glowing coals of the fireplace, where it slowly ignited.

★　★　★

She visited the library, seeking inspiration. There were more books on medical matters that primly ignored the nether regions of the human body, but were gleefully filled with pictures of bodies prickled with scarlet fever or plague. In the catalogue she discovered there were guides to love and married life, but they were not on the shelf and had to be requested. Given that the librarian was a hawk-faced man with a runny nose who watched his customers carefully, and, no doubt, made thorough mental notes of their reading habits, she was loath to make such a request. Certain books had 'For Adults Only' stamped on their covers in purple ink, the personal choice of the same librarian, reminding Tory for a moment of the heavily stamped and scored envelopes in which Donald's letters arrived, but when she nervously examined these well-worn volumes they turned out to be classics – *Madame Bovary, Jane Eyre*. She was not a literary person but she knew enough about books to realize that she would not find what she was looking for in those, and pitied the poor ranks of desperate men she imagined who had waded through their long, dense narratives waiting for the moment of abandonment that would never come.

The bookshops were no better (or worse?). There were crime and romance sections with pictures on the covers of devilish men and swooning dames. The bold lettering of the titles, written in shaded perspective, seemed to leap off the boards. But Tory knew that they would contain no writing of the sort that Donald so desired. Even so she felt hotly self-conscious as she browsed them, trying to avoid the gaze of a tweedy proprietor, only to notice a clergyman a few feet away, a leathery tome in his hands and a disapproving look on his face. She left the shop, desperately hoping she would not be remembered.

She vaguely knew that certain lewd material could be obtained on the black-market. Slim volumes of saucy stories using nondictionary words. She imagined men bought them from corrupt barbers or lavatory attendants, purveyors of filth who dwelt in filthy places to which she could never venture and so were for ever beyond her reach.

One afternoon, on her way home from an early shift, she found herself lingering on one of the benches in the square, opposite the public lavatories. From here she had a perfect view of everyone who entered and exited the underground spaces, and for a while she considered what an odd thing it was to watch these stately men and women descending the steps at their separate entrances, to emerge a little while later, visibly no different, but in some profound and indefinable way transformed. What would a visitor from another world make of it, this private, secretive yet entirely respectable endeavour? Tory herself had not visited those lavatories since childhood and would do almost anything to avoid having to use them. She recalled the moment of terror that had begun this exile, when, as a six-year-old, she had followed her mother into the lavatories without her mother's knowledge and locked herself into one of the stalls. The lavatory had seemed an enormous space to her, yellow and green tiling, a ceiling made of glass panels that let the light through, and also the sight, vaguely deckled, of people's feet as they walked above. Large porcelain sinks with fat silver taps, and the grand, polished wooden doors of the stalls, each with a large brass handle and lock. She was too frightened to call for help, and no one knew she was there. Above ground, Mrs Head must have gone into a terrible panic, and it seemed to Tory hours before she was discovered by the attendant, who'd heard her quiet sobbing.

Tory realized it was stupid of her now, as a thirty-four-year-old woman, to allow this childhood experience to influence her behaviour, but her vow of avoidance had almost reached the level of superstition. It was not that she still feared the underground lavatories on the square but it had simply become one of the rules of her life that she never used them.

The attendant who'd found her had been very kind, an enormous old woman with a long ponytail and no teeth, who'd let her sit in her office and even given her some sheets of paper and pencils and told her to do some drawing while she went above ground to look for her mother.

On this occasion, however, her focus was on the men's. There was an attendant down there too, she knew, the male equivalent of the old woman who'd rescued her from the cubicle (who must have long since departed her post and probably her life). Sometimes, passing, she saw the man emerge in his sagging blue overalls, like a miner coming up for air. He would lean against the spiked railing that surrounded the entrances to the lavatories and puff on a curled pipe. He had a sad, bloodhound face, with lots of red in his eyes (all those years of bleaching, perhaps). And, as Tory thought about this man, she tried to imagine if he was the sort to deal in illicit literature. Were there stashed somewhere in his lair, perhaps between packs of brittle toilet paper or disinfectant blocks, smudged carbon editions of stories detailing the saucy escapades of young housemaids? The thought of that sagging, lumbering old man, with his greying walrus moustache and his hands that delved daily into unspeakable mires, possessing such material was almost too hideous to bear.

She watched for about twenty minutes. The attendant didn't emerge, and Tory observed the comings and goings of the customers with a bird-watcher's avidity. There were few young men among them. Occasionally a soldier in uniform, greatcoat flapping, would scamper down the steps, or a delicate thing with spectacles and sunken cheeks, probably excused call-up on grounds of general fragility, would shakily emerge, clinging to the handrail as he lifted himself up the steps. Otherwise it was mostly older men, stout patriarchs in bowler hats and medals on their lapels to show they'd done their duty in the first war, old-timers with long beards and red swollen hands, who were too old to have fought even in the Great War, and a steady stream of sharply dressed men, just a shade too old for the draft but who seemed fit enough and were probably the most likely to use the services of an underground purveyor of smut. Tory was trying to see if any of the men emerged carrying something they hadn't gone in with. Particularly anything in a book-shaped brown-paper bag. But none did, that she could see. But, then, she didn't really know what she was going to do if she did see one. She could hardly go down into the Gents and ask to browse the shelves of the lavatory library. Perhaps it was partly because she wanted to know that ordinary men did these things, to feel assured that Donald had not, in developing this interest, turned into some sort of monster.

But the men who emerged from the lavatory in the square seemed disappointingly clean and unblemished.

There was no bench outside the barber's so she felt a little less comfortable observing its entrances and exits, and could only note that the same type of men visited this place as well, from the nearly bald to the Dickens-bearded. The only difference was that the men emerged with less than they had come with, half an inch or more from the back and sides, or a grey swathe of whiskers gleaned from the jowls. None came out with packages, or gave the least impression that they might be concealing one beneath their coats: no furtive glances up and down the street, just a bold stepping out, some fingering their newly shorn chins and temples with a satisfied air.

There was a moment when the barber's shop was empty and the barber, in his long apron, had sat down for a quick break, picking up a copy of the *News Chronicle* to read.

She had never been in a barber's before. At home she had cut Tom's hair herself, painfully, with a pair of dressmaking scissors. Donald went regularly, but to where she knew not, since his work took him sometimes far afield and he would usually visit a barber local to his job. Without giving herself the opportunity to hesitate, she entered the shop. A bell tinkled above her head as she did so, and the barber looked up from his newspaper. His hair was dark and thick, and stood up on end, like a boot brush. The shop was very bright, being lit by electricity, which burnt away in three large neon tubes hanging from the ceiling.

There must be other barbers who work in this place, Tory thought. Sometimes all four must be at work, busily shearing and shaving. Did they all deal in forbidden literature? she wondered. If not, was she now standing before the one barber who did? He seemed old and sage enough to be the owner, the employer of the other barbers, in which case it was more likely he who dealt out the filth. But looking at him, he didn't seem the sort of man to be involved in such things. He was too clean and fatherly. There was a hint of kindness in his dark brown eyes.

'Can I help you, madam?'

She looked quickly around the shop, as if there might be a clue in her surroundings. Four mirrors, four washbasins, each strewn with shaving and hair-cutting paraphernalia, little bottles of oils and lotions with silver spouts, clustered like the bottles of liquor in a cocktail cabinet, electric-powered clippers hanging on hooks with their cables dangling beneath them, scissors, cutthroats, strops. The bitter stench of perfumed alcohol stung her eyes.

Tory had been there a minute without speaking.

'I was just wondering . . .' she stammered, her eyes drawn to a little montage of photographs that adorned one of the mirrors, of film stars in revealing costumes, long legs and coy glances over shoulders. Here was the mirror of the barber who dealt in pornography, surely. But it was not the mirror of the barber she was talking to now – she could tell it had not been used recently. 'I mean I was wondering if you sell . . .' Betty Grable seemed to wink at her.

'I'm sorry, I seem to have made a mistake,' Tory muttered, and left, clumsily mishandling the door on the way out so that the bell rang louder and longer than necessary.

At home she collapsed, exhausted, in her study, and noticed, for the first time, that she had been crying on the long walk home. She dried her tears with trembling hands. She looked at her parents' engagement photo (had the expressions now changed from shock to pity?) and said to herself, 'I will never be able to do this thing that is asked of me.'

The house in which she had grown up contained few books. Donald was a great reader, but he used the library. There was a small bookcase in the sitting room of volumes that were mostly her father's. There was a complete set of Walter Scott, which she could not remember anyone ever reading, and there was a collection of poetry by James Montgomery. There were some editions of an accountancy journal, and some books of history, which, again, seemed forever unread. Tory knelt before the bookcase, fingering each volume, extracting some for a brief examination, a glance at the title page, or the first few lines of Chapter One, each of which only seemed to emphasize the rigidly correct and sexually modest nature of the prose within. Oh, Father, Tory said to herself, I don't even know why I'm looking at your library. How could I possibly think I might find what I'm looking for here? And it was then that she came across a book she hadn't noticed before. It was called *Sorrell and Son*, and the author was Warwick Deeping. She recognized the name but she had no idea what the novel was about. She only knew that it was a 'modern' novel, and that it was very popular. At one time she seemed to remember people everywhere talking about it, and she had the vaguest notion that it was somewhat 'racy'.

Her heart filled at the thought that her own house might contain the very sort of book she had been looking for, and later that evening, after writing her usual letters to the children, she began reading it.

She was quickly absorbed by the story and soon discovered why it was thought to be racy. Betrayed by his wife, the elder Sorrell devotes his life to providing for his only son, often taking lowly work in order to do so – he polishes shoes in a provincial hotel, he becomes a gardener. Reflecting on his wife Dora, he remembers 'She was not a bad woman, only a highly-sexed one, and [he] had never satisfied her sex and its various desires . . .' This in itself was enough to shock Tory. What on earth was such a book doing in the house? Whose was it? Her father's or Mrs Head's? And what did Sorrell mean by 'various desires'? She read on. Unfortunately, the language never went into any more detail. Sexuality was acknowledged but never described. The younger Sorrell, as he grew up, seemed to see women, perhaps in the light of his mother's life, as beastly seductresses, who exercised an unholy fascination and possessed a damnable beauty. 'I can't help it, Pater, but women are the very devil . . .' When he does meet a more agreeable woman, Mary, a seller of theatre programmes, Tory became hopeful that a sex scene might follow, but was rather disappointed when it came, describing Kit 'plucking the red fruit from time to time, to find the juice of it sadder and less sweet'. Shortly afterwards Mary was flattened by a bus.

Tory found herself examining that phrase – *plucking the red fruit* – over and over again. She wondered how juice could be sad. Plucking the red fruit, she supposed, meant kissing, but which part of the body? The lips, one must suppose but, then again, maybe the sad juices came from other places. Dare she think that low? Dare she write to Donald, *'I would have you pluck my red fruit, dearest (and I don't mean my lips).'* Would that do?

She tried reading more. She went back to the library and looked up more of Warwick Deeping's books. She found one that sounded promising – *The Pride of Eve,* which sounded like something scandalous starring Bette Davis and brought to mind temptresses in dark lipstick. It lacked a 'For Adults Only' stamp, however, and she was greatly disappointed when it turned out to concern the plight of a struggling female artist and her relationship with a married man who adores flowers. Tory soon realized that all the sex in the novel was contained in the flowers that filled the married man's garden. The censoring librarian had either missed this or had deemed floral writhing an acceptable substitute for sex. It was a metaphor that appealed to Tory. Almost immediately she tried applying the technique herself.

Darling, imagine me as a sagging crimson rose that wants watering. Imagine yourself as a gardener, walking up the path to my dry rose bed, with a watering-can, full to the lip with water. Now think of yourself pouring your water over me, imagine the beads of it falling into the crimson folds of my petals, seeping right down into the centre of my flowerhead. Imagine me drinking it all up, quenching my great thirst on your thousands of white pearls . . .

Tory wasn't quite sure what she had written there, and even as she posted it she pondered over what, exactly, was happening between the gardener and his rose. It had seemed simple enough to start with. But she shrugged off the meaning, satisfied and astonished, even, that she had managed, without using a single rude word, to write something so erotically charged. Moreover, the writing itself did something quite peculiar to her. She felt a warmth in the lower parts of her body, so sudden and intense that it quite shocked her. She had to go to the ewer and baste herself with cold water.

But she dreaded Donald's reply. It came as swiftly as usual, and was quite unforgiving:

I did not ask you for an essay on the art of managing my allotment. I am asking you to write about sex. How many times do I have to tell you?

This letter made Tory weep. She wept so copiously that afterwards she felt noticeably lighter. But it wasn't just the weight of tears that had gone: her imagination had been drained as well. It was as if her letter had been written in blood – why had Donald not recognized the effort she had put into it? She, who'd never written from her imagination before, not since her pitiless schooldays at least, had managed to do something miraculous: write about sex in a way that she found charged with erotic delight, at the same time as containing nothing that would raise the eyebrow of a Nazi guard.

Perhaps, husband, you could provide me with some examples of the kind of smut you require. A list of appropriate words would be useful, along with some scenarios. I am not familiar with the genre of writing of which you seem to be such a connoisseur. If not, then I do not think I can help you, and I will ask that our correspondence should cease.

CHAPTER 8

This brought a silence from the Stalag, and it was an immense relief for Tory to have this respite. For weeks now she had dreaded the blue envelopes with the prickly German writing that she found propped on the mantelpiece between the clock and the china spaniels nearly every week. There was something so relentlessly accurate and stealthy about them, the way they sought her out – dispatched from God knew where behind enemy lines, traversing a barbed and twisted European geography to land plumb in the centre of the mantelpiece at 17 Peter Street. Bombs by night, letters by day. More and more Tory began to feel that these two types of assault were linked. If the bombs didn't wipe her out, the letters, landing in her heart, would bring a different kind of death.

It seemed that with one brief, curt letter she had dammed the flow of mail from Donald, yet the continuing silence soon became its own source of anxiety. The relentless surge of unsavouriness should not have been so easily stemmed. What had she done to Donald? She pictured him in the compound, the only one among the men without a letter from his wife, the only one emaciated and hollow-eyed in a camp full of satisfied, rosy-faced prisoners. Surely it was her wifely duty to sustain, by whatever means she could, her captive husband.

The continued silence, therefore, only made her task seem more urgent. She would have to write something to satisfy him before it was too late. One evening she came in from work and went straight to her writing desk, having thought, on the tram home, of the perfect solution. It had all seemed so simple. All she had to do was write a description of the sexual act, using conventional terminology. There was no special vocabulary. There were no exotic phrases that she had to know. She could treat the whole exercise in a perfectly matter-of-fact way, just as if she was describing two people having dinner or changing a wheel on a bicycle.

In some of the letters Donald had written to her, he had referred to the writings he desired as 'bedroom thoughts'. *Please share your bedroom thoughts with me.* Perhaps he thought the term less off-putting than 'dirty letter'. *Please write to me your BEDROOM THOUGHTS!!!*
Now the phrase played over and over in her mind, so that she became preoccupied by the notion of what exactly she did think about when she was in bed.

Dearest Donald,

You have asked me many times for my 'bedroom thoughts' and now I am at last able to tell you what they are. I am sorry to have kept you waiting for so long. I now sleep alone in my bedroom, so my thoughts tend to wander into unexpected places. Last night I was thinking that I haven't seen the sea since I was seven years old. And we live on an island. How can that happen? And it is the fact that we are an island race that has saved us from invasion so far, more than anything. But most of the time I lie on my back looking at the ceiling. There is a spider up there at the moment. She spins little webs that never catch anything. How does she survive? Sometimes she folds herself up into a sort of shield-shaped blob that doesn't move for days on end. Is she asleep? Then I think about the children. I am comforted by the fact I know they are safe, but for how long must we live apart? I have not seen them for over a year now. I long to go to the Cotswolds and visit them, but there isn't the money or the time. Supposing they forget about me? They are happy in their foster homes and might be disappointed when they come back. There is no end to this war in sight. Tom might even find himself called up, if it lasts long enough. And then, of course, I think about you, my darling, and I think about what a

110

strange man you've become, in my thoughts,
at least. Are you the same man I married?
How will I ever meet your demands? You see,
I began this letter with the intention of
describing our lovemaking, but I have realized
that I could no more put those thoughts into
written words than I could undress before a
stranger in the real world (unless he was a
doctor, of course). I am afraid I can see no
difference between what you ask me to do and
the work of a prostitute.

   Yours ever

   Tory

Over the days and weeks she wrote many such letters as the above, but never sent them. She began to derive a curious comfort and fulfilment simply from writing letters she knew would never be posted. She would read them back to herself, and wonder at how articulate and profound her words sounded. She could imagine someone on the radio expressing thoughts like those. She began to use the dictionary, not in the desperate way she'd done before, searching for the smutty language that would have satisfied Donald's needs, but as a sort of kit, like a puncture-repair kit, or a sewing box, where she could find just the right thread to turn up a hem, or the perfect button to go on a dress. She began to draw words from the dictionary, extracting them carefully and then (moistening her fingertips) sewing them into her letters. The likeness of writing to embroidery startled her at this moment, especially when she remembered the agonies of labour that had gone into a sampler she'd made as a girl, with all the ruddy letters of the alphabet woven in wool. Only in its slowness did it seem much different. Real writing was so quick, so fluid, once you got into it, that the thoughts seemed to flow directly from the brain through the fingertips.

She even wrote a story. She developed the idea she had had in her gardening letter, the one Donald had been so scornful about, and wrote a story about a lonely woman who employed a gardener, whom she comes to admire from afar. Whenever she speaks to him, however, she becomes tongue-tied and awkward so she just watches him from the window. Tory tried her best to make the two characters come together, imagining some lustful encounter taking place in a potting shed, but Charlotte (the tired, wispy little woman she'd created) would never comply. She had no trouble getting Alfred the gardener into the potting shed, where his muddy hands would caress rhizomes impatiently, but Charlotte always fled back to her upstairs bedroom, locking herself in.

It wasn't a very good story, Tory realized, because nothing happened.

It was one of the curious side effects of Donald's letters that Tory's mind was permanently filled with sexual thoughts she was unable to express. She could not look at anyone without trying to imagine them unclothed. Once a week she and her mother ventured out of doors for an evening, visiting the saloon bar of the Rifleman for a quick drink, and then going to the pictures for a newsreel and a double feature (they would usually watch only the main one). It had not occurred to Tory before – at least, not in such an immediate and vivid way – that everyone in the pub or the cinema owed their existence to a moment of shocking physical propinquity, not just a touching of skin against skin, but a sort of melding of skins, a peeling back and folding over of skins, and the memories of her own such moments, their rhythmic intensity and occasional discomfort, seemed to thunder in her head. She would glance at the stout gentleman at the bar and his heavy-bosomed wife, or the thick-chinned couples sitting side by side in the Gaumont – surely they never did such things. She would peer miserably into her gin and French and wish, even though she was an atheist, that the Lord had devised a sweeter and more dignified way for people to enter the world.

But the real horror was left for the moments when Tory considered her own conception. Papa, Mr Head, Arthur, the frowning patriarch with his complicated whiskers and rotund, waistcoated belly, who'd managed to extend a portion of the Victorian era well into the twentieth century, and Mrs Head, with her thin, brittle body. Was it really

113

in this universe, in this very house, that they had performed that melding of skins? Sometimes Tory found herself helpless before an unfolding vision of her father and mother in the back bedroom that hadn't changed noticeably in thirty-two years, with its Seacunny wallpaper and mahogany wash-stand, soberly undressing, either side of the bed, in a perfectly co-ordinated and symmetrical way – Father's trousers lowering and that great white shirt spilling down with its two tails to his podgy knees, just as Mama's heavy skirt falls to reveal the sagging petticoats beneath. They are about to make love, but show no interest in the prospect at all. Thankfully, beyond a certain point, Tory's imagination always fails her. What happens there-after between Arthur and Mrs Head remains unimagined, something like a holy mystery, never to be explained or understood.

Mrs Head seemed to have changed since the arrival of Donald's letters. She had become quieter, calmer, less maddening. She had started to talk about returning to Waseminster. 'I don't know why I ever came back to London,' she said one evening. 'I was much happier in the land of Arthur's people.'

She wasn't referring to some mythical English past, but to the fact that her husband, Arthur Head, had sprung from that cold, windswept parish, though he had left it at the age of three. Tory thought it was rather touching, if inexplicable, the need to be close to her late husband's roots. A pity she hadn't shown more such interest and affection when he was alive, because Tory could barely remember the two of them exchanging a remark that wasn't a command or request of some sort. And Mrs Head had always seemed such a person of the present moment. Since history, for her, began about five minutes in the past, most of her own life vanished almost instantly into a vast pool of indifference.

That seemed to have changed. She thought about the past a great deal now, and she thought about Waseminster.

Since returning to London she had corresponded regularly with her old neighbour from the marsh-land village, Major Brandish, a retired army gentleman who kept her informed of local gossip. Tory had never read any of the Major's letters, but from the snippets her mother was wont to impart now and then, often with a knowing chuckle, she imagined the former army officer to be a mean, unhappy little man, revelling in the misfortunes of others, 'Oh, will you listen to this?' Her mother would say. 'The Major writes that Mrs Furlong disgraced herself in church . . .' Then a puzzled pause, 'Tory, what does 'eructation' mean?' This nearly always happened with the Major's letters because he was a man who liked to wrap his little barbs and insults, his little morsels of smut and vulgarity, in extravagant verbal paper. Thus she learnt that Mrs Philips-Hope was a *demi-mondaine,*

115

while Mr Philips-Hope was often in a state of crap-ulence (which Mrs Head assumed to be a digestive problem), the Vicar was a *roué*, and there were, it seemed, numerous seraglios in the village, and indeed all over the marshes. ('Perhaps thanks to the Armada,' Mrs Head rather bafflingly suggested.)

'Oh, how I miss village life,' she would say, after reading one of the Major's letters. 'Not that I don't adore your company, Tory, and it has been nice to renew my many friendships here, but I do have to confess to a feeling that I don't really belong here any more.'

Tory remembered the letters Mrs Head used to send that had revelled in the language and lore of the countryside, as though she had suddenly obtained a degree in Bucolics at the University of Rural Ways:

Oh, Tory, you should be here to see Mr Wormald shooting the partridges, oh he does look a treat in his knee breeches and cravat, or Mrs Woolnoth blooding the children with a fox's brush, Mr Reynard himself, I'm sure. I have made myself a cobnut pasty, quite delicious, and I am brewing sloe gin. There are house-martins nesting in the clerestory of St James the Less that have nested there since Norman times . . .

'Don't be silly, Mother.'
'No, it's true, Tory. Things have changed . . .'

116

'Because of the war, you mean? But that's only to be expected. As soon as it's over we'll be back to how we were.'

'No, it's not just the war. Well, in a way I suppose it is. But I don't think anything has been quite the same since . . .'

Mrs Head looked as though she was about to cry. Tory had never seen her cry, not even when Arthur had died. The advent of Mrs Head's tears was not a moment to be passed over. Tory sat up, watching her mother's eyes closely. 'Since?' she prompted.

Mrs Head took a deep breath. The tears had been abated. 'Since we ate Mr Dando.'

Mrs Head had been convinced for some time that the pork of doubtful origin had been a section of Mr Dando's lower thigh, ever since she had heard the news that the butcher had indeed died in the bomb blast.

'I do wish you wouldn't put it like that, Mother.'

'Well, we've got to face up to things, Tory. There's no point in trying to hide anything any more. That's what war does to you. A bomb lands on your house and throws your secrets to the world. I am a cannibal. And so are you.'

'There is a great deal of difference between a wilful cannibal and an accidental cannibal.'

'Not so very much. Not when we had the advantage of considering both options. We both knew there was a chance that it was human meat, but we ate it anyway.'

Mrs Head had earlier made some tea and the pot was on the table, a stout brown betty, reflecting the room in its glaze.

'I feel such terrible shame,' said Mrs Head.

'What's done is done,' said Tory. It interested her how the tables seemed to have turned. On the evening of the meal itself, it had been Tory who had resisted, while Mrs Head had pragmatically chosen to ignore the ethics of the situation. Now, a few weeks later, Mrs Head seemed to be in a turmoil of anxiety about the incident, while Tory had lost all interest in it. She supposed it was because of the problem with Donald and his letters. She had no time for thoughts about cannibalism now. For her the problem had only existed while the food was in her gut. Now that it was gone, she felt no queasiness about the subject at all.

'How can I play bridge with the ladies when I know what I've done? How can I sit in Mrs Lippiatt's living room, dealing out the hands, when they don't know that the lady sitting with them is a cannibal, no better than one of those blackfellows with bones through their noses?'

'For goodness' sake, Mother, let it rest. It's in the past now, and what we've done can't be undone. You can't change what happened. And apart for that, there's no proof that the meat we ate was Mr Dando.'

'I'm surprised at you, Tory. Are you telling me you feel no shame? I'd thought you were such a good person, and you were so reluctant to eat

118

Mr Dando that evening. Why didn't you stand more firmly against my delinquency?'

'Well, perhaps I'm not as good as you or anyone thinks.'

Mrs Head sat back, a look of distraction on her face, as though she was trying to understand the implications of what her daughter had just said.

Instead she found her thoughts directed, yet again, back to the morning after the bombing and the scene of devastation at Old Parade. She recalled the façade of the confectioner's, Timothy's, those little pieces of mince and offal she'd seen stuck to the wall. They, too, she supposed, could have been pieces of Mr Dando. That he had, by a horrible violent process, become exactly the thing he sold. She found herself trying to imagine a bomb that, on exploding, would turn greengrocers into cauliflowers, or drapers into rolls of twill and chiffon, and found it quite impossible. Yet Mr Dando, unpacked and dispersed – an ounce here, an ounce there – over the confectioner's wall, had, in his gory stucco, told her something very disturbing about the nature of human existence. 'Thinking meat' was the phrase that came to her again and again, one that she would have claimed as her own invention, if it had not sounded so clever. She imagined she'd heard it in a snatched moment, listening to *The Brains Trust*. And she thought back to the black pudding she had eaten at the beginning of the war, which Tory had warned her was likely to have been made from human blood. Only now did

119

she begin to feel nausea rising, as though, a year later, the pudding was still down there, silted up in some deep corner of her gut.

The cat arrived to distract her, as he often seemed to do.

'It's all your fault, Sambo,' she said, to the sprightly little thing. 'Why didn't you stop us?'

The cat purred and rubbed its arching back against Mrs Head's leg.

'You certainly haven't shown any remorse. And you ate Mr Dando with more eagerness than any of us. But then, in a queer way, that makes you better than us, doesn't it? Because Mr Dando was not a cat, you are not a cannibal. The only non-cannibal in the room. Tory, how does it feel to be morally inferior to a cat?'

Tory didn't answer, except for an indignant grumbling sound as she tried to read her evening newspaper.

'I'm only trying to make light of the matter,' Mrs Head went on. 'If we lost the power of laughter, where would we be then?'

Another incomprehensible burble from Tory, who was secretly amazed at her mother's latest turn-around – she had never laughed much at anything in her life. If cannibalism had woken sensitivities and sentiments hitherto suppressed, then perhaps there should be more of it. Bring more butchers to the table.

'No word from Donald for a while?' asked Mrs Head. She no longer made any attempt to read Donald's letters, but she had noticed their absence.

'No,' said Tory quietly, wondering how she was going to explain, if called upon to do so, Donald's silence.

'Strange,' said her mother.

I have starved him, Mother, Tory wanted to say. My own husband, a prisoner of war, he wanted food and I denied him.

'Men are the very devil,' Mrs Head said after some moments' pause, half to herself. The remark made Tory give her a long, unacknowledged stare.

'What I think you need to do,' said her mother, quite matter-of-factly, 'is to send him some food.'

'Really?'

'Yes. Has he never asked for it?'

'No, never. Not food. Not really.'

'And is he still making his other demands?'

Tory closed her eyes and nodded delicately.

'And how have you dealt with the matter?'

'By asking that he stop making them.'

'And has this worked?'

'No. It seems to stir him up all the more. I'm at a complete loss to know what to do.'

Tory had never got round to sending the cakes and other comestibles the women at Farraway's had given her.

Mrs Head leant forward and spoke slowly, as if to make sure the words went into her daughter's ears.

'Cocoa,' she said quietly but firmly. 'Oxo cubes,

121

Typhoo, golden syrup, Camp Coffee, fish paste . . .' she was counting off the items on her fingers as she listed them '. . . Marmite, Alka Seltzer, tomato soup . . . Can you imagine what it must do to a man to know such things are out of reach? You need to make a parcel, Tory, and put as many of these things in it as you can. You could make a start this very evening . . .'

It was several weeks before Donald replied. He had moved camps and the post had taken a long time to catch up with him.

Dearest,

You have done me great wrong. I am not asking you for much, after all. I am only asking you to perform what most normal people would consider to be your wifely duties, the only difference being that I ask you to do in words what you would willingly do bodily, that is satisfy your husband's sexual needs. Why should this be considered smutty, simply because it is written down?

But you must not ask me what you should write. If I must supply you with the words and phrases, then the whole object is defeated, because the words are not coming from your thoughts. What you write must be the product of your own memory and imagination, and be an expression of your own honest desires.

122

Otherwise it will mean nothing. You must write to me honestly, Tory, but at the same time imaginatively. Do both those things and I will be saved.

Yours affectionately

Donald

PS You sent me a box of food. I have no use for it and have distributed it among the chaps. They ask if you can send another soon. Timmy the Canadian wants to know if you can get hold of any Peanut Butter.

CHAPTER 9

Every now and then Tory would be overtaken with grief for her absent children. The nights of sobbing seemed to come in a regular wave, separated by perhaps a fortnight or so, when the continual feeling of loss would suddenly clot into something bigger and more difficult to contain. It was like a refrain to the quieter, perpetual verse of her sorrow. It could be triggered by the silliest of things, the rediscovery of a token of their childhood in one of the back bedrooms, even something as flimsy as a particular colour or smell, if it prompted some more intense recollection.

It was the evenings that were hardest to bear, because those hours had been the most crowded with children. From the moment she had brought them home from school each day the house would be filled with their three-way conversations, with their feeding and bathing and playing. With the children around, the evenings had been her favourite time of day, and even now, with air raids, she still preferred the evenings. She might feel her children's absence most painfully at this time, but there were still other comforts – the withdrawal of the daytime antagonizers (bosses, shopkeepers, coalmen, tinkers), the pleasures of silence and darkness. In a strange way, the evenings of the Blitz were even more peaceful – the utter darkness of the blackout, the deserted streets. The forces of antagonism didn't just withdraw: they vanished completely, along with the city itself. Night-time had become what she had thought it was always meant to be: empty, mysterious, boundless. The bombs, both the cause of and the threat to this form of darkness, were the one sour element in the great romance of the darkened city, but they were not a challenge that had to be met. They were not to be argued with or stood up to. One simply had to endure them.

Another reason she missed her children was that she, now, was most definitely the child of the house. She didn't even have the presence of a sane husband to shore up her status against her mother, who had become noticeably more bossy as the months of the war progressed. It seemed an age ago that Mrs Head had returned from Waseminster, humbly insisting that Tory wouldn't know she was there, that she wouldn't get under her feet. How had it happened that she now found herself running hither and thither at her mother's behest, frequently apologizing, and listening attentively, with bowed head to endless dispensations of motherly advice?

At the same time, Tory could sometimes relish the comfort of being a daughter, especially in the evenings, when she and her mother would sit together in the dining room. The work of the day over, she liked listening to Mrs Head.

Her mother had a very clever way of making artificial flowers out of scraps of old material – frayed curtains, worn-out cushion covers, outgrown children's clothes. It involved sewing and folding in such ways that Tory could never follow so that she would end up with something like a squashed purple carnation where her mother had crafted a magnificent, radiant sunflower. It was an undoubted talent her mother had, and a resourceful one as well. More than once Tory had found that a pair of her faded knickers, which she had still thought wearable, had been transformed into the delicate petal of a peony or water-lily. Tory's mother had more or less given up passing judgement on her daughter's wilting efforts, but it was as they were making another little spray for the empty vases that Tory mentioned the gym at Farraway's.

To Tory's surprise, her mother knew about George Farraway. 'Oh, so it is the same Farraway,' Mrs Head said. 'I did wonder.'

'The same Farraway?'

'As the boxer. He was a very famous man around here for a little while. Did well for himself and went into business. I heard he had a pub, and – that's right – he did open up a factory of some sort. Well, I'm glad to see he's made something, after all that trouble.'

'What trouble?'

There was a half-beat's pause before Mrs Head answered, 'He killed a man,' she said, trying to sound casual. 'In the ring,' she added, as if Tory might have thought otherwise. 'Nothing he could have done about it – boxing is a brutal sport. But I think he lost his nerve after that, and was never quite the same man. One of the papers tried to pin the blame on him, and he took it to heart. There was some legal fussing. I can remember the first time I saw him fight in public . . .'

This was too much for Tory to accept, that her mother had ever been in the audience at a boxing match, and she said so.

'No, you silly girl, I've never been to a boxing match in my life. But at the fairs we used to go to, on Blackheath or Woolwich Common, they would have fight booths where you could just wander in. It was where all the young boxers used to start. They don't have them any more of course – this was back before the Great War, when you were a little girl. You used to love them, though I'm not sure I felt happy about children being let in . . .'

'You mean you took me to see boxing matches?' Tory was floundering in new uncertainties about her childhood. She did have the vaguest memories of the old fairs on the different commons and heaths around south-east London, but she couldn't remember the fight booths.

'It was more Papa, really. He would carry you into the tents on his shoulders, and you would be

127

cheering as loudly as the rest of them in there. Arthur was quite a man for the rough sports but, then, he was the son of a docker . . .'

Tory tried hard to remember. Perhaps there was the slimmest recollection of a baying crowd, with combatants at the centre, the grey dome of her father's head rising from between her legs.

She wanted to ask her mother more, but didn't want to appear too interested so let it rest.

A week later she went back to the gym.

CHAPTER 10

The room was empty this time, but unlocked, and Tory felt compelled to explore its emptiness, though she sensed it had recently been used: a mist of human sweat lingered in the air (so distinct from the other animal smells that pervaded the factory). Having crept between rotting pelts and shattered bones to gain the space, she felt as though she was creeping through the alleyways of the human body itself, or at least its masculine incarnation. The stinking leather, the saturated canvas. She looked at rows of boxing gloves hanging by their laces on hooks, then at a downcast row of padded helmets and the thick, heavy drapery of towelling robes – it was as though the warriors had abandoned their own bodies in some comically accelerated moment of retreat. Then the instruments of their increased strength: weights, dumbbells, bars. Everything seemed thick, solid and heavy. Tory felt she was almost certainly the lightest thing in the gym, and that amid such prevailing heaviness she might float away. There was a punchbag on a stand, looking like a face which, though featureless, somehow managed to appear haughty and disdainful. It seemed to give her an eyeless stare, querying her presence. Should she dare give that punchbag a punch? There was another one hanging on a sort of spring from the ceiling. All she could do, in the end, was merely to reach out and tap the punchbag with the tip of her index finger, which caused it to stir not one little bit.

Then there was the boxing ring. Even though this was a small amateur gym and not a theatre or public venue of any kind, the boxing ring possessed the same kind of aura as a religious space, like a chapel or chancel, which sometimes, she remembered, was roped off with similar cordage. The thought amused her – of boxing priests, of a bishop out for the count – and she tittered, but only briefly because she suddenly became aware that she was being observed.

She turned and saw him, George Farraway, owner of the factory, ex-boxer, millionaire gelatine magnate. He was fully dressed this time, in his business clothes, a three-piece suit, a watch and chain. He had an overcoat draped over one arm. He was holding his hat with the other.

'Are you looking for something, Miss?' he said.

Tory didn't know what to say so only shook her head.

'It was you, wasn't it, who put a nervous little head through the doorway the other week?'

Tory was angry at her own speechlessness. It was because she knew much more about George Farraway now. Because his name was written on the chimney, it was almost as if the brick vastness of that structure had condensed itself to human size while maintaining all the weight and density of its original form. The effect was enhanced by the cigar that was lazily pluming from his lips. Since talking to her mother she had learnt more about him, mostly from Edi, one of the more senior members of the packing staff and a serious boxing fan.

'Oh, he was a gorgeous fighter,' she had said, 'absolutely gorgeous. He had this tremendous way of keeping an opponent at a distance with little jabs from the left, at arm's length, so they dangled like a fish on the end of a hook, taking hopeless swipes at thin air. Then he would finish them off with a single blow from the right. I saw him do three people like that, and he hardly raised a sweat.'

It was funny to hear Edi talk about boxing, especially when she started doing the actions to accompany her words, thrusting and uppercutting with her flabby arms.

He'd been known as Joe Jupiter in his early days as a regular of Fred Goss's fight booths, which toured the open spaces of South London from Woolwich Common to Putney Heath. In the 1920s he had turned semi-professional and become known as the the Cockney Cooler, thanks to the seeming effortlessness of his fighting style. He went to America, and a string of victories eventually found him face to face with Jack Dempsey on Long Island. It was the pinnacle of his career, even though victory had never been a serious possibility. The Manassa Mauler was at the height of his powers,

131

and George Farraway was lucky to last six rounds, though he did manage to get some good punches in and even made the champion stagger a couple of times. His career had been set back by problems with his size, his body always hovering somewhere between middleweight and light heavyweight, and had ended on a low note when he was disqualified for headbutting an opponent who, through nine rounds, had been elbowing, gouging and rabbit-punching, like a street fighter, without penalty.

Edi had said nothing about him killing a man, and Tory couldn't quite bring herself to ask.

He had surprised everyone in his retirement by proving to have an astute business sense. His fight with Jack Dempsey had earned him a fee, it was rumoured, of $50,000, though he claimed the Mob and the IRS had taken most of it before he left America's shores. Whatever the truth, he had had enough money to buy a derelict factory up a creek of the Thames and turn it into the most successful gelatine business in Britain.

The boxing gym had begun as a hobby of George's, a way of keeping in touch with the sport he loved. There was a general feeling that the productivity of the factory was suffering because of the time he was putting in at the gym when he should have been giving his attention to the business. There were only two gelatine factories in England (the other being somewhere in the north), so he didn't seem to think he needed to worry about the competition. It was said he was more concerned with producing champions than gelatine, these days. The fighters who emerged from his gym had not yet got that far, but they were gaining a reputation. They were known, collectively, as George's Jelly Babies.

Oh, but he is ugly, Tory thought, as he approached her in the gym. You couldn't see it at first, but when you looked closely you noticed how damaged his face was. And he didn't care about his ugliness. That was what rendered it invisible. Vanity was an intolerable quality in a man, Tory had always thought. He had a broken nose, the tip turned almost back on itself, to face the opposite direction. He had the flat, frayed ears of an elephant. His brow was deep and heavy, as robust as the breast of a T-42. Beneath it his eyes seemed slightly uneven, as though one had been knocked back further into his head than the other. His smile revealed several gold teeth.

What frightened her more than his ugliness was that he found her attractive. She could tell instantly, from the undistracted glance of those odd eyes. It was an unusual feeling. Tory had realized quite early in life that she was not one of the world's beauties. Male heads didn't swing in her direction when she entered a dance hall, or if they did, it was to gaze upon her girlfriends. She was small and slight, and comforted herself with the thought that her beauty was too small for most people to see until they were close. Her smallness made her susceptible to bullying, which made her nervous of any dominant male. She only felt safe among small men, like Donald. If Donald had been a boxer, he would almost certainly have been a featherweight. Maybe even a flyweight (though Tory had no idea what weight qualified for these categories, and even thought Donald might belong to some as yet unclassified realm of lightness beyond that of flyweight – perhaps fleaweight, or speck-of-dustweight).

'Have I stumbled upon a secret admirer of the noble art?' Mr Farraway said, showing her an unthreateningly clenched fist.

'I got lost,' Tory stammered at last.

'Twice?' He smiled.

She felt her nerves easing. When the damaged face smiled it seemed to fix itself. He didn't look dangerous at all. She laughed, but not from nervousness. 'I never realized this was here, that's all. It seems odd.'

He took it for granted that she knew he'd been a boxer.

'Most of the chaps of my generation look like walruses now,' he said, lifting his arms slightly to display the slimness of his figure. 'Once you leave the ring your body runs to fat. But not mine. I've kept my hand in, training . . .' He patted his torso, which gave a solid thud, like a pillar. 'Keeps me fit.' Again the smile. He gave a passing jab at the same punchbag Tory had earlier tapped with her fingernail. It gave a dreadful, agonizing lurch backwards, the springs making a wrenching sound and the whole gymnasium vibrating in sympathy with the poor writhing thing, which then presented itself for more of the same treatment. George Farraway appeared to have expended no energy at all on this act and, with an ushering gesture of the other arm, swept Tory gently along with him towards the exit.

Without really knowing how it had happened, she found herself accepting a lift home from the boss – the owner – of the factory where she worked. He had steered her through the bluebottles and bone marrow at the back of the gymnasium to a little yard where his car stood, a dark, glossy thing, not quite a limousine but which reminded Tory of an enormous black pudding, causing her to titter again.

'You seem to find things funny,' he said, as he opened the passenger door for her. 'You were chuckling to yourself when I first saw you just now.'

'I don't know why,' Tory replied, entering the vehicle cautiously (she had never been in a car before, and wondered if there was something she had to hang on to). 'I don't usually laugh very much.' Then she immediately felt embarrassed by what she'd said, as though she was begging for sympathy.

'Oh dear,' said George, slightly mockingly. 'Has it been a tragic life for you?'

'I'm not sure why I said that. I'm sure I laugh too much.'

'That seems more likely. But you wouldn't be alone. Since this war started I've never seen so many cheerful people. It starts to grate on a chap a little, after a while, all this enforced jollity.'

Mr Farraway spoke well for a man who had started his career as a fairground attraction. The rough South London burr was still there (what her mother called the Blackwall Tunnel Howl, or just the Howl, which, her father would protest, for he spoke it too, was considered by the Australians to be little short of the King's English), but in George Farraway it was overlaid and nearly obliterated by a more even tone, a powerful business voice – assertive, authoritative without being superior. Tory liked it.

The interior of the car was a very comforting, reassuring space, and one filled, again, with leather. How much use we put animal skins to, Tory thought, noticing that there was even leather on the instrument panel, and feeling rather ashamed of the fact, though she wasn't sure why.

'I'm afraid to say I don't recognize your face,' said George, as the car came to contented life and moved off with almost imperceptible motion, 'though I try to know most of my workforce. What room are you in?'

'Packing,' said Tory.

'Ah,' said George, as if that explained it. She supposed it meant he spent much less time in Packing than in the other departments. 'And are you happy there?'

'I sometimes think I'd rather be doing something more exciting, but when I think of the alternatives, I'm rather glad to be where I am.'

'Yes, the manufacture of gelatine is not a picturesque process.' He glanced in her direction, and half smiled. 'Before the war I wouldn't have allowed a woman anywhere near the production rooms, but now I find it curiously heartening to see ladies getting their elbows dirty, cutting hides or working the vats. It reminds me that we're all in this together. I don't just mean the war, but the whole business of life.'

Tory remembered the glimpses she'd had of the women at work in the Skin Cutting Room, labouring over thick hides with their cutters, which were a bit like portable sewing machines but with blades instead of needles. They were doing something consummately manual, looking, apart from the hairnets and aprons, as masculine as dockyard welders, their brawny arms wielding the cutters through several hides at once, layer upon layer, so that they were sliced like enormous sandwiches. There were still a few men left in these rooms, but they were the old ones, and seemed abashed and indignant at having to share their work with women.

'The Packing Room has always been a ladies' domain. When the men left for call-up I shifted most of them to the production rooms, because they knew a bit about the work and had more of a stomach for it than I thought the new recruits might. That's why most of the Packing Room is staffed by the new lot, like yourself.'

'Very considerate of you.'

'Well, just say the word and I'll have you trained up for the Melting Room in no time . . .'

'Like I said, I'm quite happy to be where I am.'

They laughed. What an easy man he was to talk to. Once over her initial stammers she felt free to say anything she cared to . . . almost. She wouldn't have dreamt such a thing possible, to find ease in the company of a millionaire, and one who had been famous in the past at that. But they chatted freely as they journeyed through the streets of south-east London, noting, as they did, the buildings that had disappeared since the start of the Blitz. George noted that they still had not camouflaged his factory. 'If it's not there in the morning,' he said, 'you'll know why.' He said he could take her directly home, as it was on his own way home, but he discreetly dropped her three blocks away. 'We don't want anyone talking,' he said. Tory wondered what about, as she got out of the car, and George, leaning across the passenger seat to call after her, said, 'I still don't know your name.'

'It's Tory,' said Tory, 'Tory Pace,' and she hurried towards Peter Street, feeling as though she had left something precious behind in the car with George Farraway.

CHAPTER 11

From that moment on things happened for Tory with a breathtaking swiftness. The very next day George Farraway made a rare appearance in the Packing Room, having thought up, so Tory supposed, some economic pretext for discussing packaging matters with Clara, the packing manager. He had done this several times before, and each time it had caused a stir, and this time even more so because he moved across to one of the packing tables and started chatting directly with some of the girls. He wasn't at Tory's table but was at the other end, where the older, regular workers sat. There he was, chatting with Edi, his number-one fan. Not all of the old faithfuls were so in awe of George Farraway but they admired him, as much for his wealth as for his illustrious past.

The next day he visited the Packing Room again, this time casting some words in the direction of Tory's table, some idle pleasantries and humorous little jibes. The reaction here was very different: there were blushes from the younger women, some titters, but generally a feeling that no one knew what to say, or if they should say anything at all.

Only Tory rose to the occasion. When George asked, 'And how are all you fine young ladies managing?' she replied, 'We could do with some stronger thread. This type keeps breaking.'

Clara, who was nearby, looked sternly at Tory and would have wagged a finger, if she had been in sole authority. Other girls at the table stared at her in shock. But instead of the sharp retort they were expecting, the 'There's a war on' line, 'We've got to make the best of what we've got', George took a serious interest in the thread. He asked the opinion of other girls (who backed up Tory's claim). He asked Clara how long they'd been using it. He even unwound a piece and tested its strength between his hands. In his powerful arms it sundered as easily as a single hair. He departed, asking Clara to look into it. 'We can't have production slowed down by poor materials,' he said, 'and we certainly don't want bags breaking in transit. We've a big order to meet by next week . . .'

Then he began giving her lifts regularly. She thought nothing untoward at first, because George was a generous man with his lifts, and there were quite often other people in the car, sometimes other young girls from the factory, sometimes people from the gym, 'Jelly Babies', or their trainers. Then one day, when she'd finished an early shift and was on her way home, he scooped her up again, this time on her own, and drove her into London, against her wishes, ignoring the turning that would have taken her back to her mother with a dismissive spurt of acceleration, saying, as he did so, that life was too short to spend evenings alone with one's parents, and that it was about time she saw something more of what the world had to offer her. He drove her into the very heart of London, a place she'd visited rarely, and not at all since the war had started.

She was surprised to find that it was still a bustling, throbbing hub of activity, that there were still people weaving in and out of each other down busy pavements, that chugging motorbuses and taxis and trams still queued in overcrowded thoroughfares. City gents in morning coats and wing collars jostled for position with market traders lugging crates of cauliflowers to the stalls in Covent Garden, theatres defiantly advertised risqué revues and diverting whodunits, the flower markets dazzled, when glimpsed through narrow side-streets, and gave a honey smell that vied with the stewy smell of cheap restaurants that wafted along the Strand. She'd had a picture in her mind, until then, of the centre of London as a derelict wasteland, Nelson's column a shattered stump, the magnificent buildings open to the sky, with smoke drifting upwards, and starving hordes picking through the rubble. She'd seen the damage a single stray bomb could do to the shops of Old Parade, and imagined the city centre to be like that, but magnified a thousand times. In fact, Trafalgar Square was just as it had always been, with a victory banner draped across the plinth and the four lions sitting sphinx-like. The National Gallery was sandbagged and the windows, like windows everywhere, were cross-taped. But otherwise the heart of London continued to beat. The only noticeable absence was that of strong, healthy-looking young men, save the occasional one in khaki, on leave. The barrow-pushers were older men.

He took her to Simpson's, parking the car outside the imposing front door, where a doorman eagerly took care of it.

'I have brought you to the home of English Roast Beef,' he said, as they sat at a table amid oak panelling and chandeliers. Tory had dug in her heels like a puppy being taken for a bath as they entered the restaurant, convinced that she would not be allowed in, sure that Mr Farraway was making some terrible mistake in thinking they would admit her. She was, after all, in her ordinary clothes, unwashed and unmade-up, barely presentable at the best of times. Now, seated, she found herself surrounded by tables at which men of business sawed at red meat. There seemed to be no other women.

'Why have you brought me here?' she whispered hotly, after the menu had been delivered.

'Because I thought you could do with some nourishment, my dear,' he replied, smiling, 'though with the shortages they're having trouble even here with obtaining decent beef. We might have to make do with game, or venison. Don't look so frightened – why do you always look frightened?'

'I don't feel as though I belong here,' she said, surprised that she could so easily express this particular anxiety. In any other circumstance she would have suppressed her true feelings, but George Farraway was an extraordinarily easy man to confide in. In that moment she suddenly realized she enjoyed his company more than that of any other man she had ever met. Nothing she could say surprised or shocked him. Most things she said amused him.

'They may look exclusive, but in fact they'll let anyone in,' said George, adding hastily, with another smile, 'Not that you are just anyone, of course, but you see what I mean.'

'Have you brought other girls here?'

'No.'

'Why not?'

'I've had no desire to.' He followed this with an enigmatic smile, opening the big tasselled menu. Tory opened hers and was surprised to find that she could understand it. She had been expecting things in French.

Tory couldn't quite understand what was happening to her. Was George just being kind to one of his employees or were they at the start of an affair? She felt ridiculous in the restaurant, unkempt and unwashed, gauche, lustreless. But looking around her she noticed how little notice was being taken of her. She could tell that George was a widely respected regular of the establishment: the waiters and concierges addressed him by name; some of the customers gave him polite nods. He shook a few hands, casually introducing

Tory as a colleague or business acquaintance. She didn't believe him when he said he had not brought other girls here. She assumed she was one of many, all casually introduced in the same way.

If they were about to have an affair (or had they already begun one? It was hard to say), Tory felt curiously prepared. All that business with Donald's letters, his implorations for her to be bad, made it somehow easier for her actually to be bad.

'Well,' said George, once they had ordered, 'this makes a welcome change from the environs of a gelatine factory.'

'Yes,' said Tory. 'Cooked meat smells so much better.'

'I don't know how I ended up in such a grisly branch of manufacturing. It's rather like mining gold – to those few who are prepared to do the darkest work, there are the greatest rewards.'

'But it is useful, I take it, gelatine?'

'Useful?'

'Yes, for the war effort. Is it an ingredient in explosives?'

There was a pause while Mr Farraway seemed to consider this question. 'There are many, many uses for gelatine,' he said. 'You may think of it as an ingredient for thickening desserts, such as jelly and blancmange. It is also used in ballistics to provide a simulator for human flesh. Yes, they fire bullets into blocks of our gelatine in small-arms factories throughout the land.'

The thought rather appalled Tory, as though she

144

had been struck by the possibility that gelatine could suffer. 'That's a good thing, I think.'

'It's my belief that in the future all food will be made from gelatine in some form or other. It's pure protein, don't you know? Utterly flavourless when refined, it can be artificially flavoured to taste like anything. In these times of shortages I believe we can use gelatine, processed and modified, to supply up to ninety per cent of essential nutrients in the diet for a fraction of the cost. Imagine yourself sitting down to a roast dinner, with slices of beef, roast potatoes, greens, gravy. Everything on that plate could be made out of the same stuff – flavoured gelatine. We could inject vitamins and minerals into it for essential goodness. It could have all the nutritional value of an actual roast dinner yet be made from almost nothing but gelatine.'

Tory thought for a moment. It seemed astonishing, a roast dinner made entirely out of gelatine, and she was certain there was something wrong with the idea. Then she had it. 'But wouldn't it wobble terribly?' she said.

Mr Farraway seemed to find this amusing at first, then took it more seriously. 'Show me your hands,' he said. Tory did so and he inspected her nails. 'I have developed a drink that strengthens nails and hair. It tastes delicious too. I would like you to be my first guinea pig, to drink it for a month. I guarantee you will have improved nails. They will be hard and shiny, and your hair, too, will be glossy.'

'Are you saying I look ill?'

'Like I said, you're undernourished, but then we all are . . .'

She glanced across the tables as he said this, watching waiters lifting silver domes to reveal saddles of venison, then carving the same with shining knives, to fill the plates of portly capitalists.

'I see it in the gym, strapping lads all skin and bone. They're good fighters but they just don't have the fuel to build up decent muscle. These are hard times for those of us involved in food production. Most of our hides were imported from the United States or even further afield, India and the Far East. Increasingly we've had to rely on homegrown hides and bones, but there just aren't the quantities necessary. We have to cut back. Production is down. And it's true. Domestic use of gelatine is falling. The ladies of England, like your good self, have enough problems on their hands without having to find the time to make jellies and blancmanges. I suspect the evacuation programme has had an effect, and the foster mothers are disinclined to provide jellies for the children of the towns and cities. We have to explore other avenues to secure a future for our product. Hence my nail drink. In America they've come up with a plasma extender based on gelatine. Artificial blood, if you will. I have something up my sleeve too. Protein pills.'

'Protein pills?'

'As I said before, gelatine is almost pure protein. My Jelly Babies – I mean my lads in the gym – I believe can attribute their exceptional energy and strength to the regular doses of liquid gelatine I have provided for them. I have some boffins working on a tabloid form that can be swallowed easily.' He suddenly looked round with exaggerated caution, as though suspecting the presence of eaves-droppers. 'I shouldn't be telling you this, you know, trade secrets and all that. But it's going to be quite a moneyspinner. You've seen the way my lads fight – like little bulls, aren't they? – and they eat no more red meat than you or I on the ration. Think what my pills could do for a soldier out in the middle of nowhere. If he had a pack of Farraway's Protein Pills in his knapsack he could live on those and nothing else, apart from water . . .'

'For how long?'

'Almost indefinitely. If we can combine the vita-mins and minerals – like I said – we could have a complete meal in a little pill no bigger than a cough sweet.'

He pointed to a side of roast beef, which had drawn gasps of admiration from all around the restaurant when it was uncovered – the only such joint available that day. 'All that goodness and strength contained in a single pill – can you imagine? Oh, I know we have similar things already – vitamin tablets, Iron Jelloids and so forth, but they can only supplement a normal food diet. What I'm suggesting is that in the future we could do away with meat and vegetables altogether. Think of it – no more cooking or shopping, no more crouching in front of a blazing oven basting a joint for hours on end. The future of food is in pill form, Tory.'

She liked hearing him say her name, and she tried to sound approving of his scheme for the future of food. It certainly seemed to make sense on the military front, but she tried to imagine how people like her mother would react, if told their services were no longer needed, she who liked nothing more than to stare into the blazing heat of an oven and skewer a shoulder of lamb to test for running blood. What odd little world would she find herself inhabiting, in which no cooking was done, and what would she find to do in it?

'Won't your wife miss cooking awfully?'

It was the first time mention had been made of the woman whom she knew to exist.

'She may do, but the question really is, would the world miss my wife's cookery?' He gave a sideways sort of laugh, before adding, 'Given the choice between one of her hot-pots and a protein pill . . . Well, I'm being cruel, I know. I suppose you were hoping to catch me out somehow with that question.'

'No, not really. But I find myself thinking about her.'

'I wouldn't.'

'Is she beautiful?'

'Apparently. Too beautiful, probably.'

'What do you mean?'

'Very beautiful women – they're an awful bind.

They get bored easily, are suckers for temptation, prone to scheming and dishonesty. Give me a plain but presentable woman any day.'

Tory supposed he meant her, and wished she could be angry about it. 'Does your wife know you've taken me out to dinner?'

'She probably has an inkling I'm doing something I shouldn't be. When I get home there'll be a stream of innuendoes. She can be a sarky little tripehound at times.'

Tory peered into the lucid depths of her gin and French, trying to control the thrill she felt at hearing George Farraway defame his own wife, for her ears only.

'I'm quite aware that you are married too, my dear,' he said, 'and not just because of the ring on your finger. No doubt your husband is fighting the good fight. Where is he, or aren't you allowed to say or know?'

'He's a prisoner of war,' said Tory, in a voice she didn't like – too weak and whiney.

'Oh.' George clearly didn't know quite what to say. 'Is that a good thing or a bad thing? Out of harm's way, I suppose, but you might not see him again till the war's over, whenever that might be.'

'I sometimes wish I would never see him again, or that the war will never end.' This came out involuntarily, and she managed to bring forth some tears to excuse the apparent treachery in what she'd said. George changed tack immediately, took her delicate white hands in his (inspecting the nails closely when he thought she wasn't looking), then uttered soothing implorations, telling her it didn't matter if she had feelings like those. She went on: 'I don't mean to be so weak. It's just that I'm afraid my husband is being turned into some sort of monster by the Nazis. I'm dreading meeting the man who will be returned to me when we win this war.'

'Perhaps it will be sooner. Did you read about those men who escaped?'

When the meal came to an end, George Farraway drove her home. As he arrived at the usual spot for her disembarkation, he took her hand and squeezed it. She had not quite managed to recover her spirits since talking about Donald. George reached into a sort of little cupboard underneath the steering-wheel and produced a bottle of blue glass. She glimpsed an array of different-coloured bottles in that cupboard, a sort of on-board medicine chest.

'Will you take this?' he said, putting the bottle into her hand, then closing her fingers around it.

'What is it?'

'My nail drink. I'd like you to take it once a day, just for a week. To see what difference it makes.'

'Is it . . .'

'It's a perfectly harmless liquid and tastes lovely. You just need to take a small amount each day, about a half a sherry glass. Will you do that for me?'

Tory took the bottle and left George's car, saying that she would.

CHAPTER 12

B ack in the sitting room, she realized she hadn't written to her children for more than a week. She rushed to the escritoire, took a sheet of writing paper and unscrewed the cap of the fountain pen just as her mother, having creakily descended the stairs, knocked on the door.

It was quite easy to explain away any unexpected lateness to Mrs Head. At the factory they were often called upon to do a spot of overtime, a couple of extra hours for anyone who wanted it, with no warning. Mrs Head was a little put out, however, because she had had another good run at the butcher's and had procured enough good lamb to make an Irish stew, the tasting of which she had been putting off for as long as possible. She had only just eaten her share, while Tory's was still warm in the pot. This was harder to deal with. How could she explain that she was stuffed full of venison, hadn't room for a spoonful of anything more, and would even have trouble finding room for the half sherry glass of Mr Farraway's nail potion, which was waiting for her in her handbag?

151

She came into the dining room, whose walls were covered with beads of moisture from the long, steamy hours of stewing that had taken place that afternoon. Mrs Head had already laid a place for her, and a dish of stew was waiting. Illness was the only option left, her only means of explaining her lack of appetite. She took a mouthful of the admittedly rather good stew, then put an elbow on the table and rested her forehead in her hand. Tory did hate lying. It was, in a way, one of her biggest faults. If she could have lied more freely, more inventively, she could have written those letters to Donald, she could have enjoyed her evening with Mr Farraway more, she could even have found herself a better job than that of a gelatine packer. The whole richness of the world seemed to be available only through a doorway of half-truths and white lies, and the 'good' people, the people made of gold, must watch from afar, like beggars outside a banquet, spying the delights through a keyhole, while the people of lead ran amok. Tory herself wasn't at all convinced that she was good, however. It was more that she wasn't brave enough, 'hadn't the nerve', to do anything bad. She couldn't rid herself of a residual belief that bad things came back to you, that bad people reaped the whirlwinds of their bad deeds. Hitler, surely, was about to learn that little lesson.

Well, this was the moment, then, that Tory first lied to her mother (who hadn't even asked why she was late). She may have concealed things from her before, but there had been no deliberate lies, and not one, such as this, that required a kind of acting out as well.

'I'm feeling a bit queer,' she said, as her mother returned to the dining room. 'I'm awfully sorry, I don't think I'll be able to eat this . . .'

'Oh,' said Mrs Head, then suggested a range of possible treatments, all of which were contained in glass jars, not dissimilar to the one that George had given her, on the mantelpiece.

'I think I'll just have a lie-down in the study – I mean the sitting room – on the chaise longue. I probably shouldn't have done that bit of over-time . . .'

And with this she was able to retreat with her full tummy back to the seclusion of the sitting room. Oddly enough, she did begin to feel a little bit queasy when she was on her own again. She made another attempt at writing to the children, but found it impossible to make any meaningful marks on the blank paper. It was the bottle that was stopping her, the little blue bottle that George Farraway had given her. She took it out of her bag and looked at it. Half a sherry glass, George had said. There was actually a drinks cabinet in the study which, though it contained no drink, had an array of engraved glasses suitable for just about every drink that could be imagined – beer, champagne, cocktails, whisky . . . She had no recollection of any of these glasses ever being used. There was a lock on the cabinet's glass doors, and the little silver key was in the lock as always.

Tory couldn't avoid thinking about *Alice in Wonderland* as she turned it – tiny little keys, bottles of strange medicines. And the medicine did look very strange when she poured it out. A thick, creamy, pale green liquid half filled the sherry glass. She held it to her nose. Peppermint, with a faint, chalky undertone. Quite nice. Though she didn't drink it yet. She had to look at her nails first. She put the glass down and examined them closely. Mr Farraway had seemed to read them like a jeweller might read diamonds. She always imagined that everyone's fingernails looked the same, like hers, but now she thought about it (if she could remember) there were worlds of differ-ence between her own pink ovals and, say, her mother's yellower talons or Mr Farraway's – what were his like? Why hadn't she had the nerve to return his examination? Perhaps she would next time. As it was, she didn't think her own nails looked too bad. What was he talking about, under-nourished? But, then, perhaps he did have a point. There were little white flecks, little wisps, like good weather clouds over a pink sunset, marking some of the nails, which did represent a deficiency of some sort, though she couldn't quite remember of what. Perhaps there was also a lack of shine. Perhaps they were a bit – what was the word? – papery. And thin? It was true, it didn't take much effort from a pair of scissors to trim them once

154

in a while. The question was, did she think her nails bad enough to resort to Mr Farraway's experimental tonic?

But she realized it was much more than that. By taking his drink she was entering into some sort of pact, not only agreeing to be a guinea pig in one of his experiments but somehow to give a part of herself to him, if only her nails. If she took the drink as directed, Mr Farraway would be entitled to examine them again. He would run them under that glistening, perceptive but lopsided eye and pass judgement on them, and if they were improved in some way – thicker, glossier, unflecked – she would owe that part of herself to him. It would be like he had made a part of her. And, as such, he would have a right to take it whenever he wanted it. He could call on her in the middle of the night and demand access to her fingernails – he could summon her presence at any moment for the examination, the perusal, the caress of her fingernails, strengthened, reborn through his own tonic.

'It's just a silly little drink,' she said to herself, realizing that she was thinking too much into the situation, but she was contemplating this green tonic from the viewpoint of a woman who had just been wooed by a millionaire, taken to a restaurant, the luxury and opulence of which she had never before seen the like, had travelled there in a luxury car upholstered in calves' hides, with lamps on the front bigger than her head. No drink in a dark blue fluted glass bottle proffered by the provider of such decadence could be taken lightly, could it?

She drank. She knocked the glass back in one all-or-nothing gulp. The taste wasn't bad, but the texture was unpleasant. It oozed down her throat in a slippery, half-alive way. There seemed to be strings in the fluid and, for a moment, she thought she would gag. The thick viscosity of the gelatine itself was responsible, she supposed. The temptation to look at her fingernails immediately was irresistible, even though she knew there could not possibly be a difference. Even after a week there couldn't be much change, given how slowly fingernails grow. She glanced at herself in her compact mirror. Her upper lip was marked with a little Hitler moustache of green, which she quickly wiped away.

George Farraway was relentless and ingenious in his pursuit of Tory Pace. He didn't want for resources in this enterprise, after all. He had an entire factory employing more than two hundred people at his disposal; he had his wealth, his cars, his properties. When, a few days later, Clara quietly informed Tory that Mr Farraway had asked to see her in his office and that she was to accompany her there now, she meekly acquiesced, though her heart was trembling as she followed Clara through several unsightly rooms and cobbled yards.

When she was delivered to the owner and

managing director's office, it wasn't quite what she'd been expecting. She had imagined oak-panelled walls and leather armchairs, portraits on the wall, big charts of profits inclining to the right. Instead, the office bore the same general air of shabby Victorian industrial leftovers as the rest of the factory. Bare brick walls, big pipe runs down the corners, a dirty window of small panes. There were the charts she had predicted and portraits – not the oil on canvas studies she had imagined, but photographs of George in his boxing days, some posed in the traditional way, the young boxer with his guard up, peering over the top of his gloves with a determined, piercing stare, and some framed press photos of George in action, landing his famous right hook square in the face of a hapless opponent.

'My secretary has taken the liberty of going down with the blasted 'flu,' he explained, when they were alone together. 'Didn't think you'd mind doing a bit of filling in – you seem such a bright lass, wasted in the Packing Room.'

'Don't personal secretaries get paid rather more than packing skivvies?' said Tory, surprising herself with her boldness. George laughed.

'You're not one of those blasted union people, are you? Don't worry, I will pay you the extra, but for God's sake start looking like a secretary, will you? Take your hair out of those nets for a start.'

'I haven't even agreed to this yet,' said Tory,

unleashing her hair. 'I've never done anything in the secretarial line before.'

'Oh, nothing too complicated, a well-trained chimp could do it. My word, the nail drink has taken effect already, hasn't it? I assume you've started the course – otherwise why would your locks look so glossy and bright?'

Ignoring his compliment (which, she also saw, was a statement of self-congratulation), she turned towards the photographs on the wall, walking over to examine them closely. The thing that struck her most strongly about these was how little resemblance they bore to the man sitting behind the desk. The lack of beard was perhaps the most significant difference, and the much darker hair had an oily wave to it. But a subtler difference was in the arrangement of the features: the nose of the young boxer had yet to be broken, the brows had yet to sustain their heaviest bombardment, the ears were still sharp and clearly defined.

'I wouldn't look too closely at those, my dear,' said Mr Farraway, coming over to join her in contemplation of his younger self. 'I hardly know that person any longer.'

She turned her attention to the other paraphernalia, the trophies, belts and, most intriguing of all, a pair of old boxing gloves, the leather a hard, glazed deep red that, like the punchbag she had met at the gym, was crying out for her to touch it. 'Yours, I presume?' she said.

He nodded in reply. 'If you look very carefully

you'll see traces of the blood of a world champion. My greatest moment, you could say, was to lose to the greatest in the world. I cut him above his right eye. Every time I landed another punch I was splashed in his blood. He wore me down in the end, though. Jack Dempsey. A true fighter, if ever there was one. I'm sorry, have I made you feel faint? I keep forgetting not to take for granted the goriness of my life hitherto. Why don't you sit down?'

Tory was aware that she must look very pale, for she could feel the blood draining from her face. It wasn't so much his talk of Jack Dempsey's sanguination that bothered her but the sudden recollection of what her mother had said, that George Farraway had killed a man, and she found herself wondering if it had been with these very gloves that he had done the deed.

She wanted to ask him, but didn't. It was too early in their relationship for her to broach such a subject, though she was quite aware that the opportunity would arise soon. There was a grinding inevitability about what was to follow, but Tory appeased herself by imagining that nothing more than curiosity was driving her into an ever-increasing intimacy with George Farraway. If she was on the verge of betraying her husband, a British soldier and prisoner of war, and, by extension, betraying the British Army in its fight against fascism, she could console herself with the notion that it was Donald's fault for filling her mind with

159

the problem of how to describe the sexual act, and in allowing George his pursuit, she was coming ever closer to what she sensed would be a glorious revelation.

That was why she allowed him to take her out that very afternoon, and for several afternoons thereafter, initially on the pretext of attending some business meetings outside the factory, in fact to be swept away in the almost-limousine out of London altogether, through places she'd never seen before, plunging down chalk escarpments, through a landscape of furrowed richness, dotted everywhere with fruit trees, hop fields, lazy, meandering rivers. Oast houses, thick-set churches with erect little towers. It was a landscape she had known to exist, and surprisingly close by, but which she had never visited. George had visited it many times. In fact, he had a house in the midst of it, a kind of country retreat, not a particularly grand place, more a classic roses-round-the-door thatched cottage that he used, she assumed, almost exclusively for illicit romantic convocations. The furniture was mostly under dust covers.

Tory came to know this cottage rather well over the ensuing weeks. It seemed such a remote place that at first she wondered if anyone, apart from she and George, knew of its existence. There was a village nearby, but this also seemed undiscovered, with its tiny village green, which had just enough room for a knuckly sweet chestnut with a corkscrew trunk to spread its branches. If it wasn't for the odd glimpsed figure turning into a doorway, she would have wondered if the village was inhabited at all. It was more like something that had been built as a reminder of what would be lost if the Germans won.

There was a woman who looked after the cottage, a wispily grey-haired creature with a shawl and dusty boots, sometimes accompanied by tousled, rough-and-tumble children. She could sometimes be seen besoming the leaves from the path where there weren't any leaves. It occurred to Tory that if ever she wanted to know about George's private life, she should speak to that woman. Other than that, Tory felt the cottage was so remote that she and George could have done anything there, and no one in the world would know.

At first George treated the afternoons at the cottage like jolly days out. He liked to take a little wicker hamper down there, filled with chilled champagne and packs of sardine sandwiches. They would pull the dust covers from a couch and chat while drinking. Tory noticed that if she drank too much champagne at the cottage, she nevertheless sobered up the moment they left. It was as though drunkenness was a property of the cottage rather than the champagne. And Tory was quite aware of what was happening.

'Have you brought me here to seduce me?' she said, emboldened by alcohol.

'Yes.'

'But there are prettier women in the factory.'

'Are there?'

'I'm sure of it.' Tory said this in what she realized was a too-doubtful voice, which George took for a marvellous joke.

'There you are – you've realized that you're beautiful. Let's drink to your beauty.'

He raised his glass and chinked it against Tory's. She didn't seem to notice. She was thinking about what George had just said. *Beautiful* was a much more powerful word than *pretty*. *Pretty* was what her mother and Donald might have called her, if they'd had to. *Beautiful* was for famous paintings and sculptures, for poems by the great Romantic poets, for Shakespeare's sonnets. By his use of that single word, Tory later realized, she had permitted herself to become his mistress.

A shiver of doubt remained right up to the moment, however, when George made his move. Standing in the centre of the lowceilinged sitting room, on their third visit to the cottage, he had taken the champagne glass out of her hand, as though he was plucking the bud of a white rose, and brought his face right up to hers. She felt the bristles of his beard and experienced, at first, disappointment. The uncomfortable prickliness of it reminded her of Donald, but then, from the centre, a pulse of warmth and softness, his mouth opening into hers.

Then he did this thing – he touched her in a very special way. It took her so by surprise that she couldn't help uttering a little squeal. He had placed one of his hands on her behind. '*I imagine you taking me in your manly arms, my love, and placing one of your hands on my behind.'*

'Pardon?' said George, withdrawing and looking at her quizzically.

She had not realized she had spoken out loud. 'Nothing.'

'It sounded like you were quoting something.'

'Just a silly romantic novel I once read.'

'Oh.' George sounded a little doubtful, but his hand was still there. He squeezed her. Then he kissed her again. He moved down to her neck and began unbuttoning her blouse with his teeth. Tory was struggling for breath. She felt she must be blushing so much she might weep tears of blood. She couldn't help it, only barely thinking about what was happening to her, and struggling under the influence of the champagne and other intoxications, but she blurted out, as George continued to maul her buttocks, squeezing them alternately, as though pumping the pedals of a bicycle – in the whirl of gorgeous sensations she blurted out, in little more than a whisper, *'Not good enough! Not good enough!'*

CHAPTER 13

It was as though it was her first time. And every time thereafter with George, it was as though it was her first time. She was in a permanent state of virginity, deflowered again and again and again. Every time she saw George naked she thought, *So this is what a man looks like with no clothes on* – not as horrifying as she'd thought. In fact quite . . . pretty. Somehow that word, applied to George, gained new power. The lopsided features of George Farraway's face were mounted on a body of burning symmetry. He appeared to be filled, just like a thoughtfully packed suitcase – there wasn't a square inch of his body that was not crammed with useful things, though muscles and organs rather than rolled-up socks and thimbles. And perfectly balanced. Slice him in half down the middle and weigh the two halves, there wouldn't be an ounce of difference. What had the boxers thought when their fists crumpled against this solid torso? Imagine, in return, the glove coming at you, knowing there was this much solid weight behind it. At times she was embarrassed by her admiration for George's body, aghast that she could find beauty in such a thing. But it seemed to defy nature. Wherever she touched with her tongue she found sweetness, even in those most sour places. Whatever she expected to be soft and fragile proved to be solid and robust. Contrarily, things that seemed rigid and hard felt like petals in her hands. If a statue could come to life, it would surely feel something like this.

She felt no guilt. She regarded the whole affair as entirely Donald's fault. Her union with George was simply the culmination of a research project that had begun the very first time she visited a library to peruse the 'For Adults Only' books, to examine the language of carnal desire. As such it proved to be most productive, because George Farraway had one very special quality as a love-maker: he liked to talk his way through the whole process. For most of the time, he described aloud what they were doing, rather like a commentator at a sporting event, sometimes in the third person, referring to himself and Tory by name, at others, taking the role of a minute observer of the female body, describing the journey through Tory's realm as though he was a voyager in a land of giants. Most of the terms he used were new to her, as were most of the words he used to describe their various procedures, as were the procedures themselves. But they stayed in her mind as she was driven back to the factory in the late afternoons, back through the gorgeous orchards with their stiff red fruits, through the tall hop poles with their entwining wreaths, along the oozing meanders and finally back into the brick-built corpus of the city, there to finish her day's work at the factory just as though it had been a normal day, to return home (George had avoided giving her lifts now, for reasons of discretion) to a warm, hearty meal of her mother's latest gleanings from the new butcher, then to the study, this time, almost trembling with eagerness, to write letters to Donald, meeting his demands as requested, filling them with long descriptions that mostly used George's rich sexual language but which, with a subtle and deft change of tense and viewpoint, became passionate, erotic missives from a wife to her imprisoned husband.

This, she quickly realized, was a kind of magic: to redraft the real world, to replace, simply by words, one person with another. And what a funny shock that was, to have the hollow, skinny torso of Donald appear where George's sixteen-stone bulk had been, to have his balding scalp emerge from down there, when it had been the lush grey locks of George that had first descended. By a mere play on words it could have been Donald firing these new feelings into her.

He was getting what he asked for. More than he asked for. More than he'd bargained for. Tory had launched a spring offensive of sexual narrative, she had let him have the whole artillery of sexual expression full in the face, the dirty words falling like dirty bombs square on that little hut in the middle of a German forest. She wrote her

166

letters in a kind of erotic, literary frenzy. Sometimes she didn't even begin with 'Dear Donald' but would plunge straight into a narrative of body against body, in all its possible permutations. She didn't think to revise or polish her letters – the words poured out of her, each letter like a successive wave in a storm at sea. She didn't know how many she had written, but in a matter of just a few weeks she had had to visit the stationer so many times for new writing pads that she exhausted his stock and had to go elsewhere.

Dearest Darling Tory

I told you you could do it, if you just put your mind to it. You are doing me proud, my love, I think your letters are the nearest a man can have to the real thing. You have found the voice I always knew you had. I always knew you had it in you, darling, to be a really dirty girl.

Such language, Tory. Where did you learn those words? I had to ask some of the fellows here what some of them meant (though I didn't show them your letters, you can rest assured). Some of those deeds you describe are of a kind that I think never happened in our bedroom, did they? If I had known you wanted me to do those things, or for you to do those things to me, I would willingly have obliged. I have never desired more strongly for this war to be over so that I can come home and we can bring your letters to glorious life. I am very lucky man to have such a willing wife.

I would reply in kind, but I know your mother always opens your letters, and wouldn't want her to have a heart attack – well, not really.

Keep them coming Tory old girl, you dirty, dirty girl, but still my golden girl.

Love from your man of lead

Donald

PS How did you know I have grown a beard?

What would he have thought if he'd known it was the words of her lover that formed the meat of her letters? That it was another man's words that were weaving their erotic magic? Surely that should have given her pause, she thought later. Surely that was a reason for feeling bad. If she had stepped back for a moment, seen herself from the outside (as George so often, during their love-making, seemed to see himself), she might have had the wider perspective, and maybe that would have been enough to make her end her affair with George Farraway.

But in fact the affair continued for several weeks more, and didn't end properly until Tory became pregnant, in the late summer of 1941.

PART II

CHAPTER 14

Private Donald Midlothian Pace of the 11th Royal Hussars, captured east of Tobruk while defending the Bi'r al-Ashhab airfield from encroaching Italian forces, during which he was wounded by a bullet to the knee, had, by the time his camp was liberated on 15 April 1945, been a prisoner of war for four years and twenty-nine days. About the same as what you'd get, he sometimes joked, for knocking off a jeweller's.

Having been transported across the Mare Nostrum in the light cruiser *Giuseppe Garibaldi*, he had begun his captivity at a camp beside the Appian Way, before being transported again, north by cattle truck through France to Germany. Here he was moved between camps five times, each time being forced to march up to twenty miles a day, a venture that did little to heal his wounded leg and, in fact, made it a lot worse. By the end of the war he was, effectively, crippled, being unable to bend his right knee, or place much weight upon it. He had never mentioned any of these facts in his letters to his wife.

Donald derived little pleasure from the letters

Tory was eventually able to write him, and his requests had been made purely for expedient reasons. In the camp in which he was first detained, there had grown up, in certain quarters, and among certain men, a culture of letter exchange. Captain Harry Wilde, Private Roy Smedley and Sergeant Horace Maxwell, among others, were the first to start bragging about the letters from their wives and sweethearts. They had begun swapping them among themselves, and would teasingly exaggerate the effect of reading them, giving loud moans and sighs of ecstasy that filled the huts as they read, which had the desired consequence of arousing burning curiosity among those in the hut (the majority) without such letters.

'Roy, I have to say your old girl certainly knows how to get a fellow hot under the old collar . . .'

'It's a good job the Obscene Publications Act doesn't apply to letters, Harry, old man, otherwise your good lady would be doing a stretch in Holloway.' The others in the hut, Donald included, could do nothing but imagine what the letters contained.

This led to some unpleasant moments. The merciless teasing by the men with letters led to several confrontations when the honour and morality of the writers were openly challenged. It never came to blows – there was never the energy in the huts for actual violence. Instead there were month-long sulks and endless cold-shouldering. Eventually the men started loaning their letters in return for favours or goods. A few squares of chocolate, a pinch of tobacco, a night off from cooking duties. Donald, having nothing material to offer, agreed to clean Captain Harry Wilde's boots for a week in return for an evening's loan of one of his letters. It turned out to be deeply disappointing, being little more than an innocently flirtatious description of French kissing. If only his own wife could write something stronger, he thought. Imagine what he could get people to do for that. Not only could he have almost anything he wanted, he would become part of the hut's elite. Private Donald Pace could take his place alongside Wilde, Smedley and Maxwell as a force to be reckoned with.

Other men had tried the same thing and failed, receiving cold rebukes from their wives, much as Donald had experienced when he eventually received replies from Tory. It was what he had expected. But he had the persistence that the others in the camp lacked. And it was a persistence that eventually paid off, but to an extent that Donald found quite overwhelming.

After weeks of protestations, and half-hearted attempts at compliance, there came from Tory a torrent of erotic missives that unfolded, over a few weeks, into an epic of the nuptial arts. Letters arrived daily, sometimes in batches of three or four. When Donald opened the first of these he couldn't help but shout the word 'Bingo!' at the top of his voice. Everyone in the hut could guess what this meant, that Donald Pace had finally managed to nag his old woman into writing him a dirty letter. They were crowding round his bunk within seconds, begging for a glimpse, just a line or two. Items were thrust in his direction. Archie Warhol would lend him his domino set for three days, Ricey had a tin of Ovaltine, and was willing to give him four tablespoons in a twist of paper. Corporal Howard would lend him a picture of his sister Jenny. But Donald could see that Tory had excelled herself, that she hadn't just done one of the feeble bum-pinching and thigh-stroking letters that were the best his comrades could produce. No, Tory had gone into details. Minute details. Jesus Christ, Donald could hardly contain his shock. Had she really paid such close attention to those parts of his body that she could now describe with such verve? Not even Donald could describe his own nether regions in such detail. He'd have to check when he got a moment – did it really look like that? And her own body – how had she ever been able to view those portions of herself so clearly? Not even Donald, with his detached perspective, could recall the folds and creases that shone so brightly in Tory's letter.

'Oh, but she's knows how to turn a shapely phrase,' said Second Lieutenant Orson, who'd glimpsed a few lines over Donald's shoulder before Donald had time to shield the words against his shirt.

'Wait a minute,' he said. 'If any of you blighters

want a look at these lines, you're going to have to come up with more than a few spoonfuls of Ovaltine, I can tell you.'

The explicitness of Tory's letters did at first give Donald reason to hesitate before he began loaning them, not out of any sense of loyalty but because he felt uncomfortable about having himself become common property in this way. It was as though he had not just been rendered naked before his peers but transparent as well. But it was Captain Harry Wilde who was able to secure the first loan of Tory's letter, offering a whole bar of chocolate in exchange, a transaction that shifted the power structure of the whole camp. Having read the letter Harry Wilde declared that the material was so hot he could have the whole camp on its knees at his door begging for a loan (by this time three more letters had arrived). You could make yourself a rich man, Donald Pace, a rich man in the economy of the stalag – you could have all the tobacco, alcohol and sweeties you had ever dreamt of. Not just that. You could take a fortune in IOUs for things that will be paid for when the war is over – cars, clothes, houses. Tory's letters could bring him any of these . . .

It was rather typical of Harry Wilde to get carried away like this and, in fact, no one ever offered a future automobile in exchange for one of Tory's letters, but Donald was able to secure a constant and endless supply of all the comforts and luxuries a prison camp was able to offer. Harry Wilde acted as a sort of agent, negotiating with the chaps

175

in other huts, being good at that sort of thing. He seemed to know everyone in the camp. He was an educated man, and liked to call himself an 'ever so minor man of letters'.

Tory's letters became valuable currency, or, as Captain Wilde put it, not currency exactly, more like a kind of bond. A jolly good investment for the future. Even the camp guards had expressed interest. That was the really lucrative market. Harry Wilde was able to negotiate all sorts of benefits. Soon Donald was sleeping on a proper mattress, was lathering his face with Sunlicht soap and brushing his teeth with Rosodont tooth-powder, shaving with new razor blades, wearing cotton pyjamas. He was given tins of pineapple and peaches. Even, once, a quarter-bottle of whisky. Harry Wilde allowed one of the Germans to produce a translation. 'I have to say, old boy, when rendered in the language of Schiller, your wife's missives begin to lose some of their fragrance.'

Tory Pace became a well-known name in the camps where Donald was a prisoner. She was, so Harry Wilde said, a little starlet. Many times Donald had begged for a photo (he didn't even have a decent one of her about him), but she never complied. Now the men in the camps were begging to see pictures of Tory Pace, whimpering, even. It added to his sense of power to have to deny them her image: only he would ever know what she looked like. Apart from that, he was worried that they would be disappointed with what they saw.

One hundred and seventy-two letters arrived over a period of three months. And then, quite without warning, they stopped. No one could keep it up like that for ever, Harry Wilde said. She'd have to stop some time. No one had it in them to keep writing like that every day. Donald supposed he was right, but wouldn't they have trailed off, if it had simply been a matter of her running out of stamina? Why this abrupt ending in mid-flow?

But then came another camp move, a long march in rainy weather, across peaty plains and through dripping forests, for three days. Mail was never regular from then on. The tide of the war had turned against Germany, letters for prisoners became rarer. Donald ended his days as a prisoner of war at a camp east of the Elbe, and he had not heard from his wife for nearly three years.

Donald kept his stash of erotic letters, though by the end of the war their currency had devalued. The men in the camps could only reread them so many times before their power began to wane. For Donald, their erotic charge had more or less disappeared. They had become dead pieces of paper, no more thrilling than shopping lists or laundry bills. But he kept them. New arrivals at the camp would sometimes approach him nervously, asking about the Tory Papers (as they had come to be known). Otherwise, Tory Pace, by 1945, was forgotten.

It was quite easy for long-serving prisoners like Donald to ascertain the general direction of the war. Every new arrival at the camp was, of course, a source of encouraging information, but they had become rarer. Otherwise one only had to observe the behaviour of the guards and commandant. It was widely agreed that things had not being going well for Germany since late 1942. Each battle lost, it seemed, would equate to some petty new regulation being enforced or privilege denied. By 1944 the look of impending defeat could be seen in the guards' faces, as they watched the fresh, crenellated formations of Allied planes heading east to pound the major cities. The same bombers would return with hardly any reduction in their number. Donald could almost feel sorry for the guards to see their doom written so plainly in the sky. By then they had almost ceased their bullying, and had begun instead to try to curry favour. Aware that their captives were now on the side of the eventual victors, they wondered if they would put in a good word for them. They hadn't been treated so badly, had they? Fed and clothed and housed for five years when they could just as easily have been worked to death in the coal mines?

So it was little surprise to hear the guns for the first time. Distant thumpings of heavy artillery, gradually drawing nearer. Then, one morning, the men woke up to find themselves alone. The watchtowers were empty, the guardhouses abandoned. The keys to the camp were lying on the roadway just next to the main gate. It seemed that the last guard out had thrown them back over the fence. No one knew what to do. Should they stay where they were or should they leave? After many years of longing for an opportunity to escape, and with the keys to the camp in their hands, it seemed absurd, but the general feeling was that they should stay put. There was some food in the stores. The Allies would be here in a matter of hours. Then the shells started landing, shaking the forest around them. Trees exploded. The whole camp was thrown into turmoil, men running in all directions, some trying to crowd into the defensive bunkers, five hundred attempting to squeeze into a space meant for thirty, others running into the woods to shelter in ditches and gullies. It seemed that two enormous opposing armies had come to face each other directly over Stalag III-F.

It didn't quite end with the arrival of the Russians. Donald and his fellow inmates were taken back eastwards on empty supply trucks, then laagered by a railway line with shells dropping all around them. They were as nervous and shy as deer. The only bit of fighting Donald had witnessed in more than four years, and it looked set to kill him. He felt like a child ignored during a tempestuous parental argument. Was it for this he had endured all those years of confinement, to be snuffed out in the crossfire of armies indifferent to his existence?

There came a moment, however, when the tide of conflict moved onwards towards Berlin, and attention could be paid to Donald and his fellow refugees. But the roads and railways were destroyed. It was more than a month before transport could be arranged. He had to march fifty miles to a landing strip west of Berlin, from where he was flown back to Britain in a battered Dakota, landing at an aerodrome in Oxfordshire. From there he was taken to a reception centre, washed, deinfested, given a roast beef dinner, recorded – he was told he was the thirty thousandth prisoner (or near enough) to return home – and issued with a brand new uniform. (What's the point? he thought.) A general somebody-or-other patted him warmly on the shoulder and told him he'd put on a 'damned good show'. Then he was issued with a railway warrant and told to make his way home. He was still, officially, a soldier in the British Army, and was merely going home on six weeks' leave, with double rations.

His leg had been given proper medical attention for the first time since his injury. A doctor examined it in a dismissive way and told him it would never get any better, and might get worse. If the Labour Government has its way, he said, with distaste, they'll probably give you a free wheelchair. He was given a walking-stick. In the train from Charing Cross he had a compartment to himself. Either side of the mirrors above the seats were watercolours of Scottish Highland scenery, which almost brought tears of nostalgia to his eyes, though in fact he had never been to the Highlands, apart from a single weekend, when he was six years old, fishing on the shores of Loch Lomond.

The spectacle out of the window was rather more moving; London in tatters with, to his astonishment, plumes of smoke still rising from the rubble (though he later realized they were from celebratory bonfires that were still burning). From the embankments he looked down on terraced streets with missing sections, like an old codger's mouth. Whole areas to the east of Tower Bridge had simply gone, though the destruction became less intense the further out he travelled. The thought had not occurred to him before – supposing the house in Peter Street had been hit? Supposing his wife and mother-in-law had been wiped out? Supposing all he would have to remember her by was that sheaf of letters, which now filled a good part of his kitbag. He imagined the scene when he went to pick up the children from wherever they were. *Sorry, kids, but your mama copped it in an air raid. A doodlebug landed square on her noggin. Never mind, here are some of her letters for you to remember her by . . .*

What had she been up to that she could suddenly, out of the blue, after all those measly protestations, write letters like that? He wasn't a fool. There was something going on. Must have been. Either that or she had suddenly come by the dirtiest mind he had ever encountered. There were pubs in Millwall and Cubitt Town where such language had never been heard. He had half a mind to make her bring some of her dirtiest letters to life. *You thought of it, old girl, now you can do it.*

Well, he would do, if he ever felt the slightest stirring in his loins. He had not seen a woman in over four years, but looking at the gaunt grey dames on the streets of London, he felt he hadn't been much deprived. He couldn't even really remember what Tory looked like.

As the train trundled towards Kent, he took one of Tory's letters from his bag and reread it. The dirty letters had never resumed after their abrupt conclusion, and for years no word had come from home, dirty or otherwise. He blamed it, in part, on the moves between camps and the deterioration of Germany's war, but eventually a letter had come from Tory. It was rather different from the others.

My dearest Donald,

I hope you will be as happy about this as I am, but I have gone and done an extraordinary thing. I have adopted a little baby boy. He was found in the ruins of a house after an air raid in Leicester, where I was staying with some friends. No one could be found to claim him as their own, and his existence seemed a surprise to everyone, including the surviving neighbours in the street. He was not known to be part of any of the families that were killed in the raid. So I took it upon myself to look after him. No one else was willing (I think the neighbours suspected some backstairs work), and the police were only going to take him to a hospital and from there, I suppose, to a horrid orphanage of some kind. You have heard what terrible places they are, I should think. Well, he is a beautiful little thing, and I'm sure you will be happy to have him living with us. I have left my details with the people concerned in Leicester, should the actual mother ever come forward to claim him. I have decided to call him Branson.

I don't know if you will ever get this letter, but I hope you are well, dearest Donald.

Your ever affectionate

Tory

Well, Donald thought, as he stepped off the train in a relatively undamaged part of London, I suppose I would prefer it, all in all, if she was alive.

CHAPTER 15

For Tory Pace the prospect of victory approached with the slow, unstoppable certainty of death – with every dawn, a whole day nearer. She followed the progress of the war in the newspapers and on the wireless, her heart sinking further as each new piece of territory was won. Then she would check herself for having such treacherous thoughts. Immense sacrifices had been made, countless lives lost. But again, when the second front was opened and the beaches of northern France received an invasion force of staggering proportions, she found herself drawing comfort from thoughts of the long road to Berlin, and of how the Germans would surely not just give up, not now. Again she checked herself. *I am in danger of no longer being capable of telling good from bad.* All around her wives were losing their husbands on distant battle-fields, mothers were losing their dear sons, but it seemed to Tory that all of this agony and bloodshed was taking place for one reason and one reason only: so that Private Donald Pace should be reunited with his wicked, wretched, wastrel wife.

What alternative was there for her to hope for? Did she really crave victory for the Nazis, if it would save her from the awfulness of having to face Donald? Did she really long for the end of civilization as a means to rescue her from social embarrassment? Once or twice, Tory confessed to herself, she thought that she did. Or at least not victory, because that might also lead to eventual reunion, albeit under a different regime. Instead she longed for the indefinite prolongation of the war, that it would never end. Apart from the difficulty of having to explain her child, what sort of man was Donald Pace now? She had a vision of the returning soldier carrying her upstairs, salivating like a dog, stripping her and throwing her on the bed and not letting her go until four years of stored lust had been expended in one interminable coital event. Then, spent, lifting his red face from her body, he would suddenly remember that there was one more child in the house than before. *Explain that, please, wife!*

Tory had managed to keep her pregnancy secret from all but her mother, and she had managed to conceal it even from her until the sixth month. Then suddenly Mrs Head was all for poor Donald, and how he would feel coming home from however many years he was to spend in captivity to find that his wife had produced a child in his absence. 'I must have known about this in the back of my mind for weeks, Tory Pace, but was unable to believe it. I heard you retching in the mornings, I saw your abdomen swell, but nothing could have persuaded me that you were the sort of woman capable of such a thing, such a low, sordid, unchivalrous crime . . .' Indeed, so unlikely did Tory's capacity for adultery seem, Mrs Head couldn't help feeling that her daughter had conceived her child by post. But what an odd word to use, 'unchivalrous', Tory thought, as though she had betrayed both mankind and womankind in one single action.

George Farraway had offered to have the thing destroyed. He knew a doctor, a real, qualified doctor, a Harley Street man, not some back-street wise woman, who could do the whole thing, she'd never know it had happened, no questions asked, he wouldn't even know her name. If she didn't take up this offer, she was to understand that George would play no further part in the child's life, and that she must not come to him for support. He said it with the measured, calculated tones of someone who'd had to deal with similar situations before, wagging a plump pink finger in front of her face, taking charge of the newly formed life as though it was just another item on the production line. Oh, she had been such a fool. He probably had an account with that Harley Street abortionist. God knew how many little lives he'd paid to be flushed away into the sewers of Fitzrovia. It was her choice, he had said. But there had never been any choice available in Tory's mind.

All kinds of wrongnesses had set this new life going; the least she could do now was to give it the best possible chance of happiness. At the same time she could not see any means by which Branson's existence could be established in such a way that Donald, on his return home from his terrible ordeal, would not be heartbroken.

This was Mrs Head's main concern as well. 'If only we could have you sent away somewhere . . .' she said.

'Away?'

'Just so that you could have the baby out of the range of prying eyes and the Peter Street gossips, then bring it home when it's three months old, saying you'd found it on a bomb site.'

Tory couldn't help laughing. 'Mother, your capacity for deception is extraordinary.'

But it could work, Tory supposed. Mrs Head said she would cover with a story of Tory being away, staying with friends up north. Didn't she have connections up there somewhere? One of her old school friends had moved to Leicester, hadn't she? Yes, Mary Frost, twenty years ago; she'd married a sign-writer and moved to Leicester, never to be heard of again. There was your cover. But Tory couldn't stay with Mary – she didn't even have her address. No, Mrs Head said, Mary could just be the cover. We could send you somewhere else. But where? Of course, that was the problem. A mother-and-baby home was tentatively suggested, one of those horrible places where little harlots go, the hapless girls who've fallen pregnant under age and out of wedlock. It was absurd, though. They don't take middle-aged women in places like those. That's what I mean, said Mrs Head, there's nowhere to send you.

Tory was so keen on the idea of going away that the solution soon presented itself to her. George Farraway's cottage, the little Wealden hideaway. The place where this little thing had been conceived. Now it could be born there as well.

George was not pleased. Only a few days before he had been trying to persuade her to visit his man in Harley Street. Now he was being expected not only to agree to his child's existence but to provide shelter and comfort for its mother and the thing itself for the first few weeks of its unwanted life.

'Perhaps you would like me to tell your wife about it,' she said. 'The woman whose cookery skills you have so often mocked would, I am sure, like to know what you yourself have cooked up.'

'What an ugly turn of phrase you have, my dear . . .'

But he agreed, and within days Tory was a resident of the Wealden cottage.

It was the best time of year to be there. She moved down in March to find the lawns and verges steeped in daffodils. Then the little wood at the back, visible from the bedroom window, soon became brilliant with bluebells. She stayed there six months in all. She saw the swallows arrive to build their daub and wattle under the eaves, she heard the cuckoos all day, and the nightingales at night, she watched the puffy roses filling the southern wall, and rabbits burrowing in the flowerbeds. She was looked after by the woman she'd seen in the distance before, the blowsy, rosy woman who minded the cottage, with her somersaulting children. She turned out to be a delightful soul, a dreamy Scandinavian, an outsider like herself. Tory never asked how she had ended up in the Weald of Kent, because she asked no questions about Tory – at least none of the prying kind. She kept her stocked up with eggs, milk, butter, cream and bread. Fresh off the land, the food there was abundant and unrestricted. She wrote to her mother to tell her of how she had grown quite used to eating rabbit. Be careful your child isn't born with long ears, Mrs Head replied.

Tory got along well with the children, Jennifer and Raymond, who did much of the eggs-and-milk delivering. Jennifer had something of Albertina's sweetness, and although they acted in part as a welcome substitute, they made Tory miss her own children even more. There was a doctor in the village as well, who took Tory under his tired old wing. Of George she saw nothing, though it was presumably he who was paying for all the supplies and care. If she mentioned him to the doctor or to Jorinda, they smiled in knowing ways. Tory tried, once, to ascertain from Jorinda how much of a Lothario George was – expecting to hear that his cottage was in constant use as a hideaway for his fancy women – but was surprised to learn that he very rarely used it these days.

'They bought it in 1931, and lived here two summers, but Mrs Farraway – would you believe it? – she finds she gets the sneezes. Hay fever. She didn't know before, lived in the city all her life. But this isn't the place to be if you suffer from sneezing,' she tittered, 'not with the meadow just over the lane. So she never comes now. Not been here for over a decade. Just as well, really. A woman like that does look strange in the countryside, like she doesn't belong.'

'I'm surprised Mr Farraway keeps the cottage on,' said Tory.

'Well, he can't sell it. He's tried often enough, but no one wants to buy a cottage out here in the middle of nowhere, not when there's no land attached – or not much.'

The image of the runny-nosed Mrs Farraway, with her reputed film-star looks, sneezing and weeping under the assault of grasses and sedges, kept Tory sustained for quite some time, and she relished her own ability to sniff the country air and feel nothing but the nothingness of it. It was a hot, dry, dusty summer as well. The trees turned pale and began sagging by July. Tory wrote constant letters to Mrs Head and the children. She enclosed her letters for Tom, Paulette and Albertina with Mrs Head's to be forwarded. She didn't want to have to explain a strange postmark, and she would wait until the war was over to let

190

them know about the new member of the family. London had been spared bombing raids for more than a year, and Mrs Head's letters rarely contained any real news. Things were almost starting to feel normal, although the blackout was still rigidly enforced, just in case. There was still nothing to be had in the shops.

At times Tory felt desperately homesick, and as her pregnancy approached full term, she began to feel scared as well. There was a good midwife who would look after her, the doctor was on hand, and Jorinda, who was the sort of person one assumed knew how to deliver a baby, but still Tory felt that perhaps she should go home, have the baby in Peter Street and let the gossips do their worst. But no, her deceit had to be followed through. It was just a pity, she felt, that she could only think of saving her marriage by telling lies.

In the end Tory had little memory of her labour. After twelve hours of gradually rising panic, her waters broke with the pop and gush of a Roman candle. For some reason she remembered that eleven large white towels were used in the process of her labour. The baby was so quiet when he emerged that everyone thought something was wrong. He didn't come out with the piercing cries she remembered from her other children. Instead he just uttered a little sigh, turned over and went to sleep.

It seemed to work. No one asked too many difficult questions when she returned to Peter Street.

The neighbours, Mrs Wilson and Mrs Allen, seemed to accept her story, though Mrs Head was now on rather frosty terms with Mrs Allen, ever since she had planted a forsythia in the one space that had acted as a chatting gap in the garden wall. Mrs Head was always waiting for the moment when Mrs Allen would trim this plant back, but to her indignation she had let it grow, so that, season by season, their over-the-wall conversations became harder and harder to sustain, until eventually they had stopped as the forsythia reached maturity. Well, if she isn't going to cut it back I'm not going to go out there to talk to a bush . . . In fact, Tory's tale of her rescuing Branson from the rubble of a Leicester suburb garnered enormous sympathy, and Tory elaborated, spontaneously sometimes, on the details of his survival and discovery, how firemen had heard him crying beneath the rubble, how no one could be sure whose he was, because no one knew of a baby living among the buildings that had been bombed, and all the children had been evacuated anyway. And then there were lots of slow noddings and slow winkings, that perhaps the existence of the 'poor little mite' was meant to be a secret, perhaps he was an indiscretion that was meant to be kept in the dark. They were getting the right idea. Tory's fictionalization of her baby's early life was becoming dangerously convoluted. Now it seemed he was the secret love child of an imagined Leicester harlot, a chambermaid perhaps, confined to a basement for the sake of the family's reputation, emerging from the rubble like a gurgling phoenix when the bombs had fallen. No one else had known what to do with him. In the confusion and despair of the rescue party, Tory had just happened to claim him. She was a respectable-looking woman. The police and ambulance people didn't seem to give it a second thought. She would look after him. If there were any surviving relations of the mother (if such a person could ever be identified), she was sure to seek them out.

'But you'll go back and look for his mother's people when the war's over, won't you, dear?' said Mrs Wilson, over the other wall. 'I'm sure they'd like to know if he's all right.'

'Oh, of course, I'll certainly do that,' said Tory, aware now of how her deceitfulness not only involved her and Donald but her and the entire world. The lies had to reach as far as ever any knowledge of Branson extended.

If it ever extended as far as the prisoner-of-war camps that Donald occupied, she was not sure. She had written to him several times to tell him about Branson, her foundling adopted baby, but he had made no acknowledgement of the news. Their correspondence had trailed off since her pregnancy, and now she wasn't even sure which camp he was in. So it was left to Tory to speculate on Donald's likely reaction.

'Please give him George's eyes, please give him George's eyes', Tory would whisper to herself, as she

looked into her baby's face, wondering who he would take after, Mr Farraway or herself. Since Donald had never seen Mr George Farraway, it wouldn't matter if Branson turned out to be his double, but any likeness to herself was liable to betray her as a most wretched liar. Finally, when Branson's baby blue eyes faded into the sombre browns of Mr George Farraway's and not the mossy greens of her own, Tory could breathe a little more easily. She was not aware of any other giveaways as to her identity as Branson's mother and, in fact, Tory was delighted to see that, by the age of two, Branson Pace was definitely of the Farraway mould, a tough-looking thing, lurching around the place, staring at things with a big square face, picking things up with big square hands.

As a baby he had been frighteningly quiet. It was almost as though he knew he shouldn't be there. He rarely cried, but he often looked as though he was about to, pouting with misery, thrusting out his lower lip at everything around him. He seemed unbearably disappointed with the world, and Tory sometimes felt sorry for bringing him into it. She breastfed him in secret, hiding from neighbours any clue that she might be lactating. In the darkened bedroom the child would take the nipple with a sigh, then look up at her faintly accusingly, as if to say, Is this the best you've got?

Tory's other children had accepted her story of Branson's arrival into their family with a heart-stopping lack of hesitation. Paulette and Albertina, at least, showed no sign that they thought their mother might be lying, and this made her cry, tearlessly and silently.

She had shed many tears when she went to Upper Slaughter to fetch them home at the end of the war. She had opted against visiting them during their evacuation, apart from that one weekend six months after their departure. The visit had been so difficult and awkward, the ending of it so sad (for her, at least, though the apparent lack of sorrow in her children had been one of the things that had made it so difficult), that she had decided against repeating the experience. She watched their receding figures on the platform at Moreton-in-Marsh, engulfed by sulphurous clouds from the little steam train, and she had not seen them since, instead trying to make up for her absence with her copious letter-writing. So when she returned to Upper Slaughter in May 1945, she was quite terrified that the children would not recognize her, or she them. And she didn't at first.

They had changed in proportion to their respective ages. Tom, the eldest, had altered the least, still with his intellectual hair, parted at the side and shaved at the back, and with his heavy, black-rimmed glasses. He shook his mother's hand without meeting her eye, examining the toes of his shoes instead. Paulette had become a woman, almost, with a full, downy face and flowing golden hair, and a buttoned-up bosom beneath her country-woman's coat. Albertina, at least, had the vestiges of childhood. She was twelve now, but still had a little girl's knock-knees and ribbons in her plaited hair.

'I suppose you want us to kiss you,' said Tom, wiping an imaginary piece of grit from his eye, which caused his spectacles to glance sideways.

'No,' said Tory, laughing, 'I want to kiss *you*.' And she took him and hugged him and kissed his freckled cheek, and was shocked by the faintest hint of whiskers there. She did the same with her daughters, who responded with respectable hugs in turn. They were crying by the time they got on the train, but not for joy. They were sad to be leaving their home.

They were sullen and disappointed when they arrived at Peter Street. Branson had been left there in the care of Mrs Head.

'I want you to meet your adopted brother, children. Branson is a little boy I found in Leicester. He was a baby then, but his family had been killed in an air raid.' Tom showed not the least interest in the boy, apart from expressing concern about where he was going to sleep.

'Well, he can share a room with you, Tom. I will share with Mrs Head, and the girls can have a room to themselves.'

This seemed like a good arrangement, and no one asked what would happen when and if their father came home.

★　★　★

196

It seemed to take the children a long time to settle back into their old lives. Tory would catch Paulette looking wistfully out of the back-door window at the concrete yard. She didn't say as much, but Tory could see that she was remembering the enormous gardens at Upper Slaughter, with their adjacent orchards and paddocks. What a prison a place like Peter Street must seem to her, she thought.

Then, one morning, Tom said to his mother, 'Has this house got smaller, Mama?'

'No, Tom. You've got bigger.'

'But there were more rooms . . .'

'No, the same number as before.'

'Didn't there used to be grass in the garden?'

'A long time ago, yes. But Daddy put cement down, and paving stones when you were about six years old.'

Tory had tried to organize a party for the children, inviting some of their old friends from before the war. It had been an awkward affair, because none of the children remembered each other or, if they did, were frightened by how they'd changed. Only one boy seemed untroubled by the changes, a golden-haired angel-faced but noisy child who helped himself to all the food (there wasn't a lot), and ended up pulling Paulette's hair.

Afterwards, as she cleared away the mess of cake, Tom spoke to her, as though the representative of her three children. 'Why didn't you tell us you'd adopted a baby?'

197

'I don't know, Tom. I suppose I thought you might be worried . . .'

'But why wasn't he evacuated like us?'

'Yes, he would have loved the horses.' Albertina said this through a full mouth.

'That's a nice thought, Albertina – and I'm glad you seem to have got your appetite now your friends have gone. I suppose the trouble was that he was just a baby when I found him. I don't think anyone could have been found in your village to take on a little baby . . .'

'But you took him on.'

Tory didn't know quite what to say, so tried changing the subject. 'Wasn't it nice seeing all your old friends again?'

'Friends? I didn't know any of them.'

Tom was following his thoughts through a fiercely logical progression. 'If it was safe enough for a baby to live here, then why couldn't we come home?'

'But I thought you liked it in Upper Slaughter . . .'

'That is not the point, Mother . . .'

All the children were now busily eating the food they'd ignored during the party.

'Well, one had to weigh the risks and the benefits. It was very difficult.'

'Weren't you even bombed once?' said Albertina, in a disappointed voice.

'Thankfully, no.'

'I find that rather hard to believe, Mother. I do read the newspapers, you know.'

'Do you?'

'That's what's happened, I can see it now. This house got bombed, didn't it, and you've rebuilt it exactly as it was, except that you've forgotten one of the rooms, and the ceilings are a bit lower?'

To Tory's horror, Tom's half-joking explanation for the diminution of the house was being taken seriously by the girls.

'You're right, Tom. This isn't the same house at all. You've rebuilt it, haven't you?'

Later, Tory heard the girls talking to each other in their bedroom.

'I don't think this is our house, do you?'

'No, it's like Tom said, it's a different house, designed to look the same as the old one.'

'But they didn't get it right.'

Then Tom's deep, breaking voice was heard.

'I don't think our mother is really our mother, either. I think she was probably killed when the house was bombed, and she's been replaced by someone from the Government so that we wouldn't get upset.'

To Tory's relief, this was going too far for the girls, and they disagreed with Tom.

'No, Mama's real, and so is Mrs Head . . .'

'But how do you know?'

'Shut up, Tom. Of course Mama's real.'

'So how do you explain the kid?'

'Simple. Like she said, she found him in Leicester.'

'Whoever heard of someone finding a kid in Leicester? It's obvious that the Government has sent a replacement, except this replacement has got a kid of her own . . .'

'Well, he can't be her own because he's got dark hair, and none of us is dark.'

'He could be wearing a wig. Let's find out tomorrow.'

'Don't be nasty to that little boy. I think he's a sweet thing, and you think how frightened he must be, with all us grown-ups in the house all of a sudden.'

Tom was so persistent in his theory that his mother had been replaced that the girls became exasperated.

'You be pullin' our leg, Thomas Pace,' said Paulette, apparently impersonating someone from Upper Slaughter. 'You see if I don't lash out wi' me whupp at thee . . .'

'I be not pulling yer leg, li'l wuzz'n, be I? Plain as day sha bain't no mother we never knowed . . .'

The conversation dissolved into giggling.

All three children had come home with West Country accents, quite strong in Albertina's case. They did not have to extend them very far to lampoon their erstwhile country cousins. In fact, none of the children realized their accents had changed, not until they went back to school where they were teased mercilessly. The accents were gone in less than a week.

It was Albertina who announced the arrival home of Donald Pace, though she did not at first imagine that the man she saw was her father.

200

'There's a soldier outside who keeps marching back and forth past the house. He's got a sword. He keeps looking at the window.'

Tory carefully placed the teapot on the table, clutched herself, then stared at her mother.

'Go on,' said Mrs Head. 'What are you waiting for?'

She saw that her daughter was thinking about Branson, who was sitting in a bored sort of way at the kitchen table, arranging spoons.

'Just go,' she said.

For a moment Tory forgot all her anxieties about Donald's return and ran to the front door. He was there, at the end of the short path. She hardly took a moment even to look at him as he came through the gate towards her. But when she put her arms around him, it was as though she had hugged a soufflé. The bulging khaki had mostly air inside it, and then a bony little body somewhere in the middle. He seemed aged, shrunken, crooked. His skin was loose around his jowls, his chest seemed scooped out, hollow, and his neck poked like a vulture's through the wide collar of his battle blouse.

'What are you doing hanging around outside, you stupid fool?' she said. 'Why didn't you knock?'

'Wasn't sure you were expecting me,' he said, and for the first time she realized that hers was one of the few houses not festooned with welcome-home banners. Even from there she could see the houses opposite, garnished with balloons and

201

the sign 'Welcome Home Dennis' daubed in black paint on a bed sheet. They had been left hanging long after the soldiers had returned.

'They never gave us any warning,' said Tory. 'I haven't heard anything . . . Why didn't you send a telegram?'

Apart from his thinness, his cragginess, there was a moustache, almost orange in colour, meticulously crafted and overmanaged so that it formed a perfectly symmetrical shape around the centre of his upper lip, like two little orange flames flaring sideways from his philtrum. It gave him an uncharacteristically rigid and disciplined air. He looked like an officer, and it was, she supposed, an officer's moustache, and probably newly formed, carved out of the remnant of the straggly beard she imagined he had grown in the camp. As he walked up the path alongside Tory she thought for a moment that he was marching, but then realized that his leg was stiff, and that he was using a stick (how could she not have noticed?). But he seemed, by his gait and general demeanour, to be someone anxious to show that he was suffering, and that he was in no mood to accept any excuses for there not being a welcome-home banner over the door. What would it have taken, for goodness' sake, to paint a few words on a bedsheet? Tom would have enjoyed doing that. Why hadn't she thought of it?

By now the others had gathered at the front door, but were watching as if from a position of safety, not quite sure what to make of the visiting stranger. The children, especially Albertina, could hardly remember their father, and when they had last seen him he certainly hadn't looked like he did now. They were used to seeing a spiky-haired man in a paint-splattered apron, not this brass-buttoned soldier with brand new boots shining like mirrors and a barely used forage cap tucked smartly into his epaulette, and certainly not someone with an orange moustache, so neatly clipped and vivid it looked as though it had been painted on.

Sensing that Donald was on the verge of being overwhelmed, Mrs Head ushered her grandchildren into the sitting room to allow him some space.

'Is that man our father?' said Albertina, once they were on their own.

'I suppose so,' said Paulette, who was holding the hand of a very puzzled Branson.

'Has he escaped?' said Albertina.

'No,' said Tom, his arms folded. 'The war's over – didn't you hear?'

'So they let him out?'

'Yes.'

'They must have said, "*Ok, you win, off you go, back to your own country*", then just opened the gates and let them all out.'

They listened carefully through the ajar door to the sounds that were coming from the hallway. Very few sounds were coming from the man, and what he said they couldn't make out. The accent seemed very strange, and he spoke in rather a whisper.

'Is our father foreign?' said Albertina.

'He's Scottish,' said Tom, remembering.

'He didn't have a kilt on,' said Albertina.

'I shouldn't think the Germans let him have one.'

Suddenly, after some moments of quiet while the adults had retreated to the kitchen, the sitting-room door swung open and their grandmother appeared, looking a little anxious.

'Children, your father is ready to see you now. He would like you all to line up and wait for him to come in.'

'Like an inspection?' said Tom, giving a slightly insolent half-laugh.

'It's what your father's used to. Now, go on.'

Mrs Head left the room and the children had to arrange themselves into a row, instinctively ordering it chronologically and from tallest down, with Tom, the eldest, nearest the door, descending through Paulette, Albertina and Branson, who could not be made to stand still and instead twined himself around Albertina.

Then the door squeaked open, and the small, smart soldier appeared, looking a little more composed than a few minutes earlier, but his expression was serious and concerned. It was as though he was about to ask them some huge favour. There was a long silence, during which

Donald walked up and down the line of children, none of whom knew what to do so just stood there, looking back at the man who was looking at them. Albertina's eyes were fixed with wonder on the walking-stick, which she had first thought was a sword. Now and then her father would shake his head very slightly, and mutter something to himself, a quiet expression of wonder. For Tory, who watched, as instructed, from the door, the silence was unbearable. The house should be filled with the noise of celebration, she thought. There should be laughter and music, not this agonizing quietness, this pin-drop silence where Donald's creaking boots were the only noise.

'Well, well,' he eventually murmured, giving promise of a full sentence which soon faded, continuing only with more quiet exclamations of wonder. 'Well, well.'

Tory could contain herself no longer and, having seen enough of the children's worried eyes as they followed their father left to right, right to left, as he paced back and forth, she blurted out, 'Don't you think Tom looks so much more like a man?'

Donald swung his head round. 'Did I ask you to speak, woman?'

Although he said this quietly, his voice was sharp enough to make Albertina burst into tears. Donald continued his silent inspection of the children, ignoring Albertina's sobbing and eventually settling his gaze upon Tom. He stood before him, and Tom wondered, for a moment, if his father was expecting a salute, but instead Donald held out his hand and they shook, firmly but briefly.

'We must not speak, in this house, unless spoken to . . .' Donald said, in a slightly embarrassed way, to Tom, but in reference to Tory, who remained distant, by the door. 'If people speak without asking, then there is no chance to think.'

He moved on to Paulette and Albertina, whose hands he didn't shake. He patted their golden heads instead.

'Fine girls,' he said, as though he was appraising specimens at a country show. 'Fine, fine girls.' He turned to Tory. 'Soon be able to marry these two little beauties off, eh, Tory?' he said. 'The young men will be forming a queue down the path before long.'

'Smile at your father,' Tory whispered urgently to the girls, but by the time they had overcome their fear enough to muster a smile, Donald's inspection had moved on to Branson, who was hiding behind Albertina's billowing dress.

The child, seemingly the least troubled soul in the room, returned Donald's gaze with a lazy sort of curiosity.

'I heard about someone who came home to find his wife had given birth to a little black baby,' said Donald, without taking his eyes off Branson, 'and the first thing he did when he saw it was throw it out of the window. And they lived on the fourth floor . . .'

'This is the little boy I told you about Donald,

who I found on a bomb site in Leicester. Poor little thing was orphaned so I took him in. Didn't you get my letter?'

'I must have lost it among all those other stories you sent me . . .' He gave her what she interpreted as a knowing glance, a glance she'd never seen on Donald's face before, which said – I know exactly what you've been up to, old girl. It seemed he was just about to say something else when his attention was caught by another object in the room. 'And what in God's name is this?'

He was talking about the typewriter that now sat rather stolidly on the escritoire, the Remington 748, nicknamed the Old Faithful, that she had been given by one of her mother's friends, Mrs Harrington, who had no more use for it. Donald lurched over to it, exaggerating his limp, it seemed to Tory, and bent down to take a closer look. 'I've never seen anything like it in my life,' he said. 'I suppose you'll tell me you gave birth to it . . .'

Apart from the wireless in the kitchen, the Remington was probably the most complicated and sophisticated machine that had ever taken up a space in the house. Tory loved it. She had been hesitant about accepting it at first, because it somehow seemed to ask too much of her. If she began picking away at the keys, filling the house with the sound of her slow, laborious clatter, then it would be expected that she would write something of value, something serious, worthy, publishable. In fact, Tory's ambitions as a writer had come upon her almost by stealth and against her will. Through her manipulations of viewpoint and time in the gushing narratives issued by George Farraway as he satisfied himself (and her, she had to concede), she saw how whole new worlds can suddenly spring into being. Intrigued by the possibilities, she had thus embarked on some storytelling on a bigger, more ambitious scale.

She had immersed herself in the works of Warwick Deeping, and wanted to write a novel about a family that struggles through wartime, the husband and wife separated by the necessities of war. She found that she could use her own family as a model, and that with those little shifts of perspective, alterations to time and space, a new family emerged, bearing only fragile similarities to her own. It was more as though they existed in a different country, one in which everything was foreign, yet at the same time comprehensible. They were different, but the same. She called the novel *The Distance*, and had written fourteen chapters, and each chapter was at least ten pages long, some a lot longer. Given that she couldn't type, she regarded this, with much concealed pride, as a colossal achievement. Only one thing worried her. The mother of the story, a character she had named Charlotte Maugham, was going irredeemably to the bad, and there didn't seem anything she could do to stop her.

'I never thought I'd see the like of one of these in the house,' said Donald, bending so low it was as though he was investigating the typewriter with his nose, but his remark wasn't approving. He wasn't in awe of the machine, as Tory had been. He seemed to regard it as some sort of invading despot. 'Clapped-out old thing, isn't it? When was it made?'

Tory regretted that she had left a sheet of paper in the machine, abandoned mid-sentence. She had been working on the novel in a few stolen minutes that very morning. Donald whacked some of the keys with his right index finger, jabbing down on the letters so emphatically that the typewriter's response seemed like a cry of pain as the type-face hit the paper and the carriage shunted one space to the left. In his carelessness he doubled some keys, and there was a jam in the barrel.

'Toddlers and typewriters. You've been busy while the rest of us have been fighting for king and country, haven't you, old girl?'

Later she was able to look at what Donald had typed. The words

don Iladsshome

were added to the sentence Tory had been writing, typed so heavily the black ink filled all the spaces within the letters so that they became blobs.

It was unfortunate also that Tory had left the whole typescript on the escritoire bureau beside the typewriter. She had done a title page, which read

209

THE DISTANCE
by
Victoria Louise Pace

She had taken great care over it, making sure that the text was centred, double-typing the title so that it appeared darker. In fact, the title page had taken about fifteen drafts, each previous one ending up a crumpled ball in the wastebasket. So to have it lifted up by one corner, as though it was a sickly kitten being lifted by its ear, and have her carefully chosen words read out in a quietly mocking Scottish accent, with an awful emphasis on her rarely used middle name – it was almost too much to bear, and she was only thankful that, after the surprise of the title page, Donald felt no inclination to pursue the opening lines of Chapter One.

It was a bright purple evening in October when Charlotte Maugham came home from her first day of working in the Glue Factory. I'm not sure I can stick this, she thought.

She couldn't resist that little joke in the opening sentence, but with the way the novel was beginning to take shape, it no longer seemed appropriate, and what would Donald think of such a thinly disguised reference to the gelatine factory? He would immediately think that she was writing a novel about her own family, and he would begin looking for himself in there. But all she wanted to do was to write about a woman who had the same, or similar, thoughts and feelings to her own. And even that was proving difficult. Charlotte Maugham had already worked as an artist's model, posing nude for a sculptor who wore a red bow-tie. She even drank Dubonnet.

But Donald replaced the title page with exaggerated care, then simply said, 'Well, Tory *Louise* Pace, famous author, you're going to have to shift all this junk somewhere else. I will be requiring this room.'

He said he needed a downstairs room, because, with his bad leg, he could not manage the stairs. He intended to use the sitting room as his bedroom, saying he would sleep, for the moment, on the chaise longue, which was almost exactly the right length for his not very 'longue' body.

The typewriter and manuscript of *The Distance* were removed at once. There was nowhere else in the house Tory could type. She couldn't use the small dining-table, as it was always being used for other things, and she would have felt awkward typing in the dining room, even if most of the others were out of the house. There was a small dressing-table in her bedroom, but it was not suitable for writing at. There was really only one place for the typewriter and the novel that had slowly emerged from it to go, and that was under the bed. So that was where it went, and work on *The Distance* came to an abrupt stop.

Just as well, Tory comforted herself. Now she didn't have to worry any more about what poor old Charlotte Maugham was going to get up to. Just as well.

CHAPTER 16

Donald was different. In some ways, the differences were obvious – he was thinner, greyer, craggier. He limped and used a walking-stick. He was quieter, in that he spoke less, but he was also louder, in that when he spoke he shouted. He seemed to have developed a need for solitude, and would spend hours on his own in the sitting room with the door firmly shut, barking at anyone who disturbed him.

In other ways, the differences were less obvious, and they filled Tory with unease. Donald had never been a passionate man, and had always struggled to show affection or express joy. But, all the same, one had assumed those feelings were there, deep down. Tory had always said that if you dug deep enough into her husband, you would eventually find a warm, beating heart. But not any more. Since that first hug on the front path, they'd hardly made physical contact. It was true that sometimes he would hold on to her arm for support, particularly when they were out walking, and try to pass it off as an affectionate conjoining, but even though they were touching, there was no connection.

To touch without connecting. What an odd, unnerving experience, thought Tory.

They would go to the shops together. There was a new butcher's in Old Parade now, though not where Dando's had been. That gap had yet to be filled. The new butcher's was further down, next to Bon Voyage. It was called Hughes. Passing this shop, Donald had noticed a large lattice-topped Grosvenor pie in the window. Such a thing had not appeared in a butcher's shop window for many years. He went in and bought the whole pie, but he ate it immediately, on the pavement outside the shop. Sometimes he would do a similar thing when passing a baker's – buy a whole cake and eat it immediately. Tory had to remember that for four years Donald had lived on nothing but prison-camp rations. She didn't know what they were because Donald said nothing about life in the camp, but she assumed they must have been dreadfully meagre. What must a pie look like to a man deprived of proper food for so long? Old Parade must seem like a sort of paradise, a teeming thoroughfare, every window laden with riches.

'Donald, you could wait until we get home . . .'

'What?' said through a muffler of pie.

'You know, take it home, eat it there, perhaps share it out.' Donald looked for a moment as though he wasn't going to answer, but then he said, 'It might get wasted.'

★   ★   ★

214

They hadn't had a proper celebration of his homecoming. The day of his arrival, people had gathered at the house. Word had spread. Old friends of the family arrived with bottles of ale in their hands. Someone suggested they have a singsong round the piano, before Tory pointed out that they didn't have such an instrument. But Donald didn't want to see anybody anyway, and she had to send them away. Since then he had become increasingly solitary.

Tory supposed that Donald considered food and people to be very different things. He had been deprived of both for many years, and yet he did not want to gorge on company in the same way he gorged on food. The sitting room very quickly became Donald's private room, into which no one else was allowed to venture. Tory missed the room that had been hers throughout the war. When she asked Donald if she could look at her books, he didn't invite her in to browse her little library. Instead he dumped the books in the passageway. It was as though he was fashioning his own house within a house. He had no use for books of any description, so she didn't just get her Warwick Deepings and the complete works of Walter Scott: her father's accountancy journals were expelled from the sitting room as well. There were no other bookcases in the house, so these books went under the bed, alongside the typewriter and *The Distance*.

At times Tory felt – there was no other word – *homeless*. She realized that if she wanted to have the slightest chance of feeling that she belonged anywhere in the house, she would have to occupy the kitchen and dining room with a zeal she had never before possessed. She had to give herself to the kitchen, embrace the brass and iron of the gas range. She had to set down kitchen roots.

The problem was her mother. All through the war she had been saying that when this thing was over she was going to go straight back to Waseminster, just as soon as another property became available. But she had aged in the years since her return to London, and the prospect of a solitary life in a marshland village did not seem so attractive as it once had.

So it seemed, for a while, that the kitchen would become a new battlefield for the two women. But Mrs Head was losing physical strength rapidly: she bowed out of the contest gracefully and Tory became the undisputed cook and shopper of the household.

It seemed also that Donald was not troubled by the presence of Branson in the house, but then again, it was hard to tell because he did spend an awful lot of time alone in his room. It could not quite be said that he ignored Branson in particular because he seemed to ignore everyone in the house, including his children.

Tory thought it best to leave Donald to himself for a while. He needed a period of adjustment. Of acclimatization. She had tried a few times to see if he wanted to talk about the years that he had spent away from his family, but the only thing she could manage was once placing a reassuring hand on his shoulder when they had a moment alone together, 'Donald – was it really very bad?'

To which his answer was only a simple nod, a desolate glance, and then an immediate retreat to the sitting room.

He will come out soon, she thought.

Indeed, there was an enormous air of expectation about the house in the days and weeks following Donald's return. Everyone, it seemed, was waiting patiently to see what he was going to do. But no one was inclined to ask him that question directly, and there were very few opportunities for such a question to be asked. Donald took his meals alone in the sitting room. He would make appearances in the dining room, but these were only transitory visits as he journeyed to and from the outside lavatory. Occasionally he would pause on his way there or back, and perhaps spend a half-hour in the armchair reading the newspaper, and he would politely return any friendly remarks from Tory or Mrs Head (the children usually disappeared to their rooms or the yard when their father appeared), but any attempt to engage him in more extended conversation would find him stiffly walking back to the sitting room, closing the door behind him. He hasn't even told me what happened to his leg, Tory mused despondently.

It was little over a month after Donald's return that there was a knock at the front door one evening and Bill Welch made his appearance. So rare was the sight of a face from Donald's working days that Tory hugged him like a long-lost son. The war had treated Bill much better than it had treated Donald. He seemed to have grown, whereas Donald appeared to have shrunk. He, too, had a neat little moustache, where before the war he'd had a thick drooping one (the effect of the Second World War on moustaches, Tory thought, could be a whole book). He looked suntanned and muscular, even though she could see nothing of his body because he was wearing his working clothes – white apron splattered with paint, cloth cap, speckled boots.

By chance Donald was in the midst of one of his dining-room sojourns, so Tory merely had to usher Bill in there and introduce him to his old partner.

'Donald, there's someone to see you . . .'

At last, Tory thought, Donald would be going back to work and everything would be as it was before the war. Money had been very difficult in the last few years. At times it had been a struggle to survive, and on several occasions they'd had to draw on Mrs Head's savings to make ends meet. Oh, the indignity of walking with her mother down to the bank to cash that carefully written cheque, but there was nothing else for it.

To her surprise, Mr Farraway hadn't kept his word about not being involved in Branson's life, and he had several times provided Tory with funds, sometimes by anonymous post, sometimes by surprising her as she was out walking Branson or wheeling him in his pram, by swooping down on her and walking alongside her for a little way. Sometimes he would put one of his big square hands on the pram's handlebar, alongside Tory's elegant fingers (the nails looking as papery as ever), and they would push the pram together, George bending every now and then to coo and gurgle at the infant, who returned the enormous gaze of his father with a frightened stare. Then he would depart as suddenly, and Tory would find, later, that he had slipped a note into her pocket, a folded-up five pounds, or ten pounds sometimes. So he is one of the good people, Tory thought. He is taking an interest after all. But the money was irregular and could not be relied upon. There were times when she would wheel Branson for hours so that George would have the opportunity to do one of his swoops, but she never tried to contact him directly. Such a thing could not have been done. Otherwise she and her mother took in laundry, and Tory did some cleaning. And now there was a prospect of an end to their money worries.

But Donald didn't look very pleased to see his old partner. He squirmed awkwardly in his chair, and cast cross, accusing looks in Tory's direction, as though he suspected the whole thing had been a set-up.

'Hallo, old mate,' said Bill. 'I heard you were back.'

'Word gets around,' said Donald, quietly.

They briefly exchanged summaries of their war experiences. Bill, it seemed, was able to condense the whole episode into a little mime show, firing an invisible Tommy gun and lobbing a few invisible grenades. Donald was a little less enthusiastic when called upon to report his own adventures.

'Me? I was unfortunate enough to be captured alive at Tobruk. Spent the next four years locked up. Wish they'd finished me off in the desert, I can tell you.'

This remark shocked all those in the room. Bill, having settled down on a dining chair and lighting his pipe, as if in preparation for a long, entertaining yarn from Donald, tried to brush over the silence. 'Oh, well, it's over now. History, isn't it? We've all played our part in history, whatever we were doing.'

Donald didn't say anything.

Bill puffed. 'So you'll be ready to take up the old brush again, Don? I've already done two jobs, but I can't cope on my own. Wasn't expecting it to happen so quick, but everyone's redecorating. There's a hell of a lot of work out there. And by this time next year, so long as Attlee wins, there'll be new houses going up everywhere. They're all going to need decorating.'

In the expectant pause that followed, Donald said, 'I don't suppose the gossips who told you I was back also told you about this,' and, as if it was a log, lifted his damaged right leg and dropped it to rest perfectly horizontal on a vacant dining chair next to him.

'No, Don, they didn't.'

'No, well. I don't suppose they gave a damn. Bullet from a Karabiner 98 through the kneecap, left untreated for four years, with several sessions of marching between camps . . . Fact is I'm a cripple. I couldn't stand up to hang a piece of wall-paper. I couldn't climb a ladder or even carry one. Can't ride a bike. Can't walk. Can't carry anything. Sorry.'

The leg remained in position on the chair, an unanswerable statement of Donald's disability. Tory was compelled to say something. 'But you can walk a bit, Donald.' Ignoring another cross glance from her husband, she continued, 'We walk down to the shops, you walk up and down the yard, I've seen you—'

She was interrupted by Donald bringing his walking-stick down with force on the back of the chair, nearly breaking both. 'Are you calling me a liar?' he barked. Then, to Bill, 'You'd better clear off, old boy. Hop it before I boot you out – if I could. You shouldn't have come round, but you weren't to know. Good luck to you, sprucing up the homes of the conquering heroes, but I won't be taking any part in it.'

Bill, by now, looked only too eager to make his exit, but he delayed as long as possible to make it seemly, fiddling with his cap, which he was holding meekly in both hands, asking Donald if he wanted to think again, and that if he should change his mind or that his leg might, you know, get better, he should come round and give him a knock. And with more apologetic looks, he was gone.

'Well, Donald,' said Tory, 'I think you could have been a bit nicer to your old partner. I think you treated him disgracefully. After all those years you worked together.' It was the first time she had felt able to express her anger towards him. It was now too long since his return for his behaviour to be easily excused.

'What do you care?' he sneered.

'We need to live, Donald. We have very little money coming in.'

'Well, if you can find a job for a one-legged war veteran . . . Don't you worry. I've got plans. I've got plenty of plans. Just give me time to get my strength back . . .'

'But how long? We need money for food and clothes for the children.'

'Well, why don't you take your mother's pearls down to the pop shop, if you're so worried? Or go back to the jelly factory, Farraway's, where you used to work. You liked it so much there, you were telling me.'

It was odd hearing him say George's name. Odd also, she thought, that his name was also the name of a factory, and that the two were so easily interchangeable.

'The men are back now, they've taken up their

old positions. Besides, I haven't worked there for years. And now I've got to look after the children. Mother's too ill to manage with four of them.'

'Three,' said Donald.

'No, Branson's one of the family, Donald. I know he's adopted.'

Here Donald gave a derisive laugh, and shook his head, as though full of pity for poor, lying Tory. 'Adopted,' he said. 'I like that. How long are you going to keep this up, Tory? You know your little tale's a lot of cock. I admit I was surprised you'd done the dirty on me at first, didn't think you were the sort of girl to do that to me, not at all . . .'

'It's true,' Tory protested, surprised at how fervently she had decided to stick to her story. 'I know it might look suspicious from the outside, but I swear Branson is adopted . . .'

'Well, if he's been adopted he can be bloody well unadopted. You picked him up out of the rubble of some burnt-out shack in Leicester, you can send him back there for someone else to pick up.'

'But he was a baby then, it was different. He knows us now – it would be cruel to give him away to other people.'

'But there are plenty of couples who would like a little boy. Only three doors down, didn't you hear? They sent their only son to Canada, and his ship got torpedoed. They'd like the boy, so why don't you give him to them? Anyway, who's to say he's yours? You just picked him out of the ruins and claimed him, like he was a suitcase. Where's

223

his birth certificate? Which house, precisely, was he found in? He's probably got relatives, uncles and aunts, who would like to claim him. You've stolen him, in effect, haven't you?'

'It's all in the past now, Donald. We can't talk about that – there's no point. Branson's part of our family.'

'Well, I can look after him well enough . . .'

'No, I don't think it would be a good idea.'

'Why? Don't you trust me with him? You think I'm like a daddy lion that eats all the cubs that aren't his own? You think I'm some sort of dangerous monster? Look at me, Tory. I'm a little broken thing, like a tin soldier that's been stepped on. If I wanted to boot that kid out of the house I'd only fall over in trying. No, I'm not going to do the kid any harm, but I'm not going to do him any good either. I'm not going to play any part in raising another man's children under my own roof. I'm not going to take any notice of his existence at all. And the only reason I'm not booting you out of the house as well is that I need someone here to look after me. I haven't got anyone else. And I expect you to be on your best behaviour, old girl. After what you've done you owe me.'

So Tory wasn't as good a liar as she'd thought. Or was it simply that Donald chose to believe she was a liar because that gave him a stronger position in the household? It was his undisputed right, as the wronged husband, to take over the sitting room and shut himself in there for hours on end, to refuse to make any effort to find a job or any attempt to earn money. Mrs Head was most indignant, after several weeks, that Donald had not done anything since his return home. The family would be crowded into the dining room, while he remained alone in the sitting room, taking up ten times his share of the household space, and Mrs Head would suddenly exclaim, 'This is too bad. I'm going to sort this problem out once and for all,' and disappear through to the passage. They would hear her knocking loudly on the sitting-room door, then delivering her usual harangues, to return this time to make the shocked announcement, 'He's locked it! He's gone and locked himself in.'

No one quite understood how he'd done it. There was a lock on the door, but they had never known of a key to fit it, and it had never been locked in the many years the Heads had been in residence. Somehow Donald had acquired a key.

CHAPTER 17

Bathing had usually taken place in the sitting room, in a zinc tub before the fire. Lack of access to this room now made things rather difficult. The only answer was to erect a screen across the dining room, and to bathe in privacy behind it. This seemed to be a manageable, if slightly awkward, solution to the problem, and the family quickly became used to going about their business in the dining room, while splashing and trickling noises came from behind the faded Oriental fabric of the screen. And then the bathtub disappeared.

Tory rapped loudly on Donald's door. 'Donald, have you got the bathtub?'

Donald's voice came from behind the door, sounding very distant, as though the room had become enormous and he was at the far end of it.

'I need to have a bath like the rest of you. It takes a long time to get rid of four years' worth of dirt.'

'Well, when are you going to bring the bath back?'

'When I've finished with it.'

'I can't hear you.'

'When I've finished with it!'

When, after three more days, the bath had not been returned, Tory asked again: 'Donald, can we please have the bathtub back? The children need a bath.'

'I need it.'

'But you can't keep it all the time. It's not fair.'

'I need it.'

'How are we going to wash?'

'You can use the sink in the kitchen.'

Mrs Head protested again, but it was useless. He simply ignored their voices.

After another week or so, he began to leave the house in the evenings. His claims of immobility turned out to be somewhat exaggerated, it seemed, and he could manage to walk all the way down the road to the Rifleman on his own, leaning heavily on his stick and swinging his stiff leg after him. He would return at half past ten, sometimes with companions, shifty-looking men in dark, pulled-down trilbys, so that only whiskery chins were visible as they shuffled after Donald into the sitting room to have the door carefully locked after them. They would stay sometimes for an hour or more, not leaving till after midnight, and sometimes rather noisily.

Tory would go downstairs and knock on the door, asking them to be quiet. Her voice would immediately silence those within. Then she would hear Donald muttering something unintelligible, which would produce laughter among the guests, to be followed by Donald calling, 'All right, my treasure,' to more stifled laughter.

Catching Donald in the hall one morning, she asked him who those men were. Donald looked affronted by her questioning 'They are heroes,' he said to her, 'warrior-heroes, every one of them, returned from the war to build a better life for us all.'

'Do you have to bring them home every night? I don't like the house being full of strange men.'

'It's not every night, my dear. And, anyway, that is why we confine ourselves to my room, so as not to disturb anyone else . . .'

She had meant to ask him about the bath as well, but as always, she was brushed aside.

Tory had been putting off a confrontation for as long as she could. She knew she should tell Donald that things couldn't go on like this for much longer, that he couldn't claim to be unemployable because of his leg when he could manage to walk down to the Rifleman and back nearly every night, and spend money on drinks (of course he claimed that his drinks were always bought for him – that was one of the advantages of a gammy leg, he said) while the rest of his family were having to scrape by.

Donald's increasing privacy about his activities in the sitting room raised the suspicion that he was doing something nefarious. Strange, sweet smells emanated from behind the door. Friends of Donald's would lug heavy objects into the room late at night. Tory once met a man in the passage with a sack of apples in his hands.

All the while money was dwindling.

'What do you think he's doing in there?' said Mrs Head. 'Why don't we break the door down when he's out?'

'Don't be absurd, Mother.'

'Well, do you know how to pick a lock?'

'Why should I know such a thing?'

Weeks went by, then months. The family became used to the secretive but regular pattern of Donald's life – alone in his room all day, then to the pub in the evening. Still the dark-hatted people visited. Sometimes they came over in the morning. Aways they seemed furtive. Then, suddenly, Donald started providing Tory with money. He came into the dining room one morning, his braces dangling down over his trousers, and slapped a sheaf of notes on the table. 'There you are, old girl. Don't say I never give you anything.'

There was ten pounds altogether, in crumpled, dirty notes.

'Where did you . . . ?'

'I told you I had some plans didn't I? I'm a businessman.'

'But what—'

'Don't ask any questions and you won't be told any lies.'

And then he did another extraordinary thing. He kissed her, full on the lips. Donald's lips were dry and chapped, his moustache stubbly and brittle. It was like being kissed by a bottle brush.

The money was gratefully received by Tory, and the regular stream of pound notes that followed, but she felt a sense of dread every time she opened her purse to fill it with Donald's money. It was more than apparent that Donald was becoming rich by very dubious means.

'He's probably dealing in arms,' said Mrs Head. 'Since the war the country's awash with armaments – I read about it. Mostly German guns our boys have brought home with them, taken them off dead soldiers.'

The thought appalled Tory, all those little revolvers, the most meagre and undignified spoils, the sweepings-up of the war.

'You go in his room and I bet he's got guns stuffed under all the cushions. There was a shooting only last week in Deptford. Donald probably sold them the very gun.'

'No,' protested Tory. 'Donald would never be involved in anything like that – you forget what a decent man he is.'

'Was,' corrected Mrs Head. 'You tell me if he's been behaving decently now, taking over the sitting room and never coming out except to go to the pub, stealing our bath, having those rowdy coves over nearly every night – a bunch of cutthroats you never saw the like of, then pretending to have a bad leg so he can avoid doing any proper work. Oh, yes, I agree he was a hard worker before the war, and never touched a drop of drink, but I always thought he had a darker side, and it's taken the Germans to bring it out.'

Tory took a moment from listening to her mother (she had put her hand anxiously to her neck at the word 'cutthroat') to reflect on how Donald had changed. It was almost as though he'd been Nazified by the Germans, as though a certain portion of their badness had rubbed off on him. Just a portion. He was not a thoroughly bad person – he hadn't caught the full Nazi disease, he had just absorbed some of it. What must it have been like, for four years, to see those ugly uniforms, those tin-pot commandants swaggering around, to be in close daily contact with pure evil? For the entire war she had not come face to face with one of them. They had remained as distant and as unreal as figures in comic books. She had to make allowances for that, surely, even now.

It was not guns Donald was dealing in, however, but liquor. This fact was revealed when two constables and a detective called at the house one evening while Donald was at the pub. The policeman asked Tory's permission to break down the sitting-room door, revealing for Tory an entirely new room in the house. Apart from the wallpaper, she did not recognize anything about it. (How strange, she thought, that the only thing the former painter and decorator hasn't changed is the painting and decoration.) All the pictures had gone from the walls. Every other piece of furniture in the room had been given over to whisky production: the table, the whatnot, the escritoire, the chairs, all were piled to the brim with bottles and stone jars, some empty, some full. All the floor space was taken up with bottles as well. There were now two tin baths on the floor (When had he got that other one in? Tory wondered), and a whisky still, which looked like an old oil drum. In one corner there was a sort of nest made of cushions, pillows and bedclothes, where presumably Donald curled up and slept at night.

The two baths were filled with a thick, scummy substance that the policemen referred to as 'wash'. Donald was to be prosecuted for having a still and for retailing spirits without a licence.

Donald was defiant. He claimed he was not making whisky but merely 'condensed wine', and that if he had made any whisky, it was purely by accident. He had started out by making fruit juice, he said, and this had, of its own accord, fermented into wine. The problem was that the wine had become stronger and stronger.

It was certainly strong. When Donald was taken to court, the jury was told that the substance he had produced was 56 per cent proof alcohol. One of Donald's customers was also prosecuted, for failing to pay duty. He had been found by an excise officer carrying mysterious-looking bottles into a public house. When asked what they contained he had replied, quite openly, 'Whisky,' and that he had bought them from Donald Pace, whose address he gave them. They found forty gallons of wash in the two tubs, along with a still, some stone jars and some apples. The friend was quite certain that Donald knew he was making whisky, because when he had a cold, just before Christmas, Donald had invited him to drink some that he had made.

The wash was so thick that it could not be poured down the drain but had to be buried in the garden. There was a patch of bare earth at the end near the privy, and a constable arrived with a spade to dig a grave for the alcohol.

Donald was fined twenty pounds with the alternative of a month in prison. His distinguished record as a war veteran was taken into account, and he claimed to have been suffering severe distress since returning from incarceration in Germany. He was only trying to make an honest living, he said to the magistrate. He'd fallen foul of the law by accident rather than design. He wasn't to know that what he was doing was illegal. He had been in a prison camp for four years, he had forgotten the laws of the country. He was suffering from malnutrition, he was trying to support a family when there was no work for cripples. He could no longer practise his highly skilled trade. His wife had cheated on him. He was owed compensation by the British Government, by the German Government, by the British Army, by the German Army. He was a decorated war hero, and they were taking away what little money he had and threatening him with prison. He claimed he had sent his medals back in protest.

'Well,' the magistrate had said at the end of this long tirade, 'your defence is certainly a "spirited" one,' to chuckles around the courtroom.

He was given two weeks to pay the fine, but refused. When the police called to take him into custody, he protested by setting fire to his hair, which he had primed by combing it through with cognac. 'Take one step nearer,' he'd said, holding the flame of a lighter close to his head, 'and we'll all go up like November the fifth.'

The policemen didn't understand quite what was being threatened so were shocked when Donald Pace ignited his head, which burned brightly for several seconds before anyone thought to snuff him. The confused, trembling constables took him to hospital, where he was treated for burns, then to a mental hospital, where he stayed for six weeks.

CHAPTER 18

T ory felt that she had survived the first wave of Donald's return home. She had not undergone the continuous rape she had dreaded; Branson, while not exactly welcomed, had been tolerated; the crazed, hedonistic, delinquent self she had poured into her letters appeared to have been forgotten, while her infidelity had been put to one side. And now that Donald's own delinquency had reached its climax and had achieved a type of resolution, she was able to feel that the worst had passed, and that at least she would have time to regroup before the second wave of Donald's homecoming began.

She checked herself, sometimes, for thinking about the whole episode in such literary terms, of climaxes and resolutions, but she could not help remembering her novel, *The Distance*, and Charlotte Maugham's situation, which was so very similar to her own. How she longed for a chance to retrieve the typewriter from under the bed and pick up the thread of the story. But it seemed inappropriate now, to start tapping away while her husband suffered, even though the yearning to do so was greatest for that very reason. Charlotte's husband is called Eric and he is also a prisoner of war, but in the Far East, and she has no communication with him at all, so that she does not know, in fact, if he is alive or dead for the entire duration of the war. Most of this was in Tory's mind, for she had not written much beyond describing Charlotte's daily routines, and her work in the glue factory.

'Is glue important in the war effort?' Charlotte asks her manager one day.

He replies enthusiastically, 'You would not believe just how important glue is in the war effort, Charlotte. What do you think keeps the wings of our Spitfires attached to the main fuselage?'

'Surely not our glue?' says Charlotte, breathlessly.

'No, of course not, but every rivet is coated with a rust-resistant resin in which our glue is a vital ingredient . . .'

Would people believe that? Tory wondered. Oh, why had she chosen a glue factory for her heroine to work in?

But what would they think if I set fire to her husband's head? No one would believe it. Not unless I made him completely mad, but then what is the use of a mad character in a novel? They might do anything. She had imagined a happy reunion for Charlotte and Eric, a welcome-home party that lasted for weeks on end, as had so many she'd heard about, with people sitting on top of a piano as it was constantly tinkled. But perhaps if she began writing those scenes, tried imagining Eric's ordeal, the agonies and torments he had suffered (she had heard very terrible things about the treatment of prisoners out there), she might begin to understand how Donald had come to be so unhappy.

It worried Tory greatly that the children (apart from Branson, who had been upstairs at the time) should have witnessed their father's act of self-immolation. It had happened in the dining room, in full view of Tom, Paulette and Albertina, and it had been such a pitiful and macabre spectacle. His head had ignited in the most spectacular fashion, a burst of light that lit up the gloomy room. Donald's reflex response was to attempt to put out the flame with his own hands, and in trying to suppress this response he had performed, instead, a peculiar arm-waving jig. He might have been a figure in a pagan carnival, with a fiery headdress, doing the dance of the burning lobster. The girls had screamed at the top of their young voices at the spectacle, and for a few seconds the house had become a house in Hell. Then the fire was out. Tory herself had snuffed the candle of her husband with the aid of a thick tablecloth.

Tom wondered which was more horrifying: the sight of his father's head alight, or the sight just after of his father's head giving off a plume of blue smoke, like a factory chimney. The smoke lingered in the dining room for many days, if not weeks, after that. It made everyone take the utmost care when cooking, because to produce smoke in the kitchen would be to rekindle an aspect of the horror of that evening.

'What happened to Daddy's head?' said Albertina, in the grim silence that followed Donald's exit.

'It exploded,' said Tom, who had recovered himself and could speak with the calm authority that was his characteristic voice.

'Why?'

'Daddy's ill,' said Tory, not wanting to wait to hear what Tom had to offer by way of explanation. She could see, by her daughter's round eyes, that Albertina was even more confused, and was trying to imagine what sort of illness would make one's head explode.

'Perhaps it was something he ate,' said Tom.

'Listen,' Tory said, trying to take charge of the conversation, lightly gripping Albertina's shoulders and turning her so that they faced each other squarely, 'when you go to war, it can make you very unhappy. When you are very unhappy, you can do strange things.'

'People cry when they're unhappy,' said Albertina.

'Yes, they do. But sometimes crying isn't enough.'

Mrs Head, who had been listening with impatience, felt that enough was enough. 'Your daddy was drunk,' she said. 'That's all you need to know. And when people are drunk they do even sillier things than if they were sad.'

'No,' said Tory, 'there's more to it than that.

238

They were going to put Daddy in prison, when for four years he's been a prisoner of war. The thought of going back to prison, after what he's been through . . .'

She believed it. It wasn't as though Donald had done anything so very bad – dodging a bit of duty on homemade spirits. The hard irony was that he'd learnt his brewing skills in the prison camp, and in that environment, making whisky had been an heroic act of defiance. Tory could not but agree that he was suffering an injustice.

She visited him in the asylum and it was an awful shock to see him there among the truly mad. She found him playing rummy with a twitchy young chap in stained pyjamas, but she didn't recognize him at first because he had lost all but a few wisps of his hair. The sight of her husband's smooth, shiny cranium reduced her to tears instantly, and she knelt down beside him, her arm around his shoulders, sobbing into his body. He just carried on playing cards.

A doctor told her that Donald was suffering from severe depression, common among ex-servicemen, and that if it persisted they would recommend surgical treatment. Tory hadn't given this remark much thought until she got home and spoke to her mother, who nodded approvingly – 'So they're going to give him a lobotomy?'

'Oh, no!' Tory said, finally realizing what the condescending doctor had been referring to. 'They can't do that!'

'Well,' said Mrs Head, thoughtfully, 'I've heard quite good things about lobotomies. Mrs Lippiatt's brother-in-law had one. She said he used to smash the furniture, but now he just sits in his chair all day, looking at his parakeet, quiet as a mouse.'

This was one thing on which her mother could never persuade her. She went straight to the hospital the next day to bring Donald home. She had heard that doctors sometimes performed lobotomies without giving any prior warning and she was not having a partial Donald sent back to her. She wanted the whole Donald, even if he was behaving strangely. She walked into the ward, packed his things, checked his forehead for any sign of scarring, then virtually fought her way through a cordon of doctors and nurses to the waiting taxi outside.

'You seem to forget that your husband is facing criminal proceedings. He needs to stay here so that we can report on his state of mental hygiene . . .'

'So that you can cut out pieces of his brain?'

It was true that Donald's legal situation was complicated, but in the end it was settled by a curt letter from the psychiatrist affirming that Donald had mitigating mental problems and the prison sentence was suspended.

Now it was as though the children had to get used to another father, the one returning not from a prison camp but from a lunatic asylum, and looking as strange and as different as it was possible for a man to look.

'Is it the same man?' Albertina asked of her siblings.

'He's got the same moustache, so I suppose it must be.'

'Anyone can grow a moustache,' said Tom.

'I can't,' said Albertina.

'I've never seen anyone so bald,' said Paulette.

'No, even babies have hair. He looks younger than a baby.'

'He has got a bit of hair – there was an orange bit sticking out the side. Did you see it?'

'I told you, this isn't the same house, our mother isn't the same mother, and now our father has been replaced.'

'Perhaps he'll be better than the last one.'

'Do you think they're going to replace us?'

While Donald had been away, Tory had taken the opportunity of restoring the sitting room. It was a long, laborious process. At one point it seemed there was no more room for bottles even in the yard, which had been turned into a horrible, inside-out sort of version of Donald's life, the two filthy bathtubs upended, along with the bottles, stone jars and still. They had no choice but to wait for the weekly visit of the dustmen to take away a little bit at a time, though the rag-and-bone man took the two baths. (He said he could get nothing for glass, and the dustmen weren't keen on the

241

bottles either.) The area of the garden where the wash had been buried remained slightly raised. Surely a liquid could not be so resilient? She hadn't thought of the many consequences of the burial, though she had clumsily joked that the worms would be coming up with hangovers for years to come.

It took weeks for all the traces to disappear, the last few bottles pushed neck first into the single swollen dustbin that took care of all their rubbish, the ground finally settling over the fermenting morass of Donald's failed whisky. Every time thereafter when she saw a sprouting shoot of something, she imagined the tree it might turn into, the vomit-flavoured fruit that might hang from its boughs. As it was, things did grow there with more vigour. The chickweed and the fat hen, the ragwort and the thistle, they all emerged from the suffused earth with a prickly vitality, before Tory scythed them with an old bread knife (she had no gardening tools).

They did what they could with the living room. The carpet was beyond saving: drenched in spilled substances, it had dried into a tough, cracked sheath, reminding Tory of the seasoned hides that had sometimes arrived at Farraway's, rejected from the tannery. She tried applying carpet cleaner, carbolic, borax and lemon juice, but they merely ran across the surface and drained away. When she lifted the carpet altogether she found that the floorboards beneath were also saturated. There seemed nothing she could do but air the boards and hope that as they dried the smell of fermentation, the reek of yeast and decayed fruit, would disappear. The soft furnishings were also badly damaged. The chaise longue had tidemarks of beer, sweat and possibly urine, though Tory tried to think not. These, at least, succumbed to scrubbing, as did the other surfaces. She paid particular attention to the escritoire, whose varnished mahogany was scarred with the interlinked circles of bottle and glass stains. Beeswax restored some of the lustre.

When Donald returned he was keen to take up residence in this downstairs room again, and within minutes was asking Tory to leave him alone in there and to shut the door.

'Donald, do you think it's a good idea to shut yourself away again, after all that's happened? Why don't you come upstairs and sleep in a proper bed?'

His reply, as always to questions of this type, was to tap his bad knee with his stick.

'But at least spend some time with your family, or with me. Let other people share this room. Don't shut yourself away.'

'You heard what the doctors said,' replied Donald. 'I'm a broken man, Tory, and I need time to heal. What do you do with a broken toy? You glue it back together, but you don't start playing with it straight away. You leave it on its own, some-where no one will disturb it, so that the glue can set and harden . . .'

How odd, thought Tory, that he should talk about glue, with Charlotte Maugham working in a glue factory. She tried to think of ways of working what Donald had just said into her novel.

But it didn't bode well that Donald should so quickly resume the character of his previous life and start shutting himself away again. It seemed so odd that, after all those years of confinement, he should want to continue it. Why didn't he crave company and revel in companionship? Was this to become a regular cycle, repeated for ever? She could do nothing but wait and see.

CHAPTER 19

Tory was very proud of her son, Tom. Even though his education had been disrupted by nearly five years as an evacuee, and he had had to make do with a tiny, crowded village school, where all the ages sat together in one classroom and cows jostled at the open windows in summer, as though for a glimpse of the blackboard, he had managed to attain an excellent mark for his exams, on the basis of which he had won a place at Blackdown Grammar School, one of the best schools in the area, and one that Tory thought would be for ever out of reach for her own children. Here, by all accounts, he had settled in quickly and was doing well in all his subjects. His teachers expected him to achieve a very good grade in his school certificate. He was displaying scientific leanings, and had ambitions to be a physicist or an engineer.

She was a little bit worried about his relationship with his father, however. It wasn't until Donald was away in the hospital that she had realized how frightened of him Tom seemed. With Donald out of the house, Tom thrived. Reduced to silence, usually, by the mere presence of his father, suddenly he was the oldest male in the house, and he seemed to relish his position. He would sit at the table at mealtimes and talk endlessly about some scientific fact or other, or larkingly tease the girls for their pigtails and their dolls. He would pick his mother up on the smallest solecisms, correcting her English and arithmetic whenever the opportunity arose, and siding (to Tory's delight) with little Branson in any of the teasing arguments that erupted in the house. Branson had an ally in the family now, and Tom seemed to treat him as a genuine little brother. Tory almost wept.

But as soon as Donald returned, Tom was back to his quiet, reclusive self, saying not a word at the dinner table, scuttling off to his room or the yard whenever his father appeared. And his father, on return from the hospital, did look strange, with his smooth, scarred head.

There was an outhouse in the garden, which no one had used for many years. It was next door to the privy, a slate-roofed lean-to set against the high wall at the end of the yard. Tom had soon appropriated this space as a kind of laboratory or workshop. He had done much the same thing in the Cotswolds, where he had had the use of a whole barn full of redundant mechanical equipment, including an entire car, which he had dismantled down to its last nut, then put back together again. He had played about in the farmyard forge and

246

had even done some welding. He had started making Heath Robinson-style contraptions that performed simple tasks in complicated ways. He claimed to have learnt, by such practice, that there is no such thing as a simple task. He had spent a whole year trying to produce a perpetual-motion machine, an elegant device that made use of many bicycle wheels and should have worked in theory but failed miserably in practice.

Now, back home in Peter Street, his main ambition was to build a robot. So, in the company of woodlice and spiders, he accumulated junk and scrap of every type, and would hammer, saw and solder all the hours that he had. The girls had little interest in their older brother's hobbies, and were particularly averse to visiting his dank, cobwebby laboratory. Six-year-old Branson was fascinated, however, and would sit cross-legged on the dirty floor watching his older brother at work. Tom was kind and patient enough to let him clumsily help, and he never tired of providing the younger boy with instruction on matters of physics and mechanics.

The robot was built around the upturned frame of an old folding pram. After some months of work, Tom produced hinged upper limbs that could be worked by pulleys strung with cable that did look unnervingly like a pair of wildly waving arms when the ends of the cable were tugged. The robot's head was an upturned zinc bucket, a temporary measure, Tom said. He needed more

247

time to think about the head, which was surely to prove the trickiest part. As for power, Tom had extracted the petrol engine from a lawnmower that had rusted solid at the back of the outhouse.

'Why on earth there's a lawnmower here I don't know,' he said to Branson, as they examined the engine, which had evidently been a home for mice quite recently. 'There's no grass.'

It was true that, apart from the bare patch where the wash was buried, cobbles, paving and cement stretched all the way from the back door to the gate at the end of the yard. But there must have been grass once, they supposed. What an awful thing to be that lawnmower, Tom thought, and see the world that gave you purpose and meaning laid waste beneath a mantle of cement. It must feel like a ship that had run aground.

'Perhaps they used to mow the concrete,' said Branson.

'Yeah,' said Tom, laughing, 'that's a clever thing to say Branson, but you didn't mean it to be clever did you? I like the thought –' (Here he did a shrill rendition of his mother's voice.) '– "*The concrete's getting a bit long, dear, why don't you go out and mow it?*"'

The robot was called Mr Briggs, after the name embossed on the lawnmower engine. Bit by bit he slowly emerged from the rubbish of the outhouse, Tom adding a piece here and there as he found just the right thing in a scrapyard or junk shop, and always Branson would be Tom's assistant, holding his instruments for him, handing him whatever he needed (but he was never allowed to actually make any part of Mr Briggs himself).

As the weeks and months passed, Branson slowly came to realize what his much cleverer older brother seemed not to: that the robot would never do anything. No matter how intricate and elaborate the contraption became, with its pulleys and cogs (how many old clocks had been eviscerated for this purpose?), no matter how many old nutcrackers, radiogram valves, springs and piano wire went into its construction, it would never amount to anything more than a representation of the human figure, a sort of sculpture, rendered in scrap.

Tom could be quite convincing, however, whenever Branson raised the question of how it would work.

He would talk about electronics, transistors, computational engines, and so on. At one time he decided that the nearest the human race had come to devising a thinking machine was in the common shop till, or cash register, the sort that could be found in any butcher's or baker's. They then spent some time scouring scrapyards and junk shops for such an item, but never found one. 'Our robot's brain is waiting for us on the counter of every grocer's in the land,' said Tom, with the air of a frustrated genius.

At other times he would concede that he didn't have the technological know-how to construct a fully operational robot, one that could walk and talk and perform simple tasks. But that shouldn't be a disincentive for making it because, he reasoned, by the time they had finished the body of the robot, science might have come up with an affordable artificial brain.

'And once they've done that, Branson, well, there's no limit to what Mr Briggs could do. He could be our servant – we could send him to the shops to buy us a bag of lemon bonbons, or we could make him make other robots, and then we'd have an army of them, to do our will wherever we pleased. We could take over the house with them.'

'Yes,' said Branson, excited without quite knowing why. 'We could invade it.'

Tom liked to elaborate a vision of a children-versus-adults world. He persisted with his theory that both his parents were impostors, identical replacements for his real parents, who had both died in the war.

'We're all orphans in the house, but we don't know it. Apart from you, Branson. I think you're the real son of our fake mother. That makes you the only non-orphan in the family, and a very lucky boy.'

'Do you think our father isn't our father as well?'

'Well, he's certainly not *your* father, and I very much doubt if he's ours. For a start, if he was our father, he would have noticed that his so-called wife was an actor, wouldn't he?'

Tom said this in a triumphant tone, though Branson didn't seem convinced.

The construction of Mr Briggs took more than two years, a project that soon overspilled the little outhouse, and began to fill most of the backyard, which was continually strewn with the workshop debris, tools and raw materials of Tom's ingenious invention. The robot became a celebrated local sight. His slightly comical demeanour (Tom had constructed a face with two small light bulbs for eyes and a harmonica for a mouth) and his rather bulky size, which meant he had to be handled with care when he was being moved from one spot to another, made him a spectacular curiosity. During the long, hot summer holiday of his completion, Tom had friends from school round almost every day to help with Mr Briggs. The scattered yard would be full of dishevelled, inky grammar-school boys, sitting on their haunches, labouring with hacksaws at squares of zinc plate, or filing away to smooth a jagged edge of something. The seriousness and solemnity with which they performed their work – rarely joking, rarely even speaking, unless to discuss a technical matter, seemed only to accentuate the comicality of Mr Briggs himself. He stood erect and as stolid as the statue he was, gazing with his unblinking eyes at whatever was set before him, grinning (was it a grin or a grimace?), while at his feet boys seemed curled in acts of earnest devotion.

'I can't get over how lifelike that thing looks,' said Tory one day to her mother, as they both happened to glance out of the back window.

'*Lifelike* is not a word I'd use,' said Mrs Head.

'No, I don't mean it looks alive, exactly, but it looks like it's got its own mind. It's funny but I've got so used to seeing its face staring at me from the bottom of the yard that I forget what an extraordinary thing Tom has done.'

'*Mr Briggs*,' said Mrs Head, as though correcting her daughter's *faux pas*. 'I don't like to look at him myself. He looks a bit sarcastic.'

'Don't be silly, mother. How can a robot look sarcastic?'

'Well, I just hope he doesn't ever get as far as making it speak. If Mr Briggs ever spoke, I'm sure he'd be most high-falutin' and hoity-toity. He'd look down on us because we're just human beings.'

Donald expressed similar misgivings about Mr Briggs. 'It's a pile of junk with a face on it,' he said, 'and I don't like the way it looks at me.'

The day came when Tom wanted to unveil the completed Mr Briggs officially. It was the last Sunday of the summer holiday and he had invited all his friends over. The backyard had been cleared of its debris and Mr Briggs draped with a sheet. The family were gathered near the house – Tory and Mrs Head, Donald, Albertina and Paulette, who complained all the while: 'We've seen his stupid face staring at us all summer, why do we have to come out and look at him again?'

'That's no way to talk about your brother,' Tory joked. (Oh, they had become awkward, obtuse and contrary girls. Tory was getting quite fed up with them.) 'Tom has worked very hard at Mr Briggs. He deserves some respect. And what have you done all summer, I'd like to know, apart from hang about in the streets like a couple of urchins?'

'Come on,' Donald called to the boys at the other end of the yard, as they fiddled with the figure behind the sheet, and he leant heavily on his stick to make a display of his discomfort. 'We havenae got all day.'

Donald and Tom, it seemed to Tory, had become a little closer in recent months. She had seen the way Donald would chat to the boy on his way to and from the privy, and he had dropped heavy hints that he had prepared a reward for all the work Tom had put in to Mr Briggs. No one could imagine what such a reward might consist of because Donald remained as penniless as the day he had returned from the war, having refused to look for work in the two years since. Tom and Branson were aware that this was a cause of friction in the household because they could hear the frequent arguments between their father and mother on the subject.

'So you think I should be a bus conductor eh? With my leg? Or what about a milkman, then? That's a laugh . . .'

He seemed to think that all their problems would be solved once his claim for a veteran's pension and compensation payments had been made, but these had been very slow in coming, and most of the family doubted that they were ever likely to materialize.

Tom, for his part, was very nervous. He had not thought, when he arranged this day, how he would feel if it all went wrong – if Mr Briggs's engine failed to start, or if he fell over or ran amok. He glanced at the gathered family as they stood by the poorly pointed brickwork of the house, his father's grooved face and bald head, so glaringly bald.

Only the night before he'd said to Branson, 'It's such a pity our dad's mental.'

Branson nodded slowly in carefully considered agreement, before saying, 'What do you mean?' He only had a vague memory of the time their father was in the asylum. It was never talked about in the house, and it seemed a very long time ago now. But for the fact that their father wore the scars of his madness on his head, they might all have forgotten about it.

Donald's head had become an object of horrified fascination for everyone in the house. The loss of hair seemed to transform him completely, far more than one would have thought. The whole shape of him seemed different. He did not, in fact, have a very good-shaped skull. It lacked a convincing roundness, especially at the back, which seemed to rise a little, like a pterodactyl's. Even without the application of ointment it would have been a shiny thing, but with it his skin became not just shiny but glossy, almost to the point of transparency. Branson looked at it sometimes and thought, If I touched it I bet my finger would go right through. To him, Donald became his head in a way that was uniquely his. Branson could only think, when his father came into the kitchen, Here comes my father's head; Father's head is eating its dinner; Father's head is talking to Mother . . . And some-times, Father's head has come out into the yard, and is looking at me.

And that was what he was thinking now, except that, as ever, Donald was not quite looking at him. Donald had never looked at him, as far as Branson could recall, or ever spoken to him. Only now was he beginning to feel that this was odd behaviour for a father towards his son.

Tom tugged at the starting cable of the old petrol engine that sat rather awkwardly in Mr Briggs's chest. On the fourth pull it caught, and gave its familiar, urgent throb. The sheet was drawn back by Tom and Branson, and Mr Briggs was revealed for the first time in his full, completed glory. There was a gasp of genuine delight from the observers because, although they had seen Mr Briggs many times before, in his various drafts of construction, Tom had managed a very special feat as a finishing touch to his robot. By hooking the engine up to a bicycle dynamo he had made the light bulbs

255

that served for Mr Briggs's eyes actually light up, and the bright stare that greeted the spectators as the sheet fell really did make it seem that he had gone some way towards creating a true automaton. Even more so as it began to move.

Tom had long before given up on the idea of a walking robot, and Mr Briggs was carried on a set of wheels. Instinctively the family, although nearly thirty feet away, took a step back as the robot trundled forward. The old lawnmower engine sounded unexpectedly powerful in the walled space of the yard and gave the impression that Mr Briggs could, at any minute, break into a terrifying sprint. Instead his progress was agonizingly slow and, thanks to the unevenness of the cobbled yard, lurchingly unstable. Again, this seemed to give him a human quality because he rolled from side to side as he progressed, like a drunken sailor (as Mrs Head quietly remarked). Perhaps most unnerving of all, however, was the way Tom had rigged the arms to the wheels so that they swung as the robot advanced. With a little too much free movement in the elbows and wrists, they were a little ungainly, gesticulating in a rather undisciplined way, as though the robot was frantically directing traffic or (Tory quailed at the thought) trying to put out a fire in its clothing.

The idea had occurred to Tory before that Tom had constructed a mocking simulacrum of his father in Mr Briggs. Donald, on the other hand, had been struck by a quite different and unexpected

256

resemblance. He wondered if his son had intended to mock the figure of Winston Churchill. It wasn't only something about the squatness of Mr Briggs's body, the flatly rounded head, the pear-shaped torso, he was convinced that the fingers of the flailing hands (consisting, as far as he could tell, of ten neatly soldered teaspoons), occasionally offered a V for Victory sign to the observers by the house. Donald was particularly sensitive to ignorant remarks about Mr Churchill and could still not quite believe that the nation had ditched him so readily in favour of someone who looked like a headmaster of a third-rate elementary school, and who seemed hell-bent on bankrupting the country.

Mrs Head, on the other hand, couldn't help but be reminded of Major Brandish, her neighbour in Waseminster, and a proper soldier. He had played the cymbals in a marching band, and liked to clash them together whenever he got the chance. He had performed many cymbals recitals in her little cottage (the variety of sounds that could be drawn from such a crude instrument was remarkable); the climactic moments often had the major waving his arms in similar fashion to Mr Briggs. Paulette detected signs of their old schoolteacher in Upper Slaughter, Mr Davis, the jovial old bean who would describe historical episodes with arm-waving vigour – 'And at the Battle of Prestonpans, when Bonnie Prince Charlie fought King James's men, it was every man for himself . . .'

Only Albertina was able to see the robot as

nothing other than the robot, Mr Briggs, and for this reason she was the most scared of him, out of all the family. As he came nearer, his eyes winking and his arms swinging, she searched blindly for her mother's hand, then held it tight.

'Are you going to make it stop?' said Tory, a little quaveringly, as the robot approached to within a few feet of the spectators. Tom, who had walked alongside the robot for the entire journey, like a groom escorting a mechanical bride down the aisle, checking carefully for anything coming loose, reached for the motor and turned it off. The sudden silence that befell the yard was filled instantly with applause. It was begun by Tory, who nudged everyone else to join in, which they did, the girls somewhat reluctantly. Even Donald hung his stick on his forearm and clapped, slowly and loudly. The applause seemed to take Tom entirely by surprise, and he struggled to conceal the joy he was feeling at being so noisily appreciated. He couldn't prevent the blush that coloured his half-downturned face as he pretended to adjust a vital part of Mr Briggs's body.

Donald stepped forward. 'Well, son, I've always said you were a clever bugger, and now here's the proof, a mechanical being. All you need to do now is to teach it to cook, and we can kick your mother out of the house.' No one laughed at this, apart from Donald.

'I think Branson needs some thanks as well,' said Tory, quietly. 'He helped Tom a lot.'

That Donald should ignore this remark without a pause for breath, that he should ignore Branson so completely, surprised no one. Donald had not acknowledged Branson's existence in two years. Tory did find it difficult to bear the little boy's evident disappointment, because after she'd made her remark, she had noticed how he squared himself up, put his little chest out and his shoulders back, as if ready to absorb the impact of praise from his father, then deflated immediately the moment he saw it wouldn't come. She regretted saying anything.

'I've got a special prize for you, Tom,' Donald went on, 'one that I think you will appreciate for the rest of your life.'

Tom was still looking down at something in Mr Briggs's insides, unable, quite, to bring himself to turn his face fully into the stream of fatherly appreciation.

'Aren't you going to ask me what it is?'

'What is it?' Tom said, without lifting his head.

Oh, such a shy boy, Tory thought, such a modest, abashed and awkward boy.

'I've got you an apprenticeship at Bolan's,' Donald said, slapping a hand on Tom's shoulder, so that he swayed a little. There was silence. The only response from Tom was the slightest frown of puzzlement.

It was Tory, eventually, who spoke. 'Bolan's?'

'Yes, Bolan's. Starting tomorrow, in fact . . .'

'But Tom's going back to school this week.'

'School? The boy's sixteen. He doesn't want to stay at school when he's a grown man, do you, boy?' He shook Tom's shoulder.

Tom swayed so much he had to hold on to Mr Briggs. 'I rather thought I was going to stay on,' he said at last.

'Yes,' Tory said. 'He's doing very well – all his teachers have said so.'

'In two years he could be earning twice as much as any of those teachers. Anyway, it's all arranged. There'll be a van calling at half past seven tomorrow morning . . .'

Donald looked again at Mr Briggs before turning back to Tom. 'Well, what do you say to your old man? I went to a lot of trouble to get this apprenticeship for you. Just lucky one of the foremen there is a former comrade-in-arms, an old soldier. Even so, I had to go down on bended knee – not the right one, obviously. So what have you got to say to me?'

'Thank you,' Tom, said. He appeared to be close to tears.

'That's the spirit, son,' and with that Donald stepped back into the house, back into the sitting room, and closed the door.

The crowd in the backyard slowly dispersed. The grammarschool boys, many wearing their uniforms, gave Tom a consoling pat on the back as they went. Such brief, intense valedictions for the friend they might never see again.

★   ★   ★

'You don't have to go if you don't want to,' said Tory, once they were alone in the garden, apart from Branson, who lingered nearby.

'But Dad's arranged it.'

'Without asking anyone else, least of all you. I think it would be quite reasonable for you to go to school tomorrow.'

'It doesn't actually start till Wednesday.'

'In that case, you could go to the factory, see if you like it and, if not, go to school on Wednesday, just as normal.'

Tory had her arm around her son's shoulders now. He was not an embraceable boy, normally, and flinched at any physical contact from his mother, but not this time. He accepted the compromise, but didn't seem really to think that once he had put himself into the hands of his apprenticeship, he would be able easily to break free.

Later that evening, just after it became dark, Tom and Branson were on the roof of the privy, side by side, observing the stars through Tom's telescope, bought from a junk shop on Scarborough Road with carefully saved pennies. The privy was the best place for observing the stars and the boys had spent many evenings on its roof, squinting at the night sky. Tom's ambition was to find a new comet. As he had told little Branson, if you're the first person to discover a comet, you can have it named after you.

Occasionally someone would come out to use

the privy while they were on top, stargazing. If it was their mother, she would insist that they get down and go indoors before she would even enter it, and the same went for the girls, but Donald didn't care in the slightest, to the extent that they sometimes wondered if he was even aware that they were on the roof while he was inside. The boys were the more embarrassed, and continued their astronomy in silence to the sub-noise of their father urinating or defecating, which he often did explosively, so that the roof of the privy seemed to shake.

Sometimes he would appear in the garden in a more contemplative mood, standing motionless by the back door, smoking his pipe, looking intently at nothing, or as though he was examining the night air. Sometimes he would attempt some exercise by walking up and down the backyard path without his stick, between the house and the yard gate, bending under the washing-line to do so.

He would stand in the yard right below the children, working his neck back and forth so that his head swung slowly about. It was almost as if he was bathing his head in a stream of water, but there was nothing there but cool air. At night Donald's head reflected any light that was near. The distant light bulb shining in the back room of Mr Sawbridgeworth's house opposite, would shine on Donald's head, just as though he'd had an idea. Once, Branson could distinctly pick out the belt of Orion passing across the top of his father's cranium, or so he thought. The moon was easily visible in Donald's glossy, hairless skin, and suggested, to Branson at least, that it wasn't as far away or as big as everyone thought.

On this particular evening Donald came out just as Tom and Branson had found Saturn and could see four of its moons, if not its rings, and stood below them at the privy door. He was silent for a while, as though ignorant of their presence, before suddenly speaking. 'I know you have some nonsense thoughts about going to university, Tom, and I know you've got a good brain, and determination – Mr Briggs is ample proof of that – but the sad, squalid truth of our family is that we have no money because I, as an invalid, am not able to go out and work. I've tried my best – you know how hard I've tried, what with the brewing and the other deals I've put my hand to – but the law has no pity for a crippled man trying to feed his family by what-ever means he can. As a result, I am crippled further, crippled right down to my heart, Tom, right down to my heart. I had a good brain too, once, you know. You can ask me anything you like about Charles Dickens, or Aristotle, or Plato, and I can give you an answer. There is no money to put you through university so you can forget about that. Bolan's is a much better option, a good place to work, with good prospects for a clever young man. Apart from that, well, you'll be called up to do your national service in a year or so. University was never on the cards . . .'

Donald's speech seemed to drift off, as though he was unable to finish it, and after lingering a while, as if in expectation of a reply from Tom, who all the while had not taken his eye from the telescope, he went back indoors.

Even after his father had gone, it was some time before Tom said anything. 'You wouldn't think you could see so far from the top of a shithouse, would you?' he said, still looking through the eyepiece, relishing that last noun, and using it as often as he could in the subsequent sentences. 'I wonder what the people who live on Titan would think, if they knew they were being watched by people sitting on the roof of a shithouse. Mind you, perhaps they're watching us from the roofs of their own shithouses.'

Branson was made a bit uncomfortable by the word Tom had used, because his older brother never usually swore or used dirty words of any kind. 'What do they make at that factory?' he said eventually.

Then he noticed that his brother, having put the telescope down, was sobbing into his knees. Branson's discomfort increased. He had no idea why he should be crying but reached out to pat Tom's shaking shoulders, in a vague apprehension that that was what one did with sobbing people.

The contact seemed instantly to gather Tom's wits and he stopped crying. Instead he said, as if to himself, but really for Branson's hearing, 'Well, if they could see me now, those ninnies on Titan, they'd be having a proper laugh. I expect they're

264

laughing this minute, to see me have my life taken from me on the roof of a shithouse. They'd be laughing so much they'd probably fall off of their own shithouses. Goodbye, Titans, go back to your shitty little shithouses.' The tears had returned by the time that final phrase was added, so that it was said stutteringly through gritted teeth, from the back of the throat, in a surprisingly manly tone. Tom let the telescope drop from his hands, and it rolled quickly across the slate and dropped again, onto the cobbles below. The lens popped out and spun like a coin.

The next morning at half past seven, a small green van parped its horn outside the house, and Tom, wearing his ordinary clothes and with a round of cheese sandwiches wrapped in news-paper tucked under his arm, left the house, watched anxiously by his mother from the front door. There was something about the boldness and lack of hesitation with which he had walked down the path to greet his new life that suggested to Tory that perhaps he would enjoy life as a working man after all.

When Tom came home that evening, he seemed a different person. His hands were shaking. His face was blank. He ignored anyone's questions and, with a sort of rigid shrug, went straight to his room. Tory went after him but he had wedged the door shut. She could hear him sobbing within, though he was clearly struggling to keep silent. She imagined he had wrapped his face in a pillow, it sounded so muffled.

'He's probably been given the initiation,' Donald said.

'What initiation?'

Donald mimed sharpening a cutthroat razor on a strop, then gestured towards his crotch. Tory had to sit down, feeling faint.

She would have stood firm in her insistence that Tom should stay on at school, had not Tom himself seemed, despite his apparent shock at his situation, loyal to his father's wishes and continued working at Bolan's. He obediently went the next day when the little green van called for him. It amazed Tory that he should be so stoically set upon winning his father's approval when his father's motives were so very shabby.

When Tom's headmaster called, a week or so later, to ascertain whether the rumours he'd heard were true, that one of his most outstanding pupils had left the school for good, Tom could not be made to come down from his room and face his former mentor. To her own dismay, Tory found herself siding with Donald in the discussion that followed, simply in order to present a united front and to give an impression of a settled, stable household.

Mr Wythenshaw was a slightly vague, kindly man with round, steel-rimmed glasses and a wispy moustache. He extolled at some length the exceptional abilities of young Thomas Pace, and how they had had very high hopes for him at Blackdown's, and that they should try not to think of the short-term gain they might make by sending Thomas out to work at the expense of the long-term benefits for his future if he stayed on at school.

'I must ask you to reconsider, Mr and Mrs Pace. We are very disappointed that young Thomas will not be completing his studies with us. He is one of the most able pupils we have ever had at the school . . .'

'Ableness doesn't make any difference. We can't afford to send him to university. If he's so clever he'll soon climb the ladder at Bolan's and be managing director,' said Donald. Donald then asked the headmaster what he had done in the war (he had been a captain in the First World War, he said, commanding soldiers on various perilous missions throughout the conflict), at which Donald grumbled, wishing he hadn't sent his medals back.

'I can't understand it, Donald,' said Tory, after the headmaster had gone. 'You were so keen on learning when I first met you, always reading a book, and you knew so many things – yet you don't seem to value education.'

'I learnt all I needed to know without having to go to university. They're a waste of time, Tory, when you've got public libraries full of books. Why would anyone need to go to university just to listen to a professor reading out from books that you could just as easily read for yourself? Einstein never went to university. Think of that, my dear. And now you can do my head.'

Tory didn't have an answer so settled into what had become one of the new routines of the house: applying ointment to Donald's scarred scalp.

It was the end, it seemed, of Tom's interest in scientific matters, even though he was now working in an engineering and chemical establishment. Now that he was part of the industrial world, it seemed robbed of all interest for him. When every day the knock came, he would obediently answer the door and walk out to the little green van. Then, at the end of the week, he would put his pay on the kitchen table (as instructed by his father), and he would be allowed to keep a few shillings for himself, while the rest was divided between Donald and Tory.

Mrs Head, now increasingly frail and spindly, could still muster enough energy to harangue her son-in-law. Usually when this happened Donald hobbled back to the sitting room and locked the door, but this time she banged on it incessantly for two hours, shouting through the panelling: 'You're using that boy to do the work you should be doing. I don't know why you don't go down to the factory and work yourself – you've got perfectly good arms, why don't you use them? That boy could have been anything if he'd stayed on at school. You say there was no money to pay for him but if we were inventive enough we could have found a way. You're treating this family like your own little kingdom . . .'

And so on. It made no difference. The problem was that, now that he was a worker in one of the biggest factories in the area, Tom seemed to have lost any desire to return to school. He no longer showed any interest in Branson, and if Branson asked him any scientific questions, which he was always keen on doing, Tom would reply with words like 'What are you asking me for? Save it for your teacher . . .' He had begun to comb his hair straight back from the forehead, losing the scientific side parting that he had worn since early childhood. He also grew a small ginger moustache, very similar to his father's.

Tom became noticeably older. It was as though he had been put through some sort of time accelerator. A year ago he had been a schoolboy getting used to long trousers, with yo-yos in his pockets and beetle collections in his bedroom. Now he read the *Daily Sketch* in the evening, and would drink a bottle of ale, poured carefully, at an angle, into a glass. He would talk about politics just like one of the grown-ups. Since his mother and grandmother rarely read newspapers they began to regard him as a sage authority on such matters – the futility of the Berlin Airlift (the city should be handed over to the Russians), the devaluation of the pound, the situation in Korea. He even criticized Mrs Head for not joining the dock workers' protest meeting in Trafalgar Square – when her own father had been a stevedore in the Surrey Docks. Father-in-law, corrected Mrs Head, as if that distinction absolved her from any responsibility towards the plight of the current dock workers. 'I don't know why you don't go and live in Moscow,' she said one day, pronouncing that city's name as though it was a type of bovine farm animal.

Branson, still stranded in ground-level childhood, watched this transformation with curiosity and awe. He still shared a bedroom with Tom, the smallest of the three small bedrooms, at the back of the house, overlooking the mossy concrete of the yard, but there was little conversation between them because Branson was usually asleep by the time Tom came to bed and hadn't woken up by the time he'd left for work. Sometimes he'd be woken by unusual sounds. Once, Branson woke to hear the sound of distant water falling, and it took him a long time to realize that Tom was being sick into a shoe. He didn't do anything to clear it up, and the sulphurous zest of vomit stayed in the air all night.

Another time Branson woke up with a start to find the room illuminated and Tom sitting at the end of Branson's bed in his striped pyjamas. Branson didn't say anything, but rubbed his eyes, looking at Tom, waiting for him to explain himself.

'I've just discovered something rather strange,' he said, without looking at Branson.

'Have you?'

'Yes.'

There was a long silence during which Branson gradually realized he was expected to speak.

'What is it?' he said.

'Oh, well. I was down the public library the other day – one of my favourite places. And I happened to be looking through the archive of the *Echo* – they've got them all there, you know, all the way back to 1869.'

Branson knew only vaguely that the *Echo* was their local paper.

'And I was merrily looking through the issues covering the years of the war, when me and my sisters happened to be living in a little paradise a hundred miles from here, and what do you think I found?'

'I don't know.'

'Well, I found an article that described an air raid on London on the fourth of March 1941. Many parts of London were heavily bombed that night, but it was the eastern half of the city that suffered the most. There were houses destroyed in Erith, Foots Cray, Plumstead, Blackheath and Dartford. Stapleton's was hit – they make screws – and the Pegasus factory, which made incandescent mantles, was completely destroyed. How that place must have glowed!' He looked as if he was about to laugh at this, but didn't. 'There were bombs in this area too. In fact, there was a bomb that fell here, in Peter Street. Not only that, but the report in the paper says that numbers thirteen, fifteen and seventeen were completely destroyed.'

Tom gave a long pause, during which Branson again felt he was expected to say something, especially since Tom was now staring at him with wide-open eyes and his mouth pursed in a rather strange way, somewhere between a grimace and a smile. Then it clicked with Branson. 'But this house is number seventeen.'

Tom nodded slowly. 'Haven't I always said it? This isn't the same house? Well, you wouldn't know, because you're a little boy who never knew the old house. But that isn't the most shocking thing. The most shocking thing is that the report announced the deaths of the occupants. It said Mrs Emily Head and her daughter Victoria were killed in the blast.'

'Who's Victoria?'

'Mummy, silly. She's always been called Tory.'

'So Mummy was killed by the bomb?'

Tom nodded. 'The woman who was my mother was killed, yes. The woman who lives here now, and who calls herself Tory Pace, and her mother, Mrs Head, are actors.'

Branson laughed cautiously, as though not sure whether his older brother was fibbing, as he often did about things.

But Tom went on: 'They're good, I have to admit. Very good. You have to be very observant to spot the difference. The girls haven't noticed, and you mustn't tell them, because they'll just tease you. When I try to tell them, they think I'm being fanciful, but then I didn't have the proof. Now I've got it, in the newspaper article, in black and white.'

'Show them the article. They'll believe you.'

'How can I? I can't take the paper out of the library. They won't bother to come down to the library to see it.'

'I bet they would.'

'Anyway, you need special permission to see the archives. They wouldn't let the girls in.'

'But I don't understand why they've replaced Mummy.'

Branson noticed for the first time that, all the while Tom had been talking, he had been fiddling with a pencil. He now raised the pencil to his nose and ran it several times, very gently, beneath his nostrils, as though it was a cigar.

'Who's to say what governments get up to in wartime?' he said. 'We're just pawns, Branson, little pieces in a giant chess game. I bet the government did this all the time, rebuilt the bombed houses, replaced the dead with lookalikes, so the Germans would think their bombs were having no effect, so that neighbours and families weren't demoralized by the loss of neighbourhoods and loved ones . . . The Germans must have thought their bombs were just swallowed up by the city, as though they'd dropped them into a pool of syrup.'

Although Tom was speaking in a grammatically

sensible way, Branson could tell, even at eight years old, that he was talking nonsense. It wasn't so much what he was saying, but the way in which he was saying it. Four o'clock in the morning, sitting on his bed with his jacket over his pyjamas, whispering loudly and fast, shaking all over with a curious energy and staring all the time with those wide-awake eyes.

He tried to change the subject. 'Tom, what's it like in the factory?'

Tom had never spoken about his work, and Branson was desperate to know because he presumed that when he was old enough he would be sent there in just the same way that Tom had been. But now it seemed he was prepared to explain, and took a moment to settle himself.

'We make car tyres,' he said quietly, with a sort of resolute laugh. 'Car tyres. You wouldn't think such violence goes into the making of car tyres, Branson. When I first saw the inside of the factory I thought I was in the middle of a battlefield. Tongues of flame, clouds of smoke, the smell of sulphur in the air. And figures of men, just shadows really, running back and forth through the smoke. And everything you touch is coated with a waxy sort of grease. We're supposed to wear masks to protect us from the fumes, but they're too uncomfortable so no one wears them. That's why I've started to smoke a pipe. It helps clear my lungs of the smoke from the factory.'

'Will I have to work there?'

'No, Branson.' Tom reached out to touch Branson's knee and shake it reassuringly. 'You must never work there.'

'Why not?'

Tom held out his hand as though offering, in his palm, an answer, but then he turned the gesture into one of restraint, the palm up and facing out, like a traffic policeman. 'Let me show you something very beautiful and very precious,' he said.

Branson sat up, excited, but all that Tom gave him was the pencil he'd been holding.

Branson took it and examined it. It wasn't even a very good pencil, no rubber, and chewed down half its length.

'Beautiful, isn't it?' said Tom.

'I've got a better one,' Branson replied, after some thought.

'Oh, I don't think so, Branson. It's just not possible. I think you're not looking at it properly. Look at it closely.'

Branson looked.

'Tell me what you can see.'

'Just toothmarks . . .'

'Exactly. But then you, poor creature, have not met the maker of the toothmarks. They were made by one of the most beautiful girls ever to have set foot upon the earth. I won't tell you her name, not yet, but she lives in a house in the village of Upper Slaughter, an Eden to which you have never been admitted, and never will be now. It's too late . . .'

★   ★   ★

275

Tom didn't come home from work the following day. Tory waited up till past midnight. She waited up till two o'clock in the morning, then went to bed, but didn't fall asleep properly. She got up every hour to check in Branson's room to see if Tom had returned without her hearing. On one of these occasions Branson woke up, and was told quietly to go back to sleep by his mother.

The next morning, when the little green van called, Tory went out to speak to the driver. She had only spoken to him once before, the one time that Tom was ill and couldn't go to work and she'd gone out to explain. This time she asked the driver to take her to the factory. She wanted to see if Tom had come in to work directly from wherever he'd spent the night. It was the first time she'd seen Bolan's close up. Its jagged roof of sloping skylights and its many chimneys, already spewing black smoke at that time of the morning, presented a gaunt, thorny outline against the dawn sky. She went to the office and a girl took her down to check the clocking-in cards. No, Tom Pace's card had not been stamped. Could she be allowed to wait for a while by the clock to see if he arrived late? The girl shrugged and went back upstairs.

Tory lingered in the chilly, tiled entrance vestibule, watching the square, roman-numeralled clock ticking. Every now and then a huddled figure would enter through the swing doors, take their card from the large rack that said 'OUT', insert it into the clock and pull a brass lever, which produced a noise rather like a cash register chiming, then place his card on the large rack labelled 'IN. These people gave Tory no acknowledgement. She looked closely at the beige card marked 'PACE, T.', which sat in almost complete isolation on the 'OUT' rack. She then wondered if the girl had made a mistake. Perhaps there was another Pace, T. (Terry? Tim? Tobias?), working at the factory. So she carefully looked through all the cards on the 'IN' rack but, to her disappointment, discovered that Pace, T., was unique among the employees of Bolan's.

Tory waited until ten o'clock, then made her way back alone. It was a long walk along puddly roads that wound through the enormous trading estate, back to the main road. She felt an acid sensation beneath her breastbone. She sneezed into a tissue and saw that her mucus was black. She noticed her hands, also, were black, yet she hadn't touched anything, as far as she could recall. She had merely leant against the wall, once or twice. She might have let her hands wander over the tiles behind her. She arrived home feeling exhausted. On the way she had been hoping to find Tom safely returned, and his continued absence crushed her, so that she could only sit down and pant. No one else seemed worried. Mrs Head said he had probably gone for a drink with friends and had one too many. He was old enough to do that sort of thing now, not that she approved. Donald took much the same line. But he would be home by now, surely, Tory thought. It was midday.

After lunch, which she didn't eat, she went to the police station to report her son missing. The officers were as unconcerned as Mrs Head and Donald. He was a man of eighteen, they said. There was nothing they could do. Nothing? Supposing he never comes back? The policemen shrugged. A lot of eighteen-year-olds go missing, these days, Mrs Pace. Something to do with National Service, I shouldn't wonder. But Tom was looking forward to his National Service. It would get him out of that filthy factory he's been stuck in for two years . . . We'll let you know if we hear anything.

And that was it. They would keep an eye open for him, keep an ear to the ground. If they happened to notice him as they went about their routine business of directing the traffic and telling people the time, they would let her know.

'Well, what else can they do?' said Mrs Head. 'He could be anywhere . . .'

'But surely they could ask people at the factory, ask his friends, ask anyone who knows him where he might be or where he might have gone.'

And that was what Tory ended up doing herself. She went back to the factory, asked to speak to people Tom worked with, to see if he'd told them anything about going away. But it broke her heart to speak to them, as they emerged from the factory floor (where she wasn't allowed) into the grimy locker rooms, because it became evident that Tom had had so few friends in the factory. Most didn't even know who she meant, and those who did knew nothing about him. She persuaded a manager to open his locker, which only contained the expected things: his overalls, breathing mask, boots and a mug with his name written in enamel paint on the side.

By now, at least, Mrs Head and Donald could not pretend that it didn't matter. Days had passed and Tom had not reappeared. None of them could think of where to look. They had already asked his old school friends, but they hadn't been in contact since Tom had started at the factory. Oh, why did you send him there, Donald? Why did you send him to such a dirty, ignorant, friendless place?

Then Tory wondered why she hadn't thought to ask Branson. Perhaps it was Branson's curious ability to disappear, so that he went about the house unnoticed. But he had shared a bedroom with Tom, right up until his last night in the house. If Tom had confided in anyone, it would have been Branson.

She found herself taking a strange sort of comfort from the fact that Branson was so little concerned about his older brother. She had taken this comfort many times before, especially when the raids were still happening. The flying bombs could not have bothered little Branson less. Her children made her feel safe. But Branson didn't know where Tom was.

'But he thought you weren't real,' he said, as an afterthought, in a hoping-to-please voice.

'He thought . . . ?'

'He thought you died in the war and that you were an actor.' Branson paused as he became slightly confused by his own information. 'I mean, he thought the person you were pretending to be had died, and also that the house wasn't real, but that it had been bombed.'

'Oh, God,' Tory couldn't help saying, putting a hand to her mouth. Had Tom really believed those silly stories she'd overheard him telling the girls?

'Are you?' Branson said, with an eagerness suggesting he'd wanted to ask this question for a long time. In truth Branson was excited by the idea that his mother might be an actor.

'Don't even ask such a silly question, Branson. I'm me, and Tom is my son.'

'Well, Tom didn't think so.'

This conversation took place in Branson's bedroom while Branson was in bed. He didn't like sleeping alone and had got into the habit of waking in a panic at around ten o'clock in the evening and coming downstairs. Tory had to take him up again and sit with him until he was asleep. She didn't mind; in fact, she liked it. She looked forward to the appearance downstairs of Branson's worried little face every evening, and of their quiet, soothing conversations upstairs later. She always felt disappointed when he did finally fall asleep, and would sometimes cough or clear her throat to prolong his wakefulness a few seconds longer. (How she loved the response in his eyes when she did this, their sudden opening without focus, and then, by ever narrowing degrees, their slow reclosure.)

It was three weeks before Tom's body was discovered. He had hanged himself in a large disused barn in the village of Upper Slaughter.

CHAPTER 20

Apart from the fact that he was kept off school, Branson might not have known that anything unusual had happened. His mother went about her business shopping, cooking, laundering and mending just as she always had. The only difference was that now she did these things with a silent, almost mechanical efficiency. The fact of Tom's death was not fully explained to him. His mother was only able to report that Tom had had an accident and that he wouldn't be coming home. Branson couldn't understand his mother's expression as she told him this news. She had her eyes screwed up, as if against smoke, then seemed to wink at him. Then suddenly her face was open, and the eyes appeared damp and troubled. Then she would wink again. She ended the conversation by kissing him on the forehead, which Branson found funny and laughed, but quietly. The girls went about the house in tears, but wouldn't say why. Their faces were as red as if they'd been slapped, and they looked as angry as sad. Branson kept out of their way. At the funeral, he found himself passed from person to person, each of whom would speak to him seriously and firmly, as though passing on important instructions, but all they were saying was things like 'How are you?'; 'How's school?'; 'How's your mother?' Branson observed the funeral from afar, he was kept at the back among people he didn't know, and only saw the coffin once, as it passed down the aisle of the church on the shoulders of six young men in black. It seemed to tower above him, like a liner passing out of port.

At home, things continued in this silent, efficient way for another week, and then, one night, things changed.

The first Branson knew about it was when he was lying awake in his bed in the darkened room with its empty other bed. Out of the great engulfing silence of the house there came a very small sound, like an enamel plate being rolled across the floor downstairs, its course becoming more wonky as it slowed, until it collapsed, like a coin, into a slowly increasing spin that gathered speed until, with a sort of metallic glissando, it stopped.

There should have been no one awake to cause such a noise, and Branson tried hard to get himself to sleep. But he was awoken again, this time by heavier sounds. As though someone was delivering sacks of linen. They were crashing softly downstairs. Or it was like very fat men, so fat they had lost the use of their limbs, falling over each other, pulling and squeezing past each other in the passageway . . . Then, the crisp, brittle sound of a small glass object falling onto a hard floor. Branson looked at the foot of his closed door. There was only a dim line of light there, which meant the landing light was off but the passage light was on. No shadows had moved past it. No one had come out of their room to see what the noise was. Then there was a colossal sound, so loud it was as though a part of the house had fallen down, except that it was a wooden, rather than a stony sound. As though there was a tree growing in the middle of the house, and someone had just chopped it down. Branson tightened the bedclothes around him, watching with one straining eye, too scared to blink, the line of dim light under the door. Surely that noise would have brought Mrs Head out of her room, or the girls, but there was no movement on the landing. Perhaps they had all gone and left him alone in the house. Perhaps he was the last surviving member of the household, which had been invaded by some sort of consuming demon, and he was the last one remaining to be eaten.

Then came laughter, a tinkling, brittle peal that was so uncharacteristic Branson couldn't be quite sure that it was his mother's. It seemed to Branson to be a perfect example of laughter such as you would give to demonstrate to someone who didn't know what laughter was. Then other voices, a sort of conversation, though it was difficult to tell between how many. In his half-awake state Branson thought that they were rehearsing a play.

That would explain the range and speed of the voices he could hear, the way they were punctuated with other noises – shrieks, wails, laughs, and the rumble and judder and thud of scenery being shifted, props being tested and discarded. That was surely the explanation. Branson went to sleep.

In the morning he went downstairs to an apparently normal house, except that the door to the sitting room, where his father had lived as a semi-recluse for so long, appeared to have been smashed through. All that remained were the stiles and one panel on the hinge side. The rest hung in jagged shreds, or lay in dagger-shaped splinters on the sitting-room floor beyond. And there, in the kitchen, was his father Donald. As it was so unusual to see his father in the kitchen at this time of the morning, Branson couldn't help but stare. His father looked extremely crestfallen, sitting hunched, like a dog that had been whipped, not meeting anyone's eye, his lower lip drawn in. Branson's mother was standing behind him, and she was gently and very tenderly applying ointment to his fused scalp.

A china spaniel lay in pieces on the floor. As with the debris of the door, Branson wondered why no one had yet picked up the pieces. They seemed to have been deliberately left where they had fallen.

Mrs Head was at the kitchen table. She smiled in a serious way at Branson as he came in, and then she turned to his father and said, 'And this is Branson.'

It was as though she was introducing him for the first time. It was as though his was the last name on a long list Mrs Head had gone through that morning, a list in which she'd been saving the best until last. Then Branson's father did a most unexpected thing. He held out a hand towards him. It was a long-fingered, bony hand, and Branson found it slightly repellent. His mother continued her balming of his father's head, and appeared to take no notice of Branson. It was such a peculiar reversal of roles that Branson didn't know what to do. But he stepped forward because the hand was beckoning in quick, shaky finger movements.

When Branson stepped within reach of the hand, which in his mind seemed somehow disembodied, a big, bony, gesturing shape hanging in the air, it came to rest on his shoulder. And tears were falling down his father's face. But Branson's mother was still not looking at him.

CHAPTER 21

There was the question of what to do about Mr Briggs. He had been sitting in the yard in the same position as he'd been left at the end of the day of his unveiling, right at the far end, by the back gate, facing the house. Tom had not worked on him at all since that day, and he had not moved since, his bucket face turned slightly to the left, one arm raised, the other lowered, frozen in mid-stride. Weeds had grown up in-between the cobbles and woven themselves through the rusting framework of his lower torso. Birds used him as a perch and as a site of defecation. In the winter he was the armature for an instant snowman, and in the summer months the anchoring point for many spiders' webs. His rigid stance at the end of the yard had become so commonplace that it was no longer observed. Like the ticking of a clock, he failed to register on the senses. Now, with Tom's death, he had become resolutely alive. He was noticed every time anyone looked out of the window or went to the privy.

Mrs Head's first instinct had been to get rid of Mr Briggs: he was a constant reminder of Tom.

But Tory wanted to keep him for the same reason. She even went so far as to clean him up a little, yank the weeds out of his chest, pull the cobwebs from his ears, brighten up his eyes. Seeing her from the window, going at the robot with a scrubbing brush, Mrs Head didn't know quite what to think. She supposed it wasn't a bad thing for the robot to remain in the yard, as a sort of memorial to her grandson, but on the other hand, it was such an ugly brute of a thing, and with that sarcastic, condescending expression (that, thankfully, wasn't turned fully on the house), that she couldn't help feeling there was something unhealthy about allowing it to remain in the yard. She wondered how she could tactfully broach the subject of removing it. The rag-and-bone man would be more than happy to take it, she thought. She was aware that she was not a tactful person, and that the rag-and-bone cart might not be the most sympathetic way to dispose of what Tory considered to be her son's memorial, his only surviving mark on the world.

'Tory, I wonder if it's about time we did something with Mr Briggs.'

'Like what?'

'Well, perhaps we could give him to one of the schools around here, for their science projects or something.'

Mrs Head was very pleased with her idea, and it seemed to strike Tory as a possibility. But she dismissed it anyway. 'No, I like to have Mr Briggs, he reminds me . . .'

'Perhaps now is the time to let the past go, and to let Mr Briggs move on to better things.'

'You're talking to me as though I'm a fool,' said Tory, with the air of sudden realization, 'as though I'm a little child.'

'No, Tory, I'm just trying to be considerate.'

'Well, have you considered what it's like to lose a son?'

'I'm your mother, Tory. You seem to forget. I've lost a grandson.'

'I'm sorry.'

Tory believed she was suffering from too much knowledge, that she knew things no mother should ever have to know, and which she had to keep to herself. A space had been created in her mind, which was continuously present and which she could not help but visit. It consisted of a disused barn in a remote Cotswold village, a young man rigging up the apparatus of his own death with the painstaking care and precision of an engineer. He had used a block and tackle. This was what the police had decided she needed to know. They also told her that the farmer had been led to his discovery by the unusual activities of jackdaws on his farm.

She felt that she understood Donald now, because when she had chopped through the sitting-room door with an axe she had found bandaged with cobwebs in the outhouse, and had discovered her husband unconscious on the chaise longue hugging an empty whisky bottle to his heart, sleeping like a babe in the wood, she had stood over him with the axe in her hands and raised it above her head, as if she was about to chop a difficult log. But she didn't kill him. He had opened his eyes and looked at her with a jolting sense of recognition, as though he had been expecting this moment for a long time. And then, having taken in the whole picture, he simply closed them again. For a moment Tory saw herself as he must have seen her, axe lifted, a trembling tower of anger and grief. And he had just closed his eyes as if ready to take it. The axe wilted in Tory's hands and she sank to her knees and wept.

Later, when the acrid fog of Tory's grief had cleared a little, he emerged slowly, and cautiously, and did his best to appear remorseful and contrite. The morning after Tory had contemplated splitting him in two with an axe, he emerged from the living room, brushing aside some shard of door-wood that stuck out awkwardly from the frame, and, with a teetering, tippy-toes walk, entered the kitchen and said, in his quietest, shakiest voice, 'Tory, dear, I think my head needs doing.'

Donald's head had not been balmed for several days. Usually the absence of just a day's balming would have him in agony, claiming that his head felt like it was on fire (and he should know), and crying out for water to quench a desiccating thirst. And so Tory balmed her husband's head, and the tenderness of the process, the slowness and the light-ness of the task, started to ease the need to blame him for Tom's death. Whatever had driven Tom to take his own life couldn't be laid at the feet of his father, Tory said to herself one night, and repeated it to her mother, who didn't agree. He'd robbed him of the person he was going to be, she said. He stole his son's future to pay for his own idleness in the present . . .

But Tory went even further than merely absolving Donald of blame. She apologized to him for not having understood the agonies he had gone through, both during the war and after. It was around this time that the first survivors' accounts of the concentration camps came to be published, which Tory read reviews of in the newspaper. She realized that a prisoner-of-war camp did not dispense suffering on anything like a comparable scale, but the descriptions of things that had happened made her feel that to be in such close proximity to the brethren of the deathcamp guards must have been to experience even a fraction of their horror, and even the merest fraction must be dreadful beyond comprehension.

She apologized for having believed, sometimes, that he exaggerated the injury to his leg and played on his disability, that she had told him off for spending time in the pub, when in fact he had been consoling himself with the company of former comrades, the only people on earth who could understand his suffering. It was true, what she'd heard spoken by others, that the comradeship of the regiment and of the prison camp was a closer bond, in some ways, than that of family. Families may go through their tests and trials, but they rarely have to lay down their lives for each other. Understanding Donald in terms of the life he'd led as a soldier even helped to explain why he might have been so keen for Tom to work at Bolan's: many of his pals had been recruited from there, so Tom had been inducted vicariously into the brotherhood of veterans. It was not that he had been using Tom as a way of enabling himself to remain idle: he had used Tom to do the work he might have been doing himself, had he been fit. It was a theory that Tory found satisfying and gave her some consolation.

Eventually the shreds of the shattered sitting-room door were removed, the remains of the frame taken off their hinges and discarded. The door was not replaced, and the doorway remained perpetually open. It seemed to be an unspoken understanding between them that Donald should no longer be allowed to shut himself off completely from the rest of the family. He didn't ask for the door to be replaced, and he did nothing himself to replace it. He still spent most of his time in the sitting room, however, and even without a door it was difficult for the rest of them to cross the threshold. Though, since a large portion of his domain was visible to anyone passing, it lost its power to mystify and threaten. The room became ordinary and unsecretive.

★　★　★

Tory went so far in her forgiveness of Donald that she insisted he should not even think about trying to earn money. Now that Branson was old enough to take himself to school, she would find a job for herself. Mrs Head was rather shocked by this new development, even more so when she discovered what sort of job her daughter had taken.

'Have you lost your marbles completely, Tory? You cannot possibly work as a lavatory attendant.'

'It's done, Mother. I am a lavatory attendant.'

'You seem to have an insatiable appetite for disgust. Why must you always submit yourself to the basest, most abject occupations? One would have thought you had learnt your lesson with the gelatine factory, but at least the war could excuse you working in such a filthy place. Now there's no excuse. You've chosen your occupation of your own free will. What is it? Are you trying to martyr yourself? Are you trying to punish yourself? For what? You've done nothing wrong.'

'It's a very good job, Mother. The hours are convenient.'

'I don't think this is an appropriate time for jokes.'

'But the hours *are* convenient, and the pay is much more generous than Farraway's. I'm my own boss – I even have my own office.'

'Office? You call that little cavern an office?'

Of course, Mrs Head knew the public lavatories on the square very well, having made use of them from her earliest days. Up until this moment she had regarded them as very civilized, with their

293

mosaic floors and oak panelling, the large brass fittings on the stall doors, the copper pipework, now rather green with verdigris and a little mossy. She had never paid any attention to the attendants over the years, though she was conscious that they tended to be the elderly, overweight, hoarse-voiced wives of market traders, just a step up from gypsies or fairground people. Now that her daughter was to be one of those people, she couldn't help but see the public lavatories as a malodorous, leaky underground cavern, each stall spewing forth a fountain of human manure and even more unspeakable things. How could her daughter dwell in such a place, then come home and with those same hands prepare dinner for her family?

'My hands spend most of their time bathed in disinfectant and soap. Those lavatories are probably cleaner than most restaurant dining rooms.'

'Now you *are* talking nonsense.'

In truth, Tory had never felt more content than in the ladies' lavatory on the square, where she had an office all of her own. She only spent three hours a day there and, once her regular cleaning duties had been performed, had little else to do but sit in her office and read. And it *was* an office, despite what her mother might say. For the first time since Donald had come home, she had a space for herself. There was a small desk with brass-handled drawers underneath, a comfortable, though very worn leather chair to go with it. It wasn't long before she realized that she now had somewhere in which she could work on the manuscript of her novel.

Tory had hardly stopped thinking about Charlotte Maugham. She went to bed every night with a sense that underneath it a hostage was tied up and gagged. Through the muffled handkerchief she could sometimes hear, *Write about me! Write about me!* Even if she could have managed to bring herself round to extracting the typewriter and continuing with her novel, she balked at the thought because she was terrified by the notion that she might not be able to give Charlotte the sort of life she wanted to. She might have to be cruel to her. That was why she had been so wedded to the typewriter as the sole instrument of literary production. She could have written the rest of *The Distance* with pen, or pencil, in little notebooks. She could have scribbled away at the kitchen table – no one would have taken much notice and Charlotte Maugham could have watched as her family sadly disappeared. She had longed to deal with Charlotte's oldest boy, the clever one, with his chemistry set, his cat's-whisker wireless set and his train set – Peter, with his bent, wire-rimmed spectacles and his books on bird-watching, his collection of conkers. What sad little road should she map out for him to follow? She might use the death of his father as a starting point for his decline. This was one of the reasons she hoped Donald would never ask about *The Distance* because in it he died, killed in action. The trouble was it gave

Charlotte no one to blame. There was nothing for her to put right after the death of Peter.

'Oh, Charlotte Maugham,' Tory said to herself, 'what am I going to do with you?'

It was an odd thing, but it was Donald who had encouraged her to carry on with her novel.

'Didn't you use to have a typewriter?' he said to her one day.

'Yes. You made me take it out of the room.'

'You were writing a book on it, weren't you?'

'I was trying to.'

'You should have finished it.'

Tory was quite taken aback. It was probably the kindest thing he'd said to her since his return home. Her spirits were dampened a little by what he said next, though.

'You could have had it published by now, if you'd finished it, and we could have made a bit of money.'

So it was just the usual thing, everything coming back to how the rest of the family could support Donald in his unemployment.

'I don't suppose anyone would have published it,' she said.

'Oh, I don't know. Everyone's getting published these days – have you looked in the papers? War memoirs, everyone's writing them, and probably making quite a few bob.'

'Well, I don't know. I wanted to write about the war, but I don't suppose my story was very interesting compared to what other people went through.'

Donald had smiled to himself. 'Oh, I think you

had a pretty interesting time.' Then, as though struck by a sudden thought, 'Tory, do you still have that typewriter?'

'Yes.' She thought he was going to tell her to get it out and get on with her money-making novel. But no – he wanted it for himself.

'If these people can write their war memoirs, then why can't I? My memories are worth just as much as anyone else's . . .'

She wanted to say, *Well, it would be a bit boring, wouldn't it? I mean, you spent the entire war, apart from the first few weeks, in a prison camp, behind barbed wire.* But instead, she said exactly the opposite: 'It would be a very interesting read, I'm sure. I don't suppose many men have written about their time as prisoners, but it would be just as interesting . . .'

'Yes,' said Donald, with a touch of mistrust in his voice, as though he suspected, but couldn't be quite sure, that Tory was mocking him.

So the Remington was brought out from under the bed for the first time in nearly seven years and the dust was blown from its keys. Tory carefully carried it downstairs and placed it on the writing bureau, exactly where it had been before.

'You know you don't have to type it out, not the first draft?' said Tory, a little breathless.

'I want to do it properly don't I? What's the point of writing it out with a pen then typing it all out again? All right, you can clear off now.' He smiled to show that he was only being jokingly rude. 'I need to get my memories sorted out.'

But I would like to work on *The Distance*, Tory wanted to say. What about my book? She listened for a while, leaving the kitchen door open. There was silence for a long time, except for the rustling of paper, coming through the open doorway of the living room. And then, quite unexpectedly, even though she had been expecting it, the sharp, punching sound of a key on the typewriter being decisively pressed. Just one key, on its own, which caused Tory to marvel, for a moment, at what a horribly violent noise it was. So unlike the piano, its distant relation, the typewriter cannot take a light touch. It responds to only one level of pressure. She remembered that from her own first experiences of typing. Her very first attempt had been soft and tentative: the key had lowered but the sequence of subsequent movements, all that leverage and counterbalance, couldn't be pushed into action. She'd had to press harder. The typewriter had demanded decisiveness and commitment. Every letter, it seemed, had to be placed with energy and resolve. There was no such hesitation in Donald's first letter. There was the emphatic stabbing of the key, the throwing forward of the lever to smack against the white paper, the carriage shifting one space to the left, the lever falling back into its bed. It must have been a full thirty seconds before the second key was pushed. Another longish pause, then two keys in quick succession. Another pause, shorter this time. And so the faltering rhythm of Donald's typing filled the house. The long pauses were gradually elided, and after a few days the keys were being pressed at a steady trickle. He was certainly busy. He could type for several hours at a time.

Now that she was working in the lavatories, however, Tory realized she could write her novel without the aid of a typewriter, that she could simply use pen and ink, or even pencil. She had never realized quite what a pensive place a lavatory was, how conducive to thought. It wasn't simply that it provided her with long stretches of solitude, punctuated only by the echoey clip-clop of some old girl coming down the stairs to spend a penny, but that it was a place removed from the real world in a most decisive and concise way. A bit like a nunnery, Tory imagined. It was also a good place to manage grief. Surely no one, no matter how sharply bereaved, can dwell too long on their loss when they are confronted with such sights as a public lavatory affords.

She might only be there for three hours every day, but she was the only person who could deal with many of the problems that arose. And such problems were many and varied, from the lack of toilet paper to the jamming of money in the cigarette machine to minor plumbing difficulties. She could even cope now with an overflowing cistern. And to think she had been afraid of coming down here for all those years, that it had taken the death of her son to enable her to overcome such fears. She even liked to spend time in the exact cubicle of her childhood fright, sitting on the seat imagining her six-year-old self sweating in panic at the big bolted door. It hadn't changed since then, in nearly forty years. Nothing down there had changed, but had been silently waiting for her return.

One day, as she left the public lavatory, passing the small brass sign that said 'PUBLIC LAVATORY' at the top of the steps, she could not help but amuse herself by covering up the first ten letters with her gloved hand and forearm, to leave just 'TORY' exposed.

And when she re-emerged into the everyday world of shops and daylight, everything seemed lighter and sillier than it had before, but in the most affirmative way. The soaring civic buildings of the square seemed made of lace – even the town hall looked as if it was about to launch itself into the sky. Though she always rather dreaded that her masculine counterpart from the Gents would emerge at precisely the same time and that they should, with due solemnity, do some symmetrical bowing and hat-tipping to each other before walking off in opposite directions. In fact, she very rarely even saw the male attendant, although she had been told to call on him in any emergency (she prayed there would never be one – how could she ever be expected to set foot in that underground world of dripping male members?). An emergency, she soon realized, usually took only one form: that of the lock-in, when some frazzled dame

300

would either jam or break the bolt on the inside of the cubicle, or else render herself incapacitated, would faint, have a hot flush or, more rarely, die.

'A very high proportion of deaths occur on the lavatory,' Tom had once said, during a phase of hypochondria.

'Do they?'

'Yes.'

'I suppose you're going to tell me why.'

'Because the symptoms that are associated with a catastrophic internal disorder that may cause sudden death, such as a heart-attack or aortic embolism, are very similar to feelings associated with an urgent need to evacuate the bowels.'

'Really?'

'Yes.'

It had worried Tory for weeks. Every time she felt an urge to go to the lavatory, she wondered if she was about to die. Going to the privy had felt like the long walk to the guillotine. What a way to die – for one's last moments on earth to be spent in contemplation of the WC, collapsing forward, dead on the floor with one's drawers around one's ankles.

But it was true. She had wondered why her predecessor had made a point of telling her to use the public telephone box that was not ten yards from the entrance to the lavatories, in case of a *real* emergency, but within a month of starting she was having to do just that, dealing with her first fatality.

301

She had learnt that a lockin can usually be solved with a step-ladder and a broomstick, but not this time. It was a woman of rotund anatomy and roseate complexion, and she hadn't even got as far as lowering her bloomers. She was sitting on the lowered lid, fully clothed, slumped sideways against the cubicle wall, her plump hands gathered in her lap in a way that seemed rather contrite and humble, like a child in church. When Tory phoned for the ambulance it surprised her that the operator seemed familiar with the public conveniences and, indeed, so did the ambulance men, when they arrived. A grinning couple of chaps with their caps set back on their heads, as chirpy as milkmen. Down in the lavatory they found the dead woman and searched for a pulse. One of the men, after they'd heaved the woman on to a stretcher, took the opportunity to flirt with Tory.

'Hullo, you don't look like the usual sort we find down here. When are you knocking off?'

Tory was furious with herself for blushing at this (think of running water, her mother had said, and the colour will go), which only encouraged the ambulance man, until he was beckoned on by his colleague, who asked him if he wouldn't mind taking the other end of the stretcher. 'Oh, I do hate doing the below-grounds. Why do they have to build these places underground?'

It was as though it was part of a regular routine, as though once a month they called to collect a dead woman. But, in fact, it was almost the last time someone died in the Ladies' lavatories on her shift.

Should she send Charlotte Maugham to do the same work? Tory thought she might as well, though to give it a twist she had her heroine taking a job in the Gents. Tory was thrilled at the turn her novel had taken: she was quite sure that no English novel had ever contained a heroine who was an attendant in any sort of lavatory, let alone a male one. Though she supposed such a novel might have been written by a member of the Communist Writers Committee of the Soviet Union, or whatever it was called, celebrating the heroic struggle of a urinal-wiping, headscarved babushka. Well, hers would be a decadent version of that. She wrote the scene of Charlotte's first day, in which a red-faced colonel enters the clammy rooms below ground and reddens further at the sight of Charlotte in her headscarf and overall (neither of which could quite conceal her understated beauty). He makes to turn around, believing himself in the wrong place, then notices the urinals, at which other men are already standing.

'I – I – What is the meaning of this outrage?'

'Outrage? This is 1949. Haven't you heard of socialism?'

After some months in the job she came to find the presence of males in the Ladies a most unwelcome intrusion. In fact, it was more like a distortion of reality. When old Clive made his occasional visits to check on some plumbing malfunction, it was as though something impossible had happened: a baggy-eyed, grey-moustachioed man, sagging in every aspect of his being, entering this female space, a space more feminine than any other in the world, a place *chemically* feminine.

One quiet afternoon a scream brought her from her office. A woman in artificial fur with a leopardprint headscarf and long mauve gloves was standing by the door of a stall, leaning one hand against it for support, the other struggling to find a handkerchief in her deep pocket, which she then brought to her nose. She looked at Tory as she approached, her face zigzagged with distress.

'What is it? What's wrong?' Tory asked.

Shaking her head, the woman moved to the washstands, her handkerchief still to her face, then gestured with her other hand towards the stalls. 'In there,' she gasped. 'Oh dear . . .'

Tory, expecting that she was about to discover the second dead body of her career, cautiously opened the heavy wooden door, only to find the stall within empty. There was a strong smell, however, of an unusual provenance. Not the usual stink of defecation, something more laden and weighty. As she approached the pan of the lavatory, she had an inkling of what had happened. The bowl was filled with red, and in the middle of it a translucent, curled form, maybe limbed, she couldn't be sure. She stepped back, trying to keep calm. The woman in furs had gone, saying she needed air. When Clive arrived, he dealt with the problem by lighting a rolled-up newspaper and holding it before him as he entered the cubicle, then a horrible churning sound, like a paddle-wheel plying the Mississippi, before he emerged again, more saggy than ever, mumbling something about the jobs he had to do.

'Some woman's dropped her guts down the lavatory,' he said, shuffling off, shocking a lady as she entered.

That was the second death she had witnessed in the Ladies, though this time of the smallest, saddest kind, and when she went home that evening, she couldn't help but feel that she was contaminating her own home with the colour and smell of death. It's not fair of me, she thought, to bring these things back to a house that is still in mourning. But what things? Why did she have the curious feeling, when she arrived home, that she had dragged a sack behind her all the way? In fact, she carried nothing. Her overalls and headscarf hung on a little brass hook in the underground office and were left there.

Mrs Head, at first adamant that Tory should not even enter the precincts of the kitchen until she had washed herself thoroughly, had become a little more relaxed recently, no longer insisting on the full bath. But now it was Tory who felt she needed purifying, and could not even enter the dining room but remained in the hall for some time, looking at herself in the hallway mirror, whose ugly, coffin-layered shape was such an unkind frame for her face. Then came the sound of a typewriter key, like a distant gunshot.

But in other ways the job at the lavatories continued to have a cleansing effect. Why was it that proximity to so much that was awful about human beings, tending to the far, rarely visited end of the deglutitive experience, should feel so nourishing? Then she realized. Everything was being washed away. It didn't matter how much dirt was produced, the continual flushing of the cisterns, the nod of their ballcock levers like an affirmative peck of a lavatory bird, was a constant reminder that most things, no matter how dark, malodorous, vile or inhuman, can be washed away in a stream of clear water and never be seen again. That was why (she recalled) the people had looked so bright on emerging from the lavatory, when she had observed them that day years ago, so brisk and bright as they re-emerged into the fresh air. They had been given a new lease.

The woman in artificial furs came back.

'I want to thank you.'

Tory almost jumped out of her chair: she was unused to people speaking directly to her when she was alone in her office and she had been deeply absorbed in her novel at the time.

The woman went on, in a quieter tone, 'I'm sorry, did I frighten you?'

It had been a week since the blood incident, and

306

Tory had not seen her before or since, up until this moment. 'No, I was just . . .'

'Crikey. I didn't realize being a lavatory attendant involved so much paperwork.'

Tory's little office was decked with pages of *The Distance*, Draft One. The typescript, now vigorously annotated in red and brutally scored so that barely a paragraph survived, was spread out, chapter by chapter, across the floor at the back. Draft Two, entirely handwritten on loose leaves (of several different sizes), was overspilling from an upturned crate along the side wall. Her desk was cluttered with the third draft, again handwritten, using a specially purchased fountain pen with a marbled shaft and gold-plated nib that blotted freely over her copy.

Tory looked up, not quite knowing what to say. Her office was never visited, and so never had to be explained. The woman, still in her leopard-print headscarf, took a step back, as if suddenly realizing she was encroaching. Tory took a moment to observe her. She was very beautiful, in a modishly regal sort of way; she had the tapered, streamlined look that was beginning to prevail. She wouldn't have looked out of place with a cigarette holder between her lips, and Tory kept thinking she was wearing jewellery, but every time she tried to look directly at her necklace or earrings, they weren't there.

'Well, like I said, I just wanted to thank you for your kindness.'

'I didn't really do anything,' Tory said, once she'd collected herself.

'Oh, I think you did. I think I would have fainted if you hadn't come over to me. It was very kind of you, to wipe my brow like that . . .'

'Wipe your brow?'

'Yes. Perhaps you've forgotten. You were such a kind dear, dampening those paper towels and then applying them to my forehead.'

Oh, well, if that was what the woman remembered, perhaps Tory had done such a thing. 'Think nothing of it,' she said.

The woman dared start forward again, placing her foot across the threshold.

'I'm afraid I can't stand the sight of blood, you see. I can hardly even say the word. I've always felt ashamed of the fact, especially as my mother was a nurse.'

'Well, it was enough to make anyone feel giddy . . .'

'But not you. I suppose you're toughened against things like that. I suppose your job makes you a little bit like a nurse.'

A toilet flushed, and Tory blushed. A bolt was emphatically drawn. 'I wouldn't say that.'

'I must say, I've never seen an attendant quite like you before.'

This was the third or fourth time such an observation had been made, and Tory was beginning to find it a little tiresome. How was she supposed to respond, after all – with an apology? With a promise to be someone else? But coming from this elegant young woman's lips (the first time a female had made the observation), Tory felt rather flattered. 'How do you mean?'

'Well, not that I'm a professional observer of lavatory attendants, but they tend to be of a similar type – a certain age and . . . deportment, shall we say? Now I'm going to sound like a terrible snob, and you'll hate me.'

The woman was well-spoken, prosperous-looking, but with a timidity, self-deprecation and deference towards Tory the Lavatory Attendant that Tory herself found utterly compelling.

'The very fact that we're having this conversation is proof that you're an unusual lavatory attendant,' she continued. 'I've never had a conversation with a lavatory attendant before in my life.'

'Perhaps you've never tried.'

'Well, that's probably true, but then it takes two people to have a conversation. You don't mind me talking to you, do you?'

Tory had just put down her pen in what might, she now realized, have looked like a gesture of exasperation. 'No, I don't mind.' She wondered if there was something she could say to emphasize the truth of this statement, and thus cancel out the pen-throwing gesture, but instead she allowed a little bubble of silence to form.

'Now that I've started talking to you,' the woman said, with a forced laugh, 'I realize I'm not quite sure what I want to say. And I do hate people who talk but have nothing to say.'

'In my opinion,' said Tory, helpfully, 'it's a rather extraordinary skill, when you think about it. I wonder how people do it, and I wish I could do the same.'

The woman produced a laugh, a genuine one this time, but it ended with another silence.

'Well,' the woman said, 'thank you again.' There was an awkward moment of prolonged eye contact, and she left, her footsteps echoing for what, to Tory, seemed like an hour.

The woman became a regular visitor to Tory's office, the frequency of visits gradually increasing as the weeks went by. At first Tory was worried that she would become an intrusive presence, disrupting her work on the novel. At other times she welcomed the chance to put it aside. The woman was called Grace, and it was true that she never talked about nothing, it was just that the things she said were sometimes rather odd.

'Do you know what, Tory? I must have come here twenty times now, and I haven't used the lavatory once. I was going to, on that first day, when I saw the . . . you know . . . but all my subsequent visits have been to talk to you. I suppose that makes me a rather strange woman. I would now count you among my best friends, but I have never seen you anywhere except in a public convenience. Don't you think we should meet in the outside world, just once in a while?'

'We might not like each other above ground,' said

Tory, who had come to enjoy Grace's conversation because she could say anything to her and still be understood.

Grace laughed. 'Yes, we might be like ferrets, who co-operate when hunting through tunnels but attack each other in the open air.'

Once Grace's visits had attained a certain level of regularity, Tory allowed her into the office and even made a little space for her, using the crate that had once contained Draft Two as a makeshift chair. Here Grace would sit and talk for half an hour or so, always a little nervous, breaking into little peals of jittery laughter, or else falling into pensive silences, when her beautiful eyes would seem to lose their focus, or else focus on something not in the real world. It seemed to Tory, on these occasions, that Grace could actually watch her own thoughts. Tory found herself being uncharacteristically open with her. She had soon told her things about herself that she had never told anyone else. The writing was the first quarter of her private world to fall to Grace's charms.

'What are you writing?' Grace asked one day.

'Oh, nothing. I just like scribbling things down.'

'Don't call it scribbling, that makes it seem thoughtless, and I can see you have put a lot of thought into it. What is it? A book?'

'It might be, one day.'

'Tory, I think you're so wonderful, sitting here in the back of a public lavatory, writing a book.

311

There can't be another woman in the world doing the same thing.'

'It isn't anything, really. I don't know why we make such a fuss about writing – it's just scribbling things down. Anyone can do it. The only thing that distinguishes writers is they can do it for long stretches at a time.'

'Well, that can't be as easy as it sounds.'

'My husband is also a writer,' said Tory, surprised at the sound of pride in her own voice. Though why shouldn't she be proud of Donald? He might be an awful typist, still pressing the keys at the slow rate he had started with, but he had persistence, a dogged determination to get to the end that was admirable.

'Does he write in a public lavatory as well?'

When Grace asked the inevitable question – what is your book about? – Tory again felt perfectly comfortable talking about her novel, which would have been impossible with anyone else.

'It keeps changing. At first it was about a woman whose husband is killed in the war, and she remarries. But at the end of the war it transpires that her husband was not dead at all, but had merely been held prisoner in the Far East. This is true – it happened quite a lot, because the Japanese often didn't let the Allies know if any of their men were being held prisoner, and they would be declared missing in action or dead. Well, like I said, this woman – she's called Charlotte – remarries and has a child during the war, but at the end of the war, her husband returns. So what does that mean for Charlotte's marriage? If her husband was never dead, then her second marriage isn't legal.'

'What a pickle,' said Grace.

'And what about the child? Who had legal custody of it – the illegally married natural father, or the legally married stepfather?'

'So, what happens?'

'Well, poor Charlotte is pulled this way and that – she's overjoyed that her first husband is alive, but she's now deeply in love with her second husband.'

'Things could get very difficult.'

'To make things worse, her first husband has been mentally damaged by his brutal treatment in the prison camp and has developed a violent tendency.'

'What does he think of the second husband?'

'He despises him, and is even violent towards him. For a while, Charlotte is afraid that he'll kill her second husband, or even her child.'

'And does he?'

'Well, this is what I can't decide. My original story had the first husband killing the child, then Charlotte and her second husband taking revenge on him in rather sickening ways. But now I'm thinking that the first husband should be saved, and that there should be a happier ending.'

'Perhaps the three of them could live together in what they call a ménage!'

'Grace, you are saucy. It started off being rather closely based on my own life, and now it's veering off in different ways because my life is changing so much. I have a husband who was a prisoner of war and who changed in peculiar ways. I had an affair and had a child, and I was afraid that my husband would kill my little boy. In fact, it was my older child who died, in such a way that I blamed Donald. But now Donald is rediscovering his good side and I can see that his behaviour wasn't all his fault.'

'How very touching. I think I prefer the revenge story, But, Tory, I didn't know you'd lost a child. Now I can see why you have a tragic look about you. You must be weighed down with sadness.'

How was it that she could talk to this woman about Tom's death, even telling her those aspects of it that she found most difficult to contemplate – its dreadful loneliness, the macabre tableau it must have presented to its discoverers, the inge-niousness of it, the efficiency? The manner of his death so rejected the possibility of life, gave it no chance, no corner. When she thought about that, Tory couldn't help but feel that life itself was, in the end, a broken, badly designed, inefficient, wasteful thing. In which case, why should any of us be troubled by it? Non-existence, now there was efficiency. The perfect uninterrupted span of blackness and silence that goes on for ever, and which is our ultimate destiny anyway. All of this she told Grace, who listened with the calm focus of someone who is unsurprised. Though at the end Tory couldn't quite believe that Grace was kneeling beside her, kissing away the tears that were rolling down her face.

Tory blushed. Running water, she thought. Running water.

CHAPTER 22

Donald's typing went on for so many weeks and months that the noise of it slowly disappeared. The jabbing, punching sounds of the keys that had so disrupted the regular music of the house (clocks ticking and chiming, sinks filling and emptying, gas rings thumping into life, pots bubbling, stairs creaking) became just another of the background sounds that one only heard when they stopped. Tory found great comfort in the sound. It didn't matter to her if Donald was writing something that would ever be published, and in fact she thought it very unlikely that he actually was or, even if he did, that he would ever make much money from it. She was comforted by the simple fact that he was occupied in something productive, and it helped to alleviate the pangs she felt at having her own ambitions as a writer checked and brushed aside. It could only be good for the family, after all, that Donald was so busy. He had even cut down on the frequency of his visits to the Rifleman, and the sinister miscreants he used to bring back with him no longer visited.

His mood and temperament were also softened.

She began to think that his writing of his memoirs was a way of coming to terms with Tom's death. More than anything, she hoped he would explain himself. That he would present her with a document that would account for the sort of person he had become, or had been in danger of becoming. She would forgive him even if it turned out to be a self-pitying account, so long as it gave evidence that he had thought about himself and the effect he was having on those around him.

He did not show her any of his writing, but he did eventually begin to talk a little more freely about his experiences during the war.

He described some of his fellow prisoners, what a good bunch of chaps they were, like brothers to him, some of them. He talked a little about a man who wrote poetry as good as Rupert Brooke's.

Tory remembered an occasion when she had encountered Donald and one of his guests in the passageway, and he had introduced the fellow as a war poet. 'This is Harry Wilde. We were in the Stalag together. Harry's what's called a war poet, aren't you, Harry?'

'Well, I can't deny that I was on occasion moved to turn out some verses in response to the great débâcle . . .' He gave an exaggerated, drawling French pronunciation to that last word. Tory remembered him because the fellow didn't conceal his face with collar and hat brim as the others did, but instead presented her with a rather dignified, elegant countenance, which did look very like what she imagined a poet's face to be – delicate, pale and pretty.

At times, Donald would even be forthcoming about life in the prison camp, though she began to wonder if he wasn't inventing some of it. 'We slept on bunks with bare slats, no mattress, just straw-filled burlap sacks. you traded *Zigaretten* for favours from the guards . . .'

'But how did you fill your days? What did you do?'

'I made a piano.'

'A piano? Are you mad?'

'No, over the years I made a piano. Not that hard. I scavenged bits of wood from all around the camp – no one was going to miss the odd slat from a bed, and there were hundreds of beds, little bits of skirting, anything really. I used glue reconstituted from the carpenter's glue that had been used already on the beds and other furniture, scraped it off, ground it down to powder, mixed it with water and heated it on the stove – good as new. I used a bit of broken glass for a modelling knife. For strings I used cat gut, from a real cat, Fritz, we called him, though his real name was Hermann, one of the guards' cats, used to give a Hitler salute when he was washing his ears, used to give us proper uppity looks, and definitely used to smile when the guards were shouting at us, or beating us, so we had no qualms when he came into our hut one night. We tortured the little Nazi moggy to death and ripped his intestines out.

318

Made super strings for my piano. We buried the body to avoid detection, and didn't half laugh to see the guards panicking about where little Fritz had gone – '*Wo Hermann ist?* Wo meine Katze ist?' Would you believe it? Big guard in jack boots holding out pieces of cat food under the huts to tempt out his missing moggy, then sobbing when no Nazi miaowing came in reply. Honestly, they snuff out six million Jews without a second thought but start weeping over a missing cat.'

It seemed odd, to say the least, that Donald should have filled his time with such a project. He was not a musical man; he never had been. He certainly couldn't play the piano.

'I thought I could make a piano, then learn to play it. The war poet could have taught me because he could play. You don't understand, Tory, what it does to a man to have his days emptied of everything except a morning roll call – *eins, zwei, drei* – when there are people dropping dead from starvation and sickness all around you, chaps walking about with half their faces blown off, trying to whistle merry little tunes through burnt lips just to make it seem like nothing's up, who politely decide to take their meals on their own – if you could have called them meals – sawdust bread and black sauerkraut – because they know it makes you sick to watch them putting food into their tongueless mouths, poor blighters. What do you think it does to you, Tory, a life like that? That piano was the only thing that kept me going. I could see you looked shocked when I talked about Fritz, but you grew to hate everything about the Germans, everything, even their animals . . .'

He had brought himself close to tears by telling her these things, so that Tory regretted, not for the first time, asking about them. The intimations he gave of a terrible life (someone had estimated there were seventeen barbs of barbed wire for every prisoner in the camp) lived over those five years softened her heart a great deal, and she felt ever more strongly the need to forgive him for his behaviour since his return.

'What do you think it does to a man, Tory? Look at my hands . . .' He held the two jointed plates splayed before her, each digit shaking like a mouse. 'How can a man be expected to just take up his old life and pretend none of it ever happened?'

'Is Daddy writing a book?' said Branson, one day.
  'Yes, he is.'
'What's it about?'
'It's about his time in the army.'
'Did Daddy kill anyone?'
It made Tory feel very strange when he referred to Donald as 'Daddy'. Stranger still, when Donald referred to Branson as 'sonny'.

For Branson's tenth birthday, Tory had made a very special effort. She had left the public lavatory early and had rushed around the shops, buying presents and food for the party. She had

320

rushed home and decorated the dining room with balloons and paper chains, more festively even than for Christmas Day itself. She had made a large cake in the shape of the Bluebird, and a large jelly in the shape of a rabbit, using the three-pint mould. She had allowed Branson to invite some friends around after school. It was a bigger party than usual, to mark Branson's entry into double figures. She was hopeful, very hopeful, that Donald would attend.

Up until Tom's death Branson had been a blank space in Donald's notion of his family, an un-contoured part of the family map. It broke Tory's heart when his cutting of Branson became so evident, as it did at Christmas and birthdays. She had always done her best for the children on these occasions, and Donald, even, could be mustered to exit his sitting room and make an appearance for the little celebrations that marked the anniversaries of Tom, Paulette and Albertina. He would sing along with 'Happy Birthday', and would shock everyone with his atonal gusto, always dominating the verses with a growling, over-emphatic pronunciation of the particular child's name – *Alber-TI-NAAAA*! (It had always struck Tory how he could turn anyone's name, just by stress, into a kind of insult, as though to say, There, I didn't choose that stupid name for you.) As the girls grew older he would embarrass them by making reference to their developing bodies, as though he only ever noticed their physical presence on their birthdays.

'Well, my little dear, you're getting round and soft in all the right places – or is that cotton wool I see tucked into your bra?'

The girl would redden, glance at her mother, unable to speak from embarrassment.

'Come on, now, you're a woman, near enough . . .'

'She's twelve, Donald, and I don't think you should speak to her like that.'

'Well, what about a birthday kiss from your pa?'

And he would swing his stiff leg around the table to kiss his daughter on the lips, an experience from which she would shrink back as far as it was possible to shrink.

Christmas was the time that his cutting of Branson became most evident, when Donald would again emerge from his room to make an elaborate show of minor gift-giving. It was he who gave Tom his first pipe, wrapped up in a little box. He always thought it a good joke to wrap a small gift in outsize wrapping, so that he would present Albertina with an enormous parcel decorated with Christmas trees, and she would unwrap a box (just big enough, everyone thought, to be the doll's house she longed for) to find that within it, in the centre of a lot of weighty padding, there was nothing but a steel thimble that wasn't even new. He would laugh a nasty, mocking laugh. 'Now then Alber-T I-NAAAAA, are you saying you don't like my present?' Tory was thinking, If only you could wrap up something large to make it seem small. Imagine the delight on Albertina's face if she was given a present the size of a thimble, which would unfold, when unwrapped, into a magnificent doll's house.

Tory wondered how she could have allowed her husband to be so hurtful to Branson, remembering all those birthdays he had snubbed, either making no appearance or pointedly leaving the room the moment the cake appeared, slamming the door behind him, or all those Christmases when he had given a present to everyone except the little boy, who bore his exclusion with stoical resolve.

'He's trying to make him feel as though he doesn't belong,' said her mother.

'For what purpose? Does he imagine I'll say, yes, Branson can go back to wherever he came from, which is nowhere?'

Now Tory was hopeful that things were changing. Donald had begun to acknowledge Branson's existence, even if he had not gone so far as showing him any affection. She hoped he would take the opportunity of the tenth birthday party to do this. But as she and Mrs Head made preparations for the big event, Donald was not in his room and had, it seemed, left the house

The party was a delightful event and seemed to take Branson entirely by surprise. He had not been expecting anything like the spread that filled the dining-room table, or the gaily nodding balloons that hung from every corner of the room, and he could not help but let out a gasp of delight. In fact he was more taken by the food on the table, and the giant jelly rabbit, which was the centrepiece, than the little stack of presents beside it.

The rabbit was a marvellous thing, the biggest jelly Tory had ever made, lime-flavoured, with blades of grass visible around its feet, even noticeable stippling on its body to represent fur. And the whole thing swayed and bobbed, undulated and quivered. When the children arrived they gasped and tittered, jiggling and jogging the table to make it wobble even more, laughing more loudly as the wobbling grew. They bent down and looked through its transparent body at their distorted friends on the other side.

Nothing wobbles quite as well as Farraway's gelatine, thought Tory, wondering if she had just coined a lucrative advertising slogan. But it was true: it seemed of a lighter, looser structure. Other jellies might simply shiver and shake, but the Farraway's jelly did a sort of belly-dance and fandango, an exotic, chaotic, squirming, writhing rumba. As she watched the jelly-rabbit leaping and jumping, surrounded by the excited children, she couldn't help laughing at the idea that it was there as a sort of jelly-proxy for George, Branson's real father.

She was having lots of odd thoughts. She wondered whether she could write a little story about a woman who, spurned by her lover, renders him in fruity gelatine, then consumes him, spoonful by spoonful, from the top down.

The rabbit had lost his head and most of the front half of his body by the time Donald appeared.

His presence could not have produced a silence more instantly had he been a headless spectre. The children, even those who had seen him before, were frightened. His now very pronounced limp, his smooth, hairless head (apart from those devil-like tufts), caused some to think that he was a particularly macabre clown. They edged closer together, as if for protection.

'I hear it's some little boy's birthday today!' he said, in a growly but friendly voice, which made the children laugh. They had by now noticed that he was holding a present. 'Who's the birthday boy?' he said.

Branson was too shy to give any acknowledgement, and a slightly dopey schoolfriend, not aware that Donald was joking, said seriously, 'It's Branson's birthday today.'

'Branson's birthday,' said Donald, breathlessly, as if it was a truly astonishing fact. 'Branson's birthday.' And he held out the present for Branson to take.

The thing contained in the gaudy wrapping was not a piece of rubbish but something new, pretty and delightful. It was a little brass telescope.

'Isn't that a darling little thing?' said Tory to Branson, who was glowing with appreciation of the present. 'What do you say to your father?'

'Thank you, Father,' said Branson, without a moment's hesitation, the words falling easily from his tongue, as though they had always been there, waiting.

Tory, under a pretence of clearing the table, went to the kitchen and wept.

CHAPTER 23

George no longer swooped. Now that Branson was out of his infancy and approaching adolescence, the surprise visits and benevolent ambushes had stopped. It seemed that George couldn't resist the charms of a baby or toddler (picking him up from his pram, exclaiming at how he wobbled) but was indifferent to the older child. Oh, if we only treated each other with the care and devotion we give to little children, the world would be a wonderful place, Tory thought. She missed the trickle of George's cash, the pound note discreetly tucked into the bedding of the pram, the fivers. Once Mrs Head had found one when she changed the blankets in the pram while it was parked in the passage. 'What's this?' she exclaimed, as the note fell like a leaf to the floor. 'Tory, you're becoming careless with your cash. Good heavens,' unfolding the five-pound note, 'where on earth did you get this?'

She not only missed the money. She missed George and was worried that he would forget about his son altogether.

It had been more than ten years since her last

visit to the factory, and the whole place seemed to have become more disgusting. Perhaps it was simply that she had, in the post-war years, become less accustomed to horror, but the piles of bones and stacks of hides now seemed to give off an overwhelming stench of rottenness. They looked less like raw materials for something new, more like the remains of some corrupt, perverted activity. In general the factory seemed less productive, less busy. There was no sound of machinery. There were just the boxers, pounding each other in the gym, Mr Farraway in his vest, a cigar in his mouth, urging them on. He looked significantly older now, frighteningly old. How could she ever have fallen for such an old man? But he was still strong. When he saw her enter the gym he sprang down from the ring like a cat, prowled the floor towards her, sparring jokingly with a trainee on the way, then came up to her.

Tory realized she hadn't thought where to start and, in trying to find the words, became overwhelmed and so let out her emotions in one long stream of sobbing. Boxers in the distance dropped their fists and turned in her direction. George put a consoling arm around her to steer her towards the door and the privacy of the yard beyond.

'This reminds me of the very first time you came to my gym, all those years ago. You were so nervous, do you remember? Like a little mouse creeping into a den of cats. But now you breeze in as though you've been visiting boxing gyms all your life.'

Yes, he was an old man but, gosh, those muscled limbs of his, the strength in them. She remembered how vast he had seemed, nude in the little cottage bedroom, like a giant folded up and tucked into a shoebox.

'I have become stronger,' said Tory, abstractedly, almost to herself.

'Well, that's what gyms are for. I must say, your prettiness hasn't diminished one bit. It has increased, if anything.'

'I prefer to be called beautiful.'

This stumped George for a moment. He seemed unsure if Tory was being serious or not. It was apparent he saw no difference between the words. 'Pretty, beautiful. I'll use any words you like. They are sincerely meant.'

'Tom has died.'

She didn't know why she had said this. George could scarcely have known who Tom was. This was not what she had come to tell him at all. 'He killed himself,' she went on, when George made no reply.

'I'm sorry,' he said. He was leaning with one arm against the factory wall, as if sheltering Tory, who was resting with her back to the brickwork. Bluebottles were going crazy somewhere nearby.

'I was so proud of him, but he was never happy after he was taken out of school. That was Donald's doing, sending him out to earn money before he was ready. He'd wanted to go to university, you know.'

'I remember you saying he was a bright boy.'

328

'I need your help, George. I really do. We have no money coming in, apart from my job, which doesn't amount to much. Mother's taking in washing, and that's all we've got to live on.' She left out details of Mrs Head's generous widow's pension, and the money from her various investments.

'I thought Mr Attlee had provided for everyone in need.'

Tory sobbed again, even though she didn't feel like it. George was a big man and only responded to big emotions. So she didn't exactly feel she was exaggerating when she said, 'I can hardly afford to feed the family. The girls are nearly women now and take a lot of feeding. Branson is ten – think of that. I can sometimes see a frightening thinness in him, and I think – the boy is actually undernourished – what with polio about, I'm terrified he won't even live to be an adult.'

The thought of his own flesh and blood being denied nourishment and going lean seemed to stir George. 'I'll tell you what I'll do,' he said, after a moment's thought. 'Wait here.'

He disappeared inside the gym and returned a few moments later with a small brown glass bottle. 'These will help.'

'What are they?'

'I want you to give one to Branson every day.'

She unscrewed the top and peered into the neck of the bottle. Brown, torpedo-shaped tablets nestled within.

'Protein tablets,' said George. 'This is what I'm feeding my young boxing champions on.'

'Is that the best you can do?' Tory was furious and felt like throwing the bottle of pills right back at him. In fact, she raised her hand as if about to do so, but in a flash George had caught her hand in his own. He examined her fingernails.

'It's the same with everything,' he said. 'If you don't persist with it, it won't have any effect. Protein pills, Christianity, I daresay even socialism. They'd all work if we devoted ourselves to them. Well, unlike the latter two, my pills take very little by way of commitment. Just three a day. And a pint of water. You might live for ever like that.'

Tory couldn't help letting out a half-giggle of incredulity. He seemed to really mean it. Eternal life in pill form.

'Try them,' George said. 'I guarantee you, if you feed these to Branson you won't need to feed him anything else. They're not just proteins, they contain everything you need for a nutritious diet. I'll supply you with enough to feed your whole family, for ever. Think of the saving, Tory. You will never have to buy food again. These pills and some water, that's all you'll need.'

'Well, I don't want to appear ungrateful, but I was hoping you could give me some money to help raise Branson.'

'Money? Are you off your trolley? I haven't made any money for years. The factory's being run down. We'll be closing for good before the year's out.'

'I thought things had been going well for you since the end of the war. I saw you've got your own brand of gelatine in the shops now. Farraway's gelatine – I bought some the other day. For Branson's tenth birthday, in fact. I made a three-pint rabbit.'

Tory noticed a bluebottle land on George's bare shoulder and start to suck the sweat there, as if through a straw. She thought that the insect looked as though it was wearing boxing gloves.

'Ten years,' said George, thoughtfully.

'So you can't tell me things are going downhill when you have Farraway's gelatine on every birthday-party table in the land.'

'Yes, stronger and bolder.' He smiled. 'Packet jelly was the last roll of the die, Tory, and a way of using up our stocks once the price of gelatine fell through the floor. It hasn't been a great success, I'm sorry to say. The market has been saturated with cheap imported gelatine for some years now. We've put everything into these protein pills. I call them the food of the future. It's very sad. We aren't even using our own gelatine, but are buying it from abroad. Much cheaper than making it ourselves. I'm converting this factory, slowly, for protein and vitamin production. It's costing us dearly, investing in new machinery and processes. Have you any idea how much scientific research costs? Boffins are dearer than lawyers. And with all the testing that has to be done, thanks to your darling Mr Attlee, who has completely scuppered the market for medicines, I'm wondering how I'm ever going to make any money out of it. What we need, you see, is firm evidence that these pills can replace food. My boxers are part of that proof but they're not very scientific. They tell me they eat nothing but my pills, but how am I to know they don't go home in the evening and scoff heaps of pies?'

'You're using your young boxers as laboratory mice?'

'Hardly mice, my darling, hardly mice. More like laboratory bulls, or steers, or bucking broncos. Come on, take a look, take a look.'

He steered her back through the doorway into the cavernous gym, where the trainee boxers had resumed their sparring. The young men fighting looked pale and thin, but were clearly very strong, and could jab with their arms as fast as cats.

'I'm afraid I seem to be running a gym that specializes in light-weights. I'd give anything for a good, meaty welterweight, not to speak of a heavy-weight or two. But that's the war and rationing for you, I suppose. A starved nation can produce nothing but these waifs. Still, good muscle there, and all on nothing but Farraway's pills and water – well, near enough. Listen, I'd like you to feed Branson these pills, three times a day, breakfast, lunch and supper.'

'Are you quite serious?'

'Absolutely.'

'You think one of these pills will do for a plate of bacon and eggs?'

'Yes.'

'And roast beef with Yorkshire pudding?'

'Yes, and no washing-up afterwards.'

'And no proper food?'

George shook his head, then gestured towards the distant fighters.

'But you yourself just said you don't know what they eat when they go home. I don't believe a growing boy could survive on three of these little pellets.'

'If you think the bulk of the body is related to the bulk of the food we eat, then you're deluded, my dear. How much mass do you think a growing boy gains in a single day? If he puts on a stone in a year, that amounts to less than half an ounce a day. Three of my pills weigh more than half an ounce. Moreover, it's the density of the goodness contained in the pills that matters. Each pill contains the equivalent amount of protein that you'd get in a small fillet steak, It also contains the same amount of vitamin C that you'd get in a bag of oranges, the same amount of calcium as a quart of milk, the same amount of iron as in a bowl of spinach – and much more – all in a single pill. To put it bluntly, if you weigh the food and drink we take in, then weigh what comes out of the other end, the difference will amount to the weight of one of my pills.'

It seemed that George had become a visionary. He spoke of an end to hunger and an end to poverty. Food production for the entire population could be provided by a few farms. The population of the entire world could be fed from an acreage not much greater than England's existing dairy farmland. Class barriers and racial divides could be bridged because we could all be eating fundamentally the same thing, and the opportunities for social conflict are so often based around what we eat, he said.

'Quite a potential market for your pills.'

'And I'd like you to weigh Branson at regular intervals, measure his height and note them down in a book. Would you do that for me?'

'So you want Branson to be another of your little laboratory mice.'

'You can call it that, if it pleases you. I need as much scientific evidence as I can if I want these pills to be a success. The fact that they work is not enough. They have to be seen to work.'

Tory knew from the moment she examined the pills that they would not offer an alternative to food. When she came home that evening, Branson was at the dining-room table, drawing circles freehand on a sheet of brown parcel paper. They were surprisingly good circles, which, seen from a distance, seemed perfect. Branson did seem to enjoy pointlessly intense activities. She was late and Mrs Head had been out all afternoon attending the funeral of one of her friends. Everyone was hungry. She thought, for a moment, that she might simply sprinkle some of George

Farraway's protein pills on the table and say, 'There, that's your dinner,' and imagined the baffled look she would receive in response. As for secretly feeding her youngest son concentrated protein and nothing else, the idea was quite insulting.

He's always trying to make me eat or drink something, Tory thought. She had tried his nail drink, remembering the vile peppermint concoction that clung to the sides of the lavatory when she'd vomited it once. It was nothing more than liquefied jelly. She didn't think that the protein pills would be much better. He wants to make us all into jelly. He wants to turn us all into things that are soft, indifferent, transparent. That's what he's after. For a moment a vision filled her mind, of the human race converted to jelly: rows of jelly people standing at bus stops, wobbling slightly, jelly people sitting in seats at the picture palace, jelly armies going to war with each other, not moving, apart from a slight wobbling, fixed as if from a mould, holding a jelly rifle, strawberry flavoured. A sweet world, all glisten and sheen, but a dead one.

She heard later about George's ventures with the protein pills, when they reached the pages of the national press.

He had persuaded one of his protégés to adhere rigidly to a regime of nothing but flavoured fortified gelatine. Alec Stott, his name was, destined for great things. George had visions of him holding aloft the Lonsdale Belt while proclaiming that in the last six months nothing but Farraway's Protein Pills had passed his lips. *What? No food at all?* He imagined the astonished reporters exclaiming. No, no food at all. Just pills and water. Gentlemen, the new world lightweight champion is the product of the Farraway Food-free Diet.

Alec Stott himself was keen for glory in any form, and so was quite willing to forgo the grey stews his mother set before him every evening in favour of a torpedo of compressed sustenance. He gulped down twelve pills a day as part of his training regime, and swore that he was feeling stronger than ever. And it was true – he was on magnificent form, punishing his sparring partners, the punchbags, the skipping rope, the mats. In the gym he gave off energy like a two-bar fire – the equipment and people were considerably warmer after his visit. He flattened a string of opponents to work his way up to a South of England Championship title, the furthest anyone had progressed from the malodorous environs of Farraway's gym. He fought at York Hall, Bethnal Green, before a capacity crowd of more than a thousand. Stepping into the ring to a roar of applause, he looked every inch a champion. Then, before he'd even received a blow, he took a swing at his opponent, missed, spun round, fell on the floor and died.

The post-mortem came to a conclusion about the cause of death that had the coroner looking with puzzled eyes at all about him for weeks.

This apparently healthy, ambitious young athlete had all the symptoms (the blackened lips, the shrunken stomach, the fungi in the oesophagus) of one rarely seen cause of death: starvation.

There was an inquiry. George Farraway's little experiment came to light. Yes, he had fed Alec Stott on nothing but these so-called protein pills for the last six months. Alec Stott's mother had trusted Mr Farraway completely, and believed with him that the pills were a perfect food substitute – better than food. The chemical composition of the pills was analysed. A conclusion was reached that cartilaginous protein was virtually useless in the human diet, and could not be used as a substitute for meat-based protein. The boffins that George had paid so highly were now turning against him. Alec Stott, they said, had survived on nothing but will-power and self-belief for the last six months of his life, along with a meagre trickle of vitamins and minerals.

Business from then on was difficult for George. He escaped prosecution but was given a strong warning about his training practices. He sold the gelatine factory to an American firm, but had enough money invested elsewhere to save him from disaster and, indeed, he was able now to devote himself entirely to the training of young boxers. He bought new premises on the Dartford road. A fully equipped, brand-new gym. He invested in

337

some of the holiday-camp businesses that were springing up in the coastal resorts.

He used the Wealden cottage as a warehouse to store nearly a million protein pills, enough to feed the entire population of the county of Kent for three days.

CHAPTER 24

After what felt like years of slow, steady progress, the heavy mechanical stutter of Donald's typing came to an end. It was some time before anyone noticed. Tory wasn't sure how many days it was before she suddenly became aware of the new silence at the back of their lives, as sweet and as even as a layer of fresh snow.

There was no other indication that Donald's work was finished. Tory wasn't sure what she'd been expecting – perhaps that her husband would stagger from the room that had become known as Daddy's Study with a pile of papers in his arms and slam them on the dining-table, saying, 'There you are, the product of all that work – My War Memoirs, The Keys To Freedom.'

But nothing like that happened. Mrs Head claimed to have known all along that the typing had stopped, and that the typewriter had been silent for some days.

'He has either finished his book or broken his typewriter,' she said.

Tory flinched at the word 'his'. 'Oh, I'm sure

he's finished it. If he had broken the typewriter, we would know about it. He would have made the same sort of fuss he makes when he runs out of paper or ribbon, gets us all in a panic to go into town to replenish his stock. I should think the typewriter breaking down would have caused havoc in the house.'

'Well, if he's finished his book, perhaps he'll let us read it.'

Yes, surely now Donald would allow his memoirs to be read. She looked forward to the evocations of barbed wire and sandy compounds, the thoughtful depiction of confinement and its frustrations, the soldiers longing to fight or to be home with their loved ones. It would be so important for Branson and the girls to know what their father had gone through, and why he was the man he had been when he came back.

Donald emerged from his study and limped through the dining room on his way to the yard. At first it seemed he would make this journey in his usual silence, but by the door he paused and turned, as if about to make an announcement. 'You know, I've been thinking. It's about time we had a television set in this wee house.'

The eyes of the children brightened.

'I don't think we could afford one of those,' said Mrs Head.

'Well, perhaps you won't have to afford one,' said Donald.

'Why? Have you come into some money?'

Donald unfolded the newspaper he'd been holding under his arm. 'Wright's, the electrical shop on the high street. They're renting them for two shillings a week.'

Tory came straight out with the question: 'Donald, have you finished your book?'

'Two shillings a week.' He avoided Tory's eyes, and was looking, for some reason, at Mrs Head, who in turn was looking at the bulrushes that had recently been installed in a vase on the dresser. Mrs Head was the least likely candidate for an ally in his campaign for a television. 'And with the coronation coming up, we wouldn't want to miss the crowning of the new Queen of England, would we?'

'I don't think we should be allowed to have a queen,' said Branson, who had recently taken to teasing his older sisters. 'It should be a "kings only" country.'

The sisters, who lately seemed much older than their years and had even acquired boyfriends, didn't rise to his bait.

'Donald, I asked you a question.'

He dropped his paper in exasperation. 'What are you asking me about my book for when I've got pressing matters on my mind like when we're going to get a television so we can watch the beautiful Princess Elizabeth be made queen of this country?'

'But have you finished it?'

'Well, as a matter of fact, I have.'

'When can I read it?'

'That will be rather difficult, dear Tory, because I have already passed the manuscript on to my agent.'

'You've got an agent?'

Even Mrs Head was drawn away from her contemplation of the bulrushes by this news.

'Of course. Every author has to have an agent.'

'But who is he?'

'He is none other than Mr Harry Wilde, former prisoner of war, and former war poet.'

It was noticeable that everyone, including the children, sank back into their chairs at this information.

'Oh, Donald, I thought you meant you'd got a proper agent.'

'Mr Harry Wilde is a man with very good connections. He is an educated man and a literary man. Put those three things together and you have got an agent.'

Tory thought otherwise. She did not like Mr Harry Wilde at all. On the few occasions that they had met (he was a frequent visitor to the house, though rarely made himself known to anyone other than Donald, who seemed to hide him away, like some sort of contraband), she had thought him sly and slippery and very condescending. He seemed to despise the female sex, as she could tell just by the way he looked at her. And she remembered now that she had overheard them making lewd remarks once about the princesses, whose pictures must have been in the paper.

There had been only one occasion when they had ever talked at any length, and that was when Harry Wilde had called while Donald was out and had accepted Tory's grudging invitation for him to come inside and wait. To her surprise, instead of waiting alone in the study as she would have expected, he had come through to the dining room and sat himself at the table.

She had known that Wilde had been assisting Donald with his book. Donald had only half jokingly referred to Mr Harry Wilde as his editor. They certainly seemed to spend hours together in the study, presumably going through what Donald had written. If she listened carefully, she could hear papers rustling and comments being made, though very quietly, and when she could interpret something it seemed of the trivial sort – 'Do you think we've spelt this right, Harry?'

'So, you're helping my husband with his book?' she said to him, on this occasion.

'I'm offering my services, such as they may be, to my friend and brother-in-arms, yes.'

'He doesn't say much about it to me, you know.'

'I'm not surprised.'

'Why?'

'You husband's memoir does contain some rather – how shall I put it? – unsavoury material.'

'Unsavoury?'

'Or perhaps *visceral* would be a better word.'

Tory paused. She wasn't a hundred per cent sure she knew what the word meant.

Mr Harry Wilde could see this, and enjoyed her uncertainty. 'If you understand what I mean.'

'Yes.'

'We want to make it a straightforward, honest and open account, and that means not shying away from the details.'

'I see. And I suppose you think I'm too fragile to read such details.'

'Well, I would have thought so, yes.'

This was before Tory had started working at the public lavatories.

'We had our share of 'visceral' moments here on the home front, you know.' The penny had suddenly dropped for her, and she enjoyed throwing the word back at this paper-thin man of letters. His face visibly dropped, scarcely less so than if she had lobbed a little piece of offal at him. 'Yes, a bomb landed on the butcher's just round the corner from here. I suspect we saw more blood than Donald did in most of his time as a PoW.'

'I wouldn't bank on that, my dear.'

'Did you ever see his piano?'

'Piano?'

'Yes, the piano he made in the camp. He told me all about that. One of the few things he was willing to talk about.'

Mr Harry Wilde was obviously having trouble recalling the instrument, helping to confirm Tory in her belief that he had never taken up arms in his life, let alone been an inmate of a prisoner-of-war camp.

'Surely it must take up a large part of Donald's memoirs, making that piano, finding the glue, then killing that poor Nazi cat . . .'

Wilde looked at her as though she was a mad woman, his mouth hanging slightly open. Without changing his expression he somehow managed to say, 'Yes, of course. The piano.'

'I suppose lots of the men filled their time with things like that, didn't they? Did you make anything?'

Wilde crossed his legs, evidently feeling uncomfortable. 'Well, as a matter of fact, yes. I made a bird table.'

'That can't have taken long.'

'Out of matchsticks.'

'That sounds a little more impressive.'

'My only mistake was to use live ones. Swan Vestas. Unfortunately, when a Nazi blackbird with a particularly abrasive beak landed and started pecking at the seed, the whole thing went up like a firework, toasting several Nazi sparrows.'

'I see you must take me for a fool, if you think I would believe such a story.'

'Not at all.'

Harry Wilde was annoyingly handsome, though in a way more suited to his former Nazi captors: he looked like a paragon of Aryan breeding, with blue eyes and golden hair. Curls fluttered across his forehead, to be swept back with a single finger. His moustache was small, hardly worth bothering with, and certainly not worth the amount of

345

attention he gave it, constantly preening with that same single finger, maintaining the all-important symmetry. Though she couldn't help but find Mr Wilde visually fascinating, Tory was immune to his appeal. She was wary that her interest would be misinterpreted as attraction.

'I must say,' he went on, 'from Donald's descriptions, I had no idea his wife was so pretty.'

Tory was so shocked by the sudden praise, coming from this sullen, bored man that she couldn't reply but felt herself blushing. *Running water*, she kept thinking to herself. *Running water*.

'Not that he did you a disservice, you understand. It's just that he never described you at all. Never brought you to our attention, in the way that some chaps did. They liked to talk endlessly about their supposedly beautiful wives. I'm sure in nearly all cases the reality would have been a mighty disappointment. But not you, my dear, no description could have done you justice.'

Never had Tory been so pleased at the return of Donald to the house, when his limping entrance brought an end to this ghastly serenade.

'I am quite against the idea of a television,' said Mrs Head. 'Mrs Lippiatt's sister has bought a set. She says she and her husband do nothing all day but sit and stare at the thing, even when it's switched off. I don't think it can be very good for the brain.'

'Well, if you're saying you're not interested in

346

watching the dawning of a new Elizabethan Age, then I think you're not only being unpatriotic, you're being a traitor as well. I suppose you don't even care if we no longer have an empire . . .'

Donald went off on one of his increasingly frequent rants. He had never seemed quite the same since Churchill was kicked out of office, and even though the Labour government had proved itself incapable and Churchill was back, he sometimes seemed to regard himself as the only true patriot in a nation of traitors. In the ensuing debate the matter of his memoir was forgotten, but Mrs Head's frailty became very apparent.

'All this talking is making me weak,' she said, and sat down. She rarely sat down during the day, but this time she sat down and didn't get up again for any length of time, ever.

CHAPTER 25

T ory began to think that old age and childhood were similar in more than the obvious
ways. The rapid changes that occur in the
body between birth and adulthood, when children
seem to be continually racing out of their own
skins, are echoed at the other end of life when the
body, which has been in a state of barely percep-
tible change for forty or fifty years, suddenly goes
into a state of accelerated collapse. This, at least,
was what seemed to be happening to Mrs Head.
While it was true that Tory's mother appeared to
have been an old lady for a very long time, recently
she had started to look more than just old.

It had been happening since Tom's death, Tory
now understood, which must have affected her
mother more deeply than she'd realized. Thinking
back, it was shortly after the funeral that she'd first
noticed Mrs Head's slight decrease in energy: a
certain slowness in climbing the stairs, a loud gasp
of relief whenever she sat down, as though merely
being upright was the most exhausting thing in the
world. Then came the reluctant appeals to her
daughter for assistance in minor tasks. She needed

help taking the rugs out into the backyard for beating. She had trouble with the mangle, whose wheel had become too stiff for her thinning arms. Soon she simply couldn't do these things and restricted herself to lighter duties. In the space of a couple of years she was reduced to little more than sitting in her chair all day, which had to be repositioned so that she could see out of the back window, not that there was a lot to see.

This decline in her energy was equalled by a deterioration in her appearance, a simultaneous loosening and tightening of the body, which seemed to contract into a ball within, leaving a loose, ill-fitting outer layer. The slowness and weakness of her body gradually became such that before long a dilemma presented itself to Tory. Sooner or later Mrs Head was not going to be able to use the stairs. The only possible outcome of this situation was that she would eventually have to sleep downstairs.

The prospect of Mrs Head moving downstairs played on Tory's mind for many months. Perhaps she had always known it would happen at some point, that the stairs, for her mother, would become a cliff she had no hope of climbing. But Tory had always assumed that, of all the muscles in Mrs Head's body, her leg muscles would be the last to go. They had always seemed so hard and durable. Mrs Head's legs, when she showed them – which was very rarely, since she retained a fondness for the long-skirt look that had gone out with

Edward VII – were like a sprinter's: they seemed to be made of rope, plaited together, capable of taking her anywhere, and could probably, though Tory had never witnessed it, deliver a jolly good kick. Tory imagined that, like a fallen clockwork toy, the legs would carry on walking, walking, walking, right into the grave. But, no: like the rest of her body, they were becoming weak.

Every evening it became a little bit more difficult to get her up the stairs, though Mrs Head herself was determined to accomplish the task, and wouldn't ask for help until the moment came when every last vestige of strength had been used up and there was nothing left but to call Tory. And then it became a co-operative exercise, a partnership. Mother and daughter were like mountaineers tackling a tricky rockface, relying on each other for support and encouragement. Mrs Head still did most of the work, holding on to the banister with both hands, lifting a foot with careful deliberation, placing it on the next stair, then pulling herself up to meet it. At first Tory's role was simply as 'catcher', following her mother a couple of steps behind, ready to save her if she fell. Then, by degrees, her assistance became more physical. She had to take one of her mother's arms and help her lift herself on to each step.

The mornings were just as difficult, if not more so. Mrs Head was confronted with what seemed now to be a waterfall of floral treads and risers, the sight of which had begun to upset her.

'Mama, we'll have to bring your bed downstairs. There's no alternative.'

Mrs Head reluctantly agreed, though she was not so concerned about what this would entail. Donald was now occupying the only room downstairs that could be used as a bedroom, and had done so since his return from Germany. If Mrs Head was to go down, Donald would have to come up.

'Donald,' Tory said to him one day, 'isn't it about time we lived together like a proper man and wife?'

'I thought we did.'

'Well, we don't. A proper married couple share the same bed, or at least share the same floor of the house. They don't sleep one upstairs, one downstairs.'

'Tory, how many times do I have to tell you? Stairs are out of the question for me.'

'But they are also becoming out of the question for Mrs Head.' And so it went on. The question revolved around which of them, Donald or Mrs Head, would find it most inconvenient to sleep upstairs. Donald, Tory argued, at least had one good leg, while Mrs Head was becoming weak in her entire body. Donald had strength, Mrs Head had none. Mrs Head was less likely to survive a fall down the stairs. Furthermore, Donald had a moral duty to sleep with his wife.

To push the argument further, Tory began to express a physical desire for Donald. This was not entirely contrived. It was true that since his return

351

from Germany she had, against her own best wishes, felt nothing but disgust for him, which had increased as his behaviour had worsened. By the time of Tom's death, he had had all the sexual appeal of a rat. But things had changed since then. His expressions of remorse for the loss of his son, and the deep, thoughtful seriousness with which he'd undertaken the writing of his memoirs, had begun to sweeten him as a physical presence. His glossy lizard scalp and browless eyes no longer seemed so demon-like. Now they looked tender, vulnerable and expressive. Since he'd stopped drinking and had begun eating properly, he had lost the ragged look he'd had. He had filled out and softened. Now, when she finished balming his head, she concluded the process with a kiss on the lips and tasted no sourness there.

She was balming his head now, as they spoke. He was seated, as usual, on one of the dining-chairs, and she was behind him, slowly working the ointment into his skin.

'If we could sleep together upstairs we could do the things that married couples are supposed to do,' she said, gracefully stroking his neck, then sliding her hand inside the open V of his shirt to feel a healthily fat breast.

'You mean the type of things you described so well in your letters?'

Tory withdrew her hand from Donald's breast and placed it on her own to check that her heart was beating. It was the first mention that had been

352

made of those letters in all the years since Donald's return.

'Yes,' she said hesitantly. 'Yes, if you like.'

A chill ran through her body. She had rather assumed that, as they had remained unacknowledged between herself and Donald for all these years, they had actually ceased to exist. Or she would go even further, and suppose that they had never existed, or that she had simply posted those lustful, obscene thoughts into the air. Now here was the truth: Donald's memory of them. He had talked her into acknowledging them and so bringing them back into the world.

'All of them?' he said.

Tory couldn't quite remember what she had written. 'I don't know, Donald.'

'How about this? I will promise to come upstairs if you promise to do everything you described in those letters.'

'But I can't remember what I wrote in them.'

'Oh, I can.'

'Donald – you haven't kept them, have you?'

'Only in here,' he said, tapping his shining head. 'But don't try and pretend you've forgotten.'

'Donald, isn't it better that we forget about certain things that happened during the war? I didn't write those letters.'

'Oh? Who did?'

'No, I mean they were written by a different me. One who was living in constant fear of being killed in an air raid, who was separated from her husband

353

and children and had to work in a filthy gelatine factory. I realize now what happens to people when they're so frequently at risk of death. It causes them to be so delighted with being alive that they want to experience it as fully as they can, to celebrate it almost. I suspect that is why you yourself were so overtaken by a need for gratification while you were in the camp. I have to admit I was a little shocked, not to say disgusted at first . . .'

She was repeating something Grace had said, in one of their many underground conversations. Dear Grace, she was so fond of the lavatories. She didn't mind even when the bad odours emanated. They could be sitting in their little office (Tory now thought of the office as 'theirs'), talking about some profound thing or other, then suddenly, from a stall, a little explosion followed by an engulfing cloud of pungency, of such deep richness that it couldn't possibly go unnoticed – and Grace wouldn't even miss a heartbeat. And yet she had been so delicate and shockable when she had first entered the lavatories and had seen the stall full of blood. When Tory remarked on this she had replied that it had been Tory's own consolations and reassurances that had helped her get through. 'I no longer fear anything in the world, not since I met you, Tory. And nothing disgusts me either, absolutely nothing . . .'

So Tory had told her about the letters she'd written to Donald, how she had been disgusted by the very idea at first but that she had, through her encounter with George Farraway, found a voice to express the things that Donald had wanted to hear, but that now, when she thought back to it, she was so shocked by what she had done she could hardly believe she had done it or that she was the same woman at all. And it was then that Grace extolled on her theories of war and sexual desire. 'Didn't you ever hear the screams during an air raid? I don't mean screams of fear or pain, I mean the screams of people making love. You'll think I'm mad, but I loved to walk the streets during a raid – they were always so completely empty. Did you ever do it? Absolutely magical, the whole city spread around us and not a chink of light to be seen, it was like walking in an enchanted forest, and no sound but for the wailing and moaning and whimpering of the people making love. Who were they? When all the young men were at war – were there so many on leave or excused call-up or conscientious objectors that there could be so many lovemakers? Or were they the infirm and the elderly? Perhaps they were. Or perhaps it was women making love to women – that's what I like to think, that in the absence of men, the remaining women had become overwhelmed by a lust for being alive, which transformed into a lust for each other . . .'

'Grace, what funny thoughts you have.'

But this view certainly helped explain her to herself. The madness with which she'd yielded to George Farraway – not just yielded but offered herself down to the last molecule of her being – could perhaps now be explained as an extreme sense of gratitude for being alive.

Donald was, eventually, persuaded at least to try the stairs.

His leg had got much worse over the years. It had become slightly arthritic and he was not able to bend it at all, or place much weight on it. This would have made it impossible to climb stairs in the normal way, but Tory had an idea that he could get up and down by sitting on the stairs and levering himself up on his bottom, a step at a time, backwards. Scornful of the idea at first, as much for its indignity as for its awkwardness, Donald nevertheless decided to give it a go and, after a few practice runs, was somewhat embarrassed to find that it was remarkably easy and safe – a little more strenuous than the conventional method, but one so easy that he was ashamed not to have thought of it himself.

It was very odd to see Donald upstairs, on the landing, in her bedroom. Tory couldn't help feeling invaded again.

'Got it arranged nice up here, haven't you?' he said. Was he surprised by the tidiness? It did have a preserved air, the upstairs, a saved quality that she was anxious about losing if she made it available to Donald. As they moved into the bedroom, he pretended that he had been kept from there against his will.

'At last, after all these years, I'm permitted to see where my wife sleeps . . .'

There was the same iron-framed bed with the battered beech headboard in which they'd spent their first married years.

'You were always welcome, Donald, always. You know that.'

'I remember the wallpaper. What did you call him?'

'The Seacunny. That's what Mrs Head called him anyway.'

The wallpaper had been on the wall since Tory herself had been a baby and she had slept in this room with Mrs Head. It depicted the repeated image of a man in an Oriental conical hat, standing up in the prow of a small, canoe-like boat, which he seemed to be paddling by means of a long pole, like a punt. The image had fascinated her as a child, and Mrs Head had told her stories about the figure which she called the Seacunny – where he was sailing to, what he was carrying in that little boat. Mrs Head's stories of the Seacunny were usually admonitory tales, in which he would sail off the walls and into the room itself, grow to life size and sweep the naughty little girl up into his funny boat, carry her back into the wallpaper, him and his hundreds of twins. She spent most of her childhood in fear of her wallpaper, so that she was eventually moved into the back bedroom with her sisters and more or less forgot about the Seacunny until she was a married woman and took up the master bedroom once her father had died and she and Donald began having children. Yes, the Seacunny had been watchful, the hundreds of him, as she undressed before her husband for the first time, watchful as they conjoined beneath the blankets in hushed copulation, there was no aspect of her sexual life with Donald that the Seacunny didn't know about. The Lascar oarsman. It frightened her to think that the Seacunny might see out her whole life, from birth to death.

'I think we should change this wallpaper soon.'

Tory enlisted the help of Mrs Wilson's husband Derek and his strong, lazy son, Timothy, to help her get Mrs Head's single bed downstairs and into the sitting room. Mrs Head was not going to sleep on the stained mattress that had served Donald for so long. Finally, it came to the moment when Donald would sleep in her bed.

He had by now become quite agile in his stair-climbing, managing the whole journey in less than a minute. At the top Tory listened with dread to his grunting, gasping efforts. Then, swinging himself into the room, his leg like a baton, clunking against the door frame, he sat on the side of the bed, his bad leg before him, connecting the bed with the floor, as straight as the gangplank of a ship.

'You remember that bargain we made?' he said, with his back to her. 'I want you to do everything you described . . .' He was unbuttoning his shirt, which he then took off, with a sort of struggle in

358

which he was briefly held in a half-nelson by it. '. . . every last detail.'

He was talking as though to a shopkeeper or tradesman, as though he was telling a plumber not to leave out any important bits of piping. Unseen by him, Tory began also to undress, more nervous of self-exposure than she had ever been – unbuttoning her cardigan as though picking a series of locks.

'You'll have to remind me,' she said quietly.

'Will I now?' The vest beneath the shirt was lifted over the sparkling head.

'It was a long time ago.'

Donald's shoulder-blades were frighteningly visible, shovelshaped. A good oarsman's shoulder-blades. Oh, he did look like the Seacunny, that funny little Lascar with his bald head and his unlashed eyes. Donald turned to look at Tory over his shoulder. By now she had unbuttoned her blouse and it was hanging open, exposing the silk camisole beneath.

'You know,' he said, his back still turned towards her, 'there are couples our age who have decided to put all this sort of thing behind them.'

He was taking his trousers down now. Still sitting, he did not reveal anything in the process, though for the first time, Tory became aware of an odd smell. It struck her, at first, as the same sort of smell you get from a roasting joint of lamb. It took her only a few moments to realize the smell came from Donald. By undressing, he had released a pent-up flock of odours from his rarely washed body. She caught a similar smell sometimes when she passed the living room in the morning, but had assumed that it had come from some food that Donald had taken in there, perhaps a corned-beef sandwich, or a kipper.

Tory turned her back on her husband so that she could continue undressing. With their backs to each other, they slowly set about the task. Tory found an excuse to delay proceedings by having difficulty with a button on her camisole, then realized that this put her at a disadvantage. If Donald undressed first, he could get into bed and watch the spectacle of her undressing at his leisure. She would have nowhere to hide. And this indeed was what happened. She heard the sound of the covers being pulled back and when she glanced over her shoulder she saw that Donald was covered, right up to his eyes, by the blankets. Because of his slightness, there was little shape of his body evident through the bedclothes, which made it appear as though there was nothing but a pair of eyes in the bed, resting on the pillow, and looking unblinkingly at her. To her surprise, she had found that, after the long struggle with the recalcitrant button, the result was that the camisole had become buttoned up again, and that, furthermore, her blouse was slipping its sleeves over her arms and buttoning itself again too. Things had gone into reverse and Tory was dressing.

'What are you doing?'

'I forgot to get Mrs Head her hot milk.'

'She'll be asleep by now.'

'No, she can't get to sleep without it. I must just check on her anyway.'

She said all this without really looking at Donald, although she could see that he was no longer just a pair of eyes, but had sat up a little, exposing his head and shoulders. She went out onto the landing. The girls were still awake, arguing quietly in their room. She went downstairs to the darkness of the kitchen, passing Mrs Head on the way. She was snoring quietly but with the intense, unwavering rhythm that indicated deep sleep.

In the kitchen she poured herself some water from the tap, filling a teacup with it, spilling some in her eagerness to swallow. She went back into the sitting room, now Mrs Head's bedroom. How much friendlier the wallpaper in here was. Fronds of ferns and stalks of bamboo. The walnut whatnot, the mahogany escritoire, all these things had somehow survived the years of Donald's residence, and her mother on the bed, sleeping on her back with that curious spread of limbs that she always displayed in sleep, as though someone had simply flung her there. It was no good, she could not sleep upstairs with Donald. She went back up to tell him that Mrs Head was having trouble getting to sleep, and that she had promised to stay with her for a while: she wasn't used to the new room and needed time to get adjusted. There was a cat in the front garden making rustling noises in the privet, and Mrs Head wasn't used to those sorts of noises.

Perhaps he could hear Mrs Head's snoring, but he didn't seem to believe Tory's story. 'You won't be able to hide down there for ever you know,' he said quietly, as she left. 'You'll have to sleep with me some time.'

CHAPTER 26

'This may sound like an odd sort of compliment, Tory, but since I've known you, I think I've lost my sense of disgust.'

Tory reminded Grace, as they sat in Tory's lavender-scented office, that she had paid her this 'compliment' several times already. She was, she said, becoming a little tired of it.

'But it's true, Tory. Before I met you I would have gone out of my way to avoid anything dirty or rotten, without realizing that these are just natural states of being. The ugliness of matter is not the problem, it's the ugliness of people's hearts . . . Nothing disgusts me, nothing in the world.'

Well, thought Tory, you haven't met my husband.

For a week now Tory had been sleeping downstairs with her mother while Donald slept alone upstairs, under the watchful eyes of a hundred Seacunnies. In an attempt to reconcile herself with her husband she had, instead, turned the house upside-down.

'In fact,' Grace went on, 'I would go so far as to say that there is no such thing as ugliness in the natural world. In our back garden I found a bird that had died and was being eaten by maggots. I decided that this was a beautiful tableau of death and rebirth. The body of the bird was being tidied up by the maggots—'

'Who would soon become horrid bluebottles.'

'But the bluebottles are food for spiders and spiders are food for birds. It all goes round and round. If I was a writer or an artist I would extol the beauty of bluebottles, so that we should value them as part of nature's way of processing itself. I suppose it's the economist in me that delights in such efficiency. Everything is accounted for in the natural world, just like a good balance sheet. I tried explaining this to my husband. He looked at me as though I was mad.'

By now Tory knew a lot about Grace. She knew that she was Australian, for one thing, and that she had come to England after marrying an Englishman. She knew that this Englishman was an eminent academic, a professor of economics at the LSE, and that they had met while she was a student in the same subject at the University of Melbourne, and he had been her teacher. He was much older than she, too old to be called up during the war, though he had contributed on the intelligence side of things, which she still didn't really understand. They lived in a large house in Dulwich, and had no children.

When Grace said that she was Australian, many things fell into place for Tory – that accent, for instance. At first Grace's accent had been hard to place, and she had sounded like a posh person impersonating a south-east Londoner (the perfect description, Grace had said, of the Melbourne accent). Her occasionally odd word choices and her easy intimacy, which seemed so very unEnglish to Tory, were also explained.

'You know what, Tory? I'd love to meet your husband.'

'Would you?'

'Course I would. Why wouldn't I? I feel like I've met him already.'

'In which case there would be no need to have the reality.'

'But I want to check out if he's as bad as you say he is.'

This made Tory start. 'Have I really made him seem that bad?'

'Course you have. Maybe you don't realize it, but some of the words you use about him . . .'

'Well, do you know what he said to me the other day? He said that women have no souls.'

'No souls? What does he mean by that?'

'He said that there is no evidence that God ever breathed life into the body of Eve in the way that he did into the body of Adam.'

'You never said he was religious.'

'He had a religious upbringing. He likes to invoke God when it's convenient for him.'

'I never had any religion,' said Grace, brightly, as though recounting a lucky escape. 'So what does

365

it mean for women, if they don't have souls? Does it mean we don't get to Heaven?'

'I suppose so.'

'We end up in Limbo, with all the pet hamsters and still-born babies?'

'Yes – I suppose it means we aren't any different from the animals.'

This notion seemed truly to disgust Grace.

'Well, I'd much rather go to Limbo than Heaven, to be with the animals and the little children. It must be a wonderfully peaceful place – I don't suppose the tigers there are dangerous because they wouldn't need to eat – whereas Heaven must be full of selfrighteous, interfering, bossy do-gooders, and probably people like your husband. People who claim to have the keys to the Kingdom usually belong in the sewer with all the other rats.'

'Grace!' Tory was a little shocked by this sudden outburst. 'You just said that rats and sewers are all beautiful things. And apart from that, I think I might have exaggerated Donald's more unsavoury qualities . . .'

She took a long sip of champagne, as if to get rid of a taste in her mouth. Tory and Grace did have such amusing chats in the lavatory, but they had never actually had a party down there, not until today. Grace had arrived, already a little slurred in her speech, and had produced from the reptile-skin handbag that hung from her shoulder a bottle of Moët et Chandon, and two glasses wrapped in a silk handkerchief. Grace explained that it was her birthday. Grace had opened the bottle like an experienced drinker, deftly dealing with the foil and the wire contraption, making Tory jump for her life when the cork popped and allowing a little spurt of froth to splatter the office.

Tory made protestations that she should not drink on the job, while Grace pointed out that she was so rarely visited in her office, no one was ever likely to know and, besides, was she sure she wasn't allowed? So she drank, sneezing instantly on a noseful of bubbles, feeling heady as a result of the gases given off by the alcohol. Her eyes watered. 'I don't know how I ever drank this stuff,' she said. 'It's like trying to drink a beehive.' But she had another go, and was soon, along with Grace, what she called, 'a little bit tiddled'.

'You know,' said Grace, 'the thing about Heaven . . . What I've often wondered is, if they took a census up there, do you think there would be more men than women, or more women than men, or would it be exactly even?'

'Given there's no way the question can ever be answered, I don't think there's much point in considering it.'

'But you can still speculate. My guess is that there'll be more women. What do you think?'

'Well, there are people like Donald who think that Heaven is a place where only men can go.'

'Like a gents' lavatory?'

'Oh, Grace, you do say such funny things.'

'What do you think, Tory? If we had a look next door, at the Gents, we could have a glimpse of Heaven.'

'Now you're being silly.'

'Oh, I wish you wouldn't call me that so often. You begin to sound like my husband. But I'm serious. I suddenly find the thought quite preposterous that I could live out my entire life never having seen the inside of a gents' lavatory.'

Tory laughed, almost spilling her champagne. 'But what would there be to see? It must be a place like this, just like this.'

'Do you think so? No, Tory, I think you're wrong. They have these things there, where men can just stand. Do you mean to tell me you've never been next door?'

Tory explained that once in a while she did have to call upon Clive in the Gents for assistance in some technical matter, but that when she did she merely went to the bottom of the stairs and hallooed him from there. She had never actually ventured into the lavatory itself. 'And I can assure you that's as far as I ever want to go. The smell! Clive does like using his bleach – I was nearly blinded.' She paused. 'It is true that today is Clive's day off. The Gents is unattended . . .'

'Well, there you are, then. Now's our chance. Eyes closed to the effects of chlorine we could walk blind through the Kingdom of Men, a phrase that could sum up my life. The University of Melbourne was not an easy place for a woman to be. Oh, Tory, you're a pioneer and an explorer. Let me give you a little peck.'

At first, being kissed on the lips by a woman had been a surprising experience for Tory. She had been surprised by the softness of a woman's face. When she kissed Donald, it was like putting your face into a bramble bush – prickly, rigid, unyielding. But Grace's lips were the soft beginnings of an apparently endless softness. It was like kissing a cloud.

'Let's do it now,' she whispered breathlessly, into Tory's neck.

'Now?' Tory whispered back, into the sweet spiral of Grace's ear. 'You mean . . .'

'Yes, let's visit the forbidden kingdom . . .'

Wednesday was early closing in the square. There weren't many people around. There had been no visitors to the Ladies for an hour. Furthermore, there seemed hardly anyone above ground – there were no boot soles clomping over the glass ceiling tiles. It was almost as if they were alone in the world.

'So you think we could go next door, have a look around, and there would be no one there?'

'Well. I'm not sure it would be a good idea.'

Grace pleaded with her friend. 'Oh, please, Tory . . .'

'But what if we get caught?'

'Caught? We're not little children breaking into someone's back garden to steal the apples.'

369

'But it could be awfully embarrassing.'

'I won't be embarrassed . . . and you – you've got a legitimate reason. If anyone comes in I could pretend to be your boss, from the council.'

The two women found themselves holding hands as they descended the stone steps of the gents' lavatory on Union Square. Grace was unsure in her high heels: the steps seemed wetter, more narrow and slippery than the steps to the Ladies. There was no handrail either. As if men are naturally expected to be more deft step-climbers than women, she thought. They had watched the entrance for ten minutes before making their move, so felt confident that it was empty down there, but that didn't prevent them feeling nervous as they neared the bottom of the steps, the white ceramic tiles with their occasional strata of bottle green rising like a hard liquid around them.

The smell as they descended the stairwell was immediately noticeable as being different from that of the Ladies, though not particularly masculine (neither was the smell in the ladies particularly feminine, for that matter). The aroma was of some sort of menthol with an acid undertone. A sharp, spacious smell, like mountain air. As they reached the corner, Grace half expected to see a glacier stretch before them.

They paused, listening for the faintest sound that might indicate occupancy. There was nothing other than the expected echoey trickle of the cisterns slowly filling, the same sound that constantly filled the Ladies. Tory, who was ahead, turned back to Grace and gave her a reassuring nod. Grace's face was filled with excited glee, and she covered her mouth with her hand to restrain her excitement. They stepped down and rounded the final turn.

'It is different,' was Tory's first, disappointed exclamation.

'I told you,' said Grace.

Before them was a space twice the size of the Ladies. The narrow well of white tiles they had just descended opened out into a quite dazzling vista of ceramics, with green ornamentation, curlicues and foreign-looking motifs that made the place seem like a palace. There were the same wooden stalls with frosted windows and brass locks, but these were fewer. To the right the same row of porcelain washbasins with stout silver taps. But there was the additional thing, which accounted for the extra space: the long row of standing stalls, ten of them (Tory counted), raised on a step, each one tiled in Byzantine patterns of black, red and white, surrounding the porcelain troughs that rose high and as proud as tombstones.

Still holding hands, the two women approached this solemn terrace and took the step up.

'It's like being in church,' said Grace, suddenly serious.

'It's much cleaner than I expected,' said Tory. 'Clive must be more conscientious than I thought. There isn't a trace of dirt anywhere.'

371

'I feel like we're a bride and groom who've just stepped up to receive the vicar's blessing . . .'

Just then the slow dripping of the cistern reached its brim, a float-lever somewhere lifted, and the flush sprang into life, making the two women jump. They had been admiring the copper plumbing for a moment, without quite understanding what it meant. Now they saw that the water poured down the vertical stem, then branched out to feed each urinal, emerging with a shrill, squeaking rush from a bulbous, verdigris-encrusted outlet at the top of each one, then cascading down the cliff of porcelain to reach the gutter at the bottom, which became, briefly, a river.

The women had panicked at the onset of all this watery commotion, half feeling that the lavatory had come alive, or that they were not alone after all, and that a secret chain-puller was hidden somewhere, watching. But Tory had seen the insides of a cistern enough times now to know that they could be worked automatically, by nothing more than gravity and leverage.

Once the shock was over they giggled again, and feigned anger at their own silliness.

'It had just never occurred to me before,' said Tory, 'that men come in here and . . . do it together, standing next to each other, shoulder to shoulder. You could never imagine women doing that, could you? Even if they were able. That must mean something about men, their shamelessness.'

'I don't know about that,' said Grace. 'Perhaps

it says something about their attitude to disgust. At least they don't do the other thing together, but have cubicles, like us.'

Grace giggled as she wandered deeper into the space, seeming to gain confidence as she walked around, stamping her feet to hear the echoes, whistling.

'Have you had enough of a look, Grace? I think we should go before someone comes . . .' The emboldening effects of the champagne were beginning to fade. But Grace had spotted Clive's office, and the door was open.

'Let me just have a peek in here and then we can be done,' she said, then exclaiming, 'Oh, it's so much bigger than yours. Everything's bigger here – the whole place must be twice the size.'

'I'm not sure you should go in there,' said Tory, cautiously following Grace up to the door, feeling rather surprised that it was left open, and wondering if that meant Clive was, after all, around today.

Grace was already busying herself with nosing around everything in the office, before she exclaimed, 'Well, I'd never have thought of Clive as a literary man. It looks like he spends all his time down here reading while you're writing.'

Tory had never been inside Clive's office before. She saw Grace sitting in his chair, beside his desk, reading a book.

'He's got dozens of these – see?' She waved the

book cover at Tory, and then indicated a box under the table, which contained identical copies of the same small green volume. There was no title on the cover, and no author's name. Grace handed the copy to Tory while she took another from the box. A book each, they read together.

The title page carried the following, which Grace read aloud, hardly able to control her giggling.

Letters To Her Husband
By
a Naughty Housewife

Being the genuine correspondence of a
nymphomaniac wife
To her husband while he was suffering
In a German prisoner-of-war camp
Transcribed faithfully by him

'Oh, gosh, it looks like our friend Clive has got a little trade going in dirty books. Oh, you must read this, Tory! "... *I imagine you taking me in your manly arms, my love, and then inserting your little finger ...*"' Grace was now choking with shock and mirth. 'Have you ever read anything like it, Tory. Tory? What's the matter, Tory? You look quite upset.'

PART III

CHAPTER 27

Tory was a little disappointed that Branson did not look as though he was ever going to exceed her in height. On his sixteenth birthday they stood side by side at the bus stop opposite Baines, on Old Parade, waiting for the new bus that would take them all the way to George Farraway's new boxing gym, and she couldn't help wondering what she'd done wrong that her son, fathered by someone as immense as George, should be so small. Had she not fed him enough?

It seemed that she had been having the same thought almost since the day he was born. She had always regarded his body as a promise that was never kept. If he had inherited from George and become big and powerful, no one would think for a moment that he was her child, though with Donald now removed from her life, this had ceased to be important. It was simply a matter of curiosity to see how many degrees of George Farraway would become apparent in his son's body.

When Branson was very little she hadn't known what to look for, because she had never seen George at the same age, and the task of imagining George Farraway as a baby was enormous: one could only start with the bulk and weight of his present-day self and extrapolate backwards, crushing the might of adult George down to its primary form – but she could never rid the resulting little thing of its beard and its broken face. When she looked at Branson as a baby she saw something slight, smooth, intact and uncoordinated. It was possible that baby George had been these things as well, but Tory doubted it.

More worryingly, little Branson didn't have a sportsman's eye for moving objects. He had trouble kicking a ball, even more trouble catching one. His walk was ungainly. As a toddler he fell more frequently than most, and more dangerously, seeming unable to break his fall as others did. She was afraid of sending him to school because she thought he would be defence-less against the bullies she imagined lay in wait for him. She lingered outside the railings each day, observing how he was treated by the other children. To her surprise they seemed friendly and welcoming. Even so, Tory still wondered if they were merely luring him into a trap. And then she would retrieve him at the end of the day and feel baffled by his happiness. If he was ever unhappy, it was because of his teachers rather than his fellow pupils. He even started bringing little friends home, then being invited to other friends' houses, just as though he was a normal child. Then Tory would check herself for feeling so surprised. Why should it amaze her that Branson had friends? It was hardly the case that he carried around a badge of her own wifely betrayal for all to see, and even if he did, what would little children care? In everyone's else's eyes Branson was just a regular kid.

She recalled the exact moment of realization that Branson was beautifully ordinary when she attended a little presentation given by his class on the subject of Noah's Ark. It was only his second year in the school, and he was up on stage with the other five-year-olds before what must, to him, have seemed like a huge audience. He had only one line, 'N is for Nightingale', which he stood and delivered, spreading his little cardboard and crêpe-paper wings, holding, for a few seconds, the attention of the entire audience. Just for a few seconds, before the tall lad to his right mumbled, 'O is for Ostrich,' but during that time, Branson's clear little voice, so carefully enunciating the words, seemed to have the ear of the whole universe, making Tory feel, for the first time, that he existed as a real flesh-and-blood little boy, taking up space in the world, using up air and food, reflecting light. It brought a choking sensation to her throat.

The enormous but manageable leap: from a little boy dressed as a nightingale on a school stage, enunciating carefully and clearly, to a champion boxer in the ring, delivering the winning uppercut to the bristled jaw of a blood-streaming opponent, the eyes of a stadium of jubilant people turned upon him, standing on their chairs and punching their fists in the air, hailing him as the new champion of the world.

At times she felt that that was his rightful inheritance. She didn't care about George Farraway's money or his Edwardian pile in Blackheath, or his stinking factory. She cared about the near-champion's blood he had delivered into her womb one night in the middle of a world war and which she had painstakingly nurtured to the cusp of adulthood.

She even took a certain pride in his academic inability. She was used to having clever children. Since they were all clever she hadn't really noticed their cleverness but had taken it for granted. The arrival of Branson had put that all into perspective, and she had a clear view, for the first time, though too late, of how magnificent Tom's brain had been – busy, curious, able to weave together lots of different things. Tom had been clever beyond all reason, and the girls were clever too. But Branson seemed to be a little bit slow and a little bit stupid. This meant, as far as Tory could see, that he had inherited from his father rather than his mother. George often boasted of how he couldn't read and write until he'd retired from boxing and taught himself from nursery primers, with a magnifying glass. Branson may have inherited this slowness of mind, but he had not shown a fighting spirit until after Tom's death, when he regularly came home bloody around the nose or mouth, or with a bruised eye and scraped knuckles, and was given to lurchingly unpredictable behaviour.

The hands she had examined so carefully since he had been a baby were now beginning to grow into strong, square, hammer-shaped things. His body was becoming squarer and stockier. The nightingale was turning into something altogether more powerful. She might have hoped for an eagle or a hawk, but in his adolescence Branson began to look as though he was made of cardboard boxes. Or tea chests. A body designed to withstand blows. His squareness also gave him an awkwardness: he continued to have poor balance and the tumblings of his toddler days extended into his youth. A few times he had fallen completely over for no obvious reason, having somehow pivoted wrongly, turning in mid-stride, his centre of gravity going awry, and there he was, reeling on the ground, looking baffled.

There could hardly be a greater weakness for a boxer than to be easily felled. He might have strength in his arms and a solid resilience in his body, but if he lacked the agility to remain upright, then there wasn't really much hope for him. A child could have knocked him down with a little finger.

Baines was the butcher that now occupied the spot were Dando's had been. There was no reason, Tory supposed, why a butcher should not have come to replace the one destroyed in the war, but she did think it a little odd. Was there something special about that particular location, which meant it should always be occupied by vendors of meat, from now and into the future for ever? It hadn't happened with the other shops. The baker's had been replaced by a shoe shop, the greengrocer's by a branch of a building society. She had been into Baines's a few times, and she thought the new butcher a rather cold, sinister character; he had none of old Dando's joviality, none of the rosy-cheeked sauciness that had so characterized the old man. Baines was a cold, silent, efficient butcher. He wore a narrow dark tie, and had a narrow dark moustache. It was a relief not to have to face the combative repartee of Dando any more, but Tory wondered if the coldness of Baines was worse.

'It's good to see the shops rebuilt at last,' said Tory. Branson looked at her as though she'd said something ridiculous. For the last couple of years Tory had felt as though she was on a different wavelength from her son: nothing she said seemed to interest him, and most of what she said he seemed to find baffling. She was a little surprised that he had been so insistent on her coming with him today.

'Won't you feel silly with your mummy there, and all those strapping blokes knocking seven bells out of each other?' she had said.

'I don't care, you've *got* to come.'

'I don't think any of the other would-be boxers will have their mummies there.'

'I'm not going on my own.'

Another slight pang of disappointment, to add to the one about his lack of height. Branson didn't want to go to the gym on his own, but he had done other things on his own, he had caught a train all the way up to London, sneaking out of school to do so. He had walked the length of Charing Cross Road, all the way from Trafalgar Square to Bloomsbury. He had found Donald's flat, the one he shared with the educated Mr Wilde. Oh, yes, Branson had done many things on his own by now. He had even got a Saturday job as an assistant to Bill Welch, Donald's old partner, and was learning the painting and decorating trade. He came home caked in the same decorative muck that used to cover Donald – plastery fingers, hair stiff with gloss paint, nails in his shoes, and always that pong of turpentine.

She would have done everything she could to stop Branson seeing Donald, and certainly from following his footsteps into that messy profession, if she'd thought there was the least chance she would be successful. And so she didn't.

Tory stole another glance at her son, standing awkwardly beside her at the stop. Not tall, certainly. He would never be tall. By pure coincidence, it seemed, he resembled, in height if nothing else, Donald.

The bus arrived. They got on.

The task of removing Donald from Tory's life was a long and complicated one. In the end she had

383

resorted to a method that also had its associations with George – starvation. She began, simply, by denying him food. It was less immediately violent than the first method she had considered, that of killing him. On the afternoon of their discovery, in the gents' lavatory, of a stock of Donald's socalled 'memoirs', in fact a near perfect transcription of her letters with only the names changed, she had come home in a blind fury. All the way Grace had followed her (or, more accurately, walked in front of her, backwards), trying to make her stop and think about what she was doing.

'There's to be no discussion, Grace. I'm just going to kill him.' Grace had realized quite quickly what had happened, knowing, as she did, all about the letters. 'Don't you think you should think about it?'

'I am thinking about it. There is an axe in the shed. I was thinking of using it a long time ago, and I didn't. But I think I will use it now.'

Would she ever have used it? Tory thought probably not, that it was more than just an accident of circumstance that had prevented her becoming an axe-wielding murderess, crazed to a comical degree, lampooned by her own fury into something quite ridiculous. If she thought about it more she could see all the improbabilities – especially if Grace had still been with her – of fetching the axe out from the shed, marching into the kitchen (there was no refuge for Donald now – with Mrs Head downstairs he had only the dining room or the upstairs bedroom to occupy), to raise the axe above Donald's inattentive head (probably reading the racing pages – betting on the horses had become his latest interest). Then what? He looks up just in time to see the blade flash before his eyes, as it bisects them perfectly, his face falling away in two symmetrical halves (or as near as possible for Donald, whose face had steadily lost its symmetry over the years). What a terrific horror that would have been, more horrible, probably, than anything Donald himself had seen during the war, but he would have been responsible because he had proved himself to be on the side of the bad people after all, and the blow wouldn't just have been for his sneaky, sleazy betrayal, but for all the wrong things he'd done since coming home, and most of all for taking Tom's future away from him.

It wouldn't have happened. Instead the axe would have melted away in her hands at the thought of Branson, of her own capacity for betrayal.

But it had never got that far anyway. When she arrived home, she opened the door to find Donald standing in the passageway, as though he had been waiting for her. She could see by his demeanour that something was seriously wrong, and she thought she knew what it was.

'Mama?' she said.

Donald nodded before adding, quite unnecessarily, 'I am afraid Mrs Head is now Mrs Dead.'

And thoughts of axes, of revenge, of any sort of

action directed at Donald, except to say, after a moment's deep crying, 'How could you make a joke out of it?' disappeared from her mind, and instead she was filled with the appalling task of removing her own mother from her life. It hadn't occurred to her before that that was what you had to do when a loved one died – remove them. Somehow she had imagined that everything involved with the disposal of a life was organized by outside agencies – undertakers, hospitals, doctors, the borough council – but, no, these people all have to be marshalled and cajoled and would apparently be quite content to let the dead linger on indefinitely among the living. Oh, she supposed they would have done something eventually, but it was she who had to instigate everything – and then there were her mother's things, among which, Tory realized, was the house itself. Luckily her sisters, happily and prosperously married, were not insistent upon the portion of their mother's estate that was tied up in it, and Tory was allowed to continue living at 17 Peter Street.

Donald had not made things easier for her by describing her mother's dying moments in great detail.

'She was making these awful moaning sounds. I kept asking her what the matter was, but she wouldn't say anything, lying on her side on the bed, moaning, like she had a really bad stomach ache. And she kept opening her mouth wide as if she was going to be sick, but nothing came out, then another moan – really deep moans. You wouldn't believe it was a woman making those noises – she sounded like Paul Robeson, like Al Jolson. I've never heard a sound like it . . .' Donald speculated that it was not Mrs Head's voice at all but the voice of Death himself, speaking through her, because it was the last noise to come out of her mouth, but for a brief gushing sound, as a stream of near-clear liquid poured out that, for the briefest moment, made Donald think of a thing he'd seen at a funfair on the Common once, when a slot machine gave its prize of silver tokens through the glazed mouth of a clown. And then he said Mrs Head's eyes changed colour, by which he meant the pupils dilated until the whole iris became black, and since Mrs Head's eyes had, until then, been getting lighter and lighter in their shades of blue, this was a very noticeable change. Tory didn't know why she had allowed Donald to give her this information, this verbal portrait of her mother's dying moments, a cameo of her departure, an anecdote of death told with all the urgency of a saloon-bar raconteur. She supposed he was just trying to enable her to share the experience she had missed, and that he seemed sure she regretted missing.

'You should have let me know. Why didn't you get me?'

'How could I get you? You were at work.'

'You could have come.'

'Why do you always forget about my leg, Tory?

387

Why do you always forget about it?' Tory had no answer. She had never forgotten about his leg. He could have got to the lavatories by other means – he could have hailed a taxi, got a neighbour to drive him down. 'And leave Mrs Head to die alone? Is that what you would have wanted? Besides – how could I have come to tell you? You work in a ladies' lavatory.'

Tory shouted at the ceiling. 'It is not completely out of bounds – men are allowed in in an emergency. I think it would have been acceptable in such circumstances.'

'I'm not going in a Ladies, not even if my life depended on it.'

Mrs Head was buried next to Arthur, in the graveyard of St Andrew's, Clifton Road, attended by a large and respectful crowd of people who were mostly strangers to Tory, though their names were familiar when she discovered them – Aunty Emily and Uncle Albert who were younger than Mrs Head but looked twice as old, George Washington (whose family had always so revelled in the name, and which went some way to making up for his rather shabby, achievementless life), the Dunders, the Bacons, the Popes, the Hills. Tory hadn't seen the Hills since she was a child, and was amazed at how high and broad they had become – more like mountains, Donald had joked. There were friends, too. Mrs Head had somehow maintained a wide circle of friends without ever disclosing their existence to Tory.

How had she done it? There was an art to it, surely. Apart from the familiar faces of Lippiatt and Richards and Allen and Wilson, there was Mrs McGillicuddy, Mrs Pewsey, Mrs Finny, Mrs Dark, Mrs Wise, Mrs Randall, all with their jovial, chatty husbands. The church could hardly hold all the mourners. Neither could the house in Peter Street, but Tory had been able to secure the upstairs rooms at the Rifleman, who put on a decent spread of corned-beef pasties, sprout terrines and Roquefort footballs.

It was around this time that her thoughts began returning to the book. Dressed in mourning black ('extravagant, illogical and unChristian'), floating among guests with a tray of kipper pâté rolls, a thought suddenly occurred to her: how many people in this room might have read *Letters To Her Husband*? How many copies were on sale? How many public conveniences stocked them? Every attended gents' lavatory in the land?

As soon as the guests were gone, she confronted Donald.

It was hard for Tory to say what hurt her the most – the fact that he had done this thing, of publishing her letters, or that he seemed so surprised at her anger. 'I thought you'd be pleased,' he said, raising his eyebrows, showing no sign that he was embarrassed at having his little enterprise discovered. 'You always said you wanted to be published . . .'

This rendered Tory speechless. She could do nothing but fold her arms and let her mouth form an outraged oval. That he could even think of comparing what he had done to the possible future publication of her novel, as though she could derive any sense of fulfilment from that . . .

'You've got fans, old girl. All over the country, all over the world. This book is selling like hot cakes. It's being translated into French, German, Italian, Spanish. They're all paying up front. We're going to be rolling in it, rolling in it.'

By now Tory was in control of herself, and talked calmly to Donald. 'May I ask if you showed my letters to people in the prison camp?'

'Of course I did, old girl. We all showed each other our letters from our wives, especially if they had saucy bits in them. There was a racket going on. You could rent out letters in return for favours, or even food and treats – there was no harm in it. I could see these blokes getting loads of stuff from each other and from the guards just for showing a letter from their missus that didn't even say that much. I needed some letters to help me. That's why I kept asking. I was only trying to hold my own. And then you really let rip, old girl, and started writing letters like none of us had ever seen before. Those letters were like gold dust to me – I could get anything I wanted for them, anything. You were famous all around the camp, and around every camp I went to, Tory Pace, the hottest bit of stuff in the free world. I had blokes asking if they could see your photograph.'

'And did you show them?'

'No, I didn't have a picture of you on me, so I showed them pictures of Flora. Don't worry, your identity's safe.'

'Have you told your sister this?'

'Of course I haven't.'

'How many copies have you printed?'

'You'll have to address that question to my agent.'

'If by "agent" you mean that devious little wastrel Mr Wilde then I would rather not speak to him. You must tell me.'

'But I don't know anything about it. Harry handled it all.'

'You must have an idea.'

'It's a French publishing company. Harry speaks good French – he's an educated man, like I keep telling you, a literary man. He has connections, he knows people. He said something about the first print run being five thousand copies.'

Tory's heart sank even further. Her shame multiplied five thousand times, dispersed all around the country. 'You must tell me where they all are.'

'Why, Tory? No one will ever know you were the author. I changed the names – didn't you see? You're Gertie Truelove in the book.'

As though he had provided her with some sort of gift, that grotesque, horrible name. He could not have thought of a more unpleasant one if he'd tried for a hundred years. Yes, of course she was Gertie Truelove, twin sister of Charlotte Maugham, her darker side.

'I don't know what you're getting so upset about. You came up with those letters – some of the blokes I showed them to handed them straight back, saying they didn't want to read any further. Disgusted, some of them were. I had to be careful who I showed them to after that.'

'I suppose Mr Wilde took great delight in them.'

'Harry certainly has a discerning eye for the more colourful end of the literary spectrum.'

Tory had to keep reminding herself that Donald was, or had been, a reader of Plato.

'He said that this French publisher, who publishes some pretty strong stuff, had some doubts about whether to publish them or not. Anyone found with copies could end up in jail. How does that feel, to have written something illegal?'

'But the censors let them through,' said Tory, indignantly.

'Things can be said in a private letter that can't be said in a book – you must know that.'

'Well, I may have written the letters but you have written the book. That makes you the criminal, not me.'

'It's a pretty fine distinction, don't you think? If you get me into trouble over this, I'm bringing you down with me.'

'In which case our best course of action is to ensure that all copies of this book are destroyed. Donald, you need to tell me who published it and where all the copies are. I cannot allow it to be distributed.'

'Like I said, speak to my agent.'

'Damn your agent – and stop calling him that, he's nothing more than a spiv. You speak to him. Why should I?'

'It's all underground, Tory. We'll never be able to track down all the copies.'

Underground. Was it really as simple as that? A question of visiting every attended gents' lavatory in the land, every barber's shop?

She didn't get much further with Donald. It was not possible to convince him that he had done anything so seriously wrong. If she castigated him for doing it, he reminded her that she was the author of the letters, which reminded her that she had written them under the influence of her affair with George Farraway, that large parts of them were verbatim transcriptions of his lovemaking utterances, that many of the scenarios described were accounts of their own lovemaking – did Donald recognize this? It was always these things that robbed her of her full-blown ability to be outraged; she could not quite bring herself to the brink of true anger and hurt. And then Donald would add to the problem by questioning to whom the letters belonged. Who, after all, owns a letter? The author or the recipient? Tory supposed there were lawyers somewhere who could answer the question, but she couldn't. Donald insisted the letters were his own property and that he could do what he pleased with them. He was, he said, being very generous in offering to share the profits with her.

She did manage to persuade him to show her where his own stash of copies was hidden. They were in the mahogany escritoire, in the locked cupboard underneath. Thirty copies, along with her original letters in a box file.

Books are not easy to burn. Tory discovered this as she set about constructing the first bonfire ever to flourish in the backyard of 17 Peter Street. They sit in the flames like big blocks of ice, refusing to ignite. To get them to burn properly you have to break them open, tear the spines apart so that they flail with all their organs exposed. Even then you fear that chunks of text might survive, might be readable to anyone picking through the cold embers. Tory felt alarm when, once the fire had got going, large portions of text, still burning, were being carried into the air by the updraught. This act of burning might turn out to be another form of distribution, in fragmentary form, but who knew where those bits of pornography might land, how far they might be carried, and have enough surviving text to be readable, identifiable?

It took Donald to point out the irony of the situation. 'To think we fought a war just to prevent this sort of thing happening. I never thought I'd live to see the day that book-burning became a practice in my own backyard.'

Mrs Wilson popped her head over the fence. Tory hadn't given any thought to the preparations for this event, and there was washing hanging in neighbouring gardens. She could just see the top of some tightly curled heads bobbing up and down beyond the fences, as scintillatingly clean underwear (oh, these new washing powders: never before had smalls glowed so resplendently and with such little effort) was quickly rescued before the ashes and smoke of Tory's letters poured down. She apologized to Mrs Wilson, informing her that she was just getting rid of some of her mother's old things, which brought out a sympathetic response.

'No, there's no point in clinging on to things, is there, dear?' she said.

Tory could not help but notice the rising ground where the wash had been buried all those years before. It seemed that all Donald's enterprises could go nowhere but back to an elemental form, into the earth or the air. The paving slabs had never settled over that dreadful whisky but were forever uneven, and now they used buckets of water to wash the book ash down the storm drain.

Destroying the entire print run of *Letters To Her Husband* seemed impossible. Donald continued to protest that he knew nothing of their whereabouts, since secrecy was the key to the whole operation. Imagine the trouble it takes getting these things through Customs, he said. He did promise, however, to contact Mr Harry Wilde, though naturally Mr Wilde was not someone who could be easily found. He had several addresses, Tory discovered, as well as several names, but eventually she received a letter from him.

My dear Mrs Pace,

First of all I must congratulate you on your success as an author. Your book, which your husband laboured for so many months to transcribe into typewritten form, is a literary sensation in Europe. It was published in March and distributed among the more discerning bookshops in Paris, where it can be quite legally sold. It has done very well, and not just to English-speaking customers: Parisians themselves are buying copies. I have even been told that non-English speakers are hurriedly learning the language just so that they can read your book. Of course, a French translation is inevitable, and indeed is in the process of being written as I write. Italian, Dutch, Spanish and German versions are also in preparation. The publisher is so impressed with your work that he has written to me asking if I could persuade you to write a sequel. Perhaps Letters of a Naughty Schoolgirl, Letters of a Naughty Governess, Letters of a Naughty Mother Superior, *that sort of thing. He informs me that he would be willing to pay a handsome sum in advance of royalties. I am greatly shocked that Donald has not paid you*

your share of the sum he received for Letters
To Her Husband. *This was also a handsome
sum, and I am expecting the book to earn out
its advance and entitle you to royalties. But it
is not for me to put my nose into the sanctity
of someone else's marriage.*

*You do not need to worry about the legal side
of things. I think Donald has said some silly
things to you about this, but you are not in
any danger at all in this respect. The only people
who should be worried are those who have
smuggled your book into this country and are
selling it on the black market. I understand
Her Majesty's Government can impose a
penalty of five years' imprisonment in such
cases. I only wish I knew how your book found
its way into this country. It is quite disgraceful
that our decency laws have been offended in
this way, and that you have been exposed to
possible embarrassment, though of course your
identity has been quite carefully concealed in
the book. Even those closest to you would not
suspect you as the author. As to the possibility
of retrieving and destroying those copies that
have found their way into this country, I am
afraid I can be of no help here, and neither
would the publisher, since this has been done
without our knowledge, by cads and rakes and
other bad eggs. If you are thinking of going to
Paris to try and remove the copies that have
been distributed there, I am afraid it would be*

a futile exercise. Unless you have the money to buy up every copy, you have no legal right to the work. You may think you have a case of breach of copyright, in which case your dispute should be with your husband, who assured me that he had your permission to publish the work. The copyright remains yours, of course.

Should you wish to visit your publisher, I would be most happy to accompany you to Paris, and perhaps represent you in negotiations for future works. I have very good connections in that wonderful city, and know some smashing little places to eat. The publisher of your book is a respected publishing house. They have published many eminent men of letters – not just the naughty stuff but serious stuff as well. It would be a great pity if the world were to be denied future works from your pen.

Yours sincerely

Harold S. Wilde

Literary Agent
Bloomsbury Square
London WC1

PS Donald informed me that you have written a 'proper' novel as well. I suppose there is a chance that Mr Girodias would be interested in that. Why don't you let me have a look at the manuscript?

CHAPTER 28

Mrs Head didn't leave much behind that was her own. Her only possessions were things already shared with the household – her furniture was their furniture, her kitchen things were their kitchen things, her pots and pans and casseroles, her jelly moulds and pie tins, tie pins (Arthur's), even her hair pins, hat pins and rolling pins (porcelain, with a motif of violets) were things of common ownership, shared and redistributed. The wallpapers of the different rooms (Seacunny nightmare, daisy madness, soothing bamboo, bounteous bouquets) were technically hers, chosen by her in a time before anyone now alive could remember, along with the carpets and rugs (lush, knotty problems that never solved themselves), but they were everyone's as well. The walls, the roof, the yard, the whole house itself and just about everything in it – hers and not hers.

The only object in the house that could truly be said to have belonged to Mrs Head alone, that was not the common property of the house, was her 'special box'. This was a sandalwood trunk with a copper lock that her grandfather, a sailor, had brought back from India. It had elephants carved on the side ('trunks on a trunk' ran the joke), and a stain on the lid said to be a fakir's blood. Mrs Head always kept the box locked shut and close to her bed. Tory was very familiar with the box, but had never seen inside it. Occasionally she would come upon her mother on her knees before it, shuffling through whatever it contained, and if Tory tried to see inside, which she often did when she was a little girl, her mother would quickly bang the lid shut, not seeming to care if she chopped off her daughter's nose in the process.

So now, with Mrs Head's demise, a lifetime's curiosity could be satisfied in one long orgy of rummaging. Her box, the only locked part of her long, crowded life, was now in Tory's possession.

Mrs Head's will had made no reference to the box. There was no line that read *I leave my special box and everything in it to my dearest daughter Tory,* yet it seemed to be assumed by everyone that she was expected to take charge of it. She had thought she might leave a respectful amount of time before she inserted the little copper key, perhaps even a few years, but in fact she opened the box the same day the will was read, though she nearly broke her back heaving the thing out from the corner of the back bedroom where it had resided for the last decade. Extraordinary that her mother's life should amount to such a weighty object, when she herself had ended up as light as a piece of bone china. And Tory was terrified when she lifted the lid

400

because a strong smell of her father came out, a smell she hadn't caught for more than twenty years and which was produced by the little set of his favourite pipes that her mother had preserved. It made Tory cry, and she had to close the lid and recompose herself, thankful that she had chosen to perform the task alone, when the house was empty. She had thought she might have to deal only with a few notebooks and newspapers, a few old savings books and share certificates, marriage certificates and other bureaucratic litter. She wasn't prepared to meet her long-departed father's toothmarks on the stem of a pipe, his odour. She didn't think she'd have to labour through layers of preserved sweat and saliva, richly perfumed dust and their accompanying ghosts to get to the documentation. She was wheezing, even from that little exposure. All that old stuff in there had clogged up her airways. She went downstairs for a drink of water and took a turn in the yard to clear her chest.

There was a lot of stuff in the box. Not just her mother's things but her father's as well, and her grandfather's, and Arthur's father's. It seemed that this box was an amalgam of previous boxes. There appeared to be a system: you stock up your box with mementoes of your life, then hand it on to your children when you die, who sort through it, discard the impersonal stuff – old receipts, invoices and certificates – keep the photos, letters and diaries, then add their own mementoes of their own lives. The box thus becomes a sort of vehicle travelling through the generations, picking up passengers as it goes along.

At first Tory did not feel the urge to delve too deeply into this material. There was simply too much to take in – albums, scrapbooks, letters, ledgers, magazines, journals. She had too much to think about in the present to be distracted by the past. The only thing that held her attention was a batch of more recent-looking letters to her mother, and she took these out of the box to examine.

They were all from Major Brandish, the eccentric neighbour Mrs Head had been friendly with in Waseminster. She already knew the contents of many of these letters because Mrs Head had liked to read aloud from them, the Major having such an amusing way with words, and such an exotic vocabulary. The gossiping Major loved to keep her informed on the activities of her former neighbours and co-villagers, particularly if he had uncovered anything mildly shameful or scandalous. Mrs Head had read from these letters so frequently that Tory felt she had quite a clear picture in her mind of the retired army man, who'd served some time in India, keeping a forgotten corner of the empire going singlehandedly, civilizing the natives by means of the most powerful weapon at his disposal: the china teacup and pot. He evidently regarded the marshes of Waseminster as a similar kind of outpost, the natives there being only marginally more acceptable because of a veneer of civilization. Tory had never actually seen one of the Major's letters, had no idea what his handwriting was like, and was very curious to find out. It was, as she might have imagined, sturdy, black and scrolled. It could have been made nicely out of wrought iron.

It was only on a whim that she bothered. Thinking she knew their contents already, she was about to tuck them away, never to look at them again, when she was attracted by an odd phrase, half glimpsed, and it soon became apparent that the extracts from which her mother had read were very selective indeed, and that what had been going on between the two was much more than a gossipy correspondence.

Your letter of the 21st gave me a deep satisfaction that could only be surpassed by your physical presence, dear Emily. Would that you were here to do those things you describe . . .

I would love to provide you with my own thoughts in return, but understand, as you say, the risk of your daughter discovering such letters would be too great, especially if, as you say, she is such a prudish creature. It is a very odd thing if we must avoid shaming our children. Nevertheless, I can quite imagine the devastating effect on the little madam on discovering that her own dear mother has such a rich and vivid imagination . . .

This letter was dated 1941, around the same time that Tory was struggling to write her letters to Donald. As she read, she gradually came to realize that the Major was not, by any means, a mere chance acquaintance made by Mrs Head during her time in Waseminster. It appeared that their relationship went back many years before that – that they even seemed to have been lovers at some point.

You made such a foolish mistake in returning to London, my love. Your destiny is here, with me, as it has always been. Is it not a cruel irony that now that I am free of soldiering and you are free of a husband, we must yet still remain separate, because of your foolish commitment to a lost cause . . .

Lost cause? Did he mean her?

London is finished, Emily dear, you must return to Waseminster at once. There has not been a single bomb fall with in twenty miles of the village, and that one was only dropped by accident, landing on a pig sty in St Margaret Without (bacon rain). I know you have a devotion to your daughter, but what possible use can you be to her?

Elsewhere in the letters, it seemed that Mrs Head was exercised by a continual sense of guilt about eating Mr Dando:

Will you stop wittering on about your canni-balistic crimes, Emily? To accidentally eat human meat is not to sully for ever the purity of your soul, and it is silly of you to think that it has brought you bad luck. As far as I can tell, you have had nothing but good luck since then. If you want my honest opinion, you have only become a proper woman since the day you ate Mr Dando – the meatiness of your letters are testament of that. In which case, bring more butchers to the table so that we may have a feast. I would not care for you any less if you ate a hundred butchers, or any other form of shopkeeper for that matter. There are too many in this country, aren't there? Wasn't Napoleon right about that at least? By the way, Napoleon has always been my favourite French general/emperor. Who's yours?

Emily, I think you are wrong. We should become married at the earliest possible convenience (I am so sorry to use that word: in the light of your news about your daughter's new occupa-tion, I could think of no other) – I have always said that we should have been married when we had the chance, in that blissful spring of 1912. Just think, if we had taken our chance then, the whole course of our lives would have changed. You remember you said you wanted to wait two years because of your father's financial difficulties? You weren't to know that

405

the Great War was just around the corner. I
survived that turmoil to come home and find
you married to a bank clerk! Of all the
insults . . .

How could Mrs Head have read aloud the gossipy extracts, knowing that what she was reading was hemmed in by paragraphs of the most intimate kind, that she was picking a thread out of a tangle of words that would otherwise destroy the reputation of which she had been so proud? Mrs Head had gone to Waseminster not to be among her husband's people, but to be in the neighbourhood of a former lover. In fact, as Tory delved further into the archives of the special box, she began to wonder if her father had any connection with 'the church in the mud' at all. There was no mention of a Waseminster link in any of the documents she had come across in her first foray into Arthur's things.

The revelations concerning Mrs Head took her several weeks to digest, during which time she could barely put her mind to the question of *Letters To Her Husband* – not least because it appeared that somewhere on the Kent marshes a retired major was hoarding a stash of her own mother's letters in a similar vein. Mrs Head had been writing letters of that kind even into the years of her infirmity, an idea that Tory found very hard to stomach. In fact, she felt physically sick if she dwelt on the thought for too long. She couldn't help but linger on the observation made by Major Brandish: *you have only become a proper woman since the day you ate Mr Dando.*

It should be written on my tombstone, thought Tory. Then the feeling of sickness, which she realized had lingered somewhere at the back of her stomach ever since that day, went.

The first time she decided to deprive Donald Pace of food was on the occasion of their traditional Sunday lunch. In fact, this meal had more or less disappeared from the weekly routine of the house until that particular day, and as such was staged as a conscious revival of that special tradition. She had also invited the young men she recognized to be the girls' suitors, dapper young chaps in drainpipe trousers, who had begun calling at the house every other evening to take them to dances. Tory didn't know what young people did these days, or where they went. She hadn't ventured into a ballroom for twenty years, and the dance halls now were giant palaces lit with gay, coloured lights, from which frighteningly rhythmic sounds came. And the girls did look like princesses: for the first time she could even find little Albertina, with her bulging eyes, beautiful. Those frocks they wore, with the sharp busts. The elbow gloves in salmon-coloured satin. They were just like characters from a fairy story, Tory thought. It was not a comforting notion. The conscious emulation of a fictional world seemed, to Tory, a very shallow enterprise.

They would be travelling in a coach shaped like a scallop shell and pulled by a team of white dolphins, if they had their way. The house was often clammy with scent and powder, and the two girls elbowing each other out of the way of the passageway mirror, which was the only decent mirror in the house, applying lipstick to their pinched mouths.

Although the young men seemed fine, Tory was not quite sure she approved of the girls having regular boyfriends at such a young age. Albertina was only just out of school, after all, but times seemed to be changing, and girls seemed to be growing up faster than ever before.

For the Sunday lunch, furniture had to be specially shipped in, the dining-table being moved to the sitting room and a smaller table borrowed from Mrs Wilson next door, then added to the end of the table, along with extra chairs. The exceptionally long surface extended diagonally from one corner to the other.

The young men sat at the table with too much familiarity and self-assurance for Tory's liking, although she tried not to show it. They had the loud, unwarranted confidence that distinguished their generation from all the preceding ones. Too young to have fought in the war, they seemed to have dismissed it already as an historical event, of no lasting importance. Though she was quite sure that both men were hard workers, they seemed also to take it alarmingly for granted that work was available and always would be. Paulette's boyfriend was a baker with big ideas, and dreamt of being a millionaire bread manufacturer (as he liked to call it). The future of bread was in mass production, he believed. The days of rising before dawn to prove the dough and face the torture of the red ovens would soon be over. Loaves in the future would be made in huge factories, ready sliced, ready wrapped, for distribution nationwide. He intended, one day, to own one of those factories

Albertina's boyfriend was working his way up through the building trade.

'Houses for all, Mrs Pace,' he said. 'The government is building ten new towns and more are planned. With any luck there'll be a house for every family in the country by 1960.'

'I could never understand why they were so determined to build houses after the war,' said Tory. 'Surely the population has decreased drastically as a result of the fighting.'

'But what about all the houses destroyed in the Blitz?'

'Well, you'd think it would probably match the number of lives lost, and be in proportion, at least.'

'That's very silly, Mother,' said Paulette. 'Everyone knows there aren't enough homes.'

'Well, I don't see hordes of homeless refugees drifting past my windows. Everyone seems to live somewhere, just as they always have.'

'But maybe in overcrowded conditions,' said the housebuilder, then hesitated, for fear that he had inadvertently insulted his host's household. He tried to make up for it by belittling his own background. 'We lived twelve to a room at one time . . .'

It suddenly occurred to Tory that the housebuilder was too old for Albertina. 'Well,' she said, 'after all, how much space do you really need? And where on earth are they going to fit all these new towns? What I say is, just stop building so many blooming houses, and just squeeze everyone in where they can.'

'And stop having babies,' added Donald, then, looking at the young sweethearts, 'well, for a few years anyway.'

'We're set for a population explosion, Mrs Pace. Haven't you noticed all the prams?'

'Oh, I've noticed them all right.'

'Mother, are we going to actually get anything to eat?'

'Why, of course.'

A joint of pork had been roasting in the oven all morning.

'Well now,' Tory said, 'which one of you two fine young men would like to carve?'

There was a moment of hushed embarrassment as the two young men glanced at Donald, as if unsure of whether they were permitted to take the head of the house's role in such a way.

'It's no good looking at me,' he said. 'I could never stand the sight of blood.'

'Mr Pace is excused carving duties on health grounds,' said Tory.

The baker, to everyone's surprise, deferred to the builder, and so it was he who accompanied Tory to the kitchen.

'Shouldn't I carve at the table?'

But Tory had everything carefully planned. The meat was to be carved up and everything served in advance, including vegetables and gravy, and the plates taken in and served individually. By this means Tory was able to strictly control the distribution of food during the meal. Before long, everyone had a roast dinner before them, except Donald, who had a plate on which was an upturned stainless-steel dish – an improvised serving lid.

'What's all this?' said Donald, lifting the dish to reveal a pointlessly empty plate. Empty but for one thing: a torpedo-shaped pellet of a shiny deep-reddish-brown colour.

'The food of the future,' said Tory, in a half-singing voice.

Donald bent down to look closely at the pellet. Then, sitting back, he flicked it off his plate with his finger and thumb, in the same way that a child flicks a marble, and said, 'Well, you can bring me the food of today.'

The pellet had landed close to Branson's plate, and he was about to pick it up to look at, before Tory, who had not yet sat down to her own meal, placed it carefully back on Donald's plate. It chinked against the china. 'This is very special food, for a very special man . . .' She picked up Donald's cutlery and put it in his hands, 'You can even eat it with a knife and fork. You know how to use a knife and fork, don't you?'

As if realizing for the first time that his wife was being serious, and sensing danger, he said, more cautiously, 'What's going on?'

'These pellets contain all the nutritional value of a full roast dinner – not just protein but all the vitamins and minerals as well.' Tory said this as she took her seat at the opposite end of the table to Donald.

'Really?' said the baker, who seemed genuinely interested, and peeved that he hadn't been given one. 'You mean in the future there won't be any need for all of this . . .' He waved his knife vaguely at the loaded plates around the table.

'No, not at all. No more carrying heavy shopping bags of food, no more peeling potatoes or shelling peas, no more trips to the butcher's shop, no more cutting up bloody beef . . .'

'That's incredible.' The baker was clearly preparing to say something like, Can't we all have one and be done with proper food? But attention was drawn towards Donald, who had caught Albertina's eye and had said, in more or less an undertone, 'Be an angel, sweetheart, and go out to the kitchen and get me some grub. Your mother seems to have flipped her lid.'

Albertina obediently began to leave her seat.

'Where are you going, Albertina?' Tory voice had

acquired a new edge, a sort of sawing sound, sharp and abrasive. No one had ever heard it before.

In contrast Albertina's voice seemed to have reverted to her childish piping, as she tried to explain.

'Sit down, Albertina,' Tory said, with that unsettlingly authoritative tone still in her voice. Having made to sit down, Albertina decided to try to continue her errand, mumbling that her mother was being silly.

'I said sit down!' Tory banged her palm on the table, making everyone, apart from Donald, visibly jump. She noticed Paulette glance at her boyfriend then roll her eyes upwards, as if to suggest that this was a regular occurrence, one of Mummy's little scenes that they had to put up with.

'No one is leaving this table until they have eaten their food.'

'What food?' said Donald, with a derisive chuckle.

'I don't mind swapping with Mr Pace,' said the baker, nudging his plate towards Donald's.

'What I don't understand,' said the builder, 'is if these little pills are supposed to replace shopping and cooking, what are our wives going to spend their time doing?' He gave Albertina an endearing glance.

'You keep your food,' said Donald to the baker, in a comradely way, as if they were both suffering at the hands of his wife's foolishness. 'Tory, will you get me something to eat, or do you want me

413

to limp all the way to the bloody kitchen on my bad leg?'

'You've always kept your appetite, haven't you?' she said. 'Even when you came back from the war all shell-shocked and simple, you could still stuff your face until it was running down your chin.'

'At least you won't have to blow on it to cool it down,' said the baker, who didn't seem to have heard his hostess speak. And it seemed, as Tory stood up and walked around the table towards her husband, that the joke was now over, and that she was going to take away that silly little pill and bring him his real dinner. Nothing was said. Donald looked at his wife with a resigned expression on his face that said, *All right, you've got me, you've had your fun, you've made your point, now let's get back to normal.* But that was not what happened. Instead of taking Donald's plate, Tory took hold of Donald's head, the head that, for several years now, she had balmed with a soothing lotion to ease the scars that he himself had inflicted in a moment of madness, and yanked it back.

'You want some help, Donald, you want me to feed you?'

She had pinched his nose so that his mouth gaped. His arms came up, waving pathetically in their attempts to pull his wife's hands off, but he was held in such a way that there seemed to be nothing he could hold on to. Others at the table gasped and began to stand up, not sure what to do. With a deft movement Tory took the pill and put it into her husband's throat, but in a particularly rough way, jabbing, almost stabbing it into his gullet, then vigorously rubbing his pitifully exposed neck.

'You want some water?'

She picked up the full glass and splashed it in, so that half went into his mouth, half down his shirtfront. Then she released his head, which catapulted forward so that Donald banged his forehead on the empty plate. He was making no sound but for a quiet gasping noise. Tory began to return to her seat.

'Are you all right, Dad? said Albertina, as shocked as everyone else by what had just happened. Donald was now writhing around in his chair, his mouth wide open, as though trying to vomit, but failing.

'He doesn't look too good,' said the baker. 'I think he's choking.'

'Your dinner is getting cold,' said Tory. 'All of you, eat up before it gets cold.'

'Daddy, are you choking?' said Paulette.

Donald was hooking fingers into his gaping mouth, trying to pull out the blockage. As he bent forward, brown liquid poured from his nostrils. The baker stood up, began hitting him in the back.

'I'm choking,' said Donald, with a voice that lacked any human quality, but which sounded like a dog growling. Suddenly he leant back hard in his seat so that it tipped over and he was on his back on the floor, his face a deep red, his mouth still gaping.

'Get him on his side,' said the builder. 'Try and shake it out of him.' The room had transformed: the girls had stood up and were uncertain of what to do: the men were down on the ground with their host, shaking him like a dummy. Eventually the blockage was expelled, like a champagne cork, nearly hitting the ceiling, and Donald breathed in with a rush of suction so desperate it felt as though the whole room would enter his mouth.

Tory never fed Donald again. Any meals she prepared for the family were carefully measured out so that there was not enough for Donald, even if he went himself to the pot or the pan. He could get by, making himself toast, opening tins, but with his leg, it was difficult. The girls helped him, despite their mother's insistence that they should not, and Branson sometimes offered his father food from his own plate. It led to terrific rows, not just between Donald and Tory but between Tory and her daughters, who couldn't see the point of excluding their father from every meal, of reducing him to eating bread and butter while they ate stews and pies. They would have gone as far as cooking a full meal for their father, but they didn't dare cross the kitchen threshold while their mother was in residence.

No one asked why Tory had taken this peculiar stance. While none of the children was the least bit fond of their father, they had a certain amount of respect for him, Branson especially, and didn't think that any marital dispute warranted what seemed to be on Tory's part a systematic attempt to starve her husband out of the house.

'Stop being so bloody daft' at first gave way to 'Be reasonable, Tory' and 'For God's sake, woman, we can't live like this – this is worse than the concentration camps . . . To think of all I fought for! I never thought I'd live to see torture practised in an English family home . . .'

Eventually it worked. If the way to a man's heart was through his stomach, Tory reasoned, then the best way to dispose of that heart was through the stomach also. Donald began going elsewhere for his meals. Once he was out of the house Tory began to make a pile of his belongings in the hall, announcing, when he came back, that he had a week to make arrangements for their removal; after that she would start burning them. There wasn't much, and Tory was good at burning things now.

The No. 217B was a new bus service that Tory rather liked because it took a round-the-houses route that visited many of the places that had been special to her in the past, swinging left off Old Parade and onto the steep Dorothy Hill, past the Hamlet, down Clifton Road and round by the graveyard of St Andrew's, where Mrs Head was now buried alongside Arthur, then a winding route down Russell Lane with sycamores and cow parsley leaning out from the railway embankment (you could almost be in the countryside, Tory had

417

often thought), which came out on the corner with Randall Street, by the English Rose Tea Rooms and close to where Tory used to wait for the tram that had taken her to the gelatine factory. Then past her father's old bank (now a branch of the Midland), and to the left, there was Walsingham Avenue, at the end of which, close to an inlet of the Thames, she had spent an unhappy few weeks as a searchlight operator. Then it was a long stretch on the Dartford road to George Farraway's new gym.

Tory and Branson were sitting on the top deck, at the front, a vantage-point that Tory loved because it felt to her like riding a winged chariot, the sycamore branches of Russell Lane whiplashing against the windows, on an eye level with all the bedrooms of the houses. What a magnificent form of travel. They were sitting either side of the gangway, occupying a double seat each, against Tory's wishes, but Branson could not be made to share with her. She glanced across at him.

'Good right hooks,' she said, smiling. He looked at her with an expression of mild disgust. He didn't seem to realize that she was referring to the trees lashing against the windows, and although Tory tried nodding towards them, by way of explanation, it was too late. Branson had turned away. Was she mad? To allow that sweet, square, still downy face to be pummelled by boxing gloves? Why was he so keen? He had never shown the slightest interest in rough sports before, but when

418

she had casually remarked that he might like to take boxing lessons at a renowned gym not too far from there, he had shocked her with his enthusiasm. When can we go? He asked the question incessantly. Give me a couple of weeks to sort it out. A couple of weeks? Can't we go tonight? No Branson, we mustn't rush into something like this. On and on he had pestered her. Since he had no idea that he was the son of a man who had fought Jack Dempsey on Long Island and had drawn blood from the eyebrow of the Manassa Mauler, she could only assume that Branson's enthusiasm for boxing was the manifestation of an inherited trait.

After the death of Alec Stott, the old gelatine gym, where Tory had first set eyes on a sweaty-vested George Farraway, had closed. George had a smaller factory now, a little unit, as it was called, on a trading estate off the Dartford Road. It was here that he had planned to bring an end to world hunger with the Farraway Foodfree Diet. The bad publicity had put that project on indefinite hold. Now Mrs Farraway, the woman with the film-star looks whom Tory had never seen, had come up with her own alternative scheme. Alec Stott, she reasoned, had become thinner and thinner on a diet of George's pills. Why not turn them into diet tablets, then? The cold logic of this argument was irresistible to George, and he had already begun developing a marketing strategy.

Meanwhile the shop floor of his workshop was

deserted. But George wasn't in a hurry. He had made a fortune in selling his factory and, besides, he was more interested in what was happening upstairs at the new unit, for on the top floor he had built one of the best-equipped boxing gyms in the country.

He must have spent thousands on it, Tory thought, when she entered the space for the first time. It gleamed with newness, so unlike the gelatine gym, with its dusty windows, peeling paintwork and pipe runs. Here there was the glint of chrome and stainless steel; the heavy punchbags hung in a row from an overhead gantry and had the smooth tautness of black puddings. There were exercise machines that looked like the scaffolding for a small building project, bicycles with only one wheel, on which young men sweated frantically to get nowhere. It was like a factory of the type that lay empty downstairs, this one for the production of powerful men. In every corner trainees were shadow-boxing, others skipping or at punchbags. There were three rings, each for a different level of expertise.

George approached them through the boiling throng, wearing what looked like a skin-diving outfit, but which Tory later learned was called a tracksuit. He seemed all done up in one piece with a single zip, and looked awesomely modern.

'Aha, the famous Mr Branson Pace.'

Branson glanced worriedly at his mother, as if thinking Mr Farraway was mixing him up with someone else.

420

Father and son shook hands for the first time, and at that moment Branson's likeness to his father was confirmed for Tory beyond any doubt. Their handshake produced an aspect of near-perfect symmetry, pivoting around the joined hands, expanding into two square, stocky bodies either side, of differing height, but of a near identical stance and carriage.

'You'll be gentle with him?' Tory couldn't help saying this, and received another glare from her son, who wanted it to be known that he didn't require gentle handling.

'As a lamb.' George laughed as he led Branson away, his guiding hand on his son's shoulder, towards the back rooms where, Tory hoped, he would begin the process of transforming the clumsy boy into a world-champion boxer.

'I'll be waiting for you,' she called after them, suddenly fearing that she would never see her son again. As she sat down on one of the benches near the door, she supposed that, in a way, it was true. A different Branson Pace would be returned to her in an hour or so's time.

It was Branson who missed Donald's presence the most.

'Why did you do those things to Daddy?' he would say, in a heartbreakingly adult voice. The girls, on the other hand, hardly seemed to notice that their father was gone, just pleased that there was no longer any shouting in the house. Tory warned everyone, one evening, that if their father was to knock (she had changed the locks) they should not, under any circumstances, let him in. Afterwards Branson remonstrated with his sisters, who seemed happy to comply with their mother's request.

'What's he done that's so bad? I'm not going to stop him coming in.'

'Just don't ask, Branson,' was the girls' well-practised reply, as if to say it must be truly bad for their mother to be so adamant that Donald should be gone for good. They were young women now, with their own sights on marriage, and seemed to have entered an exalted realm, where everyone had insights into everyone else's thoughts – they liked to give the impression they knew what their mother was going through, and that their own marriages would never get into such deep and dark waters.

But Donald never tried to come back. It was almost as though he'd had a contingency plan all along. On the night of his final departure a car had called for him. Tory had never seen the driver before, a coiffed young man with a fag in the corner of his mouth, lean and chiselled, a bit like Dirk Bogarde. He helped Donald with the suitcases and the one trunk Donald had packed.

Tory made as if to take no interest in the scene, and continued to read her newspaper.

'Where are you going, Dad?' said Branson, with some urgency in his voice.

'Just away, son,' he said, taking a moment to

look into the boy's eyes, then, turning to Tory, 'I told you you were too good for me, didn't I? I told you, you're made of gold, Tory Pace, while I'm a man of lead. But I managed until the war came along, managed to be good. Didn't I? Good enough for you?'

Tory looked up from her newspaper. There were tears in her eyes and her head was trembling, as if uncertain whether to shake or nod in reply. But Donald didn't wait, he gave a little one-fingered salute, tapping the rim of a peaked cap, if it had been there, and turned, tap-tapping down the path to the car.

'Are you coming back, Dad?'

'Stop it, Branson,' said one of the girls. 'Let him go.'

'He can't just go. Mummy, you've got to tell me what he's done that's so bad . . .'

Tory blew her nose, wiped her eyes. 'He has been bad in such a way that I can't tell you. I have been bad as well, but his badness started it all. He will not be coming back to live with us.'

It took a while for Branson to understand this, and he looked at his fingers as he tried to puzzle it out. 'But he's my father,' he said, as though he had found the solution. 'You can't send him away.'

And Branson cried. He cried for the man who had despised him as a little boy, who had cut him dead at every opportunity for the first five years of their acquaintanceship and who, if he spoke to him at all, had dished out icy little insults and aspersions instead of words of fatherly affection. Tory wondered if she should say to him, *But he is not your father, Branson, you know that, don't you?* She had never actually told her son the story of his 'discovery' in a bomb site in Leicester. Of the three versions of his birth, he believed the second – which only he believed – that he was the legitimate son of Donald Pace, war veteran and hero.

'How's he going to sleep? How's he going to live?' said Branson, who couldn't get past the idea that his father couldn't survive in the world beyond the house.

'He has friends who will look after him,' said Tory. 'You don't need to worry about your father – he survived the war, after all.'

Branson was so cross with his mother that he wouldn't talk to her for several weeks. At night he cried alone in his bedroom, and by day displayed brittle anger in everything he did. Most alarmingly, for Tory, he refused to eat. He would sit at the dinner table with his arms resolutely folded, the corners of his mouth turned down as emphatically, a big dark frown in his brows, while in front of him would be his favourite – egg and chips, with the chips done just how he liked them (very brown) – and a scarlet bottle of ketchup next to it. Tory wondered what she could do, and had horrible visions of a repeat performance of that cataclysmic Sunday lunch, but this time it would be Branson's young mouth that she was force-feeding.

She could not go through her whole family like this, surely. But to her great relief it was just a phase: Branson's hunger strike soon gave way to reluctant gobbling, but the anger was still there.

The moment of revelation never came, though Tory was always waiting for it: the day when she would take Branson aside and say to him, 'Let me explain something to you, son. Donald is not your father. You were born in May 1942. The man you call your father was a prisoner of war from 1940 to 1945. How do you think you were conceived? By post?' As the years went by Tory waited for the penny to drop, for Branson to storm in and say, 'Mother, if you *are* my mother, who is my real father?' But he couldn't see it. Perhaps he wasn't clear about Donald's career as a soldier. She thought she should drop heavy hints, recount stories she'd heard of Donald's days as a prisoner, make sure Branson understood that he had been away for nearly all of the war. But whenever she talked about Donald, Branson stormed out; and whenever she talked about Donald's war record, she was drawn back to thoughts of her dreadful correspondence, Donald's book, and the fact that *Letters To Her Husband By a Naughty Housewife* was still circulating around the seedier book-shops of Europe.

On Branson's fourteenth birthday he received a card from Donald, an event that seemed to throw the whole house into turmoil. There hadn't been a word from Donald since the day he had left – he hadn't even made an appearance at Paulette's wedding, or sent a card – hardly surprising, as Tory had done her best to make sure he knew nothing about it, but this didn't assuage her resentment at his failure to make an appearance. But now a birthday card from out of the blue. At that moment it seemed the dense, dark little cloud that had settled over Branson's head was instantly dispelled.

To my little mate and comrade in arms, Branson. The only one who gave me nourishment in my time of darkest suffering. Happy birthday.
Your loving father,

Donald

Branson read this in a state of extreme excitement, his hands shaking, showing it over and over again to whoever was available. It seemed to Tory that he smiled for the first time in three years, and the smile stayed on his face.

The card, resented by Albertina ('It's not fair. I didn't get a card and I fed him as well'), contained Donald's address, a flat in Bloomsbury Square. Without Tory's knowledge, Branson bunked off school, took the train all the way up to Charing Cross and found his way to Bloomsbury. From then on he became a regular visitor, seeing his father, sometimes as much as every week. Tory didn't like it at all, although she couldn't help but be pleased that he seemed so much happier, and comforted by the picture Branson inadvertently gave of Donald's life. The elegant Bloomsbury apartment was not quite what she had imagined, but a squalid bedsitter he shared with Mr Harry Wilde (even Branson now spoke of that man as 'literary' and 'educated'), down some dank, mossy stairs in a basement. A blue plaque on the first floor of the building, according to Harry Wilde, commemorated E. M. Forster getting his leg over, and that was enough to convince them that they were now part of literary London.

There were no books at all in the flat, not even small green ones without a title on the cover. Mr Wilde liked to drink in a gin palace on the Tottenham Court Road, and would, if he was able, carry Donald up the steps from the basement so that he could accompany him, now and then.

Tory did her best to avoid becoming resentful of Branson's kinship with Donald – she had to credit her husband with being welcoming of the young man. She just hoped he wouldn't get caught up in Donald's seedy little machinations and adventures.

She busied herself, partly by way of distraction, with matters of the house. Mrs Head had had enough of an estate to make Tory modestly rich for a few months. With the aid of this money and with help from the council, she was able, at last, to install an indoor lavatory and bathroom.

Floors were lifted, holes were drilled in walls, new walls were erected, and for what seemed months the house was the trampled domain of plumbers and builders. Then, suddenly, they left, and there was a new room in the house, a room newer than all the others, which was like stepping into a new dimension. It terrified Tory at first. Walking along the landing with its Edwardian shadows, its china plant pots standing on thin-legged tables, the Turkish carpet, the shadowy alcoves with their fading, roseate wallpaper, she would open a door and suddenly be in the brightly lit space of the twentieth century, where everything was white and clean, so white and matching that it was hard, in a way, to distinguish individual objects. Slowly, out of the dazzle, a bath would emerge with silver taps, then a washbasin and a lavatory with a low flush. Above the sink was a mirror that was also a cupboard. A magnificent deception. She opened it, watching her face lurch suddenly sideways.

The wiring was done. More floorboards lifted, more walls drilled open, then an instantly summoned brightness. Every room now had its own light switch, a dark brown apple with the stalk facing out. You pulled the stalk, which gave a thick, reluctant click, and suddenly clear white light was pouring into every corner, filling the room right up to its brim. The fuse box, over the dining-room door, was like a sort of cuckoo clock without a face, behind whose door sat rows of Bakelite pins. What was she supposed to do with these? She was assured they were not her concern. The family could not only bathe in running water, but they could do so under intense illumination. This had an unfortunate effect on Tory, however: she saw, for the first time in her life, her naked body in the glare of electricity. Had she lived alone, this experience would have been enough to make her regress to gas lighting. She would happily have done without the glare of a sixty-watt bulb for the rest of her life, if it meant she could gaze once again upon the textures of her own skin softened by coal gas. In gas light she was bronze, copper, brass. In electric light she was cheap aluminium, dirty tin.

Branson emerged from the changing rooms at the far end of the gym, looking rather ungainly in his vest and trunks, both of which seemed ill-fitting, the shorts coming down below the knees. She watched as her boy was fitted with gloves by his father, holding each one out in turn, wrist up, like a sort of vase, into which Branson dipped a cautious fist, as though into a lucky dip, then seeming surprised that he couldn't remove his hand, finding that it was fastened in by laces and straps, the securing of which seemed a vigorous process that shook his whole body. When the strapping in was complete, he seemed to just stand there, motionless, as if unable to understand his new body, figuring it out, testing the gloved hands against each other, knocking them together like enormous conkers, or like a butterfly that has just emerged from its cocoon and is amazed to find that it has wings.

He doesn't fight in that first session. He is shown what George calls 'ring craft', which meant, as far as she could tell, getting used to the space of the ring, running from one end to the other, feeling the elasticity of the ropes, running sideways along all four sides, sitting in the corner, as though between rounds, bending and stretching at the ropes, running on the spot and jumping up and down to get used to the feel of the ring's strange floor. This seemed to go on for a long time, with George giving him long instructional talks between. Then it was back onto the floor and over to a speed bag, one of those body-sized bags that hangs from the ceiling, but it was a long time before Branson took a swing at it. Tory could see George instructing him on the right way to hold his body. He seemed to start from the feet up, giving long sessions on where to place his feet. Good job, thought Tory. Perhaps now he'll stop falling over. He tried many different stances – right foot forward, left foot forward, right foot forward and to the side, and so on. Each time he placed his feet in a certain way George would take him by the shoulders and gently rock him, as if allowing him to feel his own centre of gravity, to learn where his 'fall point' was. This is going to be better for Branson than I ever imagined possible, Tory thought.

She could not take her eyes off the spectacle, though remained at her distant vantage-point for the whole session. The care George was taking with the boy was so unexpected. This was not just a response to her request for gentle handling. Boxing, it seemed, was a sport founded on nurturing and caring, of understanding and protecting the body, of rooting it firmly in the ground and giving it a poised and balanced structure. Tory had imagined they would just start belting each other.

'I'm glad you didn't bash him about too much,' she said, and laughed, when Branson was returned to her at the end of his hour.

'No, bashing starts later. The first weeks we teach them how to stand up and how to walk all over again.'

Well, that must be quite nice for you, Tory thought, because you missed out on it the first time.

Tory still wondered what to do with Charlotte Maugham. She had finished her novel but had been unable to find a publisher. She tried three, two of them rejected her without explanation, the third said that they enjoyed her 'bold' writing style, but the story wasn't strong enough.

As for her other literary venture, she had given up pretty quickly on the idea of seizing and destroying every copy that had been printed. For a time she and Grace had flirted with the idea of travelling to Paris to harangue the publisher and,

431

using whatever means they could, either to destroy his stock or to find out where he had sent it. Perhaps they could save the money, she thought, to buy up the whole print run. Grace was keen on the idea. She said she could speak good French, and gave Tory a demonstration, though to Tory it just sounded like gobbledegook. In the end their ambition frittered out. Going abroad seemed like too big an adventure for Tory, let alone confronting a French publisher. In they end they decided to write.

There was a letter that Tory Pace had, for the last five years, always carried around with her. It was from the French publisher of her letters, in reply to a letter she had carefully written (translated into French for her by Grace). He replied in English. She liked to take it out of her bag now and then, whenever she had doubts about the future and what it might hold. She read it now as she waited for Branson to finish changing.

> *My dear, dear Victoria Pace,*
>
> *First of all, let me say how honoured and thrilled I am that the author of* Letters To Her Husband By a Naughty Housewife *has made themselves known to me. I should not be surprised that you write French as beautifully as you write your English. I regard your work as one of the most supreme examples of erotic art to have ever been written. It is a great*

surprise to me to find that they were published without your permission or knowledge, though this is a matter for you to pursue with Mr Harry Wilde, the agent representing an anonymous (to us) author, rather than with us. I am sure you can follow what I am saying. Your sense of hurt and anger comes through very strongly in your letter, but there is little point in making threats, and indeed, when one does so in ink on paper, one risks fouling the law. I am afraid that the letter you wrote us is libellous, blackmailing and threatening. I have not yet passed it on to the police, but if you write another letter in a similar genre, I will be forced to do so.

A much more beautiful outcome for us both, I think you will agree, is that we find some sort of working relationship together, which will be mutually marvellous. You are clearly a woman of extraordinary talents and extraordinary passions, and I am a man who is always interested in people of talent and passion. I am quite serious when I say that I would like to commission a new novel from you, perhaps in a similar genre to the one you have already written, or you might want to adopt a more conventional narrative form (not letters); it is up to you. There are countless scenarios – the convent, the girls' school. For a long time I have been wanting someone to write about the women's armed forces from an erotic perspective. Such a novel would,

I would hope, spit in the eye of what you English call the fuddy-duddy society. My father was an Englishman, I would like to add. You would not need to expose yourself – you can publish under a pseudonym, if you so wish, or no name at all. I would like to point out that the Olympia Press has published some of the most distinguished authors of the twentieth century, and that my father, who started the press, published a section of work by James Joyce – I am reminded of certain aspects of A Work in Progress in your own writing, my dear Victoria Pace. There, I've paid you the highest compliment a man can possibly make to a writer, comparing her, literally, to God. Should you be inclined to put feathers to paper again, please contact me at the above address. The world should not have to be deprived of the erotic power of your work.

Your faithful servant,

Maurice Girodias

Poor Grace; it seemed she had been right after all. Their friendship didn't survive in the surface world. She had helped Tory through the crisis of her mother's death, and the task of removing Donald from her life (it had been her suggestion that she simply refuse him food), and she had helped her in dealing with Mr Girodias – she had even gone as far as suggesting some hotels they could stay at in Paris. 'Would you like me to book a room for us both, Tory? We could make a holiday of it.'

Perhaps it was the assumption that they would share a room that put Tory off. Oh, she knew what Grace was like, and she had known for some time – the poor thing was in love with her. But Tory was afraid, and had been ever since a peculiar moment a while after Mrs Head's funeral when Grace had invited her for tea at her house in Dulwich. Tory had strong misgivings about accepting the invitation, feeling all the while that she was going to be compromised in the most uncomfortable way. She had been right: the house was empty and Grace had tried to force herself upon her, plunging at Tory's face with her lips heavily painted and pouting. The softness was gone: Tory could feel all the bones in Grace's face pressing against her own, two skulls clashing, and she ran from the house, smeared with lipstick, Grace weeping apologies as she tried to hold her back, so desperately that Tory had had to slip out of her jacket to escape, leaving the woman sobbing into the empty sleeves.

It hadn't been the end of their friendship, not quite. Grace had written long letters of apology and they had agreed to meet at the Tea Rooms (Tory had resigned from the lavatories the day her mother died). She seemed quite recovered, was sparky and bright, her old self, and perhaps the friendship could have resumed, but when Grace suggested the trip to Paris and the shared bed in Montmartre, Tory decided enough was enough.

The last she had heard, Grace was divorced and back in Melbourne.

Nothing, Tory supposed, is quite as worrying as having a son who wants to be a boxer.

In the weeks that followed, Branson was still insistent that she accompany him, and Tory had grown quite fond of the brash new gym, where she still maintained her distance, sitting on the same sweaty bench as before, watching the progress of Branson from afar. There was a heart-stopping moment when he took his first hit, after George had carefully set up his guard so that he was crouched behind his two bulbous fists. George gave a little prodding tap at the closed doors, then a little harder, and a little harder. By now Branson was also wearing the amateur's padded head guard, which gave him an even more curious shape, like a heavybodied beetle, with his big clumsy fists and his swollen head. She watched as George jabbed a little harder. Branson's body shook and he took a step backwards. He was told to lean forward more. He then took a heavier punch and hardly moved at all.

Then George turned the tables, putting up his own guard, asking Branson to come forward and throw some punches at his raised gloves. Tory felt like applauding from across the other end of the gym when she saw Branson's arm outstretched, his glove connecting with his father's, then another, little dabs, like a playful cat might give a lame bird, one after another. Then the reply: George took advantage of Branson's lowered guard and landed him a punch full in the face. The boy staggered back, looked dazed. Tory was still at the other end of the gym, but stood up and felt like shouting at George, telling him off for being a bully. She saw George pat Branson on the back, dab his cheeks consolingly. She could imagine what he was saying, that he had to learn to take it, to know what it feels like to be hit, right from the beginning. And what a useful lesson, Tory thought, sitting down again, to know what it feels like to be hit full in the face. No one had ever done it to her.

By the fourth week Branson was throwing combination punches at a training dummy held aloft by his father. He was told constantly to pay attention to his feet. He gave a one-two, then a little shuffle, a little bounce, then another one-two, then a one-two-three. By week five he was bouncing solidly, landing combination strings of five or six punches in quick succession. He was beginning to look frightening. If those punches were to hit the target of an opponent's head, instead of the training dummy, they would surely knock him out. Then he was back at the speed bag, attacking it ferociously, punching at below shoulder level now, agonizing combinations left and right around the kidney area, piston-like thumping, then onto the standing punchbag, which gave him the chance to practise some uppercuts. A flowing rhythm began to develop in his fighting; he began to combine long strings of different punches, while always moving on his feet. By his sixth week he was in the ring with a sparring partner, a beginner like himself. They were of equal size, but on his first short bout Branson had the upper hand, dominating his opponent, who stepped backwards onto the ropes.

'A natural,' George assured her. 'I've never known anyone pick it up so quickly. From not even knowing how to stand up he has developed in less than two months into an extremely promising fighter. World-champion material, definitely.'

And then Branson said she no longer needed to come to the gym with him, he was happy to go on his own. This took Tory a little by surprise, though she had long been wondering what on earth she was doing there.

'Good, well, I'm sure you'll be fine . . .' She turned to George. 'In which case we'll not be seeing each other again.'

'Well,' he said, taking her aside, out of Branson's earshot, 'there's no need to look at it like that . . .'

'Goodbye, George. You just concentrate on looking after Branson. I know you'll take care of him.'

On their way home, on the No. 217B, she wondered if she had done the right thing. She had no one in her life now, apart from her children.

'I will wonder that always, about everything,' she concluded, looking fondly across at Branson in the fairy-light glare of the upper deck, still damp from his bout, his hair shiny with sweat, clinging to him. As always, he was oblivious of her attention and interest. He just didn't realize that to her he was the most interesting thing in the world.

It was dark when they got back. There was a letter on the mat from Albertina who was halfway through her first term at King's. It must have come by the late post. Tory loved getting letters from Albertina – they were always so full of wit and energy. She wrote of a world Tory herself would have loved to know, of eccentric professors, gauche, brainy young men, dusty libraries and lectures on subjects nobody in the world cared about.

Well, at least now she could look forward to spending an evening writing a letter in reply. Albertina was a good correspondent. Tory intended to write many letters to various people. Many, many letters.